ADJOURNED

Charles Holborne Legal Thrillers
Book Nine

Simon Michael

Also in the Charles Holborne Series
The Brief
An Honest Man
The Lighterman
Corrupted
The Waxwork Corpse
Force of Evil
The Final Shot
Nothing But The Truth

DEATH, ADJOURNED

Published by Sapere Books.

24 Trafalgar Road, Ilkley, England, LS29 8HH

saperebooks.com

Copyright © Simon Michael, 2024
Simon Michael has asserted his right to be identified as the author of this work.
All rights reserved.

No part of this publication may be reproduced, stored in any retrieval system, or transmitted, in any form, or by any means, electronic, mechanical, photocopying, recording, or otherwise, without the prior written permission of the publishers.
This book is a work of fiction. Names, characters, businesses, organisations, places and events, other than those clearly in the public domain, are either the product of the author's imagination, or are used fictitiously.
Any resemblances to actual persons, living or dead, events or locales are purely coincidental.

ISBN: 978-0-85495-383-7

ACKNOWLEDGEMENTS

My thanks firstly go to Aine Astbury, indefatigable librarian at No. 5 Chambers, who continues to supply me with arcane law and long-repealed statutes from the 1960s and before, long after I ceased to be a member.

Martyn Bradish and Kevin Lane, my former and current accountants respectively, both offered assistance on the nuts and bolts of auditing procedure, and invaluable ideas on how to make the accounting part of the plot work. Kevin Lane, you may note, asked to appear in the book as a baddie by way of recompense, but I took a liking to my fictional Kevin Lane and found that he had, in fact, a heart of gold. I hope the real Kevin Lane, accountant, will forgive me for not making him the criminal mastermind of his dreams after all.

I owe a great debt of thanks to Rex Tedd KC for providing me with hilarious instalments in the story of his taking silk and details of the procedure that applied in the 1960s and 1970s. I had toyed with having Charles take silk in the course of this book but, as you will have noticed, it was already significantly longer than earlier instalments in the series and eventually I decided to leave that (and the portrayal of Charles and Sally's wedding) to another book. Rex requested that Shirley Titmarsh, his assistant for many years, be mentioned by way of recompense, and mentioned she is. I must make it clear that the real Shirley Titmarsh bears no relation at all to the blackmailed and harassed county court clerk.

Finally, and as always, my thanks go to my beta readers, in particular Debbie Jacobs, Neil Cameron, Steve Witt and Karen Crawford, to all at Sapere Books, and to Elaine for her encouragement, wise insights into the emotional facets of my characters which I might otherwise miss, and all else.

PART ONE

PROLOGUE

'What's up?' says Big Kev, leaning into the open passenger window of the removals van.

The van is old and a little battered, the words "Shoreditch Enforcement Services" stencilled on its side flaking slightly at the edges.

The driver, a thin-faced man in his forties, takes a slender rollup from the corner of his mouth, checks it's no longer alight and tucks it behind an ear. He leans across and answers while pushing open the door for his colleague.

'Demolition's starting at Tarling Road tomorrow. Got a call from the security team. Someone's moved back in. Come on.'

Big Kev nods, blinks slowly and slides into the front seat of the cab, the suspension groaning at the assault. He folds his tree-trunk legs carefully into the cramped footwell and closes the door.

The way Kevin Lane moves is unnerving. Even when dispensing his trademark violence, Big Kev, known and feared throughout the East End of London, somehow gives the impression of moving slowly, implacably, like thick, viscous oil.

The driver's name is also Kevin. Given his lifelong friendship with the man mountain next to him it is unsurprising that Kevin Streeter is known locally as "Little Kev" — although he is only small when compared with his enormous colleague — or that the two of them together have become "the Kevins".

Little Kev looks over his shoulder and edges away from the kerb into the late-night traffic.

The pavements, still radiating the heat of the day, throng with milling tourists and theatre-goers strolling the brightly-lit streets. The Swinging Sixties have made the West End the cultural centre of the world. Music, fashion, celebrities and clubs; everyone wants to be part of the 24/7 neon-lit, drug-fuelled party that is the London "scene".

A few years ago Little Kev would have relished the opportunities. The shoals of the carefree are easy prey for street-shark hustlers, pickpockets and toms. The unsuspecting tourists were even known as "plankton". But courtesy of his brains and Big Kev's brawn, he and his partner have now graduated to different, more select work; work which thrives best in the deeper, darker waters of the city.

It takes them only twenty minutes to reach their destination, but they arrive in a different country.

Tarling Road in Canning Town, the heart of the East End, still looks much like it did after the Blitz. The streets of a poor but thriving community remain bulldozed into irregular piles of rubble and there remain four rows of Nissen huts, supposedly temporary wartime accommodation but which, twenty years on, are draughty, pin-holed, bronchitic sheds.

No neon signs here. No street lighting at all in fact.

Little Kev allows the van to coast to a halt and extinguishes the lights. To their right is an eighty-yard enclosure of metal fencing containing a soot-stained terrace of derelict three-storey dwellings from the previous century, its doors and windows all boarded up. The easternmost two homes took a direct hit in September 1940, but the rest of the terrace was considered salvageable and its end remains propped by enormous wooden beams resting at a forty-five degree angle to the wall. What is now an exterior wall was once someone's lounge and bedroom, and it is possible to see where patterned wallpaper, parts of internal stairs and a fireplace now face out, redundantly, into the open night air.

The street is dark and deserted. No cars, no pedestrians. Silent, except for the echoing screech of brakes a mile or so away as a late train is forced to a halt somewhere on its route into Fenchurch Street.

Big Kev's eyes scan up and down the terrace. 'Which one?' he asks.

'Let's find out,' replies his partner, opening the driver's door of the cab silently and stepping down onto the cobbles.

Halfway along the building, faint yellow light seeps from under a boarded-up door. Little Kev leans forward and listens intently. He can detect no sound. He makes hand signals, indicating they should skirt round the back. A gate at the rear of the enclosure has been left open for them. These houses had no gardens, backing instead onto an enclosed yard into which the Kevins step quietly. It has been cleared to make space for several contractors' vehicles, a bulldozer and a half-constructed crane.

They find their quarry easily. The boarding on one of the rear doors has been removed and now leans at an angle against the crumbling brickwork. More light percolates from around its edges.

Little Kev steps back. Big Kev lifts the eight by four timber boarding as if it were cardboard and sets it aside quietly. A cocktail of unpleasant smells strikes them: mould, damp plaster, rotting timber, urine and despair. Facing them, in what might once have been the back parlour of the narrow house, is a man partially covered by a thin blanket, asleep on a wooden pallet. A faint pool of flickering yellow light is cast over his torso and legs by a paraffin lamp on the floor. He wears what might, once, have been a flower-patterned shirt and a pair of jeans, but they are so uniformly filthy that it is difficult to be sure. He wears no shoes, and the soles of his bare feet are black. Beside the pallet is a large paper bag. Little Kev peers into it and recoils as he is slapped in the face by the reek of clothing unwashed for far too long.

Their attention is drawn to a clicking sound and they both turn. Behind them water drips slowly but steadily from bowing ceiling plaster into a puddle.

Little Kev lifts the paraffin lamp and holds it up to throw light on the sleeper. His eyes meet those of his colleague, who nods in recognition. Little Kev prods the sleeping man with his foot.

'Hey! Wakey-wakey, chum.'

The man stirs and half-sits. His sunken eyes are wide and wild, but they are seeing somewhere else. He mutters something incomprehensible, swats the air with a bony hand, and backs away on his pallet towards the corner of the room.

'Acid,' says Big Kev.

Little Kev shrugs. 'Prob'ly. Get up!' he orders, prodding the man harder with the toe of his boot. 'We tol' you last week. You can't stay 'ere. Where's yer bird?'

He signals to Big Kev who takes a torch from his pocket, illuminates it, and leaves the room via an internal door. He returns a few moments later shaking his head.

Little Kev points upwards. 'Upstairs?'

'Nope. No stairs left.'

'Finally took off, has she? Come on, then. Up you get!'

The skeletal man suddenly leaps to his feet and runs barefoot for the door, oblivious to the fact that Big Kev stands in his way, as solid and immovable as a mountain. Big Kev doesn't hit him. In fact, his gesture is one of surprise and self-defence. He simply raises his right arm, elbow locked, and the man runs headlong into the heel of his palm. His head snaps back with a crack as his forward momentum is halted and he falls backwards. The back of his head strikes the corner of the pallet with a sickening crunch and his chin is forced into his chest, his teeth clacking like a ventriloquist's dummy.

He lies still, eyes wide, his head at a shockingly unnatural angle.

'Jesus, Kev!' exclaims Little Kev.

The other man's shrug isn't indifferent, merely surprised at the turn of events.

Little Kev bends to the felled man. Hearing nothing he reluctantly kneels in the puddle and puts his ear to the other's face. He stands again. 'He's dead.'

'Fuck.'

Little Kev considers the situation. 'I'm tempted to leave him 'ere. If they demolish on top of him, he'll just be one more homeless druggie buried by accident. But someone's bound to do a last sweep through the building, and that'd mean police, and delay. And above all, they don't want delay.' He nods to himself. 'Yeah. Let's pick 'im up, put him in the back of the van. I'll think of something.'

'But the furniture...'

'There's space in the wardrobe. Come on, let's get cracking.'

Nose wrinkling, Big Kev picks up the body and slings it over his shoulder like a roll of evil-smelling carpet. Little Kev collects the bag of clothes, lifts the paraffin lamp and leaps into the air with surprise.

'Jesus Christ almighty!'

He points. Big Kev turns. Now illuminated by the raised paraffin lamp is another bundle. At first he thinks it's more clothes, but then it stirs and lets out a wail.

'That's all we fuckin' need,' says Little Kev. 'A bleedin' baby!'

PART ONE

CHAPTER ONE

It is a beautiful spring morning in 1969. The Temple, a compact, self-governing enclave between the city of London and the city of Westminster, is bathed in sunshine. Until Friday 13th October 1307, from which date derives the superstition regarding all Fridays falling on the thirteenth, this crowded collection of ancient buildings, courtyards and peaceful gardens was the base of the Poor Knights of the Temple of King Solomon, otherwise known as the Knights Templar. Now sandwiched between bustling twentieth-century Fleet Street to the north and the Thames Embankment to the south, it is the professional home of almost all seven thousand barristers in practice in England and Wales.

One such, Charles Holborne, strides across the cobbles towards his chambers, one hand holding his hat on his head as a gust of wind from the Thames threatens to dislodge it, the other gripping his breakfast: bacon and fried egg sarnie on buttered white, double brown sauce. The joke amongst the clerks is that, were it not for "Mick's", the legendary greasy spoon on Fleet Street, Mr Holborne would probably starve.

Charles is happy. Today the Dickensian buildings seem less smoke- and soot-stained than usual, and the old plane trees have recently put forth fresh-minted leaves which flutter gaily in the breeze. The River Thames to his right is a white-flecked deep blue. It is a lovely day, the sort of day to lift a man's spirits.

He has many reasons to be happy. His first child, Leia, is three months old and thriving, as is her mother, Sally. Nestling in his pocket is the engagement ring he has just collected from

Hatton Garden, and with which he intends proposing to Sally, although how and when are details he has yet to work out. His practice goes from strength to strength, to the extent that he might now be a genuine contender for silk — to be made "Queen's Counsel, Learned in the Law" — in the next April round. Better still, and the thing which finds him waking with a smile every morning, Messrs Ronald and Reginald Kray, the former kings of London's underworld, have started thirty-year sentences, the longest murder sentences ever imposed by a British court. And best of all, in the process of getting them incarcerated, Charles deceived them into handing over the evidence they held against him.

For the first time in almost a decade, Charles Holborne is no longer waiting for the axe of disgrace and imprisonment to fall. He can plan for the future.

Sally, as always, is more circumspect. As she has repeatedly pointed out to her over-confident boyfriend, the murderous twins had the Metropolis by the throat, with dozens of corrupt Metropolitan Police officers on their payroll and friends in high places. Several Firm members remain at large. Some turned Queen's Evidence in return for immunity from prosecution; others were missed altogether and are still in the wind. So, while Ronnie and Reggie may be tucked behind bars, they're far from powerless. They must by now have realised that Charles tricked them, says Sally, and they have never been accused of having forgiving natures. Indeed, she reminds him, it was Charles himself who labelled Ronnie Kray "a Guinness world record grudge-holder".

Her warnings are to no avail. Charles feels lighter than he has for years. Nothing can suppress his elevated spirits.

Humming to himself and keen to start his breakfast before it congeals completely, he runs up the uneven timber staircase to the first-floor clerks' room. Barbara McIntyre, Chambers' senior clerk, looks up as he enters. All the staff are in place, working quietly at their desks. At this time of morning, just after nine, the phones are usually quiet. Barristers are at or *en route* to court. Those not on their feet that day are at their desks, addressing the backlog of paperwork, researching law, drafting pleadings and writing opinions. The unfortunates who are completely unemployed read newspapers or play cards. The clerking team may therefore concentrate on opening the day's post, bringing fee notes up to date and preparing bundles of precedents for their guvnors' forthcoming trials. Chambers recently acquired two new machines, originally named "Xeroxes" but now apparently to be termed "photocopiers", which have revolutionised the clerks' working lives. No more smudgy carbons; no more copying by hand.

'Morning, sir,' calls Jennie, one of Chambers' two junior clerks.

'Morning all,' replies Charles, going straight to his pigeonhole and leafing through the documents inside for any cheques that might have arrived for him.

This habit has been the subject of some snide references to Charles's religious heritage, but every barrister does the same. Counsel are paid by way of *honorarium*. In other words, they cannot sue for their fees and solicitors cannot be compelled to pay them. Furthermore, unlike any other sensible business, barristers cannot charge interest on outstanding fees. Accordingly, payment is routinely received (if received at all) years after cases are finished. Barristers and their clerks complain bitterly but, of course, nothing is ever done. Who wants to scare off solicitors, the source of their work, to other, less persistent Chambers?

It is therefore always feast or famine. Charles can go six months without receiving a penny or a year's income might turn up in the space of a week. Checking one's pigeonhole for cheques becomes a daily habit, another pull on the slot machine to see if one's been lucky.

Today he *has* been lucky; three cheques await him, totalling almost £700. His mind turns immediately to a potential celebration with Sally, perhaps a meal out. He will need to persuade her it's safe to leave Leia for an hour or two, perhaps with his brother and sister-in-law.

It might even be an opportunity to pop the question.

'Well?' asks Barbara, an eyebrow raised.

Charles leafs further through the papers awaiting him in the pigeonhole. He looks up at her and nods.

'I'll be up in a moment,' she says.

'Give me five to finish breakfast?' he asks, lifting the paper bag to show her.

His arms full, he leaves the clerks and runs up the stairs to the first-floor corridor which houses his room.

Peter Bateman, Charles's ex-pupil with whom he shares the room, is at court, starting a three-day burglary trial at Middlesex Assizes. Charles is pleased. He doesn't want anyone in Chambers to overhear the conversation about to occur. Among the papers Charles collected from his pigeonhole is a fat envelope from the Lord Chancellor's Department marked "Confidential". It contains the application forms for next year's appointments to Queen's Counsel. Success in applying for silk means bigger cases, higher fees and prestige; recognition by the profession that he is one of the best. Failure means *schadenfreude* by one's peers and snide gossip by one's enemies, the latter being something Charles has faced throughout his career and prefers to avoid if at all possible.

He throws the papers onto his desk, sits and, while eating his sandwich, opens his newspaper. The top half of the front page is given over to a photograph of the new aeroplane, Concorde, outside an airport building, surrounded by thousands of onlookers. Charles remembers: today will be its first test flight.

He flicks the page over. He is met with another large photograph, this time of a dapper little man with greying hair laying a commemorative stone on a building development. Charles recognises him: Sir Leo Wise, sixty-something, Auschwitz survivor and successful Jewish businessman. Born Leopold Weissman in Austria, the property developer is a little dynamo who arrived in England penniless and within twenty years built a reputation and a fortune clearing post-war slums and erecting thousands of modern homes for poor East End council tenants. Photographs of him and his beautiful wife are frequently in the national newspapers. There was even a television documentary made about him when he became Knight Commander of the British Empire. Despite the fact that Wise is reported to have lost his faith while in the death camps, Charles' parents — usually so scathing of Jews like Wise and Charles who have broken with their religion — still describe the businessman, with proprietorial pride, as a *mensch*.

The commemorative stone marks the start of construction of Seagull Tower, a twenty-two-storey, state-of-the-art block being erected in the East End of London. The article gives the background information, of which Charles is already aware. Sir Leo's company secured the contract with the London Borough of Newham amid allegations by competing tenderers, particularly the consortium led by the Earl of Menteith, of a "Jewish Mafia".

Nothing ever changes, thinks Charles, shaking his head. Despite the near extermination of European Jewry by the Nazis, large swathes of the British establishment are still of the opinion that a Jew's success against Gentile competition can only be explained by membership of a Jewish conspiracy, friends in high places, dishonesty or some combination thereof. Charles turns the newspaper over in disgust to focus on the football news.

A few minutes later the door opens and Barbara enters. She slides the "Conference in Progress" sign across the outside of the door and closes it behind her. She sniffs disapprovingly. Members of Chambers are not supposed to bring food in, particularly food which, like Charles's breakfast, leaves stale cooking smells, but they all do it and she tires of reprimanding them. Holborne, in particular, is a law unto himself, and she would be wasting her breath.

When the Scotswoman speaks, it is with a lowered voice. 'So, you're going for it?' she says, pointing to the envelope.

He shrugs. 'I have, as they say, "taken soundings". Everyone says I should.'

'Your practice is certainly strong enough, and you're better than many who've been successful the last year or two.'

'I hear a "but".'

The angular woman pulls up a chair, smooths her skirts and sits opposite Charles. 'Just bear in mind that very few get it first or second time round,' she says in her Edinburgh accent.

'I know.'

'It took Piers Prentice seven applications.'

'I know.'

He waits while Barbara formulates her next response. 'And he has a father on the Bench,' she says.

'I know. And which, to state the obvious, I don't.'

'No…'

Charles decides to let her off the hook. 'What you're pussyfooting around, Barbara, is that he isn't working-class, from a Jewish background or with a "history". And he hasn't pissed off one or two important members of the judiciary.'

She looks down and stares at her shoes. When she meets his gaze again she looks apologetic. 'You have sometimes been treated very unfairly.'

'No argument there.'

'But the facts remain. I just need to make sure you're aware of the difficulties. We need to be realistic.'

Charles sighs. 'I'm very well aware, thank you,' he replies, unable entirely to keep the bitterness from his voice. 'But I want to give it another try.'

'As long as you know it's a longshot.'

'Are you saying that my position's no better than it was last time?'

Now she sighs too. 'No, I'm not. You've done some exceptional work and since the Krays' trial the rumour mill has been ... quieter. But the fundamental problems, well ... nothing's changed, has it?'

'Do you think I'm wasting my time?' He prods the envelope, leaving a slightly greasy fingerprint. 'Not to mention money.'

'No, not at all. You *do* have some support, don't you?'

'Yes. A couple of silks, including Chugger and Rhodes Thomas. And one judge I think I can rely on.'

'Only one? You really need two or three at least.'

'It's the former Recorder.'

'The Recorder of London?' She frowns. 'Are you sure? He's notoriously ... difficult.'

'He's a complete bastard,' says Charles with a smile. 'But I think I've ground him down. I've done two or three very memorable cases before him. And he sort of ... *owes* me.'

'Very well. We've time to get our ducks in a row. It would help if you put yourself about a bit more with the Inn. I know you hate the glad-handing, but you need to raise your profile with the great and the good. Dislodge some of the adverse opinions formed over the years.'

He shakes his head. 'I hate it, you know I do. They're snobby, entitled gits, and whether I get silk or not should not depend on their good opinion of me.'

'It's those snobby entitled gits who will decide your application, will they not? The judges and the Benchers? Now the Krays are out of the picture, sir, you've a chance to wipe the slate clean. You of all people need to play the game, or you'll never overcome your … disadvantages.'

'Okay. I get it,' says Charles, resigned. He knows she's right. 'You'd have thought that doing "exceptional work" would be enough,' he adds.

Barbara smiles gently. 'When has that ever been enough?'

Charles leafs through some miscellaneous papers on his desk. 'This, then?'

Barbara leans forward and reads. 'Bench Call? Yes, that'd be perfect. Oh, it's tonight! I imagine it's too late, but do you want me to call the Treasury?'

'Yes, please.'

'Just one ticket, sir?'

'No, get two if you can, and I'll see if I can persuade Sally to lend moral support.'

'Well,' says Barbara, standing, 'she won't be the only clerk there. I know of two or three going to support their guvnors on their call night.'

'Thank you. And Barbara?'

'Aye?'

'I'm sure I don't have to say this, but *schtum* please. No one is to know in the clerks' room except you. And obviously no one else at all.'

'Of course, sir. I've done this before, you know. When are you back at the Bailey?'

'Tomorrow afternoon, after sentencing in the Andover spy case. But I've only got summing up and verdict left. I was hoping for some time off afterwards, actually.' He points to the tall pile of papers on his desk awaiting attention.

'I'll block you out of court after tomorrow. Will three days be enough?'

Charles considers the pile. 'It'll certainly help. Thank you.'

Barbara's hand rests on the door handle. She turns towards Charles, clearly with something further to say, but not making eye contact with him.

'Something else, Barbara?'

'Well, no … it's just … och, do try to keep out of trouble for a wee while, Mr Holborne, sir?'

'Me?' asks Charles in mock-innocence.

CHAPTER TWO

Kevin Lane strides into Shap Street, Hoxton, east London, and almost bumps into a horse. It has a bag of feed around its head, and stands patiently by the pavement, hitched to a cart piled high with junk.

'A'right, Vera?' he says to the old nag. 'Thought you was retired.'

'She is,' comes a voice.

Vera's owner, an ancient rag and bone man known by everyone in the area as "Picky", is exiting Mrs Snyder's front door, an old lampstand in his hand, as Mrs Snyder slips some coins into her housecoat pocket and shuts the door behind him.

'Last day today,' says Picky, throwing the lamp onto the cart and lifting the bag of feed off the horse's head. 'Wheeler Dealer fixed us up with a van. It's comin' tommorah.'

'Knackers?' asks Kev, nodding at the old nag as he crosses the road, and walking backwards to finish his conversation.

'Nah. Couldn't do it. Got anything for me, Kev?'

'Sorry mate,' calls Kev, turning and continuing on his course.

He skirts the half dozen or so lads playing football on the cobbles, goalposts of clothing piled on opposite pavements, and walks past Mrs Booth from next door. In pinafore and mop cap, she is scrubbing her front step while chatting to Mrs Perry from number 40.

Hurrying isn't in Big Kev's nature. Maude is often heard to complain that if the house were burning down, Kev'd still finish his tea before stirring from his armchair. However, insofar as moving quickly is within Big Kevin's capabilities, he is doing it now. While no one dares argue with him on the streets of London, the natural order of things is reversed in the Lane household. Maude Lane, Kev's wife of sixteen years, she who could "argue the hind legs off a donkey", rules 38 Shap Street, and Maude Lane cannot abide cold, soggy chips. Cold, soggy chips are what she's going to get unless Kev has them — and the haddock presently rolled in newspaper under his arm — back home, double-quick.

He opens the door to the narrow terraced cottage. The O'Connors are fighting again in the front room, and Kev makes use of their raised voices to slip by their door unheeded and head upstairs. He hasn't time to be collared by his landlord this evening. Tom O'Connor has been out of work for over a year and has nothing to occupy his time except beating his wife, shouting futilely at his three tearaway boys (all now bigger than him) and badgering Kevin to find him work in the Firm.

The O'Connors still have sole use of the ground floor but had no choice but to sublet their upstairs. Two families now pay rent for the upper floor, the Hammersteins and their daughters in the front room, and Mr and Mrs Lane in the back. All three families share the outside privy. Conditions have eased slightly over the last few days since the Hammersteins left to visit relatives in Glasgow.

Kev opens the door to the back room.

'Got the last two haddock,' he says as he enters.

It's a good-sized room with tall ceilings, but the space is full of their double bed, a table and two chairs by the window overlooking the yard, and the sink in the corner. There is a two-ring gas stove behind the door.

'Maude?'

The diminutive woman sits on the far side of the bed, her curved back to the door. Unusually, she gives no answer.

Kev takes two plates from the shelf and starts unrolling their fish suppers. The room fills with the odours of fried haddock and vinegar. He lifts the fillets onto the plates and divides the chips with his fingers. Only then does he go over to his wife.

"S'up?' he asks, bending to her. He starts as he sees the baby in her arms. 'Maude!' he exclaims softly.

She looks up at him, her dark eyes wide with appeal. 'Couldn't do it, Kev, just couldn't. Look at 'im! 'E's an angel!'

Kev regards the baby in his wife's arms. He does look angelic. He is asleep, his lips a perfect rosebud and his eyelids a delicate mauve. He has a pink fist curled round one of Maude's fingers.

'A little angel, sent to us...' she says softly, bending to place her lips on his forehead. 'I got to Guy's and went to the loo in Casualty. I was about to leave 'im, honest I was. But then ... he opened his eyes, and he looked right at me. Didn't cry or nuffin', just looked right into me. And I knew he was asking ... *begging* me, not to leave 'im.'

Kev sits down next to her, causing the bed to dip and the springs to *twang*.

'But, Maudie,' he says gently, 'we can't keep 'im. The law'll be after 'im.'

She shakes her head. 'But I've been thinking. His mother weren't there, right? She's probably dead, ain't she? Overdose most like. You 'ear it all the time. Or if she ain't, she obviously don't want the little mite. On the other 'and...'

She doesn't need to finish the sentence. They tried for years, losing baby after baby, until the doctors told her she'd probably never carry to term, and she should stop trying or the next one might kill her.

'But how do we explain it?' he asks. 'Everyone knows you ain't been...'

'I know, I know. Thought about that too.' She pauses. 'What if we say it's Alice's?'

'Who?'

'Little Alice, Connie's girl.'

Kev's heavy face wrinkles like a bloodhound's as he tries to place the names. 'You mean, your niece? She's only fourteen, ain't she? And in Macclesfield.'

'Exactly. No one'd ever know. We say she got in the family way, Connie wouldn't have the baby in the 'ouse, and asked us to help out. It'll work, Kev, honest it will!'

She looks up from the baby into his face, her expression beseeching. 'Please, Kev! I've never asked for nothing, in all these years. For richer, for poorer it was, and I've taken it all, ain't I?' He doesn't answer. 'Well, ain't I?'

He sighs heavily. 'You 'ave.'

'And you know how 'ard it's been on me, not having me own.'

'I do.'

Her eyes fill with tears. 'Then give me this last chance to 'ave a family, love. I'm beggin' you.'

Big Kevin Lane looks down at his fierce little wife and the scrap of life cradled in her arms, and thinks.

He is not much given to thought. Most of the time he is able to enjoy a simple life doing what he is told by Maude and Little Kev. Nonetheless, after a few moments, the slow grinding of the gears in his massive head produces a conclusion.

This is a bad idea.

Little Kev will be furious if he learns that, instead of Maude leaving the baby at the hospital as agreed, she kept it. So that means lying to his boss, something he has never done before. More worrying, the baby represents a loose end, one which, if pulled by the police, could lead to a lot of other stuff — big stuff — unravelling.

On the other hand, he adores this little woman, who he has happily allowed to boss him about since their very first meeting at the Hammersmith Palais de Danse in 1946. Over the years he saw her pain, her shame at her "failure", and he could do nothing. He watched, helpless, as part of her faded away when they told her it would be dangerous to try further. And it's true; she has suffered all the ups and downs of the last twenty-three years without complaint, never asking for anything.

Big Kev takes a deep breath. 'Okay, sweetheart. Let's keep 'im. I'll work it out.'

She sobs, a great heave of happiness. 'Really?'

'Yeah, really.' He puts his great arm around her shaking shoulders. 'So, what we gonna call the little beggar?'

CHAPTER THREE

'Are you nearly ready?' calls Charles from the hallway to the top of the house.

He looks at his watch. Unless they hurry, all of Barbara's efforts to secure the last two tickets for Bench Call Night will have been wasted

There is no reply, but he can hear Sally hurriedly opening drawers and wardrobe doors above him.

Sally agreed that Charles needed to "play the game" — cultivate the judges and benchers of his Inn if he proposed to apply for silk in the next round — but it took some of Charles's best advocacy to persuade her to drop everything and return to the Temple immediately after a long day's work. And while he could get away with a quick wash and re-polishing of his shoes, she needed to shower, do her hair and change into something appropriate. Bench Call Nights are glittering occasions, and Sally will be on display, probably more than any other woman present. In addition to being one of only three female senior clerks in the Temple, there is her provocative relationship with Charles. The profession disapproves of clerks and barristers fraternising, let alone living "in sin". The fact that Charles and Sally now have a child born out of wedlock is viewed as positively scandalous.

Sally had hoped that the absence of last-minute childcare would get her off the hook. She'd reckoned without Charles's charm.

He puts his head into the lounge. Their South African doctor friend, Irenna Alexandrova, is on the floor playing with Leia.

'All okay?' he asks.

'We're fine,' she says, looking up, 'aren't we, Leia?'

Sally clatters down the stairs in her high heels. She wears a tight-fitting black Ossie Clark maxi dress with puffy shoulders and a drop neckline. Over her arm she carries a short jacket adorned with glittering buttons which match her earrings.

'Wow!' says Irenna. 'You look fabulous!'

'What do you think?' asks Sally of Charles, spinning round. 'Too much?'

Charles's eyes open wide. Sally is petite and curvaceous, with an hourglass figure accentuated by recent pregnancy, large brown eyes in a pale oval face, and a short Vidal Sassoon pageboy haircut to her glossy dark hair.

'No,' he says, smiling. 'You can carry it off.'

'They're all going to stare anyway, so I thought I'd give 'em something to stare at,' she says, grinning.

'I agree with Irenna. You look fabulous.' He looks again at his watch. 'But we've got to go. Right now.'

Sally crosses to Leia and places a kiss on her head. 'Are you sure about this?'

'About spending an evening with my goddaughter? I'm frankly offended you don't ask me more often.'

Bench Call Night in Middle Temple Hall is one of the most important occasions on the Inn's calendar. The barristers, judges and academics being elevated to the position of "Master" (regardless of sex) are leaders in their profession, and are responsible for running all aspects of Middle Temple life, including training, mentoring and care of the estate. Callees are "called" to the Bench prior to dinner and take their places at High Table. After dinner each new Bencher gives a short speech, in the time-honoured phrase, to "give an account of themselves" to the guests.

Charles and Sally's coats are taken by the staff, and they enter the Tudor hall from the milling crowd at the entrance. Sally looks up at the hammerbeam ceiling, the ornate decorations and the shiny chandeliers. The enormous room is set for dinner with long trestle tables full of cutlery, sparkling glasses and illuminated candles.

'Not bad, is it?' says Charles softly, at her elbow.

'I get why you like it. East End boy making this all his.'

'It's not that. You know I hate all the power and prestige, not to mention the frills and fripperies. It's the *history*. The Virgin Queen dined here, at that very table over there, in 1602. Sir Walter Raleigh and Sir Francis Drake were regulars. Shakespeare acted on these very floorboards. Of the five meddlesome Middle Templars who signed the American Declaration of Independence, one became its second Chief Justice. How many people can say they work in such an environment? We're inside a living history book! Come on, let's find our set.'

'Set?'

'Seats on the benches. They're in "sets" of four, and strictly we're not supposed to speak to anyone outside the set. Although I guess that'll be relaxed tonight, with so many guests being non-barristers.'

Charles guides Sally to their places and they take opposite sides of the table.

'Not exactly comfortable, is it?' comments Sally on the hard wooden benches.

They have barely taken their seats when they are approached by another couple.

'I'm not sure we're in ze right place,' says the man, addressing Charles in a thick German accent.

Charles looks up and immediately recognises the speaker, but for a moment, out of context, cannot place him. He glances down at the menu which bears the names of the people in their set.

'Sir Leo Wise,' Charles says. 'Of course! Forgive me, I recognised you but couldn't place you. I was reading about you only this morning. Yes, you're in the right place, although one of you will need to walk round to this side of the bench.'

'I will go round,' replies the businessman. 'You sit here, Esther,' he says, indicating the place next to Sally. 'May I introduce you to my wife, Lady Esther Wise?' he says.

Charles stands and shakes Esther Wise's hand. She is even more beautiful in person than she is in her photographs. She wears a long dress in midnight blue with a white fur stole, and she is tall — considerably taller than her husband — and very slim, with shoulder-length golden hair held loosely by a clasp at the back of her head. Her eyes are a striking green-blue. She looks like the film star Lauren Bacall. Her age is difficult to judge — her pale skin is translucent and entirely blemish-free — but could be anywhere between thirty-five and fifty. Charles judges that she is probably a couple of years older than he.

Like Bacall, Esther Wise does not look Jewish, and Charles reminds himself that the German woman's father was a Bavarian aristocrat who hated the Nazis and was sent to Auschwitz along with his Jewish wife and two half-Jewish daughters. So far as Hitler was concerned, half-Jewish was quite enough to have you murdered. Indeed, a quarter was sufficient.

'I am very pleased to meet you,' she says, taking Charles's hands gently in hers. She doesn't so much shake as caress it. As soon as she speaks, the Lauren Bacall impression is dispelled in favour of a husky Marlene Dietrich. She has the deepest voice of any woman Charles has ever heard.

Lady Wise and Sally also shake hands while Sir Leo skirts around to sit next to Charles.

'You are a barrister, yes?' he asks of Charles, as he clambers onto the bench with a little difficulty. 'Or maybe a judge?'

'Barrister and a member of this Inn. I'm Charles Holborne, and this is my girlfriend, Sally Fisher, who is the senior clerk at another set of chambers.'

'Good,' replies Sir Leo with a nod of approval. 'Then we have two experts to guide us on the correct procedure.'

'How is it you come to be here, Sir Leo?' asks Sally. 'I'm guessing you're somebody's guests?'

It is Lady Wise who answers. 'We are guests of Deiter Cowan who is … what's the expression? Being…?'

'Called?' supplies Charles.

'Yes, that is right,' says Lady Wise. 'So he will be on the long table over there with all the *gunser machas*.'

Sally frowns at Charles, not understanding the Yiddish expression.

'Big shots,' he translates.

'I see,' says Sally. 'Is Mr Cowan a colleague, then?'

'He's an academic,' replies Charles. 'Isn't that right? I remember him from my degree studies. "Cowan on International Criminal Law", I believe.'

'In fact, he is a colleague, of sorts,' clarifies Sir Leo, 'as he sits as a non-executive director of the 613 Trust, but you are correct. He is being honoured tonight for his contribution to law. He played a major part in the establishment of the International Criminal Court. An old, old friend.'

'The 613 Trust?' asks Charles.

'You say you saw me in the newspaper today, yes?' replies Sir Leo. Charles nods. 'I was laying a commemoration stone, I think.'

'You were indeed.'

'I have already complained to the editor.'

'Why?'

'They used an old photograph, and it was mis-captioned. That commemoration stone was for a new care home facility for elderly Jewish people in North London. Not for Seagull Tower, which is almost complete. The 613 Trust is building the home.'

'That's an unusual name,' says Sally. 'Why 613?'

Sir Leo turns to her with a warm smile. 'You are not Jewish, so perhaps you wouldn't know,' he replies.

'I'm Jewish, and I'm afraid I don't know,' says Charles.

'Really? Tsk, tsk,' berates Sir Leo. 'Not an Old Testament scholar, then?' He winks.

Charles shrugs and smiles. 'No. My parents and brother are observant, but I'm afraid it never interested me. So, why "613"?'

'Most people think there are only ten Commandments in the Torah, but in fact there are six hundred and thirteen.'

'Really? I find ten hard enough,' jokes Charles. 'But didn't I read that you no longer follow the Jewish faith?'

'My goodness, haven't we strayed onto controversial ground swiftly?' intervenes Lady Wise. She is smiling, but there is an edge to her masculine voice.

'I apologise for the bull in the china shop opposite, Lady Wise,' says Sally, giving Charles a hard stare. 'My boyfriend is not known for his diplomacy skills.'

'I'm so sorry —' starts Charles, flushing.

Sir Leo waves away his embarrassment. 'No, no, no, it is perfectly all right. It is no secret. I'm sure you can understand, after what I witnessed — what *we* witnessed,' he adds, so as to include his wife. 'But surviving such things, against truly unimaginable odds, when everyone you know has perished and all around you are dying and, yet, for some reason ... you are not? I no longer believe in an almighty power, that is true. If there was such a power, where was it in the camps? But I have to believe I was saved for a purpose. Why would Providence save me, merely for me to live a small life and make no difference? So I devote myself to doing what I can. It is not much, perhaps, but it is all one man can do. And at this moment, that is to provide decent modern homes to the poor wretches living in the East End of London in quite appalling conditions.'

The conversation is interrupted by a man standing at the centre of the head table and rapping the board in front of him for silence.

Charles lowers his voice. 'Master Treasurer is calling us to order,' he says. 'But I'd be very interested to hear about the care home. My parents are in one, and it is far from satisfactory.'

'Shhh!' commands Sally, putting a finger to her lips.

Charles and Sally leave as soon as they can after the dinner and speeches, but it is gone ten o'clock by the time they arrive home. Although they found Sir Leo and Lady Wise charming, Charles was unable to talk to as many of the senior members of the Inn as he had hoped. The German couple knew nobody at the event other than their friend, the new "Master Cowan", who sat at the High Table, chatting to the other Masters, and Charles and Sally felt responsible for, and remained with, them.

The Wises did leave early — Sir Leo was looking increasingly tired — which allowed Charles a little while to chat with a couple of the judges, but he knew it was insufficient and he found the evening frustrating. He would have to continue attending these events throughout the year if he was to make progress. He'd also have to join a couple of Hall committees — do some voluntary work on behalf of the Inn — to become better known.

He leads the way up the stone steps to the front door of their home on Wren Street. He is fishing for his keys, only for the door to open for him. Two men rush past, obviously in a hurry. They carry instrument cases containing, in one, a saxophone and in the other, judging from its size, a double bass.

The sax player shouts as he runs past. 'Sorry, Charles! Gotta run, man. Last-minute fill-in for a late set at the Dorchester! Hi Sally!' He waves as he sprints off towards Gray's Inn Road, the bass player struggling to keep up.

The lanky American is Jordan, the semi-live-in boyfriend of Charles and Sally's lodger, Maria Hudson. Maria used to be a pupil barrister at Charles's chambers, but gave up the Bar to try her luck as a jazz musician. Originally offered the spare room as a stopgap while she negotiated the fallout from that decision, two years later she is an integral part of the household. Wren Street is now often full of young musicians brewing tea, jamming in the dining room and smoking in the garden. More than once, Charles has come down to breakfast to find an unknown artist in boxer shorts, drinking coffee at his kitchen table. He loves it. An aficionado himself, one whose face is well-known at Ronnie Scott's and other jazz venues in London, Charles is energised by these young people, most of whom are fifteen or twenty years younger than he. He can't believe his luck, listening as they practice and being included in their conversations.

They find Irenna in front of the television in the front room. Having explained that Leia settled without a murmur, she hurries to put on her coat and shoes and get back to her own home. Sally sees her off at the door with a hug while Charles heads downstairs to the kitchen in the semi-basement to make up some formula for Leia's final feed of the day.

He flicks on the kitchen light. The room has been extended out into the garden, and its glass ceiling makes it the lightest and most popular room in the house. It is, for once, empty and tidy.

He heats the formula, fills Leia's bottle and takes it upstairs to let Sally settle their daughter down for the night. Twenty minutes later Sally enters the kitchen.

'All right?' he asks.

'Out like a light,' says Sally. 'I had to wake her a couple of times to get her to finish.'

'Bed?' he asks.

'Definitely. I'm bleedin' knackered.'

'Really? It's not that late.'

'Yeah, but someone came in at just after four this morning and woke her. I couldn't get her back to sleep so I brought her into bed with us.'

'I didn't know you were up with her in the night. You should have said.'

'You were spark out,' says Sally. 'Sorry, Charlie, but I'm going up.'

She turns and departs, leaving Charles to turn out the lights and follow her up to the top floor.

He resumes talking as they undress. 'Thanks for coming tonight. I know the timing was crap.'

Sally sighs wearily as she hangs her dress in the wardrobe. 'Yes, it was.' She sits on the edge of the bed to remove her stockings. 'Charlie?'

'Yes?'

'We gotta make some changes. I'm tired of tidying up after Maria and the others. You know I love her, and we couldn't have managed without them looking after Leia during the day, but I need peace and quiet when I get in, not noise, disruption and random American jazz musicians using the phone. And they keep taking food from the fridge.'

Her shoulders are slumped and her face forlorn. Charles skirts the bed and sits by her side, their shoulders and thighs touching. He inhales her perfume and the scent of her hair.

'They always leave a note. Usually money too,' he points out gently.

'I ain't suggesting they're dishonest. But if I buy stuff and it's not there when I get in, I gotta get Leia dressed again and go out to the shops! It just makes more work for me. And I'm sick and tired of Leia being woken when they come in at all hours. Their lifestyles ain't compatible with having a small baby in the house.'

'Do you want to ask Maria to leave?'

Sally sighs again. 'I hate to say it but, yes, I think so.'

Charles nods. 'Okay. How will you manage work without her looking after Leia?'

'We'll need a nanny.'

'Live in?'

She shrugs. 'Preferably not, but whatever works.'

'All right. I'll start looking at agencies.'

'Good. Then I'll give it another six months, and reconsider.'

'Give what another six months?'

'Work. Part of me — maybe most of me — wants to be at home with Leia. I miss her so much! And I hate not being here when she does something new.'

'And the other part?'

'How can I give up Chancery Court? It's taken me years to get where I am.'

'Did you ask the committee if they'd increase the juniors' hours a little?' asks Charles. 'So you could leave earlier?'

'I asked, but the meeting ain't 'til the end of next week. They don't see it as a priority. One said, now I'm a mother, my place is in the home anyway.'

'Disappointing. And exactly your mother and sister's position.'

Sally rolls her stockings down to her ankles and removes them. 'They'll never understand. They never had careers.' She stops, still in underwear and suspenders, and turns to Charles. 'It ain't fair, Charlie.'

'What isn't?'

'Leia's your daughter too, but no one expects you to stay at home and give up your career.'

'We've discussed this, sweetheart,' he says gently. 'I still earn three times what you do. And if I get silk, that differential could double. It makes no sense for me to stop, or turn work away. And what would you say if one of your star guvnors said he wanted to work part-time?' Sally pulls a face. 'There you are then. You know the score. No decent barrister works less than full-time plus thirty per cent. What about you? You mentioned working part-time before Leia was born.'

She shakes her head. 'The committee chair said no. Far as they're concerned, they want a full-time senior clerk and no job-sharing.'

Sally looks up at him intently, a frown on her oval face. Charles senses there's more, and that what she's said so far isn't even what's troubling her the most.

'What?' he asks.

'I had a word with Barbara on Friday,' she says eventually.

'And?'

As the senior clerks of two sets of chambers doing criminal work, it would not be surprising for the two women occasionally to communicate, over returns, perhaps fees, but there is something ominous in Sally's tone.

'Your diary is very busy.'

'Yes, I know. You didn't need to speak to Barbara. I could've told you.'

'Yes, but I wanted the truth.'

That brings Charles up short. He puts a hand on her shoulder. 'Sal?' he says gently. 'What's going on?'

She spins round and glares at him. Her furious expression takes him completely by surprise. 'There are no gaps. Nothing, until October!' she challenges.

'Yes. Like I said, it's really busy.'

'So, were you planning on us going anywhere, like a holiday maybe, or doing anything at all? Except work and childcare.'

Charles still can't see what Sally's getting at. 'Yes, probably, when a gap appeared. Like last year, we got that last minute deal…' His voice tails off.

'I guess you thought that now we've got Leia, I'm tied to you for life, right? No way out.'

He frowns. 'Yes. No. Well, I didn't think you'd run off with some other bloke, but I didn't assume anything about…' He bends to look at her face. Her eyes are glistening but her expression is defiant. 'Have I missed something here? Darling, what have I missed?'

'You don't understand women at all, do you, Charlie Horowitz?'

'Erm … no … apparently not.'

'At the end of last year, you all but proposed to me. In that lovely bed in Hastings, and at least once after we got back.'

'Yes. I know.'

'So? Gone off the idea?'

'No!' he protests. 'Of course not! I've been waiting for the right moment. I thought maybe, I dunno, Paris perhaps, or that trip to Ireland we talked about…'

'A big romantic gesture?'

'Yes. I wanted to make it special.'

'And you couldn't find time to make anything "special" between December last year and October of this? Is that what you're saying? Not one weekend away, not one "special" meal out?'

He nods ruefully. 'Yes. I suppose so.'

'Well, it ain't good enough, Charlie. Do you still love me?'

'Do I? Are you serious? I adore you. I tell you every five minutes.'

He tries to put his arms around her but she shoves him away.

'Oh, no! No, no, no. You ain't getting round me this time.' He obeys and stays where he is. 'For a brilliant man, Charlie Horowitz, you ain't 'alf bloody dim sometimes! I love you too. More than I've ever loved anyone. And I want to be your wife. I don't need grand gestures; I need your fuckin' commitment! Especially now, as you've got me trapped with a baby.'

'Trapped?' he exclaims.

'And as we both know,' she forges on, ignoring him, 'commitment's always been a problem with you and women, ain't that so?'

'Well —' Charles starts to justify himself but realises, for once, that discretion is the better part of valour. He seizes her by her shoulders.

'Just wait there,' he commands. 'Don't move an inch! You hear me?'

He sees furious tears in her eyes but there's a trace of a smile on her lips too, and she nods.

Charles races out of the bedroom to his study. There is then a delay with some faint banging of drawers before he returns. Sally hasn't budged. Slightly out of breath, he bends down on one knee and opens a small velveteen box in his palm. It contains the diamond ring.

'Sally Fisher,' he says. 'You are my sun, my moon, and all my stars. I love you and the life we have built here together more than I can ever express. I cannot bear the thought of living a single day of the rest of my life without you by my side. Please, will you marry me?'

Sally looks down at him, tears of happiness streaming down her cheeks, a broad smile on her lips. She has to take a couple of breaths to steady herself before answering.

'Yes, you idiot, of course I'll marry you. Now, how hard was that?'

CHAPTER FOUR

Charles wakes to find Sally gone. He looks at the bedside clock; almost half past eight. She must have left him to sleep, knowing that his case was listed at not before two o'clock.

He showers, dresses and descends to the kitchen to find Jordan feeding Leia her breakfast.

'Morning, Jordan. No Maria?' asks Charles.

'Hi,' says the American saxophonist. 'She got in late, so I volunteered.'

'Thank you. I'm well aware you're not being paid for this.'

'You wouldn't say that if you knew how much of your booze and coffee we get through,' Jordan grins. 'We're quits. And we're having fun, ain't we, Leia?'

'Well, I'm grateful 'cos I've got to get moving. Running late.'

Charles drops a piece of bread into the toaster and races back upstairs to gather his papers from his desk.

Fifteen minutes later, wearing barristers' regulation three-piece suit and striped trousers, he is running towards Gray's Inn Road, hopeful of finding a taxi. Just as he emerges onto the main road an ancient No. 17 Routemaster bus trundles past him and slows for traffic lights at the next junction. Charles runs after it and jumps aboard the deck as it moves off.

The lower deck is completely packed. Passengers standing shoulder to shoulder in the aisle turn to stare at him, looking pointedly at his briefcase and his large red robes bag. The man closest to him shakes his head as if to say "Don't even think about it!" Charles grins ruefully and nods. With a sigh, he hoists his belongings and climbs the steep steps to the top deck, finding a vacant seat towards the front.

He watches the rush-hour traffic crawling southwards and replays his proposal to Sally in his head. He finds himself grinning from ear to ear. He is so happy, he thinks his chest might burst. He hadn't imagined that formalising what he always understood to be the position between the two of them would make much difference to his state of mind. He was wrong. He had believed that committing to somebody so completely was taking a risk. Now he has done it, or at least promised to do it, he realises that it is in fact exactly the opposite. It is *not* marrying Sally which constitutes the risk. Their agreement to spend the rest of their lives together removes the risk that he might find himself without her. Having finally come to that realisation, he cannot bear the thought of wasting time before the actual wedding.

The only little niggle in his mind is the question of how to break the news to his parents. The first time he married, also to someone outside their faith, they sat *shiva* and cast him into outer darkness, never to speak to him again. As far as they were concerned, their elder son had died. It was only Henrietta's murder and Charles's run from the police that finally caused a rapprochement, and even that (at least in the case of Millie) was grudging and temporary. He decides to call David that evening and seek his advice.

He feels a light pressure on his shoulder and, simultaneously, a voice speaks softly from behind him.

'Don't turn round, Horowitz.'

Charles's heart leaps and he realises with a shock that brings a cold sweat immediately to his forehead that Sally was right. He's been over-confident, and this is the result. What now? A bullet on a crowded bus seems unlikely, but a knife to the kidneys?

'You can't expect to get away with it,' he says quickly from the corner of his mouth. 'Not here, not in a bus full of passengers.'

'I ain't trying to get away with nothing. I jus' wanna talk.'

'That you, Billy?' asks Charles.

There's a long pause and Charles realises that he has correctly identified the voice: Billy Munday, one of the Krays' former enforcers and paymasters.

'Yeah, it's me,' he says.

'Then why the fuck can't I turn round?'

There's no answer. Charles turns slowly, his pounding heart rate slowing. 'Didn't you get eighteen months?' he asks.

'Only served half. Got out Friday.'

Charles examines the young man sitting on the bench behind him. He is very tall in his seat, with a quiff of rather greasy fair hair standing almost upright from a broad forehead. In his early thirties, he bears the grey pallor of recent imprisonment, but otherwise he would be quite a handsome young man.

'Well? What can I do for you?' asks Charles.

Munday looks over both shoulders but no one's paying them any attention. 'It ain't what you can do for me,' he whispers, 'it's what I can do for you.'

'Which is?'

'I've got information you'll want to hear.'

'Okay. Give.'

Munday leans back in his seat, smiling. 'Nah. Not now, and it's gonna cost you. I need a sub.'

'Come on, Billy,' says Charles, keeping his voice low. 'I wasn't born yesterday. I need to know what you've got.'

'What you've got, is my word. It's kosher. I heard it in the 'Ville.'

'Prison gossip?' scoffs Charles. 'Give me a break!'

'No, this ain't gossip. It's 'undred per cent kosher. About the twins. Honest, Horowitz, you need to hear this.'

Charles considers. 'Okay. I'm not promising anything, but when and where?'

'The *Blind Beggar*, this evening.'

The *Beggar*, as it's known by regulars, is an East End institution. Housed in an ugly building in the heart of one of the poorest boroughs of London, the pub offers neither ambience nor entertainment. It caters to working men who need to get drunk quickly and cheaply. It is said to be named after Henry de Montfort who was blinded at the Battle of Evesham in 1265 and who, after marrying well despite his impairment, suffered a further reversal in his fortunes and spent his remaining life begging at the crossroads outside the pub. It's a good story, and great marketing for the business. More provably however, it was where Ronnie Kray murdered George Cornell in 1966 by calmly walking up to him and shooting him in the forehead as Cornell sat drinking at the crowded bar.

Charles is not surprised that Munday has suggested it — it'll be home from home for him — and he thinks it unlikely that this is a set-up. He and Munday have known one another slightly for years, both affected by the gravitational pull of the Kray twins, but there's never been any trouble between them. Munday is not such an idiot as to try something in public, and only a few days after his release from Pentonville Prison. Charles is also aware that like many in the Firm, even before Nipper Read's task force was set up, Billy Munday was becoming increasingly uncomfortable at the Krays' descent into irrational, paranoid murder of their own associates. So Charles thinks he probably can trust him, at least as far as a meeting.

On the other hand, the *Beggar* is the regular boozer of a lot of up-and-coming young tearaways. It would only take one glory-seeker hoping to ingratiate himself to the twins, or an ambitious youngster with plans to take over what remains of their empire, and Charles could find himself in trouble.

'No,' he concludes. 'How about *Jack Straw's Castle?*'

'What, in Hampstead? It's in the bloody country! Why not somewhere in the Smoke?'

'Hampstead is twenty minutes on the tube from King's Cross, Billy. Probably only five miles from Whitechapel.' Charles smiles. 'And a bit of country air'll do you good.'

'Why there?'

'It's neutral territory, and it's...' Charles searches for the appropriate word. What he is actually thinking is, it's middle-class. The old coaching inn's clientele is increasingly made up of young professionals recently relocated to trendy Highgate and Hampstead. The food is good and it's not unusual to see unaccompanied women there. Neither Munday nor Charles are likely to be recognised and anyone hoping to have a go at Charles would be immediately conspicuous.

'It's safe for both of us,' says Charles. 'Nine o'clock?'

Munday scrutinises Charles carefully, nods, stands, and without another word walks to the back of the bus where he descends the stairs. Charles watches from the window as the former enforcer jumps off the running plate while the bus is still moving. He sits back in his seat, only to realise that they are entering Fleet Street. He hurries to follow and puts the matter out of his mind.

Jack Straw's Castle, Hampstead, at the junction of New End Way and Spaniards Road, is Charles's favourite pub in London and, accordingly, the entire world. Situated at the highest point of London, from its decorative battlements one could gaze south and east over Hampstead Heath, the historic hunting ground of many a footpad and highwayman, to most of the Metropolis laid out below. To its rear, behind its formal gardens, lies West Heath, a large area of woodland. When first constructed, the inn lay north of the village of Hampstead, and although the area is now more prosaically part of the London Borough of Camden, it remains a semi-rural haven for wildlife, dog walkers and clandestine lovers.

In truth it was not its location that first attracted Charles, but its history. Despite his colleagues' insistence that his Jewish heritage is inimical to his being "properly" English, Charles's Englishness has played a far greater part in his life than the religion of his forebears. He fought for, and was decorated by, the country he loves during the Second World War, and it was the history of that country, history woven into the fabric of the Honourable Society of the Middle Temple, that fired his ambition to be a barrister.

So it was with *Jack Straw's Castle*. Charles's favourite author, Charles Dickens, is recorded as having said that here one could always get "a red-hot chop for dinner and a glass of good wine", a sentiment with which his namesake agrees. William Makepeace Thackeray and Wilkie Collins drank at the inn, and it is even mentioned in Bram Stoker's *Dracula*. Indeed, the prospect that the pub would be his "local" was a significant factor in Charles's purchase of the now-sold house in Hampstead where Sally and he had their first, ill-fated, attempt at living together.

He stands outside the pub for a moment, simply enjoying its white clapboard frontage and the sheen on the huge lanterns overhanging the pavement. The crepuscular light illuminates the building in unreal, Technicolor, hues. The building could have come straight from a Hollywood backlot.

He is not concerned about his forthcoming meeting with Billy Munday. He made sure to arrive forty minutes early and watched from his car as Munday arrived, alone, bought a drink and stationed himself at a table from which he could see the front doors and Charles's entrance. Munday has not spoken to anyone since. Charles is reasonably confident this is not a trap.

He enters the building, sees and nods towards Munday and hangs up his coat and hat. He is pleased to note that there are over a dozen other patrons sitting at tables, several of whom are women, and more drinkers still at the bar. Munday however is at a table in the corner and is reasonably inconspicuous.

'Evening, Billy,' says Charles as he arrives at the table. He gestures for Munday to stand up. 'Do you mind?'

Munday puts down his glass and rises, allowing Charles to frisk him. Satisfied that the man is carrying no weapons, Charles says: 'Thank you. Drink?'

'I'm good, thanks,' says the other, pointing at the glass before him and resuming his seat.

'Ordering food?' asks Charles. 'I'd recommend it.'

'No. This won't take long.'

'Well, I will, if you don't mind. We can chat while it arrives.'

Charles goes to the bar, orders a rare steak and chips, and brings a pint of mild back to the table.

'Okay, Billy,' he says after taking a long draught, 'what've you got?'

Munday shakes his head. 'Uh-uh. Money first.'

'I've already explained, I'm not paying a penny until I know what you have. You're going to have to trust me.'

Munday looks down, chewing his lip. 'It's about the twins. Look, if it's kosher, is it worth a ton?'

'Hundred quid? Come on, don't be silly. A pony perhaps. *Perhaps.*'

Again, Munday pauses, undecided. Finally: 'And you'll pay me tonight?'

Charles nods. 'I've got twenty-five on me. If the information's worth it.'

'Fair enough. Ronnie and Reggie won't accept it's over. They're trying to get someone to take a contract on you.'

Charles nods. 'That's not exactly news, is it?' he says. 'And weren't you one of their top enforcers? How do I know you're not the contractor?'

Munday pulls a face and shakes his head firmly. 'Nah. Had enough of all that. I can't do it no more. It was sickening me, all the killings. Even their own mates!' He shakes his head, still disbelieving, and knocks back his drink. 'Anyway, everyone knows you can't trust 'em. They wanted Albert to take Frank's murder, you know that, don't you? And when he refused 'em, they was livid, made all sorts of threats against him and his family, which is why he turned QE.'

Charles is aware of all this, having watched the trial in disguise from the public gallery of the Old Bailey.

Munday continues. 'Even the old lags leaving prison now, you know, the ones who might've taken it for start-up money, they know the score. You can't rely on the twins to pay up, even if you go through with it. So, no, no one's keen. And I certainly ain't.'

'What're you planning to do then?' asks Charles.

Billy Munday smiles shyly, and it takes Charles a moment to recognise embarrassment. 'Gonna try and go straight for a bit, ain't I? No, don't laugh!'

'I'm not laughing, Billy.'

'Yeah, right. I saw that smirk. I've thought it through. I got a property with tenants in, which keeps me ticking by, and I do odd jobs. Painting 'n' such. Thought I might start a small decorating business, see? I want to enjoy the rest of me life without looking over me shoulder.'

'Okay, let's say I believe you, and you won't take the contract. What about everyone else?'

Munday shakes his head. 'I can't speak for everyone, but I think it's a non-starter. The word is, no one wants to get involved, especially after the twins got thirty years. I was down the Regal this weekend, but it's all changed. Only a couple of faces there, and I know they've been offered as well — even Jackie Dobbs, the barman! — but no one'll touch it. We all think it's over. Everyone knows it, 'cept Ronnie and Reggie.'

Charles ponders Munday's words. He'd been wishing to be a fly on the wall at the Regal Billiard Hall, the twins' HQ, for some weeks, to gauge the atmosphere, but decided it was too dangerous. This is the real value of what Billy has to offer: the inside track on the remnants of the Firm and their states of mind.

He nods. Munday's impression makes sense, and he couldn't have asked for a more optimistic outlook.

'Well?' asks Munday hopefully. 'That's got to be worth a pony, at least!'

'It might be, long as you keep me updated. You hear of any change, you let me know. Deal?'

Munday nods. 'Deal.'

Charles reaches into his jacket and takes out his wallet. He counts out £25 and slides the notes across the table to Munday. Munday picks them up and tucks them into a pocket.

'Always had you down as a gent, Horowitz,' he says approvingly. 'Thank you.'

'Thank you too, Billy. And I wish you luck.'

Munday stands and, without a further word, slips out of the pub.

CHAPTER FIVE

'Is that the last?' asks Big Kev.

They have spent the day delivering expensive furniture to slums. It seems odd to Big Kev but he does what he's told. Most of the tenants aren't interested. What's the point of a fancy leather three-piece suite and an American fridge when your house has no electricity and no running water? But some accept it in return for the mildewed collapsing stuff they already have, and they seem happy enough to sign new contracts.

'Yeah, that's it. Early night. I'll drop you off if you like.'

Twenty minutes later Kevin Lane opens the door to the bedsit on Shap Street to find it in darkness.

'Maudie?' he asks stupidly, because there is nowhere she could be hiding.

He flicks on the light. The room is a mess. It smells of cooking and nappies. Kevin looks behind the door and sees the grill pan protruding from the grill. He pulls it out. It contains two uncooked lamb chops. There are some carrots on the counter, some peeled — bright orange coins floating in a saucepan of water — and some awaiting attention.

Kevin climbs over the corner of the bed to look on the tiny kitchen table in front of the window. There, among the unwashed teacups and a plate bearing the crumbs from an earlier meal is a pencilled note. In Maude's regular handwriting he reads: *"Tommy's with baby. Come quick."*

He finds Maude sitting in the emergency department of St Thomas's Hospital, her face creased with worry, and the baby nowhere to be seen. Kevin strides over to her.

'What is it? What's up?' he demands, sitting next to her and taking her tiny hand in his.

'It's little Matthew,' she says. 'I couldn't get him to eat, and he kept crying.'

'Well, 'e's a baby. Ain't that what they do?'

She shakes her head. 'Not like that. This was different, kind of high-pitched and then... Oh Lord, Kev, it was awful!'

'What?'

But she is too distressed to reply. She puts her head in her hands and her chest shakes with a sob. Kevin puts his arm around her shoulders, anxious and uncertain.

A woman in a white coat comes down the corridor.

'Mr and Mrs Lane?' she asks.

Kevin answers. 'Yeah?'

'I'm sorry you've been waiting so long. I'm Dr Richardson, the on-call paediatric registrar. Can you come with me, please?'

Without waiting for an answer, she turns and retraces her steps up the corridor.

'C'mon, love,' says Kevin, helping Maude to her feet.

The woman leads them into a room with a sign saying "Family" on the door. She takes a seat and indicates that the Lanes should follow suit.

'Now,' she says, 'I need some more information from you. What is Matthew's date of birth again?'

Maude gives the date she and Kevin agreed would be the baby's birthday. 'Tenth of March.'

'So, according to you, he's just over four weeks old?'

Maude sniffs and dries her eyes with the back of her hand. 'That's right, yeah.'

'Very well,' continues the doctor. 'If you'll step outside please, Mr Lane, I need to examine your wife.'

Maude and Kevin look at one another. 'Why?' asks Maude.

'Your baby isn't well, and we think that you might not be well either.'

'Me? What have I got to do with it?'

Dr Richardson takes a deep breath, puts her pen down and locks eyes with Maude. 'If you want us to do anything for Matthew, you're going to have to be completely honest with me. Now, Mrs Lane, that baby was not born four weeks ago. I don't think he's more than a fortnight old.'

Kevin opens his mouth to speak and raises his finger to point at Dr Richardson, but she forestalls him.

'Let me finish, please,' she says. She pauses. 'And I don't think Matthew's your baby, is he?'

Again Maude and Kevin look at one another. Eventually Maude responds with their prepared story. 'No. He's my niece's baby. She couldn't look after him, so my sister asked us.'

Dr Richardson nods as if expecting a reply such as this. 'Why couldn't your niece look after the baby?'

'She's very young and they ain't got the room,' replies Kevin.

'Hmm,' says the doctor. 'That might be true, but it's not the whole truth, is it?'

'Don't know what you mean,' says Kevin.

'Well, does she have a problem with drugs?'

Maude replies. 'No. Absolutely not.'

The doctor raises her eyebrows in disbelief. 'Maybe she didn't tell you. Is that possible? Because we think she does. The reason Matthew's so sick, is because he's coming off drugs. It usually starts a day or two after birth, but I've seen cases where it starts as late as five to ten days afterwards.'

'What?' replies Kevin angrily. ''E's a baby! How can he be coming off drugs? I've never heard nothing so ridiculous!'

'Mr Lane,' replies Dr Richardson patiently. 'When a pregnant mother is abusing drugs, they go into the baby's system. So, when the baby is born they are dependent on the drugs, just like the mother. Do you understand?' She turns to Maude. 'That's what caused the fit you witnessed.'

'Fit?' asks Kevin.

Maude turns to him but is so distressed that she cannot answer. She grips his hand. 'Oh, Kev,' she says eventually. 'It was awful. I thought 'e was dying.'

'So,' continues the doctor, 'when did you first notice he wouldn't feed?'

'Yesterday,' says Maude. 'I thought maybe he was just unsettled, leaving his mother and everything.'

'And have there been any other fits?'

Maude closes her eyes as she concentrates. 'I'm not sure. Maybe. He went all rigid and looked as if he was 'olding his breath, but it passed in a minute and then he was okay. Sleepy but okay.'

'Well, then,' says Kevin. 'What can you do?'

'Matthew is very ill. I'm sorry to tell you that quite a few babies in his condition don't survive. As you've probably discovered, they find it difficult to feed, and Matthew is already severely underweight. He needs drugs to help the withdrawal, and a tube to feed him. So, we'll need to keep him in for a while.'

'Can I stay with 'im?' asks Maude.

'We would usually let his *mother* stay, but...'

'I'm the only mother 'e 'as!' says Maude fiercely. 'An' I wanna stay with him!'

Dr Richardson regards the little woman steadily for a moment, and eventually nods. 'I'll see what we can do,' she says, 'but you'll need to speak to one of my colleagues first.

She's the Children's Officer. She has a statutory duty under the Children and Young Persons Act to satisfy herself that you're fit persons to care for Matthew. We can't simply hand over a baby to you, can we now?' She stands. 'Please wait here,' she says.

An hour later the Lanes part at the hospital entrance. Maude has been found a bed in the hospital. Kevin will return home to Shap Street alone.

'Think she bought it?' asks Kevin in a lowered voice.

Maude nods. 'Think so.'

They have given the Children's Officer their prepared story. Kev left Maude to do most of the talking. She explained how they were asked to look after her niece's baby; how the niece, fourteen, unmarried and a drug addict, disappeared immediately after the baby was born; how Maude's sister is disabled and on benefits and so cannot look after it. They have been required to give their own antecedents and working histories, including a false birthdate for Big Kevin which, Maude hopes, will delay the hospital authorities discovering his criminal record long enough for them to get Matthew home from hospital. Then she has a plan for them to disappear.

'You get off, love,' she says. 'Sorry about tea. There's chops on the grill pan. See you tomorrow after work, yeah?'

The following morning the Kevins meet for breakfast at their usual place. The Wimpy at the Lyons Corner House, Coventry Street, has become their unofficial West End office. The first Wimpy Bar to be opened in England, it offers round-the-clock meals, and when they are busy the Kevins often eat breakfast, lunch and dinner there. It's also where Little Kev meets certain clients and other associates who he'd prefer not to bring back to the lockup.

Big Kev looks at his watch and raises his eyebrows to his boss. It's 8:15 a.m. and they have usually left by now.

'Got to wait for Hanrahan,' explains Little Kev.

'Hanrahan?'

'The bloke from the court.'

'All right if I order something else, then? Still a bit peckish.'

'No, you go ahead.'

A few minutes later a man walks in, scans the room, and comes directly to their table. He is in his early forties, slim and bespectacled, with dark rather greasy hair parted in the centre. He wears a dark grey three-piece suit.

'All okay?' he asks, sliding in opposite Little Kev.

'Yeah,' replies Little Kev, lighting a new cigarette.

'Good,' says Hanrahan. He casts a glance at Big Kev, but the giant's attention seems focused on his second breakfast. Little Kev shakes his head as if to say "*Don't worry about him*".

Hanrahan leans forward and speaks with a lowered voice. 'Got new orders from the boss. Change of direction.'

Little Kev considers Hanrahan through a plume of cigarette smoke. 'Oh yeah?'

Hanrahan slides a folded sheet of paper across the table. 'It's all in there. He wants you to call him. He'll explain. The number's at the top.'

'Why do I have to ring 'im? I never 'ad to speak to him before. Don't you give us our orders now?' asks Little Kev warily.

'I do as I'm told. I suggest you do the same.' Hanrahan prods the piece of paper. 'Ask for Tony.'

'When?'

'Now.' He jerks his head to indicate the callbox on the pavement visible through the window.

Little Kev considers the sheet of paper in his hand. 'Fair enough.' He stands. 'Won't be a mo,' he says to Big Kev. The latter nods.

Hanrahan also stands and, without a word, follows Little Kev out of the restaurant and walks away towards Piccadilly tube station.

On the street, Little Kev steps into the telephone box and dials the phone number given to him. The call is picked up swiftly and he presses a shilling into the slot.

'This is Kevin Streeter,' he says. 'Can I speak to Tony?'

'Tony Wise speaking.'

'Mr Hanrahan told me to call you.'

'Yes. Change of strategy. We're running out of time, so we need you to hurry things along with the holdouts on the development sites.'

'Hurry things along? What do you mean, exactly?'

'We need vacant possession, right away. No messing about.'

Little Kev pauses before answering. 'Yes, but what do you want us to do, Mr Wise?'

The line goes silent for a moment. 'Whatever you need to. We just need them out. There's only three. The names and addresses are on the piece of paper you've been given. The one on Braithwaite Street is the most urgent. Start with him this afternoon.'

'This'll cost more,' says Little Kev, after a while.

'I'm sure it will. Send your invoices in the normal way, and you'll get the same again in cash. Is that acceptable?'

'Yeah, s'pose so.'

'Good. But make sure you stick to the times indicated.'

'Whatever you say. You're the boss.'

The line goes dead. Little Kev returns to his partner inside the burger bar.

'He wants us to use force against the last tenants on the development sites,' says Little Kev, sitting down.

'Force? Why? Why can't we keep givin' 'em the new furniture? It saves all that to-do.'

'Don't ask me. It's no big deal, just a bit of persuasion.'

Big Kev doesn't answer for a while. Little Kev is familiar enough with his partner to know when he's unhappy. He waits.

'Not keen, Kev,' says Big Kev eventually.

'Why you so squeamish all of a sudden? It's never bothered you before. Is it 'cos you killed that druggie?'

'No. I dunno. Just not keen.'

'But that were an accident! And he's offering double bubble. You'll make over fifty this week. There's only three, first one this afternoon. Got to be there at five-thirty.'

'Well, that's me out.'

'Why's that?'

'I was gonna tell you. I gotta leave early.'

'Why?'

'Maude's got a hospital appointment at four.'

'You ain't got her up the duff again, 'ave yer? Thought you was told to give all that up.'

Big Kev shrugs. 'Not as far as I know. But they want me there 'n' all. I think it's women's stuff.'

Little Kev laughs. 'Fat lot of use you'll be, then.' Big Kevin doesn't answer. 'Oh, fair enough,' sighs Little Kev.

'Sorry, mate. But I'll meet you soon as I can.'

'She's got you right under 'er thumb, mate,' he says, shaking his head sadly, but not arguing further.

Big Kev stamps his feet on the cold pavement and looks at his watch. Just before five. He left the hospital much later than expected — more questions, more forms to be filled — but he might still make it.

A bus draws up at last, its diesel engine rattling loudly, and Kevin climbs aboard. He locates the last remaining seats, right at the front of the lower deck. As usual, none of the people who got on behind him are keen to sit next to him. Maude tells him off every now and then but, as he explains, he can't help how big he is or that he overlaps onto a second seat.

He descends at Commercial Street in Spitalfields and walks down Wheler Street and through the dark tunnel formed by the railway bridge. This northern end becomes Braithwaite Street. It's filthy, full of refuse, unlit and almost completely derelict. All the properties are boarded up, surrounded by wire fencing. A large sign states that the site has been acquired by Wise Property and Securities Limited for redevelopment. The only sign of life is a small corner shop just past the tunnel from which light spills onto the pavement.

Big Kev looks again at his watch. Five twenty. Mindful of his partner's strict injunction not to arrive early, he pops into the shop.

'Twenty Players please, mate,' he says to the man behind the counter.

He pays, pausing in the doorway on his way out to open the packet of cigarettes and light one. If it were not for that momentary hesitation he might have missed the car turning into Braithwaite Street. A nondescript light-coloured family saloon cruises slowly past his position, the driver leaning forward and peering through the windscreen, evidently looking for something. Big Kev's heart leaps. He recognises the driver, someone he'll never forget: Detective Inspector Woolley.

He retreats slightly into the shop, skirts a display of magazines, and gets as close as he can to the plate glass window to observe Woolley's vehicle without being seen. It's an unmarked Vauxhall Viva. There is a nodding dog on the back parcel shelf and a "GB" sticker on the back bumper.

Why's he in his own motor?

Big Kev knows his police cars, and he's never seen a Met police Vauxhall Viva, even undercover. They certainly don't have nodding dogs and GB stickers. The Vauxhall slows and comes to a halt. It then reverses quickly into the chained rear entrance of a defunct shoe factory before moving forward a few feet. Now only the first couple of inches of its bonnet are visible. If Big Kev hadn't seen Woolley's manoeuvre, the car would be almost completely hidden in the shadows.

What the fuck's he doing?

At that moment the Shoreditch Enforcement Services van enters Braithwaite Street. Big Kev watches it drive past his position. It continues past Woolley's hiding place and pulls up on the opposite side of the road. Little Kev turns off the ignition but remains in the vehicle. Big Kev can no longer see him but is sure his boss is sitting in the driving seat looking at his watch. Big Kev looks up at the windows of the boarded property outside which the van has stopped. As the darkness gathers, he now sees faint light emanating from a first-floor window.

'Shit, shit, shit!' he mutters.

He starts pacing. He doesn't know what to do. He needs to warn Little Kev, but that would entail walking right past Woolley's position. He checks the time again: five twenty-five! An idea occurs to him and he strides to the counter.

'Hey!' he calls.

The man who served him moments before has gone. The shop is deserted. Big Kev sees a door behind the counter and a staircase leading upwards. He can hear boxes being moved somewhere above him.

'Hey!' he calls again.

He had the notion that he might get the shopkeeper to take a note to Little Kev in the van, but the man upstairs can't hear him.

Almost out of time!

He returns to the window. Little Kev is getting out of the van and closing the door quietly behind him. There is something in his hand. Big Kev squints, recognising the jemmy they use for breaking into boarded-up properties.

He watches as Little Kev looks at his watch and scans the road anxiously, squinting towards Commercial Street, the direction from which Big Kev should be approaching. Braithwaite Street is deserted. He squares himself to the door underneath the illuminated window, leans backwards, and kicks hard at the door.

Little Kev is a lot smaller than his big partner, but he's a solid bloke and has years of experience kicking down doors. The sole of his booted foot lands heavily, right next to the lock. Wood splinters and the door bursts open, banging against the internal wall. Little Kev runs inside.

Big Kev turns his attention to Woolley's car.

We've been set up! Must've been!

Any second the copper's going to sprint across the road and nick Little Kev.

But nothing happens.

Big Kev waits, holding his breath in anticipation.

Still nothing happens.

Waiting for Kev to come out?

'Were you calling me?' says a voice behind him.

Big Kev doesn't move from the window. 'Nah, it's too late, mate,' he says, concentrating on the scene unfolding on the street.

'What's going on?' asks the shopkeeper, making as if to come out from behind the counter.

'Stay put!' orders Big Kev, turning briefly and raising a warning finger.

The man stays put.

The silence in the abandoned street is broken by a crashing noise from the first floor of the building. Almost instantly, the front window smashes. Fragments of glass catch the light in a short-lived starburst of shards as a dark shape comes flying out. Big Kev has time only to see arms windmilling for a second as the shape falls backwards, head-first, into the pavement. It lands with a heavy thud and is immediately still.

Finally, there is movement from the factory access where Woolley's car is parked. The vehicle's interior light illuminates as the driver's door opens and Woolley sprints across the road as fast as his bulky frame will allow. He arrives beside the body just as Little Kev emerges from the door. Big Kev sees his partner raise the heavy jemmy but the copper says something to him.

Why ain't he blowing his whistle? And why ain't Kev legging it?

Little Kev pauses, arm raised, then slowly lowers his weapon. The policeman is crouching by the body, speaking urgently.

This looks all wrong! Why ain't Woolley arresting him?

Woolley is still speaking but Big Kev is too far away to hear the words. Little Kev rises, casts another look at Woolley and goes to the van. He opens the passenger door, throws the jemmy inside and scurries round to the back to open the double doors. He returns to Woolley and the two of them lift the body and carry it to the back of the van.

What the fuck...?

They throw the body inside and, as Little Kev closes the rear doors, Woolley runs back across the road to his own car, slams the driver's door and locks it. He then returns to the van and climbs in the passenger seat. Little Kev joins him in the cab. The engine starts, Little Kev executes a neat three-point turn and sets off, back up Braithwaite Street. Within seconds they have gone through the tunnel and are turning the corner onto Commercial Street.

Kevin Streeter, DI Woolley and the body of the tenant have disappeared into the City of London's evening traffic.

CHAPTER SIX

Charles spends the next couple of weeks out on Circuit. The case is a good one, he is well-paid and he defends with success, but it comes at a price. His paperwork in Chambers has seriously backed up again; he hasn't had the opportunity to speak to David to tell him of his engagement or discuss how to break the news to their parents; and Sally has made a couple of comments, only half in jest, concerning cold feet and commitment.

Always a terrible sleeper when anxious, he rises shortly after five a.m., showers in the family bathroom so as not to wake Sally and, foregoing breakfast, walks into the Temple as the sun rises. He is at his desk before seven.

By noon he has completed two sets of Instructions — one, in particular, a devilishly complex schedule of loss in a construction dispute — and, having missed breakfast, he decides he owes himself a treat. He announces that instead of eating sandwiches at his desk he is going for a "proper lunch" in Middle Temple Hall. Peter Bateman throws down his pen and says he's coming too, and they pick up two other young barristers in the clerks' room who are at a loose end. It's the Friday before the May Bank Holiday weekend, and everyone is looking forward to three days off, hopefully with better weather.

The four of them make up a convivial set on the wooden benches. The conversation is lively, particularly amongst the youngsters, who have just finished their first stints at the Hastings annex. The proposal to open an annex outside the Metropolis was passed by Chambers, in full plenary session, by a single vote, with most of the senior members of Chambers opposing the plan. Charles, as ever, led the group advocating change, and he has been vindicated. There has been a gradual influx of new work to Chambers via the annex from solicitors' firms on the south coast, and the younger members of Chambers are the principal beneficiaries. They are being exposed to higher quality and more frequent work than they could have hoped for in London and there is now fierce competition at the junior end of Chambers to spend time there.

Charles's mind drifts as the youngsters chatter about their early successes at Lewes Assizes. He looks around at the bustling Hall. It is full of barristers eating quickly, sharing gossip, discussing their current cases and complaining about reductions in their fees applied by the Legal Aid Board. They flap around in their black gowns, hurriedly pouring cups of coffee and queuing to pay their bills, before racing back across the Strand to the Royal Courts of Justice or up the hill to the Bailey. They remind Charles of a murder of crows.

He looks up at the portrait of Queen Anne above him.

'All your fault,' he mutters.

'What's that?' asks one of the junior barristers.

'Oh, nothing,' says Charles. 'I was just blaming Queen Anne for these ridiculous gowns we're still wearing.'

'Why?' asks the other, looking confused.

'Because, before her death in 1714, we wore different coloured robes at different times of year. Much more interesting. But then the old queen died, the court went into mourning, and the Bar never came out again.'

'I thought it was Charles II,' says Bateman.

'Hmm?'

'Wasn't it mourning for Charles II? Sixteen-something?'

'No, don't think so,' says Charles. He looks to his left at the portrait of Charles II on his horse. 'On the other hand,' he says, 'you never know, given *that* dress sense. "*Next on the runway we have King Charles Stuart, wearing the very latest in silver nappies, matching bed sheet draped subtly over the right shoulder*".'

The others laugh.

'Right,' says Charles, standing, 'I've got to get back.'

Before he can leave his place, Clive, the Chambers junior rushes up to him. 'Sir, you're needed in Chambers urgently!' he says breathlessly.

'Why? What's happened?' asks Charles, suddenly anxious. He and David often speak about "*that*" phone call; the one they're bound to receive sooner or later.

Mum or Dad?

'It's a Mr Stephenson from Waterfields,' replies Clive. 'Wants to speak to you urgently.'

'Waterfields? What do they want with me?'

Waterfields is a huge solicitor's firm with offices in London, the United States and Hong Kong, boasting a client-list that includes governments and listed public companies. They have their own high-flying briefs at Essex Court and other prestigious commercial sets, and have never, to the best of Charles's knowledge, instructed anyone in Chambers.

'They want you for an urgent con, sir,' replies Clive, eyes shining. He's only the office junior, but even he knows the significance of this.

'Okay. Let me pay and —'

'No, sir! Barbara says you're to come back immediately, please, sir. If you give me your money, I'll pay for you and bring the change.'

'I'm sure he'll wait another ten minutes for me to call him.'

'He doesn't want you to call him. He's already here — in the waiting room.'

Clive holds out his hand.

'Okay,' replies Charles, handing a five-pound note to the young lad. 'Sorry, chaps,' he says to his colleagues, 'looks as if I have to run,' and he strides through the crowds and out of Hall.

Charles is intercepted as he reaches the top of the steps by Barbara, who has evidently seen him jogging across the courtyard.

'Right, sir,' she says urgently and in a low voice. 'There are no papers. He wants a quick chat about a conference. It's apparently extremely urgent, and I've returned your burglary plea to Miss Sinclair. I've given him coffee and biscuits and he's in the waiting room. I don't need to emphasise what an opportunity this is.'

'No, you don't. I get it.'

'Especially bearing in mind next April.'

'Yes. Give me thirty seconds to get upstairs and tidy my room, then show him up.'

'Jennie has already been up and removed the old coffee cups and tidied your desk, sir. She also opened the window for some fresh air,' she chides.

'Thank you.'

Charles races up the staircases to his room on the second floor. Jennie must also have dusted the shelves and the desks, as the room smells pleasantly of furniture polish.

Perhaps I should do that too, once in a while, he thinks distractedly.

He has time only to settle himself behind the desk and take out a fresh counsel's notebook, when Barbara knocks on the door and ushers in his new client.

'Mr Holborne, sir, may I introduce you to Mr Stephenson, a partner in the London office of Waterfields? Mr Stephenson, Charles Holborne of counsel.'

Charles offers his hand to the solicitor, evaluating him. He is about Charles's age, but he is very tall and thin, with a slightly bent posture which reminds Charles incongruously of a heron. He wears gold rimmed spectacles on a narrow face and an old-fashioned well-cut suit which, had it resided in Charles's wardrobe, would have been thrown out by Sally years ago.

'Mr Stephenson,' greets Charles, 'please take a seat. How can I help you?'

Stephenson comes directly to the point. 'I think you know our clients, Sir Leo and Anthony Wise?'

'I met Sir Leo last month at Middle Temple. I don't think I know Anthony Wise.'

'He's the son. Very odd young man, but apparently some sort of genius. Took a starred first from Cambridge at the age of eighteen. He's now twenty-two or twenty-three and has recently joined the board of Wise Property and Securities Limited.'

'Okay. And how can I help? I do some commercial work, but I have to say I'm surprised —'

'They've been arrested. They actually pulled Sir Leo out of treatment at hospital. I don't know the medical details but he's very unwell which is why Tony has stepped in. He suffered some form of collapse a few days ago.'

'What are the charges?' asks Charles.

'Suspicion of conspiracy to harass and unlawfully evict tenants. Two are, or were, supposedly in hospital themselves. I got the call at ten this morning,' says Stephenson reaching into his briefcase for his notebook, 'from West End Central police station. I've worked with the company for several years and they were asking for me. I confess I wasn't comfortable going, but we haven't got anyone who deals with this sort of work.'

'That must have been quite an experience,' says Charles with a grim smile. 'First time at West End Central?'

Stephenson shakes his head. 'First time in any police station. Those C8 officers are appalling! I don't mind telling you, I found it rather frightening.'

'They're known for it, the Sweeney. Arrogant, violent and corrupt.'

'I had no idea. I mean, you hear stories, but I always imagined that they were made up by villains. Or, at least, exaggerated.'

Charles shakes his head. 'We in the trenches know otherwise. Enter a Met police station, especially in central London, and you're rolling the dice. They'll verbal you...' Charles sees Stephenson's puzzled expression. 'Concoct a confession you didn't make. Or manipulate the evidence, beat you into signing a statement or threaten your children with being taken into care. Some are not beyond putting the frighteners on defence solicitors either.'

'But there's no recording of anything that happens!' says Stephenson in astonishment. 'It's like descending into Hades!'

'Exactly.'

'Anyway, once I'd spoken to Sir Leo he said I should instruct you, so here I am. You must have made quite an impression.'

'I guess so. Were they interviewed?'

Stephenson nods. 'Yes, both of them, separately. I sat in. I tried to take notes, but they went very quickly. I don't suppose you can read this, can you?'

He shows Charles his notebook.

'I can make out some of the words, but it might be better if you read it to me.'

'Okay. I'll summarise. They brought Sir Leo in first.'

'Do you have the names of the officers conducting the investigation?'

'Yes. The chap in charge was a Detective Inspector Woolley. He had a detective constable with him called Truman. They asked him about three properties where tenants say they've been muscled out. The first was in … hang on a tick … yes, Braithwaite Street. The tenant in that case has disappeared. They didn't ask much about that one. The other two were in Rochester Avenue where WPSL are building something called Macintosh Point. It'll be the largest high-rise housing estate in Europe once completed, so they say. They didn't give the names of the tenants, but apparently one is in hospital with a broken jaw and another, a woman, was dragged out of the property by her hair.'

'What was Sir Leo's response?'

'I advised him to say "No comment" but he wouldn't listen to me. He said he had nothing to hide and wanted to help. He claimed to know nothing about any of these events, and he does appear to have a cast-iron alibi. He was in hospital at the time of the evictions. We've requested his medical notes.'

'I don't suppose they're saying he did it himself,' comments Charles. 'They'll say the three tenants were holding up the company's construction projects, and he had the most to gain by getting them out quickly.'

'Exactly. But surely we can say it makes no sense to bother taking possession proceedings at the county court if you're just going to use force anyway?' asks Stephenson.

'Possession proceedings?'

'Yes, sorry, forgot to mention that. The company has been working with the London Borough of Newham to bring proceedings in Bow County Court against the remaining tenants who are holding out.'

'Bow County Court? I know the senior clerk there, Shirley Titmarsh. Are you acting on those matters?'

'No. Formally, the landlord is the London Borough of Newham, but they've been delegating some of the work to the legal team at WPSL. The clients' instructions are that Newham have sent several claim forms to the county court, but that nothing has happened.'

Charles makes some notes. 'See if you can get dates and copies, but the county court is swamped with work. It's one of the busiest in the country. I'm afraid delays are inevitable. I'm more interested in the alleged forcible repossessions. When did that happen?'

'Braithwaite Street last Friday and the others this Monday.'

'What, all three?'

Stephenson checks his notes and nods. 'Yes. Why?'

'Well, firstly, it's a little surprising the tenants reported it at all. Many of these people are squatting. They break back into boarded-up properties awaiting development. Not the sort of people to complain to the police if they're found out. But even assuming they were lawful tenants, it usually takes weeks for the police to pull the threads together. This is amazingly quick. Any idea who interviewed the tenants?'

'I'm not sure, but I got the impression that it was Woolley himself.'

Charles frowns and stares through the tall windows at the River Thames. He lights a cigarette and offers one to Stephenson, who declines.

'Well?' asks the solicitor.

'I don't know DI Woolley, but I can't at the moment see why the clients would be interviewed at West End Central, where the Flying Squad are based, and not at a local police station near the investigation. Why would injured and frightened tenants *schlep* into the West End when they could report it round the corner at Stratford? And this isn't Flying Squad business at all. It may be nothing, but I think we need to find these witnesses. What was Sir Leo's story?'

'He denied knowing anything about it. He said companies listed on the stock exchange don't use bruisers in this way.'

'And Tony?'

'He did as advised and answered "No comment" to every question. He wouldn't even look at the policemen. Woolley said something about faking an insanity defence, although I think he was joking.'

'Insanity?' asks Charles.

'Woolley got quite aggressive at times and Tony started rocking backwards and forwards on his chair and making odd noises. It was … bizarre.'

'A lot of so-called geniuses are a bit odd, though, aren't they?'

'I haven't met enough to form an opinion,' replies Stephenson drily. Charles can't decide if the solicitor is joking or not.

'Were they released on bail?' he asks.

'Sir Leo was, and went straight back to hospital. Tony was still in custody when I left, but Woolley said they'd probably agree to police bail on conditions, like surrendering his passport and not interfering with witnesses.'

'Good. Let me know if that doesn't occur today, and we'll make an application.'

'Will do. Next steps? I know the clients want to meet you as soon as possible, although I'm not sure if Sir Leo's going to be fit to travel.'

'We can't do much until we know the charges and what evidence there is. But it would be handy if we could track down these tenants and get some more detail.'

'They're prosecution witnesses.'

'Not yet they aren't. And, in law, there's no property in a witness. Meaning we can take statements from them too.'

'What about the bail condition? Not interfering with witnesses.'

'Taking a voluntary statement, without payment or duress, is not "interfering". Do Waterfields have investigators they can use?'

Stephenson shakes his head. 'Not really. Certainly not investigators who do this sort of work. Can you recommend anyone?'

'Someone who's familiar with this part of the East End, won't stand out,' muses Charles, 'and knows these people.' His face brightens. 'Actually, you know, I might have just the chap. If I can get him to agree, shall I instruct him on Waterfields' behalf?'

'You think he's the right man for the job?'

Charles answers with a smile. 'I doubt there's anyone more suitable. He's perfect.'

The solicitor pulls a face. 'It's a bit unconventional, but I suppose so. I'd be more comfortable if I dealt with him direct, but … sure. At least at the outset.'

Charles pushes open the door to the *Blind Beggar* pub on Whitechapel Road. He wears a raincoat over paint-stained overalls, a flat cap pulled low over his brow and carries a rolled-up newspaper. The bar is crowded and full of noise. No one pays him any attention as he buys a pint and a whisky chaser and finds a table in the corner between the brick fireplace and the window.

He unrolls and flattens his *Evening Standard* to read about Leeds United's first ever First Division title and their chances in the European Cup. He lights a cigarette, the smoke drifting towards the red-painted ceiling moulding where it joins a band of fug so thick it could hide a squadron of Messerschmitts.

Charles has misgivings entering the pub, but arriving unannounced on a busy Friday night in disguise seems a reasonable risk. He's looking for Billy Munday. On the eve of a Bank Holiday, with the football season over but summer weather still around the corner, he calculates that there's a good chance Munday will come in for a pint or two.

The ex-member of the Firm grew up in Canning Town. He went to St Helen's Catholic Junior School (since bombed to rubble by the Luftwaffe and now rebuilt) which is only a few minutes' walk from Rochester Avenue. He will know everyone in the area and if anyone can locate the tenants supposedly evicted by the Wises, and persuade them to talk, it will be him. And it will pay much better than painting and decorating.

Charles has a secondary motive. Getting Munday some well-paid straight work might help earn his trust, and Charles needs to be kept in the loop as to the goings-on at the Regal Billiard Hall; in particular, any plans that sore losers from the Firm might have for retribution.

Half an hour passes and Charles buys a second pint. The bar is now even more crowded than it was when he came in. It is becoming so hot that he fears arousing suspicion, wearing a raincoat and hat. He slips out of the raincoat but leaves the hat on.

Voices are raised in song at the far end of the bar. There is some good-natured jeering, but one or two other singers join in, and soon the bar is ringing with "My Old Man Said Follow The Van" to the accompaniment of an ill-tuned piano.

Charles smiles. When he and David were children, Millie's parents, old Shimon and Ada Cohen, used to take the boys to the New Royal Pavilion Theatre in Stepney for birthday and other special treats. The grandparents went for the Yiddish performances, but Charles and David looked forward particularly to the musical interludes, which were typically comedy musical numbers in English. This song takes him back immediately to when he was eight years old, sitting in the dark of the theatre, a ha'penny bag of sweets passing back and forth between him and David, both singing along with the audience to some of the up-and-coming talent of the music halls.

It is because he is so distracted by his memories that he fails to notice Munday taking a seat opposite him.

'Thought you said this place was too dangerous,' says the big man, smiling.

'All right, Billy?' replies Charles.

'I'm okay. You looking for me or something?'

Charles nods. 'Yes. Drink?'

'I'll get 'em, seeing's you're on my patch.' He nods at Charles's pint. 'Same again?'

Charles knocks back the last inch or two of his beer and hands the empty glass to Munday. 'Yes, please.'

Munday pushes his way through to the bar and returns several minutes later with two pints. 'Okay,' he says, sitting down again. He looks around him and lowers his voice before speaking, but the carousers have started another song, and the din is such that Charles has to lean forward to hear. 'What d'ya want?'

'I'll come straight to the point,' says Charles, having to raise his voice slightly. 'I've got some work for you, if you want it.'

'What sort of work?'

'There's a firm of solicitors who need some witnesses tracked down. Locals.'

Munday grins. 'You want me to work for lawyers? You taking the piss?'

Charles smiles, having foreseen this response. 'No, it's straight up. I reckon you could get ten shillings an hour.'

'Really?' Charles watches as the man opposite him calculates. 'How many hours' work?'

Charles shrugs. 'No way of telling at the moment. There are supposedly three witnesses, all tenants who the Filth are saying were unlawfully evicted. I've got addresses, although one tenant is supposedly still in hospital somewhere. Another has done a runner. Tracking them down might take a few days. Taking statements, if they'll give them, takes a while too. I'd say a week's work, maybe a bit more. And if you do a good job, well, solicitors are always looking for good investigators, and not just this lot. Most importantly, it keeps you straight. You're out on licence, right?' Munday nods. 'So your parole officer's going to be well impressed.'

Munday doesn't answer at first. 'It's tempting, and thanks, but I don't think so. I've got a bit of decorating coming up. I just can't see myself working for solicitors. Goes against the grain, you know?'

'They're not the Filth, Billy, just solicitors. They're guns for hire, work for everyone, including people you and I know. In fact, I could name half a dozen villains who work for solicitors now. You know, poachers turned gamekeepers? Remember Ozzie Sinclair?'

'The tall tea leaf?'

'Yes. He's got a record twice as long as yours, but he started working for Harry Robeson when he last came out, outdoor clerking. When Robeson went inside, Ozzie was snapped up by another firm at twice the pay. He's been straight for six years now, got a mortgage and everything.'

Munday reconsiders but again shakes his head. 'I can see the upsides, and I might enjoy the work. But I just can't see myself in a suit.'

'You don't need to wear a suit.'

'And I'd be no good with time logs, expense receipts, tax returns 'n' all that. It's all too … official for me.'

'You've got the wrong end of the stick. You don't have to deal with the solicitors. You'd be reporting to me, just doing a bit of digging around.'

'For cash?'

'Cash?' Charles gives that a moment's thought. 'I can't see why not. I suppose I can deal with the paperwork.'

'I wouldn't want you to be out of pocket, though. Would you be repaid? Is the client good for it?'

Charles grins. 'Mate, he's probably the richest man you or I will ever meet.'

Munday nods. He delves into his pocket and takes out an old bus ticket, turns it over, scribbles an address and telephone number on the back and slides it over the sticky table.

'There's me details. Now; tell me exactly what you want.'

CHAPTER SEVEN

Bow County Court is located in one of the poorest boroughs in the country. It's daily diet of litigation is precisely what one would expect for a court servicing the needs of hundreds of thousands of underprivileged, impoverished and dispossessed citizens: divorce, child custody, housing disputes, evictions and personal injuries.

Charles's former chambers at Chancery Court used to receive instructions from a dozen firms in and around Bow, and Charles cut his teeth on that work before he began to specialise in criminal cases. During his pupillage and for two years thereafter, he often spent two or three days a week at that county court, and he became familiar with everyone working there. The staff, most of whom lived in the borough themselves, were overworked, underpaid, invariably stressed and always friendly. They shared a team spirit that, in Charles's experience, was almost unique in the court service, and they were unusually kind to a green and inexperienced barrister whom they saw as one of their own. More than once a discreet steer from one of the clerks or an usher prevented him making a fool of himself.

For twenty years this jolly team has been led by Shirley Titmarsh, a vastly experienced solicitor, who rose through the ranks to senior clerk. Even judges sitting at the court were wont to say that, without Shirley, the civil justice system in East London would probably have collapsed. Charles dealt with her on many occasions in the early years of his practice. His move to specialist criminal chambers meant that he did less of this sort of work, and as a result he lost touch with her over the intervening years. He is therefore looking forward to renewing their acquaintance.

He has deliberately timed his arrival to shortly before 1 p.m. when the courts would rise and the public counter would close for an hour. He knows that at any other time of the day, Shirley will not have time for chat.

He arrives at reception in the main office. There are still a few people waiting, but one of the two counter positions has already closed and Charles notes that the young man at the one still open is shooting glances at the clock above the door as he deals with his instant query.

Someone's anxious for their lunch, thinks Charles.

He takes a seat on the wooden bench, and waits. Eventually the last member of public with business in the office is dealt with and departs. The young man gets up from his position, opens a door and emerges into the public area.

'We're closing for lunch,' he says. 'I'm afraid you'll need to come back at two.'

Charles rises. 'Is Shirley Titmarsh available?' he asks. 'It's a … social matter.'

'Is Mrs Titmarsh expecting you?' asks the young man.

'No, but if you tell her it's Charles Holborne, she'll know who I am.'

The young clerk hesitates, again looking at the clock. 'I will need to lock the door,' he explains, 'or I'll never get away.'

'Fine by me,' says Charles. 'I'll wait here.'

The young man locks the door and returns to his position. He picks up the phone and dials.

'Shirley? I've got a gentleman here by the name of Charles Holborne, says he would like a word with you.'

He listens on the phone for a few moments and then replaces the receiver.

'She'll be right down,' he says. 'Is it okay if I leave you to it?'

'Of course.'

The clerk rises and disappears through a door into an inner office. Charles is only waiting for a couple of minutes before the same door opens and Shirley emerges. She has not changed much since Charles last saw her: a slim and elegant woman in her late fifties with voluminous greying hair held off her forehead by her pushed-up spectacles. She beams at Charles and opens the door to the public area.

'Hello, hello!' she says cheerfully. 'The famous Charles Holborne, as I live and breathe!'

'Hello, Shirley. Not that famous.'

'What brings you over this way?'

'I popped in to say hello,' replies Charles. 'It's a couple of years since I've been at Bow and I miss you. You were all very kind to a naive and overconfident young barrister.'

'And I'm sure everyone at Bow County Court misses the bumptious young Charlie Holborne,' teases Shirley, a twinkle in her eye. 'Although, from what I read, you've now got much bigger fish to fry than we can offer. Big cases, important clients.'

'Thanks to the grounding you gave me here,' replies Charles with sincerity.

She smiles again, her eyes narrowing. 'Nonetheless, quite a long way for a busy senior barrister to "pop in".'

'No, honestly I wanted to see you. But your name came up recently, and I do have a question.'

'Oh yes? What sort of question?'

She looks above Charles's head to the clock. Charles decides to cut to the chase.

'Procedural, really. When possession actions are sent to the court in the post, how are they recorded when they arrive? Is there a specific clerk who deals with that type of action, or are they dealt with by whoever happens to be opening the post that morning?'

Shirley's familiar smile continues to illuminate her face but Charles notes something different in her eyes. She looks guarded, almost suspicious.

'Why do you ask?'

'Well, I've just been instructed in a criminal case where my clients are saying that claim forms for possession for various properties in Newham have been sent here, but some weeks or months later they're still awaiting a reply. I wondered if a member of the team had been off sick or something like that.'

Shirley's smile dies further. She looks up again at the clock.

'Goodness, look at the time! I'm awfully sorry, Charles, but I've got to get going. I'm clerking a trial at two, and there are further papers for the judge.'

She brushes past him and unlocks the door to the landing, showing him out. Charles doesn't move for a moment. He tries to gauge Shirley's expression but she has her face turned away from him. After a moment he moves through the open door.

'Do pop in again soon,' she says, and before Charles can respond, the door closes and he hears the *snap* of the deadlock.

He walks back towards Stratford Underground Station, shaken and deep in thought. Shirley Titmarsh is one of the most decent people he has ever met. She says exactly what she thinks and she is one hundred per cent scrupulously straightforward. Yet he has absolutely no doubt: she has just lied to him.

Instead of going directly to the westbound platform, Charles walks to the first telephone box he finds inside the station foyer. He reaches into his jacket pocket for his wallet, and the bus ticket used by Billy Munday to scribble his details.

'May I speak to Billy Munday, please?' he says after the phone is picked up at the other end. 'Billy? It's Charles Holborne. I know it's only a couple of days, so I'm not chasing on those witnesses. I've got something else for you.'

CHAPTER EIGHT

Charles is, as is often the case, the first barrister to get in the following morning. He has at last managed to arrange to see David that evening and needs a prompt start at his desk. But Barbara has beaten him to it.

'Ah, there you are,' she says as he enters the clerks' room. 'I was hoping you might come in early this morning, sir. You have instructions from Waterfields to represent Sir Leo and his son. I've put them on your desk. I thought you'd want to look at them immediately. I have agreed fees and you're going to be very happy.'

'Thank you. Con? Committal? Trial?'

'Conference. Sir Leo has been discharged from hospital, although apparently his condition is still very poor. I'm to call Waterfields this afternoon to arrange the conference at the clients' home in North London. Tomorrow or the day after. Is that okay with you?'

'If the poor bloke can't get down to the Temple, of course.'

Charles takes his other post and proceeds to his desk. He picks up the instructions and begins reading.

BRIEF TO COUNSEL

THE QUEEN
– v –
SIR LEO WISE, ANTHONY WISE AND OTHERS

Enclosures:
1. Copy charge sheet

2. Statements of Witnesses A and B
3. Contract for development between the London Borough of Newham and Wise Property and Securities Limited
4. Statement of DI Woolley
5. Statement of DC Truman
6. Draft proof of evidence of Sir Leo Wise — to follow after the conference
7. Draft proof evidence of Mr Anthony Wise — to follow after the conference

Counsel is instructed on behalf of Sir Leo Wise and Anthony Wise who are charged with an offence of conspiracy to harass and unlawfully evict three tenants of the London Borough of Newham. Counsel will note that the clients are charged with "persons unknown", presumably the persons who actually threatened and were violent towards the tenants.

Two of the tenants have provided statements but their identities have not been revealed, on the supposed grounds that they would be at risk of further harassment. One of the matters upon which Instructing Solicitors will seek Counsel's advice is whether the Crown can continue to conceal the identity of these critical witnesses. The local investigator recommended by Counsel to locate them has yet to report. Instructing Solicitors have agreed that, bearing in mind the unusual circumstances, Counsel may act as an intermediary with the investigator, but we remain uncomfortable at not being involved directly and as soon as he can be persuaded to deal with us, the better.

Witness A and Witness B say essentially the same thing, namely, that a man arrived at their dwellings purporting to be from WPSL and used force to evict them. Witness A, a young woman with small children, was apparently bundled out of the property with minor injuries. Witness B, who appears to be a male, was struck with a weapon that he identified as a jemmy or tyre iron, and suffered more serious injuries, including a broken jaw which required surgery. Both give a description of the man who assaulted them, but the police have to date been unable to identify him. He is described as about five feet ten inches tall, dark-haired, with a solid build and a thin face. One of the witnesses noted heavily nicotine-stained fingers of the left hand and a slight limp.

Only two pieces of evidence link our clients with these attacks. The first lies in the assertions by the unnamed witnesses that the man who assaulted them claimed to act on behalf of WPSL. Instructing Solicitors are of the opinion that this evidence is inadmissible as it is hearsay, and without the attacker available to give evidence of his instructions and who gave them, this evidence should be excluded by the court at trial. Counsel's confirmation is sought.

The second piece of evidence is the alleged confession of Anthony Wise contained in the statements of DI Woolley and DC Truman. It will be recalled that during the interview attended by Mr Stephenson, Mr Wise answered "No comment" to all questions put to him. However, the police officers assert that after Mr Stephenson left West End Central Police Station, Mr Wise changed his mind and gave a second interview in which he made admissions. Mr Wise denies that the second interview occurred at all. The Defence case is that Woolley and/or Truman have made up this interview.

There is additionally circumstantial evidence, which in Instructing Solicitors' opinion is quite persuasive, namely, the common factor linking the tenants. They were all housed in Newham properties scheduled for demolition by WPSL, and WPSL is liable to pay substantial penalties for late handover of completed developments (see Enclosure 3, particularly Schedules 11 and 12). This evidence certainly provides motivation for those controlling WPSL to take shortcuts.

Counsel is instructed to advise on evidence in conference and to conduct the committal hearing. It is understood that the committal will be listed at Old Street Magistrates' Court, but no date has yet been set. Both clients are presently on police bail. Sir Leo remains very unwell and is unable to travel to the Temple. Accordingly, a conference will be arranged at the clients' home in Hampstead Garden Suburb.

Counsel should contact Mr Stephenson of those instructing if he has any queries.
Waterfields, Solicitors.

'For someone who doesn't do criminal law, those are pretty good instructions,' comments Charles to himself.

'Is this your Waterfields case?' says Peter Bateman from the opposite side of the room. He arrived a few minutes earlier but, seeing Charles engrossed, began work without speaking.

'Yes.'

'Any chance you'll need a junior?' he asks hopefully.

'Sorry, mate, but I doubt it. It looks pretty straightforward. But I will ask. Money appears to be no object. You wouldn't believe the fee marked on this brief.'

'Why do you suppose they haven't gone to one of the established silks, then?' asks Bateman. 'No offence, but you're not in silk yet, and if they can afford the best, the most prominent QC…?'

'No offence taken, you're absolutely right. It's a mystery. We dined with them at Bench Call Night, entirely by chance, but I can't believe that a good enough reason to put their liberty in my hands.'

The room falls silent as each of them refocuses on their own work. Charles locates the statements from the two policemen. That from Truman simply records that he noted the interviews and was present when the Wises were arrested. Charles picks up DI Woolley's statement. It is much longer.

Statement of Clifford Andrew Woolley
Occupation: Detective Inspector, Metropolitan Police
Address: C8, West End Central Police Station, 27 Savile Row, London, W1

This statement is true to the best of my knowledge and belief, and I make it knowing that, if it is tendered in evidence, I shall be liable to prosecution if I wilfully state in it anything which I know to be false or do not believe to be true.

Signed: Clifford Andrew Woolley

I am a Detective Inspector based at the Commissioner's Office 8, working out of West End Central Police Station. The principal interest of C8, otherwise known as the Flying Squad, is dealing with robberies and other organised crime. Unlike the rest of the Metropolitan Police its remit is not confined to specific Divisions within the Metropolitan area.

Since the passing of the Rent Acts, which gave protected status to most residential tenants, there have been reports of landlords using unlawful means, including force, to evict tenants. In normal circumstances this would not be of interest to the Flying Squad. However, some reports raised suspicions that organised crime might be involved. I was accordingly tasked to investigate further.

"Organised crime"? Charles marks this last passage. If true, this would explain why an inspector from the Sweeney was investigating. He continues reading.

The bulk of the reports came from the boroughs situated in the East End of London where large areas are being redeveloped and the sums of money involved are very substantial. In particular I learned that the company, Wise Property and Securities Limited (hereinafter referred to as "the company") had entered into a contract with the London Borough of Newham to demolish slum dwellings and erect three new modern tower blocks. The company would be paid sums between £500,000 and £850,000 on handover of each of the blocks. There is now produced and shown to me marked CAW1 the contract between the company and

Newham from which it will be seen that the company is liable to pay heavy financial penalties should effective handover be delayed.

On Monday 28 April 1969, as a result of information received…

So, thinks Charles, that explains how Woolley was on hand for these evictions, and within a day or so of one another. The "information received" which tipped him off and started the investigation is likely to pose a problem for the defence. Judges will rarely force police officers to give details of confidential informants; it puts the informants at risk and frightens off other sources of information. In Charles's experience, juries understand it too. He continues reading.

…I went to an address at Rochester Avenue, the home of Witness A and her two children. Rochester Avenue is the site of a major redevelopment where a complex of residential blocks is to be erected by the company. Several streets had already been demolished, but a terrace of forty derelict properties remained. I met Witness A. She and her children were the last tenants in the street with the exception of Witness B, who lived at the opposite end. Their gas and electricity had been cut off but there was still running water. Only two rooms of Witness A's property were habitable, the upstairs having been flooded repeatedly due to water leakage through the roof. I noted that the property contained various items of expensive furniture which seemed inconsistent with the state of the property and the means of the tenants.

"Expensive furniture"? Charles marks this passage and resumes reading.

As a result of what I was told, I decided to maintain surveillance of the terrace in the hope of witnessing the arrival of agents for the landlords, Newham, or of the company. However due to the small number in my team, we were unable to maintain continual surveillance for more than 36 hours and unfortunately none of us were there on the morning of 29 April. That afternoon I received a telephone call at C8 from Witness A who informed me that she was in hospital having been forcibly evicted from the property, during the course of which she was assaulted. I went to the Homerton Hospital and met her. I saw that she had minor injuries to her face, and a large clump of hair had been torn from her scalp. She was also complaining of chest pain. I took a brief statement from Witness A, but her two small children had been taken into care and she was very anxious to be discharged so she could locate them. While I was present she discharged herself against medical advice and before X-rays could be taken.

I immediately resumed surveillance at Rochester Avenue close to Witness B's home. The other members of my team were engaged on other duties, and I was alone. It appeared that someone was in occupation, but I did not see them enter or leave.

At approximately 18:00 hours on the evening of 29 April I was observing the property from an unmarked police vehicle. A Caucasian man in his 40s walked up to number 43. At that stage I did not see any vehicle. The male was of above average height with a thin face and dark hair. I did not recognise him. I saw that he had a length of metal, possibly a jemmy, in one hand and a large holdall in the other. He knocked on the door, which was opened by Witness B. I heard the man say that he was there "for the landlords" and that the tenant had to "clear out immediately". Witness B protested, and I saw the man raise the jemmy and strike him on the side of the head. Witness B fell to the floor.

I left the police vehicle and ran across the road to intervene. The attacker saw my approach and ran. I was concerned for Witness B who appeared to be unconscious and was bleeding heavily from the side of his head, so I radioed for assistance and an ambulance before setting off in pursuit. As I rounded the corner, I saw a white van moving off from the kerb at speed. I was not able to see the vehicle's registration plate. I returned to 43

Rochester Avenue and waited with Witness B for the ambulance to arrive which it did, at 18:25 hours.

I followed the ambulance to the hospital and later that evening when Witness B had recovered consciousness, I interviewed him.

On 2 May 1969 with other officers, I arrested Sir Leo and Mr Anthony Wise on suspicion of conspiracy to harass and unlawfully evict tenants and took them in custody to West End Central Police Station.

Charles pauses in his reading and sits back in his chair. There is something wrong here. The man who attacked Witness B said he was there "for the landlords", namely, the London Borough of Newham. There is no suggestion of any involvement by Wise Property and Securities Limited. Where is the evidence giving rise to "reasonable suspicion" sufficient for Woolley to arrest Sir Leo and Anthony Wise?

Charles writes the words "Reasonable suspicion??" in the margin of the policeman's statement, underlines the words, and continues reading.

I conducted one interview of Sir Leo Wise who was accompanied by his solicitor Mr Stephenson. A transcript of this interview is now produced and shown to me marked CAW2. Sir Leo answered all questions put to him. He agreed that until 2 February 1969 he was the chairman of the board of the company. On that date the company notified Companies House that he had stood down. In summary, he denied any knowledge of the forcible evictions referred to above, and said that formal possession proceedings had been initiated at the Bow County Court. He claimed that had he known of any such unlawful possession actions he would have stopped them. I have since made enquiries of that county court, and no record exists of any supposed possession proceedings.

I conducted two interviews of Anthony Wise. In the first, on the advice of the solicitor Mr Stephenson, he answered all questions "No comment".

Following the departure of Mr Stephenson from the police station Sir Leo Wise was taken back to Guy's Hospital where he had been receiving treatment and Mr Anthony Wise was placed in a cell pending a decision as to bail in his case.

At approximately 3 p.m. that afternoon I was informed that Mr Anthony Wise wished to speak to me again. He was taken out of the cell and returned to the interview room where a further interview occurred. I asked the questions and DC Truman who was present throughout recorded both questions and answers as they were given. A transcript of that interview is now produced and shown to me marked CAW3.

Signed: Clifford Andrew Woolley

What made Anthony Wise change his mind? thinks Charles. Having been advised not to answer questions by a solicitor and having remained silent throughout a long interview, why would he go back on that once the solicitor departed? Seems most unlikely.

Charles turns to the supposed second interview.

Q: [Caution re-administered] Do you understand?
A: Yes.
Q: And do you understand that you are entitled to have your solicitor back? For the record, you were advised by your solicitor, Mr Stephenson, to reply "No comment" to the questions I asked this morning, and you exercised that right while he was here. I don't want you saying at trial that you were forced to answer now, when you have no obligation to do so and your solicitor isn't present.
A: No, I understand. I've decided I want to answer.
Q: Do you want me to call your solicitor back before we start?
A: No.
Q: Why not?
A: Because he'll tell me again not to answer your questions, and that's not

advice I wish to take. I have nothing to hide.

Q: Very well. Since 2 February this year you have been the chairman of Wise Property and Securities Limited, is that right? Mr Wise? Please would you look at me? Are you chairman of Wise Property and Securities Limited?

A: No.

Q: Are you a director? Mr Wise, look at me please. Are you a director of that company?

A: Yes.

Q: Do you have a particular title as director?

A: Yes.

Q: Which is?

A: Acting managing director.

Q: Does that mean you're in charge of the company?

A: You obviously don't understand how publicly listed companies work. It's a very big organisation, with lots of very competent employees.

Q: Then explain to me in terms that I can understand. Mr Wise? Look, you asked to talk to us again. If you don't want to continue with this interview we will stop now.

A: I have temporarily taken over as MD.

Q: Okay. And who did that before you?

A: My father.

Q: Why have you stepped in?

A: My father's unwell.

Q: What's wrong with him?

A: You'd have to ask him. He doesn't discuss it with me. But I know he's very ill and has been receiving treatment in hospital.

Q: All right. Now the company has a contract with the London Borough of Newham to demolish large areas of slum housing and erect new residential tower blocks. Is that right?

A: Yes.

Q: Have any of the tower blocks been built yet?

A: Seagull Tower is in the process of construction and should be complete in the next few weeks.
Q: And the others?
A: Some demolition has taken place but building work hasn't started.
Q: Why is that?
A: There have been various problems, including planning in respect of new roads.
Q: Is it right that you've also had difficulty evicting sitting tenants?
A: Our company wouldn't evict sitting tenants. They are tenants of the London Borough of Newham.
Q: We've had numerous reports of tenants being approached by people and being offered expensive furniture in place of the furniture provided by Newham when the tenancies began. Do you know anything about that?
A: Yes. It's very important that possession is obtained so demolition and reconstruction can begin. There are thousands of people on the housing list, some of them living in really atrocious conditions. It was suggested that if we replaced the furniture so that it had a substantial value compared to the overall rent, the tenancies might no longer attract the protection of the Rent Acts.
Q: So you forced these tenants to take different furniture?
A: Absolutely not! The situation was explained to them and they were invited to have the new furniture or not. Those who did, signed new tenancies.
Q: The whole point being that you would then use the furniture to force them out?
A: I repeat, there was no question of forcing anyone out. The plan was for possession proceedings to be brought in court, to test the law.
Q: But you didn't take possession proceedings, did you?
A: I've just explained this. Wise Property and Securities Limited could never take possession proceedings. It doesn't have locus standi.
Q: What does that mean?
A: It means that the company is not the landlord. Only a landlord can

bring possession proceedings.

Q: Did your company have anything to do with bringing such proceedings?

A: Yes.

Q: Then explain what your company did.

A: We lent the services of our in-house legal team to the council.

Q: Why?

A: They're overloaded and don't have equivalent resources.

Q: Thank you. Were such proceedings actually started, do you know?

A: You'd have to ask the council, but it appears not.

Q: Why?

A: We don't know.

Q: So, time was going on and the company was no closer to getting possession and starting demolition.

A: Yes.

Q: And somebody authorised a shortcut, didn't they?

A: What do you mean?

Q: Come on, Mr Wise. You're the acting MD of a publicly limited company. I can't believe you'd have got your role, even temporarily, without the board approving. They must think you're clever enough. And you claim to know civil law — not to mention Latin — better than me. You know exactly what I mean.

A: Are you referring to the forced evictions?

Q: Very good. Clever boy. The only people to gain from pressurising tenants to leave would be your company.

A: And the council.

Q: Yes, but the council's protected, isn't it? If your company doesn't hand over on time, it has to pay huge penalties to the council, right?

A: Yes.

Q: So, I go back to my question. Somebody authorised a shortcut, namely the use of force to get the last tenants out. Who was that?

A: [No answer]

Q: Did you hear my question, Mr Wise? Who authorised the use of force?

A: [No answer]

Q: Was it you who used a jemmy to break the jaw of a tenant at Rochester Avenue?

A: No, of course not. Look at the size of me.

Q: You don't have to be very big to hit an unprotected man over the head with an iron bar.

A: Don't be absurd. I am not a man of violence.

Q: Well, the man who struck that tenant certainly was. Do you know his identity?

A: No.

Q: Who gave the order? Was it your father?

A: My father would never do anything like that. He would never use violence in any circumstances. You know his history.

Q: Who, then? Would someone in the legal team at your company have authorised it?

A: No. They're solicitors and clerks, not thugs.

Q: I repeat, who then? Who had the authority? [Pause] Why are you rocking like that, Mr Wise? Are you unwell?

A: N-No … I'm fine.

Q: You don't sound fine. [Pause] Please can you stop making that noise and focus on my question? Who authorised the use of force? Please look at me, Mr Wise. Look at me!

A: It was me, all right? I authorised it! I didn't know what else to do. The company's in serious financial difficulties, and we have to start building work!

Q: Did you speak to your father about it before making the decision?

A: No. He's very ill. That's why I was brought in. I didn't want to trouble him with it. It was my decision, and my decision alone.

Q: Who did you get to do it? [Pause] Mr Wise? What did you do to put your plan into operation?

A: I … I'm not going to answer any more questions. I have admitted my part in it, but I won't involve anyone else.

Q: Did you tell them how much force to use? Perhaps you didn't tell them to go cracking people's skulls? Perhaps you asked them to use a bit more persuasion but didn't realise they were going to use violence? Is that right?
A: [No answer]
Q: It would be in your best interests to tell us the full story, Mr Wise. Unless you want to be blamed for everything, even what was done by other people.
A: I have nothing more to say. Please take me back to my cell.

Charles sits back in his seat. If this was a concocted interview, it's one of the best he's ever seen. It contains irrelevancies, as authentic interviews frequently do, and it gives a striking impression of the personalities involved. It reads exactly as a genuine interview would. Charles looks forward to hearing Anthony Wise's explanation. If, as he claims, the interview didn't occur at all, how is it so authentic?

Nonetheless if Charles can discredit the interview — or perhaps the interviewer — the case against Anthony Wise will collapse. It's all the Crown has. And there is nothing at all in the case against his father. Charles can't work out why Sir Leo was arrested or charged. Somebody is over-reaching. But who, and why?

CHAPTER NINE

Charles steps out of the lift onto the second floor of Sunshine Court. This floor, named with bitter irony or, perhaps, complete thoughtlessness, "Remembrance", is the care home's secure floor for residents suffering from dementia.

A party is in progress. Charles has been present when a number of residents have celebrated birthdays and they are, by and large, sad affairs. The staff do their best. They put on music, dance with the residents who are still able, wear silly hats, sing "Happy Birthday" and dole out portions of cake and ice cream. Their ersatz cheer is, usually, wasted. Few of the residents understand what is happening and frequently the birthday boy or girl is blithely unaware of the significance of the date or of what is going on around them.

On this occasion, however, the atmosphere is different. In addition to a few residents who have not yet been put to bed, there are a dozen or more visitors who appear genuinely to be enjoying themselves. A carer is circulating with a bottle of champagne, topping up glasses here and there. Charles Trenet is singing "La Mer" from the gramophone and, in the centre of the gathering is a little man wearing a beret, laughing and talking rapidly in French.

Charles cannot see David, whom he is supposed to meet. Nor, in fact, can he see either of his parents. He apologises his way through the party guests and makes his way across the communal lounge towards his parents' suite. They have two rooms, a small but comfortable living room, and a bedroom containing two single beds. Millie's dementia continues to progress. Her sleep pattern is now so disrupted that, after almost half a century sleeping in the same bed as her husband, they have to sleep separately. In addition to the lounge and the bedroom, they share a bathroom with the other resident whose bedroom opens off the same lobby.

Charles pushes open the door to his parents' lounge, and is astonished to see two uniformed police officers.

'Sorry sir,' says one, urgently. 'You can't come in here.'

'This is my parents' room,' replies Charles.

'It may very well be, sir, but no one can come in at the moment.'

'What's happened? Where are they? Are they okay?'

He feels a light touch on his arm and spins round. It's his brother. David is quite unlike Charles. He is taller, blonder and blue-eyed. He is also devoutly Jewish and wears a head-covering at all times. Were it not for their voices, which are almost indistinguishable, they would never be taken for relatives.

'It's okay, Charles. They're here, and they're fine.'

'But what's happened?' persists Charles.

The second police officer answers. 'It seems as if their room has been ransacked, although your father doesn't believe anything's been stolen. We're just looking round.'

Charles puts his head around the door jamb. The chest of drawers under the window has had its drawers pulled out and the contents strewn on the floor. The wardrobe doors are also open. One or two of his parents' holiday photograph albums, normally stacked neatly on a small bookcase, are open on the carpet.

'Are Scenes of Crime on their way?' asks Charles, still in the doorway.

'That's not for me to decide, sir,' says the first officer. 'I've radioed the station. But we wouldn't normally trouble them if nothing's been taken, especially in these circumstances.'

'These circumstances?'

'We understand it isn't unusual for residents to go into one another's bedrooms. We suspect one of them came in, perhaps to look for something.' Charles knows that to be true. Millie has herself been known to wander into other residents' rooms and even sleep in their beds. Most of the people on Remembrance are confused to some extent.

'And given the security on the door and the lift, it seems unlikely an intruder got in,' finishes the other constable.

'Come on, Charles,' says David. 'Mum and Dad are in here.'

David leads Charles to the other room opening off the lobby, another bedroom. This resident has a larger bedroom than that of the Horowitzes, presumably because his accommodation does not include a separate lounge. Millie and Harry sit, holding hands, on a small sofa.

'Hello, son,' says Harry looking up.

Millie does not respond to the entry of her sons. Her eyes are fixed on something at the junction between the wall and the ceiling.

'Hello, Dad,' says Charles, bending to kiss his father's cheek. 'Are you okay?'

'We're fine. We didn't see anything or anyone. I was bringing your mother back here for a lie down and we found the room in a mess. Jean-Luc said we could sit in here until the police have finished.'

'Jean-Luc?'

'This is his room,' explains David. 'He's the party boy, outside. One hundred today.'

'Who, that chap with the beret?' asks Charles, surprised.

He checks the seat of an armchair to ensure it is dry before sitting down. He has been caught out before and become the unintended victim of a resident's "accident".

'He's amazing for a hundred.'

'I know,' says David. 'To be honest, he could still be on the ground floor, as his dementia is still pretty mild. Have you never spoken to him?'

Charles shakes his head. 'No, don't think so.'

'You should. Jean-Luc Pelletier. Look at this.'

David leads Charles towards a small framed photograph on the nightstand. It shows a parade of servicemen and, in the centre, the same little man in uniform being presented with a medal by President de Gaulle.

'That's him being awarded the *Officier de la Légion d'honneur*. It's incredibly rare. The *Officier* is a level above the basic *Chevalier*, which is what he received in 1919 after the First World War, and even *that* is usually only awarded for the highest service to the Republic. For anyone to have earned it twice is almost unique. Next time you come, ask him to show you his hobby.'

'Hobby?'

David grins. 'You won't believe it. Anyway, I was about to make tea. Want some?'

'Yes. I'll give you a hand.'

'Don't forget the chocolate biscuits, boys!' calls Harry after them.

The brothers walk through the party guests again to the open-plan kitchen. David fills and turns on the kettle while Charles loads a tray with cups, saucers and plates.

'What did you want to talk about?' asks David.

'I don't think now's the right time. I'd expected Mum and Dad to be in bed soon, so we'd have some time without them listening.'

'You and Sally are getting married.'

Charles frowns and pulls a face. 'Yes. How did you know?'

David smiles and shrugs. 'We've been waiting for months for you to muster the courage to ask her.'

'Yes, but…'

'Plus, you can't keep secrets in Hatton Garden. Robert Rosenberg, the chap who sold you the ring, is a member of our *shul*.'

Charles laughs. 'I should've guessed.'

'And?' asks David, pouring boiling water into the teapot.

'And what?'

'Don't be obtuse, Charles. Did she say yes?'

'She did.'

'*Mazeltov*,' says David enthusiastically, and he puts down the kettle and gives Charles a hug. 'We're very pleased for you. She's a lovely girl, and you obviously make one another very happy.'

'Thank you. My problem now is what to tell Mum and Dad.'

'I don't understand.'

'Another *shiksa*? Look what happened when I married Henrietta. You all sat *shiva* and I was banished from the family for a decade.'

'That was your fault. You did it without a word to any of us, without even introducing her, and having changed your name. You couldn't have rejected everything Mum and Dad stood for, and rubbed their noses in it, more effectively had you'd tried.'

Charles stares at his brother, astonished. 'I … I didn't know you felt like that,' he says.

'I've always supported you, Charles, you know I have. Even when Mum and Dad bad-mouthed you. And I told them that holding a *shiva* for you was a mistake and they'd come to regret it. But you don't know how much you hurt them, especially Dad. Mum was full of outrage but Dad…'

'What?'

'Silent. Utterly miserable. As if he'd actually been bereaved. But that was all different. Sally is not Henrietta. They've known her since she was a toddler, and they like her.'

'She's no more Jewish than Henrietta was,' points out Charles.

'True, but she grew up in the East End, she's known Jews all her life, and they know her mother too. And, well, a lot of water's gone under the bridge since you met Henrietta at Cambridge. Now, I think they just want you to be happy.'

Charles grunts sceptically. 'They? Dad maybe. Not Mum.'

'She'll be okay,' says David optimistically.

'But can I risk it? When she's with it, she's got no filter! You've heard some of the things she says. She's outrageous, a loose cannon, and I don't want her upsetting Sally. She could ruin the whole day.'

David sighs. 'I do see that. Perhaps leave her here? She might not be aware of it in any case.'

'I've considered that. But can I invite Dad without her? Won't he be upset? And it won't be in a *shul*. I've been wondering if we shouldn't just take ourselves off somewhere, Scotland maybe, or even the registry office on Euston Road, and do it, before a couple of random witnesses. That way nobody is offended, or *everybody* is offended, but we haven't singled anyone out.'

David doesn't reply for a moment. 'Would you mind if I discussed it with Sonia? She's very wise about these things.'

'Of course not. Maybe the four of us can get together and thrash it out.'

'Yes, good idea. Let's take this tea in before it gets cold.'

CHAPTER TEN

'Mr Holborne, sir!'

Charles is halfway up the staircase to his corridor, his arms full of law reports from Chambers' library. He leans over the banister. Clive has his head out of the clerks' room.

'Yes, Clive. What's up?'

'Just had a call from a Mr Munday, sir. He says it's about the Wise Property and Securities case, and if it's convenient to you, he'll meet you at midday.'

'Good. Is he coming here?'

'Sort of. He says he'll see you on the corner opposite. I think he means outside Inner Temple Common Room.'

Charles sighs. 'Is he still on the phone?'

'No, sir, he's gone.'

Charles shakes his head, exasperated. 'Okay, thank you,' he says, resuming his climb.

It's a week since Charles's last conversation with Munday. Billy called to say he "had something" and he'd pop into the Temple soon. Charles tried to persuade him to go to Waterfields' office in the city and give any evidence he'd obtained direct to Stephenson. As he pointed out, hoping it might act as an inducement, Munday could be paid at the same time.

However, the ex-enforcer was extremely resistant to the idea of going anywhere near a solicitor's office. Charles finished the call a little anxious. Working directly with a private investigator in this way is a breach, albeit a technical one, of his professional rules. It was the last thing Charles needed now if he was to apply for silk. On the other hand, he reminded himself, one had to bear in mind Munday's experience of solicitors, indeed probably the experience of every person the ex-con knew. Solicitors only featured in their lives when they were in trouble. Lawyers were harbingers of bailiffs, eviction, lost contact with children and, all too often, imprisonment. They were bad news; a group from which to keep as much distance as possible. They were also, in Munday's words, "up their own arses", and while Charles didn't fully share that characterisation, in the case of Waterfields he conceded that Munday might have a point. So he reluctantly agreed to continue acting as go-between, at least in the short term.

The conference with the Wises, arranged for that evening, is fully prepared, so he makes use of the morning by completing a set of papers involving a tricky point of law on foreign jurisdictions. At just before midday, he pulls on his jacket and takes his manuscript notes downstairs to the typists as he leaves. He descends the steps onto King's Bench Walk and warm sunshine and crosses the cobbles towards the opposite corner of the square.

Munday has yet to arrive. Charles looks through the Georgian windows into the common room. It is already filling up with young barristers. It was once staffed full-time by a couple of middle-aged women who had served in the war. They were employed by the Inn, ostensibly as waitresses, but in fact to nanny the cohort of boisterous young ex-servicemen then training for the Bar, many of whom were still receiving medical and psychiatric treatment. In his twenties Charles and his pupil colleagues used to take refuge here when they needed a break from the rigours of their pupillages. Released from bondage for half an hour, they would share horror stories of their pupilmasters' disgusting personal habits and the mystifying piles of legal documents placed before them for analysis. There was horseplay, teasing and welcome camaraderie.

To Charles's sadness the two ladies disappeared in the late 1950s, the Inn presumably of the view that Baby Boom Barristers required no additional safeguarding. The common room is now provided with facilities for pupils to brew their own tea and toast their own muffins, overseen by a member of staff whose duties are strictly limited to afternoon waitressing.

For a moment the smell and the memories combine to induce Charles to go inside while he waits but then, as he looks through the window, he realises with consternation that he recognises none of the young barristers within. It's a new generation. He remains on the pavement.

Five minutes later a man approaches Charles from the direction of Middle Temple Lane. It is Munday, but it takes Charles a second look to recognise him. The ex-enforcer's long greasy hair has been washed, cut and styled in a surprisingly conservative manner with a side parting. He wears a new suit and polished black brogues. He could easily pass for one of the solicitors or outdoor clerks criss-crossing the Temple; indeed, his large stature and bold stride give him an air of confident authority.

'Almost didn't recognise you, Billy,' says Charles with a smile as Munday arrives before him.

'Yeah, well, Viv thought it time I smartened up a bit. Been wearing that suit since I was demobbed.'

'Viv?'

'Trouble 'n' strife. She's well chuffed I'm doing this.' Munday grins sheepishly. 'Like a proper profession, she reckons.'

'So it is. Well, now you look the part, do you want to come into Chambers?' asks Charles. 'It's just over the road.'

'Nah, you're all right. Here.' He offers Charles a large envelope. 'There's a summary and statements in there. All typed up. Viv gave us an 'and with the spelling, but I 'spect there're still some mistakes. And she did an invoice too,' he points to the envelope.

'Very professional,' says Charles approvingly. 'Want to give me a brief rundown?'

'Yeah, sure. Witness A is Mrs Avril Connelly. Lived at number 10, north end of the terrace. She didn't know the name of the bloke who chucked her out, but she'd definitely recognise him again. About five-ten, dark hair, thin face, with a sour expression and a bit of a limp. Nasty piece of work. Didn't even ask her to go. She opened the door to him, he dragged her out by her hair and punched her in the face, right in front of her kids. Then he boarded up the door. She lost everything.'

'Did she get a name?'

'No. Said he was sent by Wise Property and Securities.'

'Do you think she'll make a good witness?'

'I do, yeah. Quiet-spoken but determined. She's now in emergency accommodation with the kids, and she's promised to let me know if they move. Witness B is interesting. His name's Mueller. Older geezer, maybe around fifty-five? German, some sort of scientist, interned here during the war. Again, the bloke who chucked him out — same description — didn't say much. Something like "You were told before", and then hit him with an iron bar. Left him unconscious. Mueller woke up in hospital, but … he had a name. Apparently, Mueller was there when his next-door neighbours were given new furniture a couple of months back. That time, the bloke, same bloke, was all smiles and schmooze. Gave his name as "Kevin".'

'Just Kevin?'

'Yeah. There's a bit more. Some of the people I spoke to came from a different development, a WPSL site on Braithwaite Street. Just off Commercial Street.'

'That's the third tenant, the one the police have been soft peddling.'

'Looks like it. Anyway, they was all talking about "The Last Holdout" at Braithwaite Street, a chap called Eddie Bartlett. Bit of a local hero. Had boarded himself in, claimed they'd never get 'im out alive, that sort of nonsense. Apparently 'e was even on the news. Well, he just disappeared. After a couple of days some mates of his took off the boarding and broke in. They found his half-eaten tea on the table. The chair was on its side. Upstairs, the front window was smashed — not just the glass, but the whole window frame. Looked as if something big went through it.'

'And Mr Bartlett?'

'That's the thing. Disappeared. He was born in the house, worked in the area all his life, was a regular at the local. Everyone knew 'im, and everyone says he'd never have left voluntarily. I tried asking round, but the area's more or less abandoned. Like a ghost town, 'cept the corner shop, which is closing end of the month. I spoke to the bloke who runs it, Mr Martinelli. A few weeks ago, early evening, he hears a commotion, big crash like a window going in. Was gonna go 'n' look, but a customer tol' him to stay back. This chap was hanging about, hiding in the shop but watching what was going on over at Bartlett's place. I stood in the window, and you can see everything. Bartlett's front door is almost bang opposite.'

Charles smiles. 'You're a natural at this, you know that, Billy?'

Munday smiles shyly. 'Actually, I surprised meself, 'cos I'm enjoying it. I've always liked talking to people, and they seem to open up to me. Probably 'cos I know 'alf of 'em. Anyway, Martinelli said the chap in the shop, the one watching, was very big. He called 'im a giant.'

'Have we got a statement from him, this Martinelli?'

Munday shakes his head. 'No. Sorry. He's a bit scared and just wants a quiet life. But I know where to find him until 'is lease runs out, so I thought I might go back, have another go at persuading him. One last thing: it may be coincidence, but a minute or two after the commotion, a van passed the shop front from the Braithwaite Street end. Martinelli noticed it because nowadays there's never any traffic down that end except contractors' vehicles. It's a cul-de-sac, and the properties are all empty. Also, it was in an 'urry. He saw the name on the side: Shoreditch Enforcement Services.'

'Shoreditch Enforcement Services?' ponders Charles. 'I wonder what they enforce.'

'I'll let you know. If you agree, I thought I might pop round their lock-up tomorrow.'

'Good idea. Yes, see what you can find. Is that it?'

'Yup. Everything I've got so far is in there,' replies Munday, pointing at the envelope.

'Anything on Shirley Titmarsh? The lady from Bow County Court?'

Munday shakes his head. 'Not really. All I've got is that her husband fell off some scaffolding a while back. He's a surveyor apparently. Nasty injuries. He's been off work for months.'

Charles ponders this information. 'Might mean they're up against it, financially,' he muses.

'I thought that too. Oh, one other thing I learned at the court. I pretended to be a landlord with a tenant in rent arrears. How could I get him out, etcetera. Turns out all new actions coming in get put in a basket, and are actioned by anyone on the team. There's not just one person dealing with 'em. So your theory that they've been held up 'cos someone's been off sick won't fly.'

'Which makes our client's story, that they've been trying to use legal means to get possession, a bit iffy.'

'Yeah. Unless your Mrs Titmarsh, or someone else, is intercepting them.'

'Well, I'll interrogate the Wises tomorrow when I meet them. Stay with Shirley. My instinct says there's something going on there.'

'Will do.'

Charles indicates the envelope in his hand. 'This is far better than I expected, Billy. Well done. I'll send the invoice to the solicitors. I can pay you the cash by tomorrow, if that's okay.'

'Vivienne says it'll be okay if they send a cheque. Me address is on the chit.'

'That's a relief. Very sensible. Perhaps next time we can actually meet in an office?' says Charles. 'What you're doing isn't illegal, Billy. Nothing to be ashamed of. It's a proper job.'

'Yeah, I know. Got to, sorta, ease meself into it. Feels funny, trusting people like…' He tails off and studies his new shiny shoes.

'Like me?' suggests Charles with a grin.

'Sorry,' replies Munday. 'No offence.'

'None taken. I *am* one of them.'

'Yeah, but at the same time, you're not really, are you, Mr Holborne? Not one of *them*.'

Charles nods sadly. 'Yeah. Never was a truer word said, mate. And from now on Billy, it's Charles or Charlie. Okay?'

Munday nods, grinning, and shakes Charles's outstretched hand.

CHAPTER ELEVEN

Charles brings his blue Rover 2000 to a halt behind a brand-new silver-coloured Jaguar XJS saloon parked ahead of him. They are in the wide tree-lined suburban road called The Bishops Avenue. Stephenson climbs out of the Jaguar, takes a briefcase off the rear seat and waits for Charles. Charles descends from his car and meets the solicitor on the pavement.

It is just before 6 p.m., the heart of the rush-hour, but this road, backing onto the prestigious Highgate Golf Club, remains silent and peaceful, a select and undisturbed enclave of leafy green in one of the most expensive areas of real estate in London. Charles remembers reading that Robert the Bruce used the hunting lodge where the golf clubhouse now stands. The only sound is the movement of the wind through the trees, although, if Charles listens intently, he is just able to make out the dull hum of traffic from the A1 at the far northern end of the Avenue.

'Hope I didn't keep you waiting,' he says.

'No, I've just arrived myself,' replies Stephenson.

Charles leads the way to the tall gates, finds a shiny intercom panel, presses a button and waits. There is no response. He leans sideways to look through the ironwork. Facing him is a circular gravel driveway of such size that it resembles a roundabout. At its centre is a pond with a fountain in the form of a Greek goddess. Beyond that is a large house in an enormous garden with many trees. Compared to most of the others in the road it is relatively modest, but above the white marble portico enclosing the front door he counts eight large windows overlooking the front, not including the smaller windows under the mansard roof which presumably house the servants' quarters. It is a very impressive mansion. He wonders what one must pay for such a property on this road. Millions, certainly.

There's a tangle of parked cars on the driveway and most of the ground floor windows of the large house are illuminated. He presses the intercom button again. After another delay there is a click, and an impatient female voice emerges from the speaker.

'Yes? What is it?'

Charles is surprised at the peremptory greeting. 'My name's Charles Holborne, and I'm the barrister representing Sir Leo and Anthony Wise. I have Mr Stephenson from Waterfields solicitors with me, and I believe we are expected.'

'What? Do barristers make house calls?' says the voice. She apparently turns away from the intercom, as he hears her shout: 'Where's Jacquetta? Madeleine? There's a barrister at the gate!' she laughs.

Charles can't hear any reply but after a short delay there is a second click, and the gate starts to move. 'Come to the front door,' orders the voice.

Charles and Stephenson crunch across the pebbles, skirting the fountain in the centre and weaving their way between the luxury vehicles. They pass a small copse of ash and birch to their left. Almost hidden in the trees stands a modern two-storey building with two further sportscars parked outside. A sign reads "The Coach House."

They reach the main property's large entrance portico. As they do so the lights above them are illuminated and the front door opens. A pretty girl in her late teens faces them. She's tall, fair and slim and wears jeans and a T-shirt. Her face is tanned. Charles immediately notes her resemblance to Lady Wise.

A daughter, I suppose.

'I've just arrived myself,' says the girl, pointing to suitcases behind her, 'and they're all in a meeting. You'd better come in.'

Charles hears raised voices and laughter from somewhere in the interior.

'Sounds like they're finishing up,' says the girl. 'Jacquetta!' she shouts again irritably. 'I have no idea where that woman gets to,' she mutters. 'Well, come in, then. I guess you can wait there,' she says, pointing towards a group of low seats around a coffee table in a corner of the marbled entrance hall. 'Someone can probably make you a drink while you wait, although I've no idea where all the staff have gone.'

Charles and Stephenson look at one another. This is one of the reasons Charles dislikes conferences in clients' homes. There is something about making the effort to travel to counsel's chambers in the Temple which focuses minds. Meeting on their "home turf" results in a collision between Charles's professional need for concentration on the case and the client's domestic arrangements, and he cannot take charge in the same way. It also becomes more difficult to challenge clients, to ask difficult questions — even, sometimes, to accuse them of lying — in their own homes.

He and Stephenson take seats at the coffee table and wait. After a few minutes they hear a hubbub of raised voices, chairs being scraped on hard floors and doors opening from somewhere in the interior. A woman's high-heeled shoes clip-clop across the marble floor towards them. Lady Esther Wise appears. The two lawyers stand. Again, she looks gorgeous, radiant. Charles notes with surprise that Stephenson is blushing.

'I am so sorry, gentlemen!' she says in her deep voice, offering her hand limply to each of them in turn. Again,

Charles is aware that she holds his, almost caresses it, for a fraction of a second too long, and there is a disconcerting intensity in the way she locks eyes with him. He finds himself anxious that Stephenson will assume from this false intimacy that something is going on between them.

She is still speaking. 'I just don't know what to do with Sir Leo. He was only discharged on the strict understanding that he would take it easy, but since then it's been meeting after meeting after meeting. Please may I try your patience for another few minutes while he has a short rest? I assure you he is very keen to speak to you both.'

'Yes, of course, Lady Wise,' says Stephenson smoothly.

'May we offer you a glass of wine while you wait?' she asks. 'Or something else perhaps? Madeleine's making Martinis.'

Charles speaks before Stephenson can accept. 'No, nothing for the moment, thank you. After we finish maybe, but I think we need to keep our focus on the issues. There is much to discuss. The prosecution evidence raises some difficult questions.'

'Oh, I'm sure Leo and Tony will be able to explain everything,' she says airily. Other voices and footsteps approach. 'Forgive me…' she says, turning to the newcomers.

A group of people arrive in the entrance hall. They carry briefcases and are chatting noisily amongst themselves, an end-of-school-day exuberance following a long meeting. Lady Wise returns to one of them, a man wearing a suit, and puts her hand on his arm. The man is striking. He is an inch or two shorter than Charles, powerfully built with a square head, a strong chin and cropped salt-and-pepper hair. He wears thick dark-framed spectacles and reminds Charles of the actor George C. Scott. Lady Wise leans into him and whispers something in his ear. He laughs. Her mood, bright and flirtatious, seems oddly inconsistent with the fact that her husband and son face serious criminal charges and have just been released from police custody. More so still when her husband is, supposedly, seriously ill.

The teenager appears again and speaks directly to her mother, interrupting her confidential aside. 'Have you seen the lawyers, over there? I invited them in, but I can't find Jacquetta. Or Madeleine for that matter.'

'Yes, thank you, Hannah,' replies Lady Wise, without taking her eyes off the face of the man whose arm she clasps.

Lady Wise continues towards the front door, arm in arm with the man, when she notices Charles's scrutiny of her. She halts in front of the lawyers, forcing the man to do the same.

'Charles Holborne of counsel, and Andrew Stephenson of Waterfields, may I introduce you to Bernard Levy? Mr Levy sits on the board of the 613 Trust. We've just finished discussing the care home, my husband's legacy project.'

Charles cannot decide if she intended to be scornful or if her choice of words was caused by English not being her first language.

Charles and Stephenson each shake Levy's hand in turn.

'Pleased to meet you,' Levy says curtly, barely paying them any attention. He turns to Lady Wise. 'I'll be in touch,' he says, disengaging her arm — rather brusquely thinks Charles — and strides out of the front door. There was something slightly performative about the man's gesture, as if done for the benefit of anyone watching.

Lady Wise bids farewell to her other guests, who also file out. She closes the door after them and walks directly out of the entrance hall and down a corridor from whence Charles and Stephenson can hear her issuing orders in German. There is a clatter of crockery being stacked, and Charles assumes she has entered a kitchen. The two men are left standing and, after a moment, resume their seats. Stephenson looks pointedly at his watch and raises his eyebrows towards Charles, who shrugs.

A few moments later the teenage girl follows her mother and enters the kitchen. Charles hears her say something to Lady Wise and, although he cannot hear the words, there is anger in her tone. Her voice continues to rise before her mother interrupts. A furious row in German erupts, with both women shouting at and over one another. Charles and Stephenson make no eye contact. The kitchen door slams, but the argument can still be heard continuing behind it.

'Good evening, gentlemen,' says a male voice.

Standing before them is Sir Leo Wise. He leans on a walking frame and is supported at one elbow by a young woman. She is a shorter, slightly younger and less glamorous version of Lady Wise, but she is very attractive. She wears a plain knee-length skirt and a cardigan and has a small briefcase tucked under her arm.

A nurse? wonders Charles.

He focuses on Sir Leo. He barely recognises the man from their meeting in Hall the previous month. His skin is grey, and the folds hanging from his cheeks demonstrate significant sudden weight loss. His luxurious silvery hair, formerly so much a defining feature of his appearance that newspaper cartoonists would exaggerate it, is thin, and patches of scalp glint through it. There is a tenseness around his mouth and eyes which suggests to Charles that he is in pain, but the eyes crinkle and a genuinely warm smile appears on his face.

'Charles, Mr Stephenson. Please accept my apologies for keeping you waiting,' he says. 'As always, Esther was right, and I have taken on too much. You'd have thought I'd listen to her, after all these years.' He pauses as the row in the kitchen crescendos again and then adds lightly: 'A lesson my daughter might usefully learn. Would you care to follow me, gentlemen?'

He turns to the woman supporting him and nods.

Charles and Stephenson follow him as he makes his slow and painful way towards the back of the house. There, two sets of double doors open onto what looks like a ballroom. It runs along the back of the property and features chandeliers and ceiling-to-floor curtains. Four pairs of French doors open onto a garden now largely in darkness. Another member of staff is in the process of closing the doors and curtains which, Charles supposes, were opened to freshen the air after the previous meetings.

An enormous oval table fills one end of the room. Sitting at it is a young man, who rises as they enter. He wears casual clothes, a pair of light slacks and a shirt. Charles notes that the slacks are ironed with a sharp crease and the shirt is, oddly, buttoned to the neck. Something about the clothes and the way he stands suggest tension; as if he were a sprinter on starting blocks.

'This is my son, Anthony,' says Sir Leo as he is guided to a chair.

Stephenson offers his hand to the young man, but Anthony Wise either does not see the gesture or ignores it, as he sits down again without speaking or making eye contact with either of the lawyers.

Charles notes that at the far end of the enormous conference table is what looks like a model village. It has neat white blocks set on undulating green baize, with miniature trees and roads winding between the buildings.

The woman pulls out a chair next to Anthony Wise, takes the walking frame from Sir Leo and helps him to sit. Then she opens the briefcase under her arm and takes out a notepad, a pen, and some other documents and arranges them in front of him.

'Thank you, Jacquetta,' says Sir Leo quietly, and he pats her hand affectionately. 'Sit wherever you are comfortable,' he says, waving at the ten or twelve chairs around the table. Charles chooses to sit directly opposite his lay clients.

'Don't you want to be at the end?' asks the older man.

Charles laughs. 'My pupil master, Wally Otkins, used to say "Never sit at the head of the table".'

'Why?'

'Because people will assume you're in charge and know what you're talking about.'

Sir Leo laughs. Charles and Stephenson begin unpacking their papers.

'Will Lady Wise be joining us?' asks Charles.

'Do you need her? She has very little to do with the business,' says Sir Leo.

Another member of staff enters with a tray of drinks, a pot of coffee and another of tea, and starts distributing cups and saucers.

'It might be helpful,' replies Charles.

Sir Leo speaks to the woman with the tray. 'Please ask Esther to join us, Madeleine. I see you are looking at the model care home, Mr Stephenson.'

'Yes. It's very impressive.'

'One hundred and twenty rooms, including two dozen suites for couples, its own swimming pool, a small cinema, an à la carte restaurant, several dining rooms including one that can be used by residents for family gatherings, and a health centre,' replies Sir Leo with unmistakeable pride.

'Health centre?' queries Stephenson.

'GP and physiotherapists on duty from nine till five every day, and round the clock nursing. I see it as a community where the elderly can be supported to enjoy their last few years, even if their health needs increase. Not an institution where they are abandoned and forgotten.'

'It sounds wonderful. I wish my parents were somewhere like that,' comments Charles with feeling.

'Do they need that sort of support?' asks Sir Leo.

'Yes. They're at Sunshine Court, which is far from satisfactory. But I doubt we could afford what you're offering.'

Sir Leo smiles. 'It is very important to me that this type of care is not only available to the rich. I have been negotiating with several synagogues in London about a form of insurance arrangement.'

'Insurance?'

'Were your parents observant? Did they go to synagogue regularly?'

'Yes, until their ill health made that impossible.'

'But I bet they're still paying their synagogue subscriptions. To pay for funeral arrangements, ya? Well, what if they had the option of paying a little extra from the day they joined the synagogue, when they were in their twenties or thirties? The synagogue would use the additional income to pay for group insurance in case members of the community require such care.'

'That's a clever idea. Too late for my parents, unfortunately. How close are you to opening?'

Sir Leo sighs heavily. 'Problems, always problems,' he says, gesturing vaguely towards the doors, from which Charles takes it he is referring to the last meeting. 'But soon. It *has* to be soon.'

The sick man speaks vehemently, as if he could push the development through by sheer willpower alone. Charles hears the unexpressed conclusion to the sentence which would have begun with "because…".

Because he knows he is dying.

'Ah, Esther, good,' says Sir Leo, looking up as his wife enters and takes a seat. She holds a half-empty cocktail glass in her hand.

'Now,' says Sir Leo, 'we begin, yes? Tony?'

The young man is scribbling industriously in a notebook, but for the first time he does look up briefly. Charles casts a glance at the notebook but can make nothing of the crowded lines of tiny writing. Anthony pushes away that pad and slides another into place in front of him. He nods.

'Okay, Charles,' says Sir Leo. 'Over to you.'

As Charles is about to speak, Anthony interrupts. 'What do they mean by saying we conspired with "persons unknown"?'

'It's not unusual,' replies Charles. 'The essence of a conspiracy is the criminal agreement, and as long as the Crown can prove that you and your father must have entered into an agreement to do the alleged illegal acts with *someone*, they don't need to prove who. We assume it's the people who actually assaulted the tenants.'

'Why are we charged with conspiracy and not offences under the Rent Act?' asks Anthony. He speaks quickly, and there is a curious lack of intonation in his voice. He sounds slightly robotic.

'Because,' replies Charles, 'a conspiracy is triable on indictment with unlimited fines and prison sentences. Maximum sentences under the Rent Act are a fine of one hundred pounds or six months.'

Anthony fires another question. 'So they're going to ask for longer terms of imprisonment. How long?'

'This is not America, Mr Wise. The prosecution doesn't ask for any particular level of sentence. That's a matter for the judge. In some cases there are published guidelines.'

'What do the guidelines say in this case?'

'There aren't any yet in respect of Rent Act offences, but conspiracy will certainly attract a longer sentence.'

Sir Leo intervenes. 'The fact that they have charged us with conspiracy, just to get an increased sentence, suggests some animus against us, don't you think, Charles?'

'Not necessarily —' starts Charles.

'Yes, it does,' interrupts Anthony. 'That inspector hated me on sight. I heard him calling me a "flash Jew boy" to the desk officer, and his whole attitude to me was arrogant and aggressive. At one point, after I'd been in a cell for four hours, I asked if I could have something to eat and he told me to fuck off and starve.'

Charles makes a note of that response. He turns to Stephenson. 'It might be worth seeing if Woolley has previous for this sort of thing.'

'How would we find out?' asks the solicitor.

Charles thinks. 'We could ask Munday to make enquiries of other people Woolley has arrested and prosecuted, especially in the East End. See if they report any obvious anti-Semitism. If we can find ammunition, it might enable us to damage his credibility over the alleged second interview on grounds of prejudice.'

He returns his attention to his clients.

'However, proving the police officer was motivated by anti-Semitism won't affect the facts of the case,' he explains. 'If the jury finds you guilty of entering a criminal conspiracy to use coercion as a business tactic, a tactic resulting in huge profits, the fact that Woolley hates Jews is neither here nor there. The judge has to act on the jury's verdict, and the penalty will be severe.'

Lady Wise speaks for the first time. 'How severe?'

'As I explained,' answers Charles, 'it's impossible to be sure without precedents. But prison certainly, and probably for some years.'

The woman's beautiful eyes widen in shock. 'Seriously?'

'I'm afraid so.'

She lifts her cocktail glass to her lips and drains it in a single swallow. Without speaking she rises and leaves the room.

'Now, if you have finished asking your questions, Mr Wise, I have some of my own. The first relates to this second interview.'

Lady Wise returns having replenished her cocktail glass. Charles watches her approach the table, and notes a certain deliberation about her movements, as if she were taking pains to hide intoxication. She carries a jug of what, Charles presumes, is more of the same. She sits and lights a cigarette, blowing smoke towards the ceiling. That produces an irritated "Tut!" and an angry movement from her son on the opposite side of the table. For a second Charles thinks the young man might be about to storm out of the room, but he appears to control himself. Charles asks his next question.

'Detective Inspector Woolley has recorded a long second interview with you, Mr Wise, in which you are alleged to have confessed to ordering that violence be used against recalcitrant tenants. My Instructions state that you deny a second interview even occurred. Is that correct?'

'Yes,' replies Anthony, not looking up.

'So it has to be our case that Woolley has made all this up,' says Charles.

'He must have,' replies Sir Leo.

'Had either of you ever met him before this occasion?'

'Never,' says Anthony.

'Any of the other police officers?' Charles directs this question specifically to Anthony.

'No. I've had no dealings with any police officers before this.'

'So he'd have had no opportunity to observe you?'

'No.'

Charles turns to Stephenson. 'You were present during the first interview when you advised Mr Wise not to say anything.'

'Yes,' replies Stephenson.

'And what was Mr Wise's behaviour during that interview?' asks Charles.

'What do you mean?'

'Was any of his behaviour odd? Any rocking? Unusual noises?'

'He said "No comment" to every question. He didn't actually look at the police officers. He stared at the desk. He did make some strange sounds and rock backwards and forwards when Woolley pressed harder. Why?'

Charles turns back to the Wises. 'Sir Leo. Have you ever witnessed your son exhibiting any of the behaviours attributed to him by DI Woolley in this interview?'

'Behaviours?' asks Sir Leo.

'Yes. Such as rocking, not looking at the speaker, making unusual noises.'

Sir Leo turns to look at his son, sitting next to him. Anthony's head is bowed. His hands are clasped together on his lap and, Charles notes, his knuckles are white.

'Tony sometimes has difficulty in certain social situations,' replies Sir Leo gently.

'Has he ever been diagnosed with a specific condition?' asks Charles. 'One that might involve the sort of behaviour described by DI Woolley?'

'He underwent many tests as a boy. One doctor thought he had childhood schizophrenia but we never agreed with that. Why is this relevant?'

Charles makes a note before answering. 'Because the police officers are describing behaviour which would not be uncharacteristic for your son.'

'I suppose not.'

'In which case one has to ask: how were they aware of them? Anthony says this interview didn't take place at all and yet the police had no means of knowing that he might act in this way. Did any of you mention that Anthony had these sorts of difficulties?'

'Of course not,' replies Sir Leo. 'It's not something one would advertise.'

'Mr Stephenson?'

'I wasn't aware of them,' replies Stephenson. 'I'd only ever dealt with Mr Wise by correspondence. Until I went to West End Central police station, I'd never actually met him face to face.'

'Mr Wise?' asks Charles of Anthony. The young man is now rocking backwards and forwards slightly in his chair. 'How would they know what you were like, to fabricate such an accurate depiction of you?'

He does not answer.

'Let me explain something to you,' says Charles, putting down his pen. 'The prosecution has almost no admissible evidence against you. In your case, Sir Leo, there's none at all and unless it's supplemented before the committal proceedings, I'm confident a submission of no case to answer in your case will be successful. As for you, Mr Wise, the only admissible evidence against you is contained in this alleged second interview. If the jury believes you gave that interview, it is certainly enough to convict you and send you to prison for some years. For them to disbelieve that interview we have to attack DI Woolley and DC Truman, both of whom were there and claim to have heard you give these answers. Whereas we might be able to attack one of them, DI Woolley for example, on some grounds, perhaps because he's anti-Semitic, it's much more difficult, more than twice as difficult, to discredit two apparently honest police officers. It is also very likely that you will have to give evidence yourself…'

'No,' interrupts Anthony, shaking his head.

'…so as to tell the jury, in your own words, that you did not say what they claim you said. From what I have seen, you're going to find giving evidence quite difficult. Furthermore, and forgive me for being blunt, but without some medical evidence to explain your … unusual presentation, juries are unlikely to warm to you.'

'No,' repeats Anthony.

Charles presses on. 'Explain to me about the furniture. Woolley has you saying that there was a scheme to give expensive furniture to the tenants, to evade the Rent Acts.'

No one answers.

'Well?' persists Charles. 'Has he made this up?'

Still no one offers an answer.

'Sir Leo, Mr Wise, nothing you say to us goes beyond this room, do you understand? I'm sure Mr Stephenson has explained this to you before. You're protected by legal professional privilege. Even if you reveal that you've committed an offence, I can say nothing to anyone about it. But I need an answer to my question.'

The silence is broken, eventually, by Sir Leo. 'We were advised that it might be possible to get protected tenants out of their properties, legally, if their rent included substantial payments towards furniture. So we offered them expensive furniture in return for the old and broken things they already had.'

'So, this interview, which Anthony says never occurred, includes details which neither of you gave to Woolley, but which are, in fact, true? How is that possible?'

'He had other information, perhaps?' suggests Sir Leo. 'From another source.'

Charles considers. 'That's possible, I guess. Who gave you this advice, about the furniture?'

'A lawyer in the company,' says Sir Leo.

'Did this lawyer provide any authority for such a proposition?' asks Charles.

'He said that the law was so new that there were no decided cases on it. It was his interpretation.'

'So the company gave expensive furniture to these tenants and then forced them out?'

'No!' replies Anthony. 'We didn't give them the furniture. That was an act of charity by Estate Clearances Limited. And there's no suggestion of forcing them out at all. We worked with the council to bring possession proceedings. It was all above board.'

'Who are Estate Clearances Limited?' asks Charles.

'They're a registered charity. They collect furniture from properties where the owners have died intestate and then distribute the furniture among needy members of the Jewish community.'

'Who runs the company? Or the charity?'

'You just met him,' says Lady Wise, her diction slightly fuzzy. She is now onto her third cocktail. 'The managing director is Bernard Levy.'

Charles makes a note. 'Can you give me details of the possession proceedings brought against these tenants?' he asks.

'No. We've been having problems with Bow County Court,' says Anthony.

'Are you saying that proceedings weren't actually issued?' asks Charles.

'It looks that way,' replies Sir Leo. 'But I believe copies of the claim forms are in the office. One of our in-house lawyers was drafting them for the borough council, who are short-staffed. But they were in the name of the London Borough of Newham, and Newham issued the proceedings. I don't know what the exact legal term is, but we needed guidance from the judge as to whether the furniture meant that we could obtain possession.'

'It's called a declaration,' says Anthony.

'Was the strategy one of your ideas, Mr Wise?' asks Charles.

'The idea came from John Yelland, but I approved it. We had to do something. We were running out of time.'

'So, to prove the motivation for providing the furniture, you would again have to give evidence,' points out Charles.

'Not necessarily,' says Sir Leo. 'Mr Yelland is a solicitor in our in-house legal team. He could give evidence. And it was he who drafted the proceedings for Newham to issue.'

'All right, let's park that for the moment. You're saying we don't know why legal proceedings were never actually issued by the county court? Is that right? So the Crown might well argue,' points out Charles, 'that the drafts produced by Mr

Yelland were concocted to cover up the fact that this was an unlawful attempt at repossession.'

'But is it unlawful?' asks Anthony. 'You don't know that. You're not a judge.'

'No, Mr Wise, I'm not a judge; but I would be absolutely astonished if the court were to say that the provision of replacement furniture could possibly allow a landlord to evade the protection given by the Rent Acts. The entire point of the legislation is to protect tenants' rights to remain in premises, to prevent them being evicted without very good cause. Does the provision of a nice couch seem to you a good enough reason to throw a family onto the street?'

'We didn't cause the housing crisis,' protests Lady Wise. 'It's because we recognise the need for decent housing that we're doing this. These people will be much better off once the new blocks are built. Have you seen the specifications for Seagull Tower? Large rooms, double-glazed windows, inside lavatories, new stoves and fridges, and views over half of London.'

Charles turns to Anthony. 'Is there any possibility that someone else from the company could have authorised the use of force?'

'Absolutely not.'

Charles turns to Sir Leo. 'I have to ask, Sir Leo: did you give that order or know who did?'

The old man shakes his head. 'No.'

'And what would be the purpose?' asks Anthony, exasperated, 'if we're taking formal legal proceedings?'

'The obvious answer is speed. But I can think of others. Have you heard of Shoreditch Enforcement Services?'

'Yes,' replies Sir Leo. 'They're licensed bailiffs on the approved list at most east London courts. All landlords with properties in the East End use them at some time or other. They do a lot of debt collection work for the London councils, especially Newham. Why? What's their involvement here?'

'None, so far as the Crown's concerned. Maybe none at all.'

'Then...?' prompts Lady Wise.

'Our investigator discovered that another tenant — different development site, but also one of yours — was also evicted.'

'So?' asks Sir Leo.

'It was the manner of his eviction. He was thrown from a first-floor window.'

There is a sharp intake of breath from Lady Wise. '*Eine Methode, die von den Braunhemden bevorzugt wird,*' she says softly to her husband.

'Yes, Lady Wise,' says Charles. 'Very like the Brownshirts in Nazi Germany.'

'You speak German?' she asks, surprised.

'Not really, but I heard enough Yiddish spoken in my childhood.'

'I give you my solemn word, Mr Holborne, Charles,' says Sir Leo, 'if that's true, my company had absolutely nothing to do with it.'

'And Shoreditch Enforcement Services?' asks Anthony.

'One of its vans was seen, as they say, "leaving the scene of the crime". It might be nothing, and this particular tenant forms no part of the Crown's case — yet. But he's disappeared. I have asked Mr Munday to make enquiries.'

'But you said it has nothing to do with the case,' says Anthony. 'Why would we start digging up material that might be useful to the prosecution?'

'You tell me that neither you nor your father, nor anyone involved in the company, authorised the use of force. Therefore, someone else did. And we need to identify that person to raise it as a possibility for the jury. Without it, the motive plus your alleged confession make a conviction likely. Reasonable doubt, remember? The only lead we have is Shoreditch Enforcement Services, and even that might be pure coincidence. Don't you think it's worth exploring that loose end? Let me reassure you, nothing we discover is disclosable to the Crown. And forewarned is forearmed.'

Sir Leo answers. 'Yes, I think we should find out if Shoreditch Enforcement Services is involved.'

'Good,' says Charles. 'Do you know who runs it?'

'No. But I'll get one of the staff to find out,' replies Sir Leo.

Charles scans his notes for his next question and hears Sir Leo sigh heavily opposite him. He looks up. The old man's grey face looks bloodless and his breathing is laboured. 'Are you all right to continue?' he asks.

'I think perhaps I need to lie down,' says Sir Leo.

Lady Wise pushes her chair back and gets to her feet. She is now obviously unsteady, and sits down again suddenly.

'*Es ist okay*, Esther,' says Sir Leo wearily. 'Jacquetta!'

The young woman opens the door so promptly the Charles realises she must have been listening outside. She walks round swiftly to Sir Leo to help him rise.

'I'm sure if you have any other questions, Tony will be able to answer them,' says Sir Leo. 'I'm very sorry.'

Jacquetta guides him out of the room, closing the door behind her.

'Shall we continue?' asks Stephenson of Charles quietly.

'I'd rather wait until Sir Leo's available. I have enough for the moment. We'll need to meet again anyway, once committal papers are served.'

Charles and Stephenson pack up their papers. Anthony Wise shuffles together his notebooks and leaves the room without a word. Lady Wise has already disappeared. Madeleine arrives and waits to escort the lawyers to the front door.

She leads them across the marble hallway. As they are about to step outside there is a call from behind them.

'Mr Holborne! Mr Holborne!'

Charles turns to see Jacquetta running down the wide curved staircase towards them. 'Sir Leo forgot something. Would you mind coming back for a second?'

'Just me?'

'Yes, please.'

Charles turns to Stephenson. 'I'll see you outside.'

He drops his case papers and bag by the front door and follows Jacquetta up the stairs and along a soft carpeted landing to a door. She leads him into a large well-appointed bedroom. It accommodates not only a huge bed but also a couch, a couple of armchairs, a dressing table and a desk laden with documents and plans. Sir Leo is lying on the bed, still clothed, his head propped by pillows and a cold compress on his forehead. He beckons to Charles. Jacquetta stays by the door.

'Sorry to delay you … again,' he says, breathing heavily. He indicates that he wants Charles to come closer. Feeling awkward, Charles approaches the bedside.

'I couldn't ask in front of my wife,' says Sir Leo quietly. 'You said that a conviction would probably lead to a prison term.'

'Yes,' confirms Charles.

'What if I were to say that *I* gave the order for violence to be used? Would I go to prison too? Given my age and ... state of health?'

'Those factors would be taken into account but, probably, yes. And, forgive me, but I doubt you'd survive it.'

'Isn't that the point? I'm not going to survive much longer anyway.'

Charles frowns. 'Are you telling me you *did* give such an order?'

The old man closes his eyes. There is such a long pause that Charles wonders if his client might have fallen asleep.

Eventually, Sir Leo does reply, but in a whisper. 'I'm extremely tired, Charles. Leave me be.'

Charles waits for a few seconds to see if his client has anything further to say. Then he turns and is shown out of the room by Jacquetta.

'Can you find your own way out, Mr Holborne?' she asks. 'I need to see to Sir Leo.'

'Yes, of course. Excuse me for asking, but are you his nurse?'

'No, I'm the ... housekeeper. Goodbye.'

She returns to Sir Leo's bedroom and closes the door. Charles finds his way back to the head of the stairs and starts to descend.

Lady Wise is climbing the staircase towards him. Now there can be no doubt: she is drunk and, judging by her unsteadiness, *very* drunk. She reaches twice for the handrail, missing both times. As they close on one another Charles sees that her eyes are glazed, some of her hair has escaped the clip at the back of her neck, and her red lipstick is smudged.

They play a little *pas de deux*, each moving to one side of the staircase and then to the other. Charles smiles, moves aside and indicates that the woman should pass him. She lifts her foot to take the next step and trips. Charles bends swiftly to catch her, and suddenly she is in his arms, trying to kiss him. Her golden hair is all over his face, and the smell of perfume and alcohol is overpowering. For a wild second or two before he can get hold of her sufficiently to disengage, her hands are everywhere, touching him.

'No,' he says firmly.

It's as if his word severs the strings of a puppet. She goes limp, rocks backwards and seems an instant from falling backwards down the stairs. Charles has no choice but to catch her again by the waist. Now she is in his arms, flopped over like a rag doll, her hair touching the carpet. He is unsure if she really is unconscious or if this too is play-acting, but he daren't let her go just in case.

'Jacquetta!' he calls loudly. 'Jacquetta!'

He hears a door opening above him, a few steps, a gasp and then the housekeeper is running softly down the stairs towards him.

'I think she fainted,' explains Charles, getting his shoulder under one of Lady Wise's armpits to lift her. Jacquetta does the same on the other side. 'Up or down?' he asks.

'Up,' grunts the young woman.

They manoeuvre carefully so they are all facing the first floor landing, and then together lift Lady Wise to the top of the staircase, her feet bumping uselessly over the carpeted stairs as they go.

'Now what?' asks Charles.

'Lie her down here,' instructs Jacquetta.

They lower her to the carpet. Her eyes remain closed. Jacquetta places her in the recovery position. 'I can manage from here,' she says. 'You may go. Thank you.'

'Yes, of course.'

'And, sir?'

'Yes?'

'Please be kind and forget this. She will.'

Charles nods. He walks swiftly back down the stairs, collects his things and leaves the house, pulling the door closed behind him.

He meets Stephenson on the pavement.

'I don't have much experience of these things, but that was an extraordinary interview,' comments Stephenson. 'What did you make of it?'

'I think one, two or perhaps all three of them are lying. But which of them, and on which subjects, I'm not sure.'

Stephenson nods slowly. 'Yes. That was my impression too. What did the old man want?'

Charles shakes his head. 'He was mooting the possibility that he would confess to giving the order.'

'But did he? Give the order, I mean?'

'No idea. Do you speak German, by any chance?'

'Me? No. Why?'

'Of all the odd things that happened tonight, the one that takes the biscuit was that row between Lady Wise and the daughter. I couldn't hear most of it, but one sentence was crystal-clear.'

'Why? What did Lady Wise say?'

'It wasn't her, it was the daughter.'

'And?'

'She said, and I quote: "*You're a whore, but even you can't fuck your way out of this!*"'

It is almost nine-thirty before Charles gets home. The lower part of the house is in darkness. He descends to the kitchen to find a note on the table from Sally saying that she's gone up, but she'll be reading for a while. She apologises, but she was too tired to cook.

Charles makes himself a sandwich and is about to take it upstairs when the telephone rings.

'Terminus 1525,' he answers.

'Charlie?'

'Yes, Billy.'

'Sorry to ring so late. Your missus said I should call back at ten.'

'It's fine. I was seeing the clients. What news?'

'I'm gonna do you a whatsit ... like a file note or something. What do you call 'em?'

'An Attendance Note?'

'Yeah, maybe. But I thought you might want to hear this straightaway.'

'Okay. Let me get my notebook ... right. Off you go.'

'I went to Shoreditch Enforcement Services. They're at 28 Charles Square, Hoxton, West Shoreditch. I got there at about quarter past six. It's all residential on that street, but the ground floor of number 28 is a lock-up garage with double wooden doors and residential above.'

'Okay. Did you speak to anyone?'

'Yeah. There was a light on inside the ground floor, so I rang the bell. The door was opened by a middle-aged bloke, between forty and forty-five I guess, about five-eleven, white, dark hair and solid build. He had a narrow face. A heavy smoker as his left hand was all nicotine-stained. Also, I think he had a limp but I can't be sure as he didn't walk around much. Said his name was Kevin Streeter, and he was a licenced bailiff and a director of the company.'

'Was he difficult?' asks Charles.

'No, not really, maybe a bit suspicious. I said I was investigating the disappearance of a Mr Bartlett of 61 Braithwaite Street, Shoreditch, on behalf of Waterfields solicitors. I asked if I could come in, and he agreed. The lock-up had a white Bedford CA van with "Shoreditch Enforcement Services" on the side. Registration plate ... hang on, I've got it here ... yes, ABL 609.'

'Did he know Bartlett?'

'He claims not. He asked me why I was asking, and I said there'd been reports of a Shoreditch Enforcement Services van seen in Braithwaite Street the evening Bartlett disappeared. I asked him if he'd seen anything. He denied being in the area, and produced work schedules showing lists with names and times against them. It was on Bow County Court headed notepaper and the last appointment was in Tottenham at 4 p.m.'

'Bow County Court again.'

'Could be coincidence. Most of the bailiff work in the East End comes from that court.'

'True. Anyway, a list of possessions running to 4 p.m. wouldn't stop him being in Braithwaite Street at half past five.'

'No. I asked where the van would have been after that time and he said, locked up in the garage. He denied anyone else had access to the keys. According to him, no one else ever drove it. I asked if he had any employees who might've taken it. That was the first time I thought he might've been hiding something.'

'Why?'

'Just a feeling, really. 'E said there had been one but he left, months ago, before any of this happened.'

'Anything else?'

'Nah. But I left my card in case he thought of anything.'

'Okay. Thank you.'

'I'm still working on Martinelli, the corner shop bloke. I'll let you know how I get on.'

'And the big bloke who was watching through the window. The "giant".'

'Yeah, still on that.'

CHAPTER TWELVE

Leia has been settled for the night. Charles and Sally are just finishing a meal at the kitchen table. Miles Davis's trumpet comes from the turntable in the background and the lights are dimmed. This is the first evening the couple have spent together for some days, and they're enjoying an hour or so of peace and quiet.

'Sonia called,' says Sally. 'They've invited us over for Friday night supper.'

'At Sunshine Court?' asks Charles, putting down his knife and fork.

'No, their place. Just the four of us, apparently. Something about our wedding?'

'Oh, yes. When I saw David we weren't able to speak for long. I thought they could help me decide what to do.'

'Help *you*?' retorts Sally. 'What about me? Isn't this my wedding too?'

'Oh, Sal, it's not like that, and you know it. I may not be your mum's favourite person in the world, but she's not going to create a scene at the wedding like mine could. And your lot aren't going to cut you off for marrying me. It's trickier for me, especially after what happened with Henrietta.'

Sally relents and puts her small hand over his great paw. 'I know. I'm sorry.'

She continues eating for a moment before also putting down her cutlery. 'It's always religion, isn't it?'

'Yes. Now maybe you understand why I hate it so much.'

'I've always understood, sweetheart.'

'And it's not just the Jewish thing. There's Mum's dementia as well. David's right, it is different this time round. They know you and like you. I don't imagine they'll sit *shiva* for me again. But I excluded them from my wedding to Henrietta, and I don't think I understood how much that hurt them. I can't do it again. But I don't know how either of them will react to a non-religious service at a registry office.'

'To be honest, Charlie, I don't see how your mum could manage, even if she was on best behaviour. You know … what if she has an accident?'

'She's wearing those pads now,' he points out.

'I know, but, still…' Sally raises an eyebrow.

'Yes. Having my stinky mum in a tiny registry office might affect the ambience somewhat.'

'Exactly.'

Sally stands and starts collecting the crockery.

'Leave that,' offers Charles. 'I'll do it. Why don't you warm up the TV and put your feet up?'

'Really? Would that be okay? I am out on my feet.'

'Absolutely. Go on.'

Sally kisses him on the cheek and goes upstairs to the lounge. A few moments later Charles hears the sound of the television. He takes the used plates and cutlery to the sink and starts running the hot water. He hears Sally calling him.

'Charles! Charles! Come quickly!'

There is intense urgency in her voice. Charles turns off the tap, grabs a tea towel and runs upstairs. He enters the lounge. Sally is standing before the television, pointing at a news report. A tower block has partially collapsed. Most of the flats in one corner are open to the air with walls, floors and ceilings completely missing. There's an enormous pile of broken masonry at the base of the building, with clouds of dust still swirling around it. The scene is illuminated by the headlamps and rotating blue lights of emergency vehicles. It looks like a war scene.

'It's Seagull Tower!' exclaims Sally. 'Isn't that the Wises' new block?'

The camera swings to focus on a reporter. Charles strides to the set and turns up the volume.

'— loud explosion. Reports of the tower's collapse began coming in within minutes,' says the reporter, breathless with excitement. 'The police have cordoned off the area. There are four … five … no, six ambulances already here and judging from the sirens you can probably hear in the background, more on the way. We've no news regarding deaths and injuries, but Seagull Tower only opened a few days ago and occupants to whom I've spoken — you can probably see behind me, there are dozens here on the pavement in their nightclothes — say it was almost full of tenants recently installed by the London Borough of Newham. The police have expressed the fear that, given the hour, most people in the tower would have been in their beds. The explosion appears to have been on the eighteenth floor. All the storeys above that, and most of those below, have been completely destroyed. As you can see, they're just not there any more! Almost the entire south-west corner of the twenty-two-storey block now lies — Oh my God! There goes another flat … and another!'

Sally and Charles watch, open-mouthed, as more corner flats collapse before their eyes. Huge chunks of masonry, furniture and belongings plunge and flutter hundreds of feet towards the ground.

Sally grips Charles's arm. 'Oh, Jesus, Charlie, was that someone falling?'

Charles shakes his head. 'I don't know. Christ, this is awful!' he breathes.

'The IRA?' asks Sally. 'He said there was an explosion.'

'I don't know,' repeats Charles. 'Possibly. They've been escalating the violence in Northern Ireland so, maybe. But even if it is, look at the way the flats are collapsing, one after another. That's got to be a design flaw, surely? That shouldn't happen.'

'Ever the lawyer,' she comments, her eyes riveted to the TV screen. 'What about those poor people?'

PART TWO

CHAPTER THIRTEEN

Hannah Wise presses a button to open the gates and watches her best friend, Priscilla, walk across the pavement to a luxury car. Priscilla waves, climbs in the front passenger seat, says something to the uniformed driver, and the car roars off up the road towards Kenwood.

Hannah remains in the doorway, looking up at the cold night sky. Her mood, slightly manic, and buoyed by music and gin for the last couple of hours, deflates. She wanted Priscilla to stay the night, as originally planned. She is one of very few people in whom Hannah can confide, and they never got to talking about her father's illness or the court case.

She is about to close the front door again when she notices lights on in the Coach House. Tony is still up, probably working. Hannah goes back up to her bedroom. She opens a window to let out the stale cigarette smoke, pulls on her jacket and shoes and returns to the front door. She closes it behind her, making sure to leave it on the latch, and walks across the drive.

She gives the Coach House bell their "special ring" — devised when they were children — so Tony will know it's her, and pushes open the door. The ground floor, which contains her brother's offices and space for his Aston Martin, is in darkness, but light shines down the open Swedish staircase from the floor above, and she follows it.

Tony is in the living area, which takes up two thirds of the space under the roof. He is hunched over his architect's drafting table, several sheets of paper pinned to it, making notes in his tiny handwriting. As always, the living space is immaculate, everything perfectly in its place. Hannah knows he ate alone in the little kitchenette, but you wouldn't be able to tell. Everything has been washed, dried and put away. The tea towel hangs next to the oven, positioned so that it falls over the rail perfectly, the front and back at exactly the same height. The apartment is as perfect as a show home.

'You okay?' he asks, not looking up from his work.

Hannah takes off her shoes and leaves them by the side of the sofa, aligned neatly so as not to distress him. She sits, looking across the wide room at his curved back as he works. 'Bit lonely.'

'Go to bed,' he suggests.

'Not tired.'

He continues to work in silence. Hannah knows better than to ask him what he is doing. He doesn't like to be interrupted. In any event, she has tried in the past to understand what it is he writes on the reams of paper he goes through, but it is beyond her. All she took from the conversation was that it was important, and that recording everything that happens to him in minute detail calms him.

'What's going to happen, Tony?' she asks softly.

'With Dad?'

'With everything. Dad, the police, the business. And Mum, I suppose.'

'Dad's going to die, I think.'

There is a long silence during which all Hannah can hear is the soft sound of Tony's pencil moving across the paper.

'Why didn't they tell me before?' she asks plaintively. 'I feel like I've been cheated out of his last weeks.'

'He didn't tell anyone at first. And then he only told me because he needed me to take his seat on the board. He swore me to secrecy. Said his illness was market-sensitive information and if I told anyone, I'd be breaching my fiduciary duties as director. Breaking the law.'

'Is that true?'

'Sort of.'

'Why did you tell me, then?'

'It all came out anyway when he collapsed. She still didn't want to tell you.'

'Bitch.'

'No, I think it was easier to pretend it wasn't happening. She must have realised he was ill, but I don't think she could face how serious it was. Calling you back from Switzerland would have meant accepting it was bad. I think his collapsing and requiring a transfusion brought it home to her.'

'Is she having a thing with that bloke, the furniture guy?'

'Levy? I've not noticed anything.'

'You never do. I bet Dad knows.'

'Leave her alone, Hannah. I know it's difficult, but their marriage is their affair.'

'You mean their marriage is her affairs,' replies Hannah bitterly. Tony doesn't respond. 'And the business? If Dad does die?' she asks after a while.

'I'll do what I can. Mum's not the sort of woman who can manage without money.'

'I despise her for that. Don't you find it odious? When you consider where she came from?'

For the first time Tony does look up. He turns and regards his sister. She is one of the few people with whom he can reliably make eye contact and, even with her, it makes him uncomfortable and takes an effort. Hannah thinks she is probably the only human being with whom Tony is able to connect emotionally.

'Actually, no. It makes sense to me,' he says. 'She uses all this —' and he waves his hand to indicate the Coach House, the main house, the gardens and the expensive cars — 'to insulate herself from what happened to her. The knowledge that that is all still there, in the world outside the gate ... it terrifies her.'

He stands, places his pencil exactly in line with the others on his drafting table and crosses the room to sit on the sofa. He cannot sit next to her as she would have preferred — in fact she would have liked him to hold her hand if that were possible — but he is quite close.

'Do you still have nightmares about being chased?' he asks.

'Yes, quite often.'

'Especially by dogs?'

'Yes.'

'So do I. But I've never been chased by a dog, have you?'

Hannah shakes her head. 'Not that I recall.'

'Mum and Dad both were.'

'I know. I've seen Dad's scars. So, what're you saying? That we're dreaming what happened to them? That's nonsense.'

'Of course not. But they *are* both terrified of dogs, and somehow, we've absorbed it. You feel enormous protectiveness of them too, don't you? Like it's your job to look after them?'

'I used to. I still do, so far as Dad's concerned. Not Mum, though. Not any more. What's this all about, Tony? What are you saying?'

He stands and walks to the far wall. It's lined with modern filing cabinets. Hannah once looked over her brother's shoulder at their contents. As far as she could see they were filled with scores and scores of dated notebooks, all fattened and wrinkled by her brother's handwriting. However, on this occasion he returns with an envelope from which he takes a sheet of paper. He hands it to her.

'It's a new group for the children of Holocaust survivors. I've been going for the last few months. Since you left at the start of term.'

'What do they do?' asks Hannah as she skim-reads the document.

'We talk. You'd be amazed at the similarities in the family dynamics. Both the survivors and their children have increased rates of suicide, depression and schizophrenia. Almost all of the survivors suffer from something similar to shell shock; so, nightmares, intrusive visions of the events and so on. They all have their own way of dealing with it, but something they call "avoidance" is the big one.'

'That's our mother all over.'

'That's my point. Faced with a stressful situation, she pretends it doesn't exist. And if that doesn't work, she hides in other ways.'

Hannah sighs. 'Like fucking all-comers.'

'I was thinking of her drinking actually, but, yes.'

'How can you defend her?'

'I don't defend her, do I? I'm just saying, it's not difficult to understand. Over-protectiveness is another feature shared by children of survivors.'

Hannah nods and is silent for a moment. When she does speak again she is more sad than angry. 'I so wanted us to be close, like normal mothers and daughters. When I was little and she spent so much time in bed, I used to think I could make her better.'

'I know. You were very sweet. Remember the omelette?'

She smiles sadly. 'I was so proud of it. And she threw it at me. I was only five.'

'I know.'

They hear the crunch of tyres on the gravel outside the Coach House. Tony stands and looks out of the window. 'It's her.'

'Can I stay?' asks Hannah.

'For the night?'

'Can I?' she asks.

She knows he finds any change to his rigid routine very difficult. He will also hate the "mess" the bedding will make on his leather couch. When he was younger this sort of change from the familiar, the routine, would cause him to close his eyes, stop his ears and scream.

He smiles at her. 'Course you can. I've only got a few more pages to do. Make up a bed while I finish off; you know where the blankets are. You'd better tell Mum though. If she wanders into your room and finds you not there, she'll panic.'

Hannah stands and looks out of the window. Her mother has made her way from the car to the house and is about to step up, under the portico, but misjudges it. She trips and staggers, preventing herself from falling by grabbing one of the pillars.

'She's drunk,' says Hannah, scathingly. 'Again.'

Tony nods without speaking and returns to his work.

Hannah makes up a bed on the couch and, still in her clothes, gets under the blanket. The gin is making her sleepy, and the sound of her brother's pencil is reassuring. She closes her eyes.

'Hannah! Hannah, wake up!'

Tony is standing over her, shaking her shoulder. He wears his pyjamas and a dressing gown.

'I fell asleep,' she mumbles, sitting up. 'What's the time?'

'Six minutes past four. Look!'

He points out of the window above her. She throws off her blanket and kneels on the sofa to look outside. The house and grounds are in darkness, and she can't see the main gates from the Coach House windows, but reflected on the front of the main house is a confused irregular flashing of blue lights.

'What's going on?' asks Hannah, her heart rate accelerating. She is now completely awake.

'Police,' says Tony. He rushes from her side towards his bedroom. 'Stay there!' he calls as he runs. 'I need to get dressed.'

'They're inside the gates!' she cries after him.

About eight men in dark clothes have entered the garden and are now spreading out around the house, moving cautiously across the gravel towards the front, side and garden doors. Tony runs past her, pulling a jumper on over his pyjamas.

Hannah listens to his feet clattering down the stairs. He wrenches open the Coach House door.

Four of the policemen have taken up position by the front door. Two hold a dark cylindrical object with handles on its side. For a fleeting moment, Hannah wonders what they are doing with a fire extinguisher, but then she realises that it's an implement to smash down the door.

Tony appears below her, running across the gravel towards them.

'Stop!' he shouts. All four men turn to him. 'It's open!'

Tony arrives at the portico. He pushes past the policemen and turns the front door handle. The door swings inwards. 'See?' he says. 'There's no need to destroy it.'

The tallest of the four men speaks. 'Are you Mr Anthony Wise?' he asks.

'Yes.'

'Then I'm arresting you on suspicion of conspiracy to murder. You don't need to say anything unless you wish to do so, but anything you do say may be taken down and given in evidence against you. Do you understand?'

'Murder?' asks Tony, stunned. 'What on earth do you mean, murder?'

'Have you understood the caution I just gave you?'

'Yes, of course, but I don't know what you mean by murder.'

Two of the policemen by the front door have already entered the building and disappeared into the darkness.

The officer speaks to his remaining colleague on the doorstep. 'Cuff him and bring him inside.' He addresses Tony. 'We are also here to arrest Sir Leo Wise. We can search the entire house, but it would be easier on everyone concerned if you told us where his bedroom is.'

'Upstairs, turn right, first door,' answers Tony immediately.

The tall policeman enters the building swiftly and Tony is dragged after him.

The upstairs of the house is suddenly flooded with light.

Hannah can stand the suspense no longer. She runs downstairs, out of the Coach House door and across the driveway. None of the intruders is now visible and she is not intercepted.

She runs through the gaping front door and halts. She can see at least two men down the corridor in the kitchen. They must have come through the side door. Almost simultaneously, she hears glass smashing at the back of the house, followed by the splintering of timber. They're coming in the back too!

The remaining policemen are upstairs on the landing, one now attached to Tony, outside her father's bedroom door. Tony senses her presence, or at any rate happens to look down at that moment. He shakes his head firmly.

Then several things happen at the same time. From one end of the landing: her father's confused voice — a shout by Jacquetta — one of the policemen saying something firmly in a tone of voice that brooks no interruption. From the other end of the landing, overriding everything else, an urgent shout, almost a cry: 'Guv! Guv! Get an ambulance!'

The tall police officer stops talking and re-emerges onto the landing from Sir Leo's bedroom. He looks to his right. 'What?' he calls to his colleague.

'I can't wake the woman! There's a ton of empty pill bottles on the floor by her bed!'

CHAPTER FOURTEEN

Despite it being almost the middle of June, it is cloudy and cool, and the queue for the Visitors' Centre at Wandsworth Prison is long and slow-moving. Charles and Stephenson hug themselves against the chill and move forward a couple of feet.

Finally admitted, they give their details. Charles starts removing his coat and jacket, and directs Stephenson, who has never been inside a prison before, to copy him. He empties his keys and loose change into a dish, opens his briefcase and spreads the papers on the table. Then he positions himself with his arms out and his feet apart. He watches a guard examining his removed clothing while allowing himself to be frisked.

Satisfied that the pinstriped jacket and woollen coat contain no razor blades, knives or other weapons, and no drugs have been sewn into the lining, the guard returns them to him. Charles allows him to feel along his trouser turnups before he re-dresses. Another guard lifts up Charles's copy of Archbold, the criminal practitioners' bible, four inches thick and as heavy as a brick. Gripping it by its spine and holding it towards the floor, he fans the pages so anything secreted in them will fall out. In fact something does fall out, a card that Charles had been using as a bookmark.

The guard reads it and looks over at him. 'Ronnie Scott's? You a jazz fan, then?'

'I am, actually.'

'Me too, though I haven't been since Christmas. A mate of mine reckons The Who played there last month,' comments the guard.

'I think they did. I missed it, but I'm told they were very good.'

'Weird, eh?'

Having established some rapport, the guard waves Charles through. Charles re-loads his pockets while waiting for Stephenson.

The interview rooms are busy, but Charles and Stephenson are fortunate. As they are about to take seats and wait, the door at the far end opens and other lawyers emerge, apparently finished.

'Take that one,' says another guard, pointing with his pen from his desk, 'and I'll have him sent over from the wing.'

Charles and Stephenson take seats around a small table in the conference room at the end of the corridor. The chairs are small, flimsy and plastic.

'It's like being back in infants' school,' comments Stephenson, struggling to get comfortable on his seat.

'Be thankful. I was once smacked over the head with one of the wooden pre-war chairs they used to have. Concussion and eight stitches.'

'Why? Who hit you?'

'A client who disliked my advice.'

A few minutes later a prison guard appears at the door with Anthony Wise. The young man has a black eye and a livid bruise on one cheek. Charles and Stephenson stand.

'What happened?' asks Charles.

'Nothing,' replies the prison guard disingenuously. 'In you go, Wise.'

The guard closes the door.

'Take a seat,' says Charles to Anthony. 'What *did* happen?'

'I objected to my new nickname,' he says as he sits. Charles frowns, and the young man explains further. 'It's "Wid". Apparently a contraction of "weird" and "Yid."'

'I'm really sorry —'

'But you're going to tell me,' interrupts Anthony, 'there's no chance of bail so I have to grin and bear it.'

'Yes. Sorry. It is vanishingly rare for bail to be granted on a charge of murder or, for that matter, conspiracy to murder. And you have money, connections abroad so…'

'They'll say I won't turn up for trial.'

'Exactly.'

'Even though my father's in one hospital, unlikely even to make it to trial, and my mother's in another, just out of a coma?'

'Even then.'

'Right.' Anthony pauses. 'Okay, then.'

'What's the news regarding Lady Wise?' asks Stephenson.

'Out of danger.'

Charles is becoming accustomed to the young man's odd behaviour, but the complete lack of any warmth, indeed any emotion at all, is shocking. He and Stephenson share a glance. Anthony Wise is looking at the back of his hand, on which Charles can see a few words written in biro.

'Question one,' says Anthony. 'Who are these men we're supposed to have killed?'

'They're not saying you actually killed them,' replies Charles. 'They say that you entered an agreement to evict tenants with the use of force up to and including murder.'

'Yes, but who *are* they?' he demands, impatiently looking from one lawyer to the other.

'Haven't you been interviewed again?' asks Stephenson. 'Didn't they tell you then?'

'Why do you think I'm asking? You told me, very forcefully, to say "No comment" to all questions, so that's what I did! They gave up after a while and didn't go into detail.'

Charles answers. 'Very well. In addition to the four tenants of Seagull Tower who died in the collapse, there were two bodies found in the wreckage that didn't belong there. The first has been identified as a man called Crozier. The pathologist reckons he was somewhere in the building, dead, for weeks before the collapse: i.e. he was there from the time of construction. At present they have no evidence connecting Crozier with you at all. From marks on his arms and feet he appears to have been an habitual drug user. How they link him with you and the company remains to be seen.

'The second body I'm much more worried about. He was Edward Bartlett. You remember when we last met I told you that a man had been thrown from a first-floor window? At that time he was just missing, and the police didn't seem to be making a big deal about him. Without a complainant, they couldn't get very far. Well, now they *can* make a big deal about him. He has a definite connection with Wise Property and Securities Limited: he was a tenant at the proposed development on Braithwaite Street; he was definitely holding out against eviction; and now he's turned up, dead, in the rubble of another of your developments at Seagull Tower. At that time I thought the case against you was pretty weak. Obviously, things have now changed. We can ask for further particulars of the charge but, whatever their final position regarding Crozier may be, I fully expect the Crown to say that Bartlett was a victim of your conspiracy to murder.'

Anthony looks down at the table, absorbing what he's just been told. Then he looks up again, glances at the back of his hand and fires his next question.

'Question two: where's their new evidence? They must have new evidence.'

Stephenson hands him a fat bundle of documents. 'Copies of what was served yesterday. There's also some accountancy evidence on its way, but we haven't seen it yet.'

'You'll have time to read it all back in the cell,' says Charles. 'One last critical point: when we last met, you doubted the relevance of Shoreditch Enforcement Services, whose van was seen leaving Braithwaite Street at speed. Well, Shoreditch Enforcement Services is Kevin Streeter, and he is now named as your co-conspirator.'

'What?' cries Anthony. 'They say we entered into an agreement with him? So he's been charged as well?'

'Apparently. However, he's given a statement to the police and it's my guess that they've done a deal with him to get him to give evidence against you and your father.'

'What does he say?'

Charles points to the sheaf of papers in front of his client. 'It's in there, but he claims he's been dealing with you for some time. According to him, you gave him the instruction to use force on certain tenants, two of whom were Witness A and Witness B. In addition, he says, you gave him specific instructions to board up 61 Braithwaite Street, believing Bartlett to have left the property. However, while doing so, Streeter's employee, a man called Kevin Lane, had a fight with Bartlett and threw him out of a window. He claims that Bartlett was alive at that stage, because he was able to run off. However, Lane drove off in search of him and Streeter never saw Bartlett alive again. And Lane's disappeared.' Charles turns to Stephenson. 'Streeter lied about this other chap, Kevin Lane, when Billy spoke to him. Said he'd only had one employee who left before all this started. That's a thread we shall need to pull.'

'But it's *all* a pack of lies!' shouts the young man. He starts rocking gently, backwards and forwards, making a little squeaking noise from the back of his throat with each forward movement.

'Well, that's what we're here to discuss,' says Charles gently. 'Do you know of Shoreditch Enforcement Services?'

Anthony doesn't answer. He continues rocking, now with his eyes closed.

'Mr Wise, did you hear me?'

He nods briefly and, without opening his eyes, speaks very quickly. 'I've never spoken to anyone called Kevin Streeter. You'd have to ask my father if he ever did, but it's extremely unlikely. The company has over two hundred employees, including twenty-two in the housing management division. The MD never deals directly with bailiffs! Furthermore, these were Newham's tenants, and we'd never get involved with physical evictions.'

'You told me that the company changed strategy and started offering recalcitrant tenants new furniture. Do you accept that the people actually effecting the furniture exchange were Shoreditch Enforcement Services?'

'It's possible.'

'But you don't know?'

'No. We use a number of bailiffs.'

'If it was that company, who would have communicated this information to them?'

'I don't know. Not me.'

'I see. So it's your case that you've never spoken to Streeter, either in person or by telephone?'

'Correct. Never. And I'd be astonished if Dad had.'

Charles pauses and makes some notes of his new instructions. He thinks for a moment and then looks up at Anthony. The young man continues to rock and make his soft distress noise, but his eyes are now open. He flinches as his gaze locks briefly with Charles's and he shuts his eyelids tightly, his face contorted.

'Sorry,' says Charles. 'I know you find it difficult to make eye contact. I'll try not to do that again.' There is no response. 'Okay,' continues Charles. 'If it wasn't you or your father who gave that instruction to Streeter, who would it have been? Like I said last time, no one else had a motive. If not someone within the company, then who?'

Anthony shakes his head. 'No idea. But question three,' he says. 'What's the penalty if we're convicted?'

He is doing something with his hands, as if he were washing them, but without soap and water.

'Depends which charge. Conspiracy to murder would attract life imprisonment.'

'So, fifty years for me and a couple of weeks for my father.'

'I doubt it would be fifty, but certainly life, and a minimum of fifteen or twenty before parole. If you're only convicted of conspiracy to harass and unlawfully evict tenants at common law, the sentence is, strictly, unlimited, but it would be substantially less. How much less depends on whether they prove that Bartlett died as a result of the conspiracy. In that case it might be as much as ten years.'

'Question four: what are our chances?'

'Slightly better from your father's perspective, but not great. The Crown can establish a motive specific to your company; we can offer them no suggestion as to anyone else who would have given an order to use force; the police say you admitted giving the order; and now they appear to have Streeter who confirms it. Add that all together, and I'd expect most juries to convict you of the lesser charge. They'll struggle more on the conspiracy to murder because it has to be proven that you actually agreed that someone should be killed. Agreeing that someone should be threatened, or even hurt, to get them to leave a property is not enough, even if they are killed in the event. There must be a specific agreement to murder, which there isn't. But one man certainly ended up dead, a tenant who'd been holding up one of your developments, and his body was found buried in another of your building sites. Too big a coincidence... That's even before we get to Crozier. You can see how the prosecution will put it, can't you? They'll say the agreement to use force was deliberately left vague, but both parties knew that it included killing if necessary. Like the Mafia. They never tell their men outright to assassinate someone. They talk about him being "removed" or "retired". Now,' finishes Charles, 'have I covered all your questions? If not, please proceed.'

'Five: I did give that interview to DI Woolley.'

Charles does not answer. He senses Stephenson's eyes boring into him, but he doesn't look up. The silence in the little conference room lengthens. Finally, Charles speaks while examining his fountain pen.

'I need to be sure I've understood you correctly,' he says evenly. 'You are now telling me that your earlier instructions, namely, that you had no second interview with DI Woolley at all, were false?'

'Yes.'

Stephenson intervenes. 'So is DI Woolley telling the truth when he says you asked for a second interview?'

'Yes.'

'And, as far as you remember, has DC Truman correctly recorded the questions and answers?'

'Yes.'

Charles pauses again before asking the next question. 'So, you asked for a further interview and told the police officers that you gave the order to use force. Why?'

'To protect my father. He was going to admit giving the order, to protect me. So I got in first.'

'I see,' says Charles.

He does not find this difficult to believe. Anthony Wise's fear that his father would take the blame to protect him, and perhaps the rest of the family, is exactly what Sir Leo suggested to Charles himself.

'Was the confession you gave to the police true?' Charles asks, seeking absolute clarity.

'No. I didn't give that order and I have never spoken to Kevin Streeter or, to the best of my recollection, anyone at Shoreditch Enforcement Services.'

Charles thinks about this for a moment. 'In some ways, that makes our case easier,' he concludes.

'How so?' asks Stephenson.

'It means we don't have to get into a battle with Woolley and Truman by suggesting they fabricated the entire thing. On the other hand, you made an admission which you now have to withdraw, and it leaves you with no choice. Mr Wise, you have no option: you have to give evidence to explain yourself or you will, certainly, be convicted.'

An hour later Charles and Stephenson step out of the prison and into weak sunshine. They pause.

'What do you think?' asks the solicitor.

Charles ponders for several seconds before answering. 'I think three things. Firstly, we should let the committal go through on the nod. They clearly have a prima facie case now, and there's no point trying to attack it in the magistrates' court. Let's keep our powder dry for the Old Bailey. That will also give us time to persuade Anthony to give evidence.'

'Okay. Secondly?'

'Even if he agrees, Anthony Wise will make an absolutely awful witness. Unless we can explain him to the jury.'

'How would we do that?'

'I'm not sure yet. But his ... I don't know how one would put it kindly ... his particular personality, the fact that he is so *different*, no matter how bright he might be — makes it very difficult to warm to him. Or even understand him. Imagine him rocking in the witness box with his hands over his ears. The jury won't know what to make of it. They might even assume he's bonkers and convict him on that ground alone. The jury usually have to like an accused, or at least understand him, before they'll acquit.'

'So, are you suggesting some medical evidence? From a psychiatrist perhaps?'

'Maybe. I'll do some research and get back to you, if that's okay.'

'Of course. And the third thing?'

'I don't care how ill he is, we need to get a signed statement from Sir Leo as soon as possible, in other words, before he dies. If he does die, it'll be admissible. You'll need some medical evidence that he is dangerously ill and unlikely to recover and it's not practicable for his evidence to be taken by the magistrates. Let me know if you need guidance on the procedure. Can you get onto that as soon as possible?'

'Yes, certainly.'

'Now we have the son saying he admitted it to protect the father, I'm interested to see if the father is going to admit it to save the son. Last thing: my Instructions mention accounting evidence to follow. I assume you've not yet received it from the Crown?'

'Correct.'

'We need to chase it. I'm not much of an accountant and it's possible we'll want to consider expert evidence on that issue. Good forensic accountants are rare, and always busy.'

'Okay. I'll get onto it.'

CHAPTER FIFTEEN

Charles wakes suddenly and completely. He lifts his head to find Sally still fast asleep beside him and turns to look at the clock on his nightstand: 6:05 a.m. He is about to settle down to sleep again when he again hears the noise which must have woken him. It's coming from the kitchen, two floors below.

He weighs the prospect of his being able to return to sleep for any useful period against the mountain of work on his desk, and decides to get up. He slips out of bed quietly, throws on his slippers and dressing gown, and pads down the stairs to the kitchen.

The door has been shut fully, which is unusual, and he opens it gently to find Maria and Jordan kneeling on the floor before a pile of their belongings, whispering. The room is full of boxes, instrument cases, clothes rails, piles of books, music manuscripts and other items: the couple's possessions ready for their move of home. Charles sees that an effort's been made to leave an aisle leading to the kettle and the sink, but it's obviously going to be impossible to use the room that morning.

Maria turns at the sound of the door opening.

'Oh, Charles, I'm so sorry. Did we wake you? We were trying to be quiet, but the van's coming at nine, and there's still so much to do!'

Charles steps fully into the room. 'You did wake me, but you've probably done me a favour as I need to get in early.'

'Can you get to the breakfast things?' asks Jordan, who is still himself barefoot in boxers and a T-shirt.

Charles considers the obstacle course and grins, shaking his head. 'I think it's a cooked breakfast from Mick's this morning,' he says. 'But you might need to make a bit more room so Greta can get to Leia's breakfast things. I don't want her complaining of a dangerous workplace.'

Greta is the new nanny, part of the household for only a week and still on probation. Charles and Sally are already pretty sure she's going to fit in perfectly. She's well-qualified, has already built trust with Leia and, because she shares a flat with her sisters in Chelsea, doesn't want to live at Wren Street. So far as Sally is concerned, if Greta's happy to commute to and from Chelsea, that suits her perfectly. They'll finally have the house to themselves and Leia.

'I'll make sure you can't be sued,' replies Maria, laughing.

Charles surveys the jumble of belongings in boxes before him. He's astonished at the amount his ex-pupil has accumulated over two years of living at Wren Street, although he notes wryly that quite a lot of it in fact belongs to Jordan who, despite not actually living there, must have been using Maria's room as a depository for all the belongings he doesn't take on tour.

'We're so sorry for the disruption,' says Jordan. 'I promise, all this will be gone by the time you get home.'

'It's fine. To be honest, I'm a bit ambivalent about the prospective peace and quiet once you've gone. I'll miss the energy you guys bring to the place.'

'You'll get used to it,' replies Maria. 'You and Sally have been brilliant, but I think we all know it's time.'

Charles shrugs, resigned. He cannot avoid the feeling that this change somehow marks the end of his youth. He still looks younger than his almost forty-four years, despite the increasing incursion of grey hairs around his temples, and he remains in good physical shape, courtesy of twice-weekly visits to the boxing gym in Kennington and regular runs at the weekend. And having a much younger partner keeps him in touch with the new generation's fashion and music. Nonetheless, he is treated with a disconcerting amount of respect by the youngsters in Chambers and by Maria's musician friends, all of whom are twenty years his junior.

Charles Holborne has reluctantly begun to acknowledge that he has reached middle-age. It comes as something of a shock.

'So I won't see you before you go?' he says.

'Not today, no, but we're back at the weekend. Sally's invited the whole band round for a final meal. Didn't you know?'

Charles smiles. 'I'm sure she told me. I've been a bit distracted.'

'Oh,' says Maria, as Charles turns to leave the room, 'please tell Greta I've left the books on Leia's changing mat upstairs.'

'Books?'

'She knows all about it. Jordan and I have been reading "Peanuts" to your baby girl. She loves them, and I'm determined she'll still have *some* American influences around her once we've gone.'

'Will do,' replies Charles.

He again makes to leave the room but Maria forestalls him for a second time.

'One more thing,' she says.

'Yes?'

'I want to give you a hug.'

She goes to him, puts her arms around him and squeezes. She is tiny, and he towers above her halo of hair.

'I'll never be able to thank you enough,' she says softly into his chest. 'You and Sally have been my family here in the UK.

Dad's eternally grateful too. I know I wouldn't have made it without your support.'

'Yeah, you would. And it's been fun having you here. Don't be a stranger, eh? You're always welcome.'

Charles runs up the steps to Chambers, gripping a brown paper bag containing his breakfast in one hand and a selection of newspapers in the other. It is so early that the outer door to the clerks' room remains locked, as are the doors to the upstairs corridors. He's the first to arrive.

He is forced to put everything down on the floor to open the huge, strapped outer door to the corridor, but within a few moments he is at his desk. He fans the newspapers out before him, opens the brown paper bag, takes out his coffee and fried egg and bacon sandwich, and starts work.

Charles always makes it his business to read a wide selection of newspapers in the run-up to a major jury trial. He knows he has the ability to connect with juries; a common touch, courtesy of his start in life and his having worked and socialised with ordinary people. Nonetheless, his days of law-breaking as a teenager and as a young working man on the river are now long behind him. He has been in the rarefied atmosphere of the Temple for twenty years and he is now reasonably prosperous.

In addition to being middle-aged, Charles Holborne has also become middle class.

So it would be all too easy to lose touch with the concerns of the group from whom the jury will be drawn, and it's essential to know what they're reading and thinking. Accordingly, Charles makes the effort to read all the newspapers, the broadsheets, the tabloids and the scandal sheets. When he comes to speak to the jury, his references and his jokes will be up-to-date; they'll be relevant to the lives of the people he is addressing. He doesn't expect the twelve jurors to see him as "one of them", but he does hope they'll see him as someone to whom they can relate; treat him as "an honest guide" through the evidence. That will be of particular importance in this case, where his clients are extremely wealthy, German and Jewish, three factors which will "other" them to most jury members.

Unfortunately, as he feared, his breakfast reading does not inspire much confidence. All the papers carry articles on the continuing investigation into the Seagull Tower collapse. There is a lot of unhelpful speculation on the same lines as Charles's own: that well-designed and well-built tower blocks should not disintegrate as this one did. Every article mentions Wise Property and Securities in the context of cost-saving and short-cuts. Every article names his clients specifically. And whatever the jury might make of the Crown's evidence regarding conspiracies, they will all certainly know that the body of a reluctant, forcibly-evicted tenant, Edward Bartlett, was found, buried, at the company's flagship development, Seagull Tower. Charles has never seen such damaging pre-trial newspaper coverage.

Stephenson and he have discussed at length whether injunctions could be brought to stifle the press — their clients have made funds available to do it — but concluded that it would be a waste of time and money. These reports concern an entirely different matter, the collapse of a building. The jury won't have to consider anything relating to that, and it's too late to prevent them learning about where Bartlett's body was discovered; millions of them watched the story unfold on national television.

Charles could well lose this case, the most important case of his career. Further, he risks the obloquy of having defended guilty clients who exemplify the cardinal caricatured feature of his own race — greed, and the merciless pursuit of profit. Hardly the sort of triumph for which he and Barbara hoped to support an application for silk.

He spends a little time reading other news stories, but eventually takes the easy way out by turning to what he hopes will be the relatively anodyne sports pages. They too are dispiriting. They include a post mortem of West Ham's indifferent season, in which they finished eighth and behind all their London rivals, Arsenal, Chelsea and Spurs.

His breakfast finished, the remains of his coffee cold and his mood now irritable, he shoves the papers to one side, checks his watch and picks up the telephone.

'Morning, Clive. May I have an outside line, please?'

'Morning, sir. I didn't know you was in. Here you go.'

Charles dials a London number. 'May I speak to Dr Audrey Felix?' he asks.

'Who's speaking, please?'

'My name's Charles Holborne. I'm a barrister, and I've worked with Dr Felix in the past. I left a message with her secretary yesterday and I believe she's expecting my call.'

'Please hold the line.'

Charles waits. It has taken him three days to track down Dr Felix, a paediatric psychiatrist with whom he has worked in the past. He has never come across anyone who presents like Anthony Wise, and he's not sure she will be able to help him, but he knows no other psychiatrists well enough to ask.

'Dr Felix speaking,' says a woman's voice.

'Good morning, Dr Felix. I hope you'll remember me, I'm the barrister —'

'Teddy Behr,' she replies instantly.

There is a short silence on the line as both of them remember the terrible case that brought them together, and its awful conclusion.

'Yes,' replies Charles.

'I think about that poor boy very often,' says Dr Felix.

'So do I.'

'I sometimes wonder how people in your profession cope when things like that occur,' she says. 'In mine we're surrounded by psychologists and psychiatrists, and those of us in clinical practice are in therapy ourselves, or receiving supervision from a therapist. But I don't think lawyers have that sort of support, do they?'

'No,' replies Charles. 'We just get on with it.'

'Yes. I suspect the accumulated burden will eventually leave marks on your psyches,' she says sadly. 'Anyway, I'm sure you didn't call to discuss past failures. How can I help you?'

'Well, you might be in a better position to help now than you were before your move. You're at the Tavistock Clinic now, is that right?'

'Yes.'

'Here's the problem. I'm representing a young man, some form of genius apparently, in his early twenties. He has trouble making eye contact, he is obsessively orderly, so that, for example, if two pens are on the table beside him he will be uncomfortable unless they are lined up minutely. And he seems to become easily overloaded by stimuli, like noise and stressful situations. In such cases he rocks backwards and forwards, makes this strange keening noise, and sometimes closes his eyes and claps his hands over his ears to block out sight and sound.'

'I see. I have some experience dealing with young people like that.'

'His case requires him to give evidence before a jury and I'm concerned that they won't understand, and might be prejudiced against, someone who presents the way he does. I'm proposing to call an expert to help guide the jury. I need them to consider his evidence rather than his unusual behaviour. I imagine the right person would be a psychiatrist, but I'm not even sure of that.'

'He's too old for a paediatric psychiatrist, even if his problems began very young or at birth. You need an adult psychiatrist with specific experience of something they've been calling "pervasive developmental disorder".'

'Is that what this is?'

'Mr Holborne, you don't really expect me to diagnose someone else by phone, and on the basis of a few sentences given by you, do you?'

'No, of course not.'

'But what you're describing could fall within that diagnosis. A few of my colleagues might think of autism, but there's no standard classification as yet. It's an evolving field.'

'Does this fall within your experience?'

'Not sufficiently to be able to help you, I'm afraid. I can give you the name of a couple of colleagues. May I ask — I'm sure they will — how the client would propose paying them? My previous experience tells me that you'd be very unlikely to get legal aid for this sort of thing, and I was only prepared to work with you on Teddy's case because it fell within my research.'

'The clients — I'm representing both the young man and his father — are very wealthy, so they'd pay the expert privately, to assist the court. That won't be a problem.'

'Very well. I have someone in mind, but I'll need to speak to him first. His name is Dr Rosenfeld, Yossi Rosenfeld. He's an Israeli but he's been working in the US and, more recently, here. If he's interested and able to assist, may I give him your details?'

'Yes, of course. As always, I'm afraid this is urgent. I need to instruct someone within the next few days. But, as I say, whoever assists will be paid handsomely.'

'Very well. Leave it with me. I hope you remain well, Mr Holborne?'

'Yes, thank you, I am.'

'Good. Goodbye.'

CHAPTER SIXTEEN

It is the following day and Charles is bored.

Although he nags Barbara incessantly for time out of court to catch up on paperwork, when she eventually gives in it only takes two or three days before he is champing at the bit to get away from his desk and perform in a courtroom. He finds churning through papers particularly tiresome when, as at present, Peter Bateman is out of town on a case. At least when they are working on papers in Chambers at the same time, they can stop for a chat every now and then, gossip, smoke, tell jokes, and retell courtroom anecdotes.

Charles thrives on the variety and excitement involved in travelling up and down the country to different court centres, meeting barrister colleagues and addressing new judges and juries. Yes, the paperwork is well-paid and of course it allows him to remain in London with Sally and Leia, but he knows that, at heart, he is a performer. He is never happier than when on stage before a jury.

Focusing on work today is particularly hard, because the weather is so glorious. Not a single cloud mars the cerulean sky and it is warm enough to go out without a coat or hat. As Charles gazes out of the window at the Thames, two coxless eights streak below him heading westwards, their oarsmen's blades flashing brightly as they dip in and out of the water. He is reminded of his time at Cambridge. He puts his pen down and goes to the window to follow their progress. He can't think where they could have come from, as he knows of no rowing clubs anywhere near the Temple. Putney, perhaps?

There is a knock on the door.

'Come in,' he calls, still looking through the window.

'Charles?' says a woman's voice.

He turns. Lady Esther Wise stands in the doorway, half in and half out of the room, her hand on the doorknob. She looks nervous, as if aware that she should not be there.

'Lady Wise,' says Charles in surprise. 'How did you get up here?'

Visitors to Chambers are expected to report to the clerks' room and are then either installed in the waiting room or escorted to meet their barrister. Members of the public are not allowed to wander around upstairs unaccompanied.

'I need to speak to you,' she says.

Her voice is plaintive and quieter than he has heard before, and she looks different. She is no less beautiful, but there is something vulnerable and unsophisticated about her appearance. She wears a loose lambswool jumper over simple blue slacks and what look like ballet pumps. As far as Charles can see she is wearing neither make up nor jewellery. If she has a coat or handbag, or any other personal items, they are not with her right now. *Perhaps in the car, with the chauffeur?* he thinks. She looks considerably younger than when in her finery.

'Are you alone?' he asks.

She nods, her eyes downcast.

Charles is acutely aware that only a few weeks ago this woman threw herself at him and then fainted in his arms like a maiden overcome. Or, more likely, pretended to faint. She is manipulative, dangerous and unstable, and he fears being drawn into some new drama of her invention. He even wonders if her appearance, so different to the glamorous woman of the world presented to him thus far, is another disguise designed to appeal to him. Indeed, dressed thus, she reminds him strongly of Henrietta, the epitome of the type of woman he found fascinating prior to Sally: slim, elegant and aloof. David used to call it his "Grace Kelly Complex".

He is about to escort her back downstairs when he reminds himself that she has just been discharged from hospital following a serious, and very nearly successful, suicide attempt. She is under immense personal stress, her world is collapsing around her ears, and she seems still to be carrying an intolerable psychological burden from her time in the camps. A wave of sympathy for her overcomes his better judgement.

'Come in and take a seat,' he says gently.

She does so, closing the door quietly behind her. He indicates the chair opposite him, facing his desk, and she sits. Charles follows suit.

'Can I get you something to drink?' She shakes her head. 'I hope you are feeling better,' he says.

'You refer to my period in hospital? Yes, I am,' she replies. 'Thank you.'

Her voice is so quiet that Charles has to lean forward to hear her. It occurs to him that she is probably on powerful antidepressants which will be suppressing her affect.

He waits and watches as she looks down at the elegant hands in her lap. She does not speak.

'How may I help you, Lady Wise?' he prompts eventually.

She answers without looking up. 'I thought we had reached the stage of first names,' she says, chiding gently.

'I'm sorry, I meant nothing by it. How may I help you, Esther?'

'I felt I had to come. I don't know what impression you have of me, but I'm sure it is not good. When you came to the house…'

'Please don't concern yourself about that. It is forgotten.'

She still does not look up but Charles sees her pale face colouring. 'I cannot forget it,' she says softly. 'You can't imagine the depths of my embarrassment.'

'Honestly, Esther, please put it out of your mind. I understand you've been under terrible stress recently. With everything that's going on … your husband's health, the prosecution, the risks to the business … people react in different ways.'

She shakes her head sadly. 'I'm sure you think very badly of me.'

'I assure you, I don't. If all you wanted to do by coming here was to apologise, it was unnecessary. But of course, I accept it. It is forgiven, and forgotten.'

She nods.

Another long silence.

'Is there anything else?'

'My husband's case…'

'Yes?'

'Do you think I will have to give evidence?'

'You? No, I don't think so. At least not on the basis of the case as it's currently presented.'

'But it's possible, if the case were to change?'

Charles frowns. 'At present I can't see any reason why you should. But I suppose it's not impossible. Why?'

'Could I … I don't know how it works here. In America, at least in American films, they say they "take the fifth". Have I got that right?'

Charles is finding this conversation difficult to follow. 'I think you mean the privilege against self-incrimination. We have a similar rule here.'

'So I would not have to answer questions?'

'Not questions that incriminated you, no. Do you think such questions might be asked?'

She shakes her head. 'I don't think so. I hope not.'

'Then you should be fine. In the unlikely eventuality you give evidence at all.' He pauses. 'I'm not sure quite what's concerning you, Esther, but perhaps I can reassure you by saying that, by and large, I find that juries come to the right decisions. I have faith in the system. It usually reaches the right result, the just result.'

To his surprise, she stands and walks back to the door. Charles has, apparently, reassured her. She turns her wan face to his, and he sees despair in her pale green-blue eyes.

'There is no justice,' she says calmly. 'We are ants. No one, no god, will save us, now or in another life. It's all just chaos and brutality, and evil always wins. I'm surprised you haven't learned that. Your faith is that of a child's.'

She opens the door, steps out into the corridor and closes the door gently behind her. Charles stares after her, his mouth slightly open.

What the fuck was that all about?

Charles returns to his desk and continues work until lunchtime. The sloping lawns leading down to the Embankment and thence the Thames have gradually filled with young barristers, clerks and office workers from the surrounding streets. They sit or, in some cases, lie, on the grass, or sit on the benches between the immaculate flower beds, warming their faces in the sunshine and eating sandwiches. Charles wishes he could join them. He decides that he will phone Sally and see if she can be persuaded to leave her desk for a walk in the fresh air for half an hour.

As his hand reaches for the telephone, it rings.

'Yes?'

'It's me, sir,' says Jeremy. 'I have Mr Munday here with a box of papers for you. On the Wise case. Shall I send him up?'

'What? He's actually in the building, is he?'

'Yes. Standing in front of me.'

'Then, yes, certainly, ask him to come up.'

A minute or so later Charles hears the outer door to his corridor bang open and footsteps approach. There is a little fumbling for his door handle, a muttered curse and a thud. The door is pushed open and a second or two later Billy Munday enters, carrying what appears to be a very full and heavy cardboard box.

'Hello, Billy,' says Charles, rising from his desk and smiling broadly.

'Where would you like these?' asks Munday.

'Anywhere you like,' replies Charles, and Munday drops the box onto Charles's armchair.

'I was at Waterfields and they was organising someone to bring these down. I needed a word with you so I thought I might as well do it,' explains Munday.

'Thank you,' says Charles. 'Well done. Solicitors' offices and barristers' chambers all in one morning. I'd say you've completed the transition to legal professional.'

'This lot is the accountancy evidence. Mr Stephenson says he ain't had a chance to look through it himself. He thought you should have it soon as poss. So you've got the only copies.'

'Okay,' says Charles, flicking briefly through the thick files in the box. 'Blimey.'

'Yeah, I don't envy you. Do you understand all that stuff, then?' asks Munday, nodding at the box.

'Accounting? Not my strong suit, I'm afraid. Given long enough I can probably work through it, but we don't have time with the trial only a week away. You wanted to see me?'

'Yeah. You asked me to make some enquiries into that copper, Woolley.'

'Yes. Any joy?'

'I asked around. Managed to track down four people he's nicked in the past, and the daughter of another one who's still inside. He's bent as a nine-bob note. They all say the same: verbals, planted evidence, all sorts of arm-twisting. But so far as having anything against Jews is concerned, nothing. But none of the ex-cons I located is Jewish, so perhaps I'm asking the wrong people.' He shrugs.

'That's disappointing,' says Charles.

'What do you want me to do? I can keep looking if you want, but I just put in a bill for twenty-six hours' work, with bugger all to show for it.'

Charles considers. 'No,' he concludes. 'It was Tony Wise who set this hare running, and I always thought it a longshot. Leave it be. Soon as I've read all this I'll be arranging to meet Sir Leo again. If there's any more work for you then, we'll be in touch. Anyway, aren't you supposed to be decorating someone's gaff, right now?'

Munday grins. 'Nah. You was right. This is a much better gig. Even thinkin' of opening me own office. Oh, by the way, I went back to that corner shop bloke, Martinelli. On Braithwaite Street.'

'And?'

''E's gone. Left early I guess. Shop's boarded up. So that looks like a dead end too. Sorry, Charlie.'

'Well well,' says David with a smile, 'a state visit. Welcome.'

'Can't tell you how grateful I am for this,' says Charles, lowering the box of accounting documents. 'You never told me you had a river view,' he says, walking to the large windows overlooking Blackfriars and the Thames.

'You've never paid me a visit before.'

'Yes. Sorry about that.'

'Only teasing. Why would you? A modern office block may be nice, but it's not the Temple. So, what do we have here?' David starts unloading the files and reports onto his desk.

'I know you can't read all of it,' says Charles apologetically, 'but if you could direct me to the most important files, it would save me a huge amount of time.'

'This is the Wise Properties and Securities case, yes?'

'Yes.'

David pauses. 'Is it all right for me to look at these papers? As in, is it ethical?'

'Well, obviously, you can't talk to anyone about it, but lawyers instruct forensic accountants and other experts all the time on their cases.'

'But you're not instructing me, are you?'

'I'm sure I can get Waterfields to send you a letter of instruction, if that makes you more comfortable. I can probably even get you paid.'

'They'll have their own experts, surely? They may not do criminal work, but their daily diet is commercial. You can't move for accountants in mergers and acquisitions.'

'I know, but none who'll do this for me today, right now, which is when I need it. Tell you what, give me access to a telephone and I'll speak to Stephenson while you're browsing,' says Charles, nodding to the files.

David takes Charles to an adjoining empty office. 'You can use the phone there,' he says. 'In fact, my colleague won't be in today, so you can wait here, and I'll organise you some coffee. I'd prefer to work without you looking over my shoulder anyway. I'll put my head round the door when I'm ready.'

'Yes, that suits me fine. I've got some work I can be getting on with. Thank you.'

David leaves Charles to it. Charles calls Stephenson but finds the solicitor out at a meeting. He leaves a message.

Later that afternoon David opens the door and invites Charles to return to his office. David takes a seat behind his desk.

'Right. Although there's a lot of documents, most of them are irrelevant and it's not actually that complex. Do you know how an audit works, Charles? The actual nuts and bolts of it?'

'No idea.'

'Okay. I'm going to focus only on the borrowing side of things, right? So, every year the company tells the auditors, who are independent accountants, what borrowing it currently has. How much the banks have lent it, and what security has been given to secure that borrowing.'

'In other words what mortgages it has?' asks Charles.

'Yes, in simple terms. So the auditors check the position. They send letters to all the company's lenders, saying *"Please send us, firstly, an account of the amounts you have lent the company; secondly, a list of the properties over which your bank has a charge securing those loans; and, thirdly, the amounts still owing at the end of the accounting year."*'

'Basically asking how much debt is outstanding?'

'Exactly. The banks send replies to the auditor, the independent accountant, and then they go to the premises of the company being audited. In this case it was a Mr Fincham from a well-known firm of auditors. Very proper, all above board. Fincham went to your client's offices and in his briefcase he had the banks' lists of loans together with lists of properties mortgaged to secure those loans.'

'Just like my mortgage on Wren Street.'

'Yes, but in the case of a company like Wise Property and Securities Limited there were numerous mortgages all secured on different properties and developments. Anyway, Mr Fincham took his list and compared it to what he found in the company's books. And he found a mortgage on one of the developments that wasn't anywhere on the banks' lists. So he went through the company's documents, making a list of all the mortgages. And he found a mortgage in favour of Lloyds Bank which was not on Lloyds Bank's list.

'Could it have been a mistake? Some bank clerk left it off the list?'

'Of course. So Mr Fincham went to central filing and looked at the company's correspondence file, looking for any letters to or from Lloyds that might refer to it. And that's where he found this.'

David points to a document in one of the ring binders and spins it round so Charles can see it.

'What is it?'

'It's a letter from Lloyds' lending officer. That's the person who makes the decision, "Can we lend this company more money or not?" Let me read it to you. "*I refer to our meeting on 17 January 1969 at which you informed me that the properties at Rochester Avenue were vacant and ready for development —*"'

'That's Macintosh Point,' interrupts Charles. 'Two of the tenants were recently beaten up to get them to move out.'

'That makes sense. Listen to the rest. "*On that basis the bank lent WPSL a further £80,000 towards redevelopment costs. However in our subsequent meeting on 21 February 1969 you informed me that the street continued to have a 15% occupancy rate by protected tenants. As we* told you then, the failure to obtain vacant possession of the entire street causes the value to be substantially less than you represented, indeed less than the sum of the further advance. In our meeting of 10 March 1969 the bank was given personal assurances by you and Mr Anthony Wise that the tenancies were not, after all, protected and that possession would be obtained of the remaining houses within days. Nonetheless, a month later, possession had not yet been obtained, and we informed you in our letter of 14 April 1969 that the bank might have to call in that specific loan and conduct an overall review of the lending on the company's properties."* Do you understand so far?' asks David.

'Yes, of course. The company is very highly borrowed. They're saying "You are — or may be — in breach of your agreed banking limit."'

'Precisely. And that would mean the company would probably no longer be a going concern. Its debts exceed its value. The entire house of cards would collapse. And, note, one of the properties already mortgaged to the hilt is the family home on The Bishops Avenue.'

'I didn't know that, but I've always understood the problem from the company's perspective. That's the Crown's case: they were so up to their ears in debt, they took shortcuts to get rid of the tenants so as to start building.'

'Yes, but now listen to this last letter. It's apparently a reply to the lending officer, and it's written by and signed by Sir Leo. *"We are using every means possible to hasten the tenants' removal. I am undergoing medical treatment but I expect the doktor to discharge me by the end of the week, by which time I expect the company to have obtained full vacant possession. I suggest we arrange a meeting to discuss the company's future borrowing requirements. In the meantime, please refrain from taking any steps to alter the company's overall lending limit. News of such action would certainly damage the company's markt value with substantial consequences ..."* blah, blah, blah.'

Charles takes the letter. 'This is dated 19 April,' he muses. 'Wait a minute…'

He opens his briefcase and takes out a blue counsel's notebook. He leafs furiously to a page on which he has written a chronology.

'No! I don't see how Sir Leo could have written that letter! He had a seizure, and was found unconscious on the evening of 18 April. That was a Friday. He was rushed to hospital in an ambulance and remained unconscious for forty-eight hours. They thought he was going to die, and called the daughter back to England from her Swiss finishing school. Esther Wise showed me a discharge letter dated … yes, here it is, 23 April.'

'Unless the letter was drafted and typed before he was taken ill, but signed and dated later. That does happen,' points out David.

'I suppose that's possible. Did you find any correspondence from the bank?' asks Charles.

'No, although I think there is a statement from a banker. Let me see…'

'There!' shouts Charles, pointing as David's fingers leaf through the remaining documents in the box.

David lifts out a Metropolitan Police statement with a fat exhibit attached to it. He hands it to Charles. Charles doesn't bother reading the contents of the statement but runs through the correspondence attached to it.

'Here it is. It's the same letter, but the original as received by Lloyds. It's got the bank's date-stamp on it: Monday 21 April. First class, so posted no later than Saturday 19 April, the date it was signed. Which rules out Sir Leo.'

Charles runs through the letter again, reading slowly. 'Look at this!' he says, pointing to a typewritten sentence.

'What, the typo?'

'I don't think it *is* a typo. Who types "doctor" with a "k" instead of a "c"?'

David shrugs. 'A poor typist?'

'No. A German speaker, that's who. Sir Leo's secretary is a very English lady called Amanda Wainwright. Whoever typed this letter has spelt "doctor" with a "k". And look! "Market" should have an "e" in it.' I don't know much German, but I'm prepared to bet that "market", in German, has no "e". This was written by someone whose first language isn't English, which rules out Tony, born and brought up in England. He's Anglophone. Why would he misspell words as if he were German?'

'So who?'

Charles's brow furrows in thought. After a while he looks up. 'Esther. It was Esther.'

'You think she gave the order to use "every means possible"?'

Charles nods. 'She came to Chambers this morning — just turned up, unannounced — and we had the weirdest conversation. About the only part of it I understood was that she was worried about self-incrimination, which made no sense. Well, it does now.' He pauses and frowns. 'Wait a minute ... wait a minute! Maybe it's not only the letter. The man to whom the order was given, a chap named Kevin Streeter, claims he spoke to Tony Wise. But then…'

'What?'

Charles slaps his head as enlightenment hits him. 'Of course! Esther Wise has the most extraordinarily deep voice. It's almost Marlene Dietrich! I think it could have been her, pretending to be Tony.'

'Has she been charged?'

Charles shakes his head. 'No.'

'What a family!'

'I feel sorry for them,' says Charles thoughtfully. 'I've never seen a more dysfunctional group of people.'

'Are you surprised, given what they went through?'

'No, but the children didn't go through it, and the whole family is being destroyed. Leo has only weeks or months to live. Esther's a drunk and a depressive who, sooner or later, will succeed in killing herself. Tony's in prison and Hannah's a terrified teenager with no support. And on top of all that, any survivors are going to be ruined financially. It's almost as if someone set out to destroy them.'

'No,' replies David, sceptically. 'Why would anyone do that? The much more obvious answer is that they were all involved. The family business was going under, and the family did what it had to, honest or otherwise.' Then he sees Charles's expression. 'You really think someone else is behind all this?'

Charles shrugs. 'I've no idea. But I find it difficult to believe one family could suffer this amount of bad luck in the space of only a few months. But if they are being set up, then by whom, and why?'

CHAPTER SEVENTEEN

There is little security at Guy's Hospital. Charles and Stephenson find a police constable stationed outside Sir Leo's private room, but the officer seems entirely relaxed, sitting at a small table in the corridor, drinking tea and reading a newspaper, his helmet on the chair beside him. He stands, a little flustered, as the lawyers approach.

'Counsel and solicitor to see Sir Leo Wise,' says Stephenson.

'Yes, sir. I was told you'd be coming. He's in there,' says the constable, indicating with a jerk of his head the room behind him.

'Thank you,' replies Stephenson, and he and Charles ease their way past the table and push open the door.

One look at the sick man in the bed makes it clear why Sir Leo Wise would be an unlikely flight risk. He has lost more weight in the four weeks since Charles and Stephenson last saw him at his home. His grey skin and his eyes, deeply sunk into his skull, make him look more corpse than human. What was left of his hair has now gone and his bald skull glistens under the bright hospital lights. He is connected to an intravenous drip and he wears nasal cannulae to deliver oxygen.

Rather to Charles's surprise, Sir Leo turns towards them as they enter, and smiles. Whatever his physical condition, thinks Charles, he still seems mentally alert. Even more to Charles's surprise, sitting on the far side of the bed, and holding Sir Leo's hand in both of hers, is the housekeeper, Jacquetta. She doesn't exactly start as Charles and Stephenson enter, but Charles sees that she had been leaning forward, perhaps saying something quietly to her employer, and on their entry she sits back calmly and releases Sir Leo's hand.

Well, well…

Jacquetta locks eyes with Charles but he can't decipher her expression. There is a faint smile on her lips and her head is tilted slightly, as if challenging him to say something.

Charles switches his attention to his client. 'Good afternoon, Sir Leo,' he starts. 'I hope you were informed of our visit.'

'Yes, indeed,' he replies.

'And are you feeling up to a discussion of the case?' asks Charles.

'Yes, I think so. They've been talking about morphine for the pain, but I know how that goes once it starts, so I'm delaying as long as I can. I shall be fine as long as we don't take too long. The pain does tire one out. Please pull up seats.'

Charles turns to see a line of plastic seats by the wall. He and Stephenson each drag one towards their client's bed.

Charles has decided not to mention Esther Wise's visit to Chambers. He is not entirely sure why. Perhaps because she is neither his client nor a witness in the case. And, in any case, what exactly would he report? He still doesn't understand the conversation that occurred.

'Is Lady Wise feeling better?' asks Charles.

No one answers for a moment and Charles sees a glance shared between Sir Leo and Jacquetta. It is in fact the woman who replies.

'She is back home. It was very frightening, as you may imagine.'

'Terrible accident,' adds Sir Leo, shaking his head and looking down at his hands.

Charles cannot help himself. 'It was an accident?'

'Of course,' replies Sir Leo firmly. 'What else would it be? She'd had a couple of drinks and took sleeping pills. She thinks she must have woken, forgotten that she had already taken a tranquilliser, and repeated the dose.'

'I see,' says Charles. If that's the party line, it's no business of his to challenge it. 'Very well. Let's get down to business. I don't want to take up any more of your time than absolutely necessary. Mr Stephenson has shown me your new statement.'

'Yes,' replies Sir Leo. He holds out his hand and Jacquetta reaches into a briefcase to hand him a document.

'And in that statement you admit that you gave Streeter the order to use force, but you say you had no idea there would be such violence or, worse still, deaths.'

'That is an accurate summary.'

'So you understand this evidence means you have to plead guilty to a conspiracy to harass and evict, but you may still contest the principal charge of conspiracy to murder.'

'Yes.'

'And there's no guarantee they will accept your plea to the lesser offence. You and Tony may still find yourself facing conspiracy to murder.'

'You told us when we last met that conspiracy to murder requires a specific agreement to kill,' says Sir Leo. 'Of which there's no evidence.'

'That's right.'

'Then I have faith in you. You will make a legal argument and show the judge there is no such evidence.'

'Very well, I now have your clear instructions. But, I would like your permission to test the Crown's evidence against you first. If, having done that, a submission of no case to answer fails, I will be unable to put forward a "not guilty" case on your behalf. You would then change your plea to guilty.'

'If that is what you advise.'

'The only downside to not admitting an offence early is that it might increase your sentence. The discount for making an admission and avoiding a trial is usually a third.'

Sir Leo smiles. 'I don't think that need concern us, do you, Charles? Whatever the outcome of this case.'

Charles sighs. 'I understand. I am curious, however. If you gave the order to force the tenants out, can you explain why Kevin Streeter claims he was speaking to Tony?'

Sir Leo shakes his head. 'A mistake he made, maybe?'

'If Kevin Streeter is told to call Tony, and the person who picks up the phone announces himself as "Tony Wise", where's the mistake? Unless you pick up and announce yourself as Tony. Why would you do that?'

No one answers.

'I visited Tony in prison last week, and he tells me he has never spoken to anyone called Kevin Streeter, and does not believe that you would have.'

'How would he know?'

'How likely is it that a managing director of a large publicly-listed company such as yours would be dealing with bailiffs? And, giving a false name, that of his own son?'

Again, no answer.

'I'd like to show you a document now, please, Sir Leo.'

Charles places on the bed the letter shown to him by David and allows Sir Leo time to read it.

'I assume, if it's your case that you were the person who decided to use force, you also sent this letter to Lloyds Bank, assuring them you were using "every means possible" to hasten the tenants' departure, so they'd be gone by the end of the week.'

Sir Leo appears to re-read the letter. He licks his chapped lips. The gesture is seen by Jacquetta who leans across and offers him a glass of water, which he takes. Further seconds elapse.

'I mean,' persists Charles, 'if you didn't write this letter and someone else did, then that person was also apparently taking shortcuts.'

'Yes,' decides Sir Leo. 'I wrote it.'

'You're sure?'

'Yes, I'm sure. That is my signature.'

Charles allows a few seconds to elapse. 'The date of that letter is 19 April. You were unconscious, somewhere in this hospital, on that day.'

'That means nothing. Letters are often drafted on one date and signed on a different one,' says Sir Leo.

'So, it could have been drafted on 19 April but signed by you after you recovered consciousness? Perhaps when you went home?'

'Exactly.'

'Do you remember where you were when you signed it?' asks Charles.

'No. Probably…'

He tails off as he sees Charles shaking his head. 'What you have in your hand there, Sir Leo, is the copy kept in the files of WPSL. I have the actual letter received by Lloyds Bank.'

Charles hands him the original and puts his finger on the date stamp. 'Received on 21 April. That was a Monday, before you were discharged on the Wednesday. It can't have been signed or posted later than the Saturday before, 19 April. While you were still unconscious.'

Sir Leo shakes his head. 'I don't understand how this is possible…' he starts.

'Sir Leo,' intervenes Charles gently. 'It is no part of my job to demonstrate that you are lying. I'm just asking the questions that will be asked by prosecution counsel. They're not idiots. They'll realise that you're admitting this to protect your son from a long prison sentence. And Tony tells us he admitted it to protect *you*. It's obvious to me that you didn't write this letter, and nor did Tony. See how the word "doktor" has been spelled? And the word "markt". They are typical mistakes made by a native German speaker, which Tony is not.'

'You cannot involve her,' says Sir Leo, his watery eyes pleading. 'You must promise me! Or I shall dismiss you as counsel, here and now!'

'Her? You mean Esther?'

It takes the sick man several seconds to compose himself. He breathes heavily, his narrow chest heaving under the bedlinen. He speaks so quietly that Charles has to lean forward to hear his words. 'You don't understand, Charles. She is very, very vulnerable.'

'I do understand,' replies Charles. It is a few seconds before he speaks again. 'Fair enough. If that's the story you want me to put before the court, that's what I'll do. It's not my job to persuade you to say or do anything. I'm just your mouthpiece. But, in my opinion, it won't hold up under serious scrutiny. The first thing any decent barrister does when he receives the papers in a case, for defence or prosecution, is to create a chronology. You must expect prosecution counsel to do the same. And once he realises that you and Tony are lying to protect Esther, he will pursue her. As would I, in his place.'

Jacquetta intervenes. 'That's enough for now. He hasn't the strength for this. We all need to leave and let Sir Leo rest.'

Stephenson and Charles look at one another.

'Very well,' says Charles. 'This may be our last meeting before the trial. If you … if you are well enough…'

'What you mean, Charles, is if I haven't died by then, ya?'

Charles nods. 'Yes. Sorry. If you are still here, and you want to give Tony a half chance of acquittal, you need to get to court and give evidence. Your statement's admissible if you have died, but it won't carry the same weight.'

'I realise that. Jacquetta is making arrangements.' He pats her hand fondly. Charles sees tears in the woman's eyes. 'But I expect to be well enough to get there.' Sir Leo sees the expression on Jacquetta's face. 'I will,' he insists quietly to her. He turns to Charles. 'It's the treatment, the drugs and the radiation. Now they're over — for the present at least — they say I'll start feeling better soon.'

'I hope so,' says Stephenson, rising, and packing away his papers.

The two lawyers shake hands with Sir Leo and nod towards Jacquetta, who is also rising and putting on her coat.

Outside in the corridor Charles and Stephenson look at one another without speaking. They start walking towards the hospital entrance.

'Station?' asks Stephenson.

'No, you go on. I have something I need to do.'

Stephenson heads into the rush hour dusk. Charles looks behind him, considers, and reaches a decision. He takes a seat at the back of the busy reception area, opens a newspaper discarded on the seat next to him and, hiding his face, waits, glancing every few seconds back up the corridor.

It only takes a couple of minutes before he sees Jacquetta approaching. She carries the small leather briefcase that Charles has seen twice before, once at the residence on The Bishops Avenue and a few minutes ago in Sir Leo's hospital room. From behind the newspaper Charles watches her progress down the corridor and through the busy reception area.

He examines the woman closely for the first time. She is, perhaps, six or seven years younger than Esther Wise, shorter and less model-slim. However, their blonde hair is exactly the same colour and there are, indeed, other similarities in their features. Her employer's film star looks would always have drawn the eye but, thinks Charles, Jacquetta is also a very attractive woman. Perhaps she always felt in Esther Wise's shadow; like a younger, less dazzling, sister.

It is that thought which propels him out of his chair as soon as Jacquetta has disappeared through the hospital doors. He retraces his steps to Sir Leo's room and looks through the door. His client's position has not changed since he left a few minutes earlier. Sir Leo is still propped on the bed, pillows behind his back, eyes closed. Uncertain whether to enter or not, Charles is still hesitating outside the door when Sir Leo's eyes open and his head turns towards Charles. The sick man raises his arm and beckons Charles to enter.

'You forgot something?' he asks.

'No. But another thought occurred to me. May I?'

'Come in. Do you want to sit down again?'

'No, thank you. This won't take long. How long have you known Jacquetta?'

Sir Leo's eyes open in surprise. 'Why on earth would you ask that?'

'Please. How long?'

'I met her at the same time as I met my wife. They were both on the boat from Europe to England.'

'Has she always been your employee?' asks Charles.

'I wouldn't say she's my employee. She is my friend. She is *our* friend.'

'But she runs the household does she not? You and Lady Wise give her orders, as if she was an employee. That's certainly how it looks from the outside,' points out Charles.

'If that's how it looks, it misrepresents the position. I would say that I am as close to Jacquetta as I am to any other living person, including my children.'

'So you trust her?'

'Completely.'

'Is there any possibility, do you think, that she would have written that letter? I notice that she has access to all your papers. Your office is in your bedroom at home, isn't it, and there are no locks anywhere so far as I could see.'

'Charles, you've got it wrong. I would trust Jacquetta Kozlov with my life. I shall tell you something that may surprise you: I proposed to Jacquetta before I proposed to Esther.'

'But you married Esther. Is there any possibility that Jacquetta is nursing some long-standing jealousy?'

'If you understood the relationship between the three of us, you wouldn't say that. We escaped Europe together. We spent months in the same resettlement camp in Kent. When we first moved to London, a tiny attic flat in Hammersmith, we lived together, as we have ever since. At that time we all had to share the same bedroom. We started what is now Wise Property and Securities Limited together. The three of us. The all-important shares, the Class B shares, are divided between us equally. We were the Three Musketeers. We still are.'

'But you and Lady Wise have all the money; it is your house on The Bishops Avenue. And, as far as I can see, even if Jacquetta is not a housekeeper then she is, what? Your factotum? From the outside it does not look like "*All for one and one for all*".'

Sir Leo sighs. 'How things look is not always how they are. People are complicated, Charles. Things have changed since 1946, I grant you, but I can tell you with absolute certainty: Jacquetta would never do anything to harm me. Or Esther.'

CHAPTER EIGHTEEN

Charles meets Stephenson outside Swiss Cottage Underground Station, and together they walk north up College Crescent and Fitzjohn's Avenue towards Hampstead.

From the day that Charles was first instructed by the gangling solicitor, Stephenson has been professionalism personified. He has always referred to Charles as "Mr Holborne" and has never in fact offered his own first name, which Charles knows to be Andrew. He has been efficient and calm, two attributes frequently absent in over-stretched and under-paid criminal solicitors, and has evidently spent time researching criminal procedure to compensate for his lack of practical experience in the field. Most particularly, and to Charles's surprise, this high-flying Establishment city solicitor has demonstrated no animosity arising out of Charles's Jewish heritage or his working-class upbringing. Charles has no idea what the man actually thinks; about the clients, about their case or indeed about him. Now, for the first time, as they walk along the wide suburban pavements in the afternoon sunshine, Stephenson starts talking quietly.

'Is it frequently like this? Criminal work?' he asks.

'In what way?'

'I never imagined it would be so stressful and so … intimate, I suppose. Of course, I realised that it would be more affecting than my usual work which, in the end, only involves money. Closer to the bone. But the … *rawness* of this has taken me by surprise.'

'I guess the risk of disgrace and imprisonment will do that. Consider yourself lucky you weren't doing this a few years ago.

At the start of my career it wasn't just disgrace and imprisonment. Men were hanged. And women. It's doesn't get more raw than that.'

'Yes, I have thought about that. I used to be in favour of the death penalty.'

'Not now?' asks Charles.

'No. I don't think so. The way the evidence comes out, or doesn't, seems such a lottery. One imagines a trial will reveal the truth but...'

'You think we won't get to the truth next week?'

'Do you?'

Charles laughs. 'Probably not.'

'And I've been surprised at how — you'll think this an odd thing to say, but anyway — I've been surprised at how one sees into the lives of one's clients. That certainly never happens in commercial work. One never knows what goes on behind closed doors, of course. Other people's families, their closest relationships — always mysterious. But watching the Wise family under this pressure, well, at times I've been embarrassed. Like a voyeur.'

Charles nods. 'One of the reasons I went into this line of work was because I'm always acutely aware that, whatever one's clients might have done wrong, now or in the past, they're like everyone else: flawed human beings, doing their best with the poor cards dealt to them, to keep their heads above water. I could earn two or three times more if I were to do exclusively civil work, and I am gradually expanding that side of my practice, but I'll never give up crime. It's too important. But I agree; this case has been unusually revealing of the personalities involved.'

Charles comes to a halt outside a modern building set back at an angle from the road. 'Here we are. The Tavistock Clinic.'

The two men enter the building and give their names at reception. They are shown to a first floor conference room and asked to wait. After a few minutes a slim bespectacled young man with a yarmulke over his dark hair enters the room.

'Good afternoon, gentlemen,' he says. 'I'm Dr Yossi Rosenfeld. Please sit.'

The three men take seats at a small table.

'I have read the papers you sent me and was able to interview Mr Wise at the prison yesterday.' He speaks English perfectly but there is a very slight accent which Charles cannot immediately identify.

American. Yes, I forgot. He's spent time in America.

'Are you in a position to offer an opinion at this stage?' asks Charles.

'I'd like to interview members of his family, if possible, before writing my report but, yes, I think I am.'

'I'll see what can be arranged,' says Stephenson. 'It'll have to be in the next day or so.'

'Yes, that should be possible,' replies Rosenfeld. He turns to Charles and then Stephenson in turn. 'How shall we proceed? Would you like me to give you my provisional opinion or would you prefer to fire questions at me?'

'I think it would help if we heard your opinion first, and reserved questions for afterwards.'

'Very well. In my professional opinion, Mr Anthony Wise suffers from a developmental disorder. In other words, present since birth. It affects the way he communicates and interacts with others. Such patients find it difficult to understand the subtext of what's said to them, the mood of the person with whom they're dealing, or their emotions. So, for example, they don't understand body language or, in some cases, even facial expressions. They can be very literal in their understanding.

However, Mr Wise has, like most adults with his condition, learned the meaning of some non-verbal communication signals. Whereas most babies and children pick them up intuitively, without even thinking about it, usually from their parents, people suffering from this disorder have to learn them, rather like you or I would learn a foreign language. They often have interests, some would say obsessions, with certain subjects or activities which they can pursue to the exclusion of almost everything else.'

'What is this disorder called?' asks Stephenson, raising his pen from his notebook.

'There is no unanimity about that. Some clinicians believe it's linked to schizophrenia, and have called it a pervasive developmental disorder. Others believe it to be something more specific, but the research is ongoing.'

'But whatever label one puts on it,' asks Charles, 'is the presentation recognised generally within the psychiatric profession? In other words, if the prosecution were to instruct its own psychiatrist, would that person be likely to reach a similar diagnosis?'

'Oh yes,' replies Rosenfeld. 'Mr Wise is remarkably high-functioning, but his presentation is almost classic.'

'And what about the rocking and whining?' asks Charles.

'That is very common with such patients. It's a sign of over-stimulation, too much input. That's why, for example, Mr Wise doesn't like shaking hands or being in close proximity to other people, particularly people with whom he's not familiar.'

'Would people with this condition find it difficult to lie?' asks Charles.

Dr Rosenfeld turns to look at Charles. 'You asked that question specifically in your letter of instruction, didn't you? I can see why it's of importance in the context of a criminal trial.

Unfortunately I cannot give you a clear answer. I've been unable to find any research on the subject. However, I can say this: people with minds like Mr Wise's like rules. Rules give them structure in a world they find chaotic. In my opinion that makes them less likely to lie, because lying entails breaking rules. Furthermore, because they frequently struggle to understand others' minds, they find manipulating those minds, by lying, more difficult.'

'Are you saying that because of Mr Wise's developmental problems, he'd be less likely to lie to protect, for example, his mother?'

'Ah, now here we encounter a different, and very interesting, factor. He told me that his parents were both Auschwitz survivors.'

'Yes, that's right.'

'There is a lot of emerging research concerning the psychiatric injuries carried by such victims. It's long been recognised as shell shock in combatants, but it's now generally accepted that one may suffer from similar symptoms even when not engaged in actual fighting.'

'What are the symptoms?' asks Stephenson.

'Intrusive memories, flashbacks to the events, intense fear, as if the events were still continuing. Many also suffer from depression. Such people are extremely vulnerable to life's shocks. When supported, they may function reasonably well, albeit with periodic relapses, but when their security is threatened, when the scaffolding supporting their existence is taken away, they can become extremely distressed.'

'Scaffolding?' asks Charles.

'If their marriage is threatened; if their economic well-being is put at risk; if they're bereaved, for example. These sorts of events affect everyone, but the impact on people suffering from what I prefer to call "war neurosis" is profound.'

Charles and Stephenson look at one another. 'Lady Wise, Anthony's mother, is suffering from all of those and more,' explains Charles. 'She made a serious suicide attempt recently.'

'I'm very sorry to hear that, but given what I've read in the press about their case, it doesn't surprise me.'

Charles turns again to Stephenson. 'I still think we need Dr Rosenfeld's evidence about the developmental disorder to put before the jury. If Wise starts rocking or making odd noises in the dock or witness box; if he demonstrates any of his odd behaviours; if he can't focus on a question being asked and instead focuses on what is obsessing him at that moment, we need the jury to understand why, and not merely assume he's being evasive, or dishonest.' Charles turns to the psychiatrist. 'Can you get us a report by tomorrow?'

'Yes. Would you want me available for the trial?'

'Yes, please. Perhaps not for all of it, but certainly for the period when Mr Wise is giving evidence. Mr Stephenson will serve a witness summons on you.'

'That won't be necessary,' says Dr Rosenfeld.

'No, it's not because I doubt your willingness to turn up. You may find it useful to ensure that no other professional obligations can be inserted into your diary that might clash.'

Back out on the sunny pavement, Charles and Stephenson halt.

'I've been thinking,' says Charles. 'We now have two clients each saying they gave the order, and the two accounts are incompatible. We're conflicted. They need separate representation.'

'Really? Oh, shit!' swears Stephenson quietly. 'Sorry,' he apologises immediately.

Charles laughs. 'No, I'm relieved. I've been on best behaviour since I first met you, and you've no idea how much effort it's cost me to moderate my language! For what it's worth, I share the sentiment. It won't be easy to find someone competent only three working days before trial. On the other hand, I don't think we can afford to adjourn, bearing in mind the father's condition.'

'Any suggestions?'

'Maybe. There are several barristers in my chambers whom I rate highly. I happen to know that my ex-pupil, Peter Bateman, is available next week as he had a three-week trial collapse yesterday.'

'Would he be up to this, do you think?'

'He is seven or eight years' call, so relatively junior, but very sound. He has built an extremely successful practice.'

'If you recommend him, I'll happily go with that. If you have a word with your clerk and let me know as soon as possible, I'll get duplicate papers down to Chambers. Which client do you want to retain?'

'There's no difference between their cases legally but, Sir Leo I think,' replies Charles. 'And Peter may be able to form a better relationship with the son than me. They're closer in age. Also, there are tactical reasons I'd like to retain Sir Leo.'

'Very well. Anything further you need me to do, Charles?' asks the solicitor. Charles notes Stephenson's use of his first name. It appears the ice has been broken.

'Someone will need to explain the situation to the Wises.'

'I can do that. I'll speak to them both by telephone and follow up with a letter.'

'One other thing. I want to interview Esther Wise.'

'You only spoke to her a couple of days ago.'

'Yes, but that was before I saw the accountancy evidence.' Charles looks at his watch. 'And I think I've time right now.'

Stephenson's eyebrows rise. 'Really? Now?'

'It's as good a time as any. And there may not be another opportunity.'

'I'm afraid I can't go now. I've an appointment in the city in just under an hour. If you're proposing to go immediately, is there any professional difficulty in you seeing her on your own?'

'I don't think so. She's not a witness for either side, so I can talk to her without someone from your office being present.'

'If she's not going to be a witness, why do you want to interview her?'

'I'm pretty sure she — or perhaps Jacquetta — wrote that letter. Further, I suspect Esther gave the order to use force. It is not impossible they're working together. Yet both her son and her husband are prepared to go to prison to protect her. She appears to have no qualms about that, which I find very surprising. I don't suppose for a moment she'll admit it, but I want to put it to her, to her face. I think I have a duty to Sir Leo to do so. You never know. Some maternal feeling might overcome her.'

CHAPTER NINETEEN

By the time Charles has returned to the Temple to collect his car and has driven to The Bishops Avenue, it is dark and raining. He finds that he is now uncertain of his mission. He sits in his comfortable Rover outside the Wise mansion, the cooling engine clicking and the rain pattering on the roof, turning the issue round and round in his mind.

He has never been in the position before of having two clients each insisting, falsely, that they committed a crime, to protect someone else. He reminds himself that he is, as he stated to Sir Leo, merely a "mouthpiece". His job is to put his client's story before the jury as best he can, not to judge it. And whereas he has a duty not to mislead the court by putting forward a "not guilty" case when he knows it to be false, he's unsure if he has the commensurate reverse duty. Are barristers prevented from misleading the court by putting forward a "guilty" plea if they know *that* is false? In any case, he might have a strong suspicion that one or both of his clients is lying, but that's not the same as *knowing*. Every barrister has had cases where they've been absolutely certain of the guilt or innocence of the accused, only to be proved wrong. So often there pops up during the trial a completely unexpected piece of evidence; an unsuspected motivation; a confident identification which proves, on close questioning, to have been mistaken. And suddenly, everything looks different. That's part of what makes criminal trials so fascinating to the public: they're real-life drama because unpredictable stuff happens all the time.

Why, then, is he here? He knows that part of the answer lies in his fascination with Esther Wise. He is not tempted by her beauty, nor her apparent availability. He would have been, in earlier years. He was irresistibly drawn to dangerous women like her, unable to prevent himself playing with fire, sometimes simply to see how far he could go without being burned. No; that high-risk behaviour is consigned firmly to his past. The thought that he might do something to jeopardise his precious life with Sally and Leia makes him shudder. That's a change in him of which he is absolutely certain, and quietly proud. It's taken a long time, but he has finally discovered what makes him happy.

So, this is not a flirtation. Nonetheless, he confesses to himself, Esther Wise fascinates him, in the same way as he would be unable to take his eyes off a dangerous snake or venomous spider. That she would sacrifice a dying husband or her own son to protect herself demonstrates a degree of ruthlessness, a ferocity of self-preservation, which Charles has never encountered before. Like a starving lioness eating her own young.

Coming to a conclusion, he reaches for the ignition key, ready to turn round and head back to King's Cross, when there is a sudden bang on the passenger window. It makes him jump, so lost was he in his thoughts. He looks to his left.

'Why don't you fuck off, you vultures!' says a woman's voice from outside on the pavement.

She hammers on the window again, and only then does Charles recognise her.

It's the daughter, Hannah, wearing what looks like a cape, its hood partly pulled over her head. Rain streams down her face and the blonde hair not covered by the hood is a collection of beige rats' tails.

Charles opens the passenger window. 'It's me,' he shouts over the rain. 'Charles Holborne. Your father and brother's barrister.'

'Oh,' she says, also raising her voice slightly to be heard. 'I thought you were another of those journalists. They've been hanging around here lately. Are you here to see my father? He's still in hospital. And Tony's in prison, although I suppose you know that.'

'No, I saw your father yesterday. Actually I came to see your mother, but more or less decided it was a bad idea.'

'Come in,' she says. 'I want to talk to you anyway.'

With that she turns away from him and runs back through the open gates. Charles draws a deep breath. He is not sure he should be talking to this young woman, and is reluctant to get drawn into a complex family dynamic he doesn't understand and where he doesn't belong.

Nonetheless he closes the window, gets out of the car and runs after her.

Hannah is waiting for him in the hallway. She has thrown off her cape and is towelling her hair dry.

'Cup of tea?' she asks.

'Sure. Thanks.'

She strides towards the kitchen and Charles follows. Hannah has the same long confident gait as her mother.

The kitchen has expanses of white marble and stainless steel. It is huge and spotless, and reminds Charles of some of the West End restaurants to which Percy Farrow, his gourmet journalist friend, has taken him, behind the scenes and before the evening shift has started.

'Take a seat,' says the young woman, pointing towards a stool at the counter.

She fills a kettle and switches it on.

'I was so sorry to hear about your mother,' starts Charles.

'You heard about that? Yes. I suppose as a cry for help it was pretty deafening,' she says cynically.

'That's what you think it was, then?' asks Charles.

'My mother has a degree in histrionics. With Tony in prison and Dad dying, she really had to pull out all the stops to get star billing, but I think she achieved what she wanted.'

'Miss Wise —'

'Please, Hannah.'

'Hannah, is it possible … do you think that your mother might actually be suffering from some…' He grinds to a halt, chary of suggesting that Esther Wise is suffering from mental illness.

'The effects of being in a concentration camp? Of course. I've lived with her for almost eighteen years, Mr…'

'Charles.'

'I've lived with her for almost eighteen years, Charles. I could write a fucking textbook on her. I bet I know more about her condition than any so-called expert. She's deranged.' She sees Charles's expression. 'You think that's harsh? I suppose it is. But look at it from my perspective. I spent the first half of my life trying to look after her, to win her attention and approval and to make her better. I was only a child! I needed a mother, and I didn't get one. I got a gaping hole of neuroses and betrayals. Any sympathy I had for her has long gone.'

Charles has no answer to that. He watches as the girl makes a pot of tea, pours two cups and slides one across the marble counter to him. She takes a stool opposite him and raises her cup as if in a toast.

'I'm sorry, Hannah. My experience is nothing like yours, but I know what it's like to have a self-absorbed mother who is incapable of giving love.'

Hannah looks into Charles's eyes, actually connecting with him for the first time. The muscles of her face relax and her shoulders sag slightly. She looks much younger, little more than child. She heaves a deep sigh, and nods.

'I know about legal privilege and all that,' she says, more quietly, 'but are you able to tell me what's likely to happen to my brother? I'm very frightened that, in a short while, I could be on my own. And he and I are really close.'

'That's good to hear,' replies Charles. 'I wasn't sure if he was able to form deep attachments.'

'Yes, he is. In his own way and on his terms.'

'Well,' starts Charles, 'both he and your father have taken responsibility for agreeing to use some pretty unpleasant methods to evict tenants from their developments. One died and two were injured. Either your father or your brother — perhaps both — are lying, either to protect the other or perhaps your mother. Maybe they've assumed she's behind all this — I admit, that's occurred to me too — but I'm still not sure. Which is why I want to talk to her tonight. The trial's supposed to start next week.'

'And if Tony's convicted?'

'Prison. For a long time. It's unlikely, but if they prove that he agreed to killing tenants, it would be for life.'

'I thought so. But thank you for being honest with me and not treating me like a child. And I guess that probably means the company will fold.'

'It might do, anyway. If the developments don't go ahead…'

'Yes. I've heard my parents talking about that.' She stops and drinks tea for a few moments. 'I suppose that's the end of Mont-Choisi.'

'Mont-Choisi?'

'A very expensive finishing school in Switzerland.'

'I see. I'm sorry.'

'Don't be. I hated it. It's only advantage was that it got me away from here. Although I did have some friends there. I suppose I should start looking for a job.'

'Any idea what you'll do?'

She shrugs. 'Nope. Mum had hopes of marrying me off to some minor member of the aristocracy. Ludicrous. I think Dad hoped I might go into the business eventually.'

'What are you good at?'

'Not much. I'm sort of semi-fluent in French and Italian. And although I was never interested in school, I always managed to keep in the top half of the class without really trying. I'm pretty bright. I guess something will turn up.'

Silence falls again. Charles finishes drinking his tea.

'Is your mother home?' he asks.

'Yes. She's upstairs with Jacquetta. We've been taking it in turns to sit with her.'

'How do you get on with Jacquetta?' asks Charles.

'Jacquetta? She's lovely. I've never really been able to work out her relationship with my parents. For a long time I thought she was … you know … with my dad. Mum was always out and she had other … interests. Now I'm not sure. But she's always been wonderful to me and Tony, and when things have been really bad with Mum, with her drinking for example, she's always been there for us. Reliable.'

'Reliable?'

'Yes. Making sure Tony and I did our homework, washing our school uniforms, putting meals on the table. That sort of thing. A bit like a nanny, or a governess.'

'She sounds very loyal,' says Charles, aware that he is fishing. 'And I gather she's been part of the household since shortly after the war.'

'Yes.'

The girl puts down her cup. 'I'll take you up now,' she says.

She gets up and walks out of the kitchen. Charles follows. At the top of the wide curved staircase they turn left, away from the suite occupied by Sir Leo. Hannah comes to a halt outside a door, inclines her head to listen and then knocks.

'Come in,' says a woman's voice.

Hannah indicates that Charles should go in, and turns away. He opens the door. Esther Wise and Jacquetta sit in armchairs close to one another. Facing them is a television on a stand. A programme is playing, with the sound off. Jacquetta has a book open on her lap. Esther appears to be looking at the television but her eyes are unfocused. Her hair is loose on her shoulders and she wears casual clothes, fawn-coloured slacks and a white top. It takes her a while to turn her head towards the door.

'Lady Wise?' says Charles. 'Hannah let me in. I wonder if I could have a few moments of your time.'

Jacquetta replies. 'I'm not sure that's possible. Lady Wise is very tired. If it concerns the legal case, I suggest you…'

She stops when she sees the other woman raise her hand. 'It's fine, Jacquetta. We have to stop meeting like this, Charles. People will talk.'

She speaks slowly and her eyelids seem droopy.

Tranquillisers?

'I won't keep you long,' he replies.

'Come in, then. Jacquetta, can you give us a few moments please?'

Jacquetta hesitates, looking from Charles to Esther and back again. Eventually she rises. 'I'll start on supper,' she says, and without looking at Charles, she walks past him and leaves the room, shutting the door behind her. Charles hears her footsteps descending the staircase.

'Sit down then,' directs Esther, pointing to the armchair that Jacquetta has just vacated. Charles complies. 'Well?' she asks. 'What do you want?'

'Comprehension, I think. There's a question about the criminal case that's been bothering me since you came to Chambers. And I think you know the answer.'

'Question?'

'Yes. I've seen a letter to Lloyds Bank which purports to be signed by your husband, but which I know he didn't sign. It wasn't Tony either. I believe you signed it, falsifying your husband's signature. That letter is going to go some way towards convicting one or both of them.'

'So?'

'So, I want to know if you did sign it. And why.'

'I've no obligation to answer your questions, do I?'

'Of course not. But you're happy, are you, that one or both of your menfolk will go to prison in your place?'

She looks down at her hands in her lap. She appears to examine her long nails — painted a startling red, Charles notes — for a long time. Then she smiles to herself.

'How can I be sure you will not use my answers against me?' she asks.

'If you were to admit the crime with which your husband and son have been charged, that is, admit it to *me*, strictly, I might have to hand over your husband's defence to someone else, as I would become a witness. So it would put me in a difficult position, professionally. On the other hand, your husband and son won't allow me to do that. And, more importantly, I give you my word that whatever you say to me will be strictly between us. You can trust me.'

She looks at him more closely. Her eyes are now wide open and a half-smile plays about her lips. 'Yes, I see you must be a good barrister. It is difficult not to be swayed by such candour. So, I shall trust you.'

'Thank you. And?'

'I wrote that letter.'

'Why?'

'Someone had to do something. We had to buy some time or else the loans would be called in. The whole furniture idea was nonsense from the start, but Leo insisted on pursuing it through the courts.'

'I thought so. And you pretended to be your son and told Kevin Streeter to use force against the tenants.'

She looks puzzled. 'No. I didn't do that.'

The answer takes Charles by surprise. 'Is that the truth?'

'I admit forging the letter. This doesn't make me guilty of telling those bailiffs to use force. And I know nothing about a telephone call.'

Charles frowns.

'You don't believe me?'

Charles hesitates. 'I don't know.'

'Well, I don't care whether you do or not.'

'All right, let's put that to one side. Are you saying you won't give evidence to the court that you wrote the letter?'

'I won't give evidence.'

'You're prepared to let your son or your husband go to prison for you?'

'I don't think the letter's that important, but Leo has agreed to say he wrote it, to tidy up that loose end. He has also agreed to say that he gave the order to the bailiffs. Tony will say that he only admitted it to the police to protect his father and me. You understand these things better than me, but if the jury is faced with two accused people, one of them admitting the crime and the other denying it, surely that's the end of it?'

'No one could guarantee that, but even if you're right, that still leaves your husband going to prison for you.'

She nods. 'Yes. He accepts that.'

Charles stares at her, disbelieving.

'What do you want me to say?' she demands. 'You want me to feel guilty? He's going to die soon anyway. So better him than me!'

'But after everything you've been through…'

Esther stands, glaring down at Charles. 'You fool. You understand nothing. It's *because* of everything we've been through!'

Charles looks up at her, shaking his head slightly as he tries to comprehend this woman, and failing completely. She is shouting.

'I've already told you this, haven't I? I'm a bad person, all right? Like you, like Leo, like the rest of the world! There is no reckoning at the end. You think there's someone there to balance your good deeds and your bad deeds and pass judgement? Fool! There is no one. There's just this … this … festering cesspit! All one can do is keep one's head above *der Scheiß* for as long as possible. If you're too stupid to understand that, it's not my fault. Now get out.'

For a second or two Charles is too stunned to move.

She screams at him. 'I said get out!'

He rises and leaves the room. As he closes the door behind him, he bumps into Hannah. She has been listening at the door. There are silent tears running down her face.

Charles halts. He takes one of the girl's hands in both of his. He wants to say something to console her. He wants in fact to take her in his arms and hold her because, God knows, someone should. But he knows she doesn't want him or his sympathy. Nothing he can say or do will help her. He's a stranger, and it would be an intrusion.

He heads downstairs and walks out into the rain.

PART THREE

CHAPTER TWENTY

Charles and Peter Bateman walk down Fleet Street towards Ludgate Circus, their robes bags, red in Charles's case and blue in Peter's, slung over their shoulders. The briefcases in their hands bulge with case papers and law reports. Ahead of them and behind there are groups of barristers making the same journey. This is the usual route from the Temple to the Old Bailey and at this time of day it is a procession of barristers, a few even robed, chatting about their cases, arguing points of law and laughing over the latest anecdotes swirling around the Bar Mess. Most of the office workers, on the pavements, crossing the road, hopping on and off buses, pay them little attention, but a couple of tourists stop, point and take photographs.

'Have you ever appeared before the Common Serjeant?' asks Charles, raising his voice over the busy traffic.

The Common Serjeant is the second most senior judge sitting at the Central Criminal Court, the deputy of the Recorder of London, and has been allocated to try their case.

'Not the new one —'

'You need to watch out for him. Llywelyn-Jones is absolutely charming to your face and comes across as a very pleasant tribunal. Then, when you least expect it, he slips the knife in and destroys your star witness or nobbles the jury. I call him the "Smiling Assassin".'

'What I was about to say is…'

Charles turns to his former pupil, seeing embarrassment in his expression. 'What?'

'Well, although I've never appeared before him, I do actually know him rather well.'

'Oh? How come?'

'He's a sort of family friend. When pater was Lord-Lieutenant of the county, Llywelyn-Jones was one of his deputies.'

Charles smiles wryly and shakes his head. 'Course he was.'

'So they've known one another for years.'

'And I suppose he dandled you on his knee when you were a little chap in swaddling,' says Charles.

'Not exactly, but I have known him since I was a boy. It wasn't a close relationship — he's not my godfather or anything — but I have been to his house, and he to ours.'

Charles grimaces. 'At least one of us is likely to get a warm reception, then. You never know,' he adds bitterly, and more to himself than to Bateman, 'maybe some of your "Old Pals Act" conviviality will wash off in my direction.'

They cross Ludgate Circus and climb the hill towards the Cathedral. The dome of St Paul's glitters in the sunshine ahead of them and Charles promises himself, yet again, to make time to pay another visit to the magnificent building one lunchtime, and finally climb to the Whispering Gallery at the top. They turn left onto Old Bailey and are faced with a large crowd spilling off the pavements and into the road. Two lines of tall City of London police officers in their distinctive dark blue uniforms are holding back the crowds. There must be over a hundred members of the public, pushing and shoving to get a view of the parties and witnesses, or queueing for the public gallery. As the group of barristers approaches, the officers have to create a path through the jostling people to enable the lawyers to enter the court building.

'Did you expect this circus?' shouts Peter.

'No, I didn't. I thought there'd be some press — because of the collapse of Seagull Tower — but nothing like this.'

The two men climb the steps and cross the polished marble floor of the Great Hall. The noise of the crowd outside fades behind them. As always, as he enters the courthouse Charles looks up at the mural above his head. It was painted after the building was restored from the bomb damage received in the Blitz in December 1940. Many people lost their lives that night. Harry Horowitz, back in London on business, volunteered to work some shifts as fire warden, and he and his colleagues were responsible for carrying many of the dead out of the rubble. Over the years, while waiting for juries or for cases to start, Charles has often sat beneath the mural, looking up at the faces painted above him, wondering if he might spot someone with a likeness to the little tailor.

He and Peter climb the stairs to the robing room and push open the oak doors. Inside, it is as noisy and busy as always: locker doors bang and barristers juggle for position at the polished dressing table, shouting across the room to one another. A small queue has formed before the full-length mirrors as robed barristers take turns to examine their reflections before heading down to court or, if they have time, up to the Mess for a final cup of tea. Peter does insufficient work at the grand old court to warrant the rental of a locker, so Charles has offered to share his.

They have changed into their stiff wing collars and bands when Charles hears his name called.

'Charles! Holborne!'

Charles turns. A dark-haired woman in her early forties wearing a wig and a silk's gown is pushing her way through the male barristers towards him. Women have their own robing room, and her appearance here causes a stir, with one or two men in their vests hurriedly pulling on tunic shirts to cover their embarrassment.

'Hello, Calli.'

Calliope Allinson is well-known — some would say "infamous" — at the Bar, and her barging into the male robing room is typical of the woman. A brilliant student, she was one of only two female undergraduates to study law at Cambridge in her year, and having graduated with a First, found it impossible to find chambers prepared to take her on. At that stage there were no more than a handful of women at the Bar. Much to her embarrassment, she was forced eventually to rely on blatant nepotism to secure a tenancy. The pupil master to whom she was forcibly assigned, although charming on a personal level, suffered excruciating embarrassment every time he was forced to appear in court with a female pupil behind him. She was so unwelcome in her chambers that, on her entry, new locks were fitted to the lavatories and, of the thirty members of Chambers, she alone was refused a key. If she needed access to such facilities, the senior clerk informed her snootily, she would have to go to the Kardomah restaurant on Fleet Street.

Over the years she managed, despite these and other obstacles, to build a successful and busy practice and, having taken silk three years before, has recently been appointed Senior Treasury Counsel, one of the small handful of barristers trusted by the Crown to prosecute the most serious cases.

'Oh, have I missed the famous pecs, darling?' she teases Charles, her eyes sparkling.

'Just too late, I'm afraid. But private viewings can be arranged.'

'Really? I heard your lucky ex-clerk has exclusive rights nowadays.'

Most of the Temple views Charles's relationship with Sally as scandalous, but this is typical Allinson banter and her smile is genuinely friendly.

'I gather you're representing one or both of the Wises?' she says.

'I am. The father. Are you prosecuting?' asks Charles with some surprise. 'Surely this case doesn't merit Senior Treasury Counsel.'

'I don't suppose it merits the Common Serjeant either, but you seem to have drawn the short straw,' she says, still smiling. 'Not for us to fathom the inscrutable workings of the Lord Chancellor's Department, eh? So, if you're for the father, who's for the son?'

'I am,' says Peter, turning to her.

'Peter, darling!' exclaims the prosecutor.

Charles spins round swiftly. 'Oh, for fuck's sake, Peter, don't tell me you know her too?' he says, only half-joking. 'What, hunt balls? Polo matches? Or were you also a debutante?'

'Now, now, Charles,' chides Allinson. 'Put your dusty working-class prejudices back in their box. We sit on a fundraising committee together, that's all. *Noblesse oblige*, you know?'

'Yus, missus. I knows me place, missus,' replies Charles, giving a good impression of Alfred Doolittle.

'Silly ass,' says Allinson, patting Charles affectionately on the cheek. 'Now, gentlemen, I need a serious word. Is this still a fight?'

'It is,' confirms Charles. Bateman nods.

Allinson turns to the younger man. 'But your client has admitted giving the order — not murder I agree — but the order to use force. Or are you saying it was a "verbal"?'

Bateman smiles. 'All to be revealed in due course.'

'And your client, Charles? Is he here?'

'He'll be here.'

'We understood him to be at death's door. No?'

'He'll be here,' repeats Charles.

'Okay. Have you seen Roger Butler yet?' she asks.

'From 1 KBW? No, why?'

'He's representing Streeter, your co-conspirator. We're accepting Streeter's plea to the lesser conspiracy, and he'll be giving evidence for the Crown.'

Charles and Bateman share a glance. 'We guessed as much,' says Bateman.

'So we'll have him arraigned, he can plead, Roger will mitigate, and I'll ask Llywelyn-Jones to sentence him before we start your clients' trial. Okay? Now, I'm off to grab a cup of tea before we start, if that's all.'

The barrister is about to turn but Charles puts a hand on her arm to stop her. 'Can I give you this, please, Calli?' he says, offering her a document.

She takes it and starts reading.

'It's a medical report from the consultant at Guy's treating Sir Leo,' explains Charles. 'He's been bouncing between hospital and home for the last couple of weeks. As I understand it, he's coming here directly from hospital. As you can see, he's in a bad way. I'm told he will attend, but probably in a wheelchair, and I may need to seek the court's indulgence for occasional breaks in the evidence.'

'Professor Sir Robin Clarke?' says Allinson, reading the signature at the bottom of the medical report. 'Well, you've certainly got the top chap. I'll take instructions, but I don't expect this to cause any problems.'

'Thank you. Oh, and to give you a heads-up, Calli, we're proposing to call psychiatric evidence relating to Peter's client.'

'Psychiatric evidence? On what issue?'

Bateman answers. 'Mr Anthony Wise suffers from an unusual neurological condition which may need explaining to the jury.'

'I think not,' says Allinson. 'The evaluation of witnesses is for the jury, not for medical expertise.'

'Let's see how matters unfold,' says Charles smoothly. 'We're making no immediate application, just giving you a heads-up.'

Allinson nods. 'Fair enough. See you in court.'

Charles and Bateman watch her heading towards the Bar Mess and share a glance. Charles winks at the younger man.

Over the weekend, during their last strategy meeting at Wren Street, the two men spent some time arguing over the evidence of Dr Yossi Rosenfeld. Despite hours spent in the library, neither had found any legal authority where psychiatric evidence had been admitted to explain an accused's demeanour in court. The reason, Bateman argued, was because it related to a collateral issue: bizarre behaviour in court had no relevance to a confession made in a police interview. More importantly, he thought, such evidence would usurp the jury's function, namely, the assessment of witnesses. He could see no way of getting the evidence in, even with the most relaxed of judges.

'But,' argued Charles, 'there's no difference in principle from cases of children or others with low IQs and high suggestibility. Victorian judges called them "imbeciles", "cretins", or sometimes "feebleminded". There's a long history of psychiatric evidence being admitted in such cases. We simply show that Tony falls into the same category.'

Bateman had scoffed. 'How the hell do we persuade a judge that the acting managing director of a publicly limited company, a supposed genius with a Cambridge degree and an IQ of 160, is feebleminded? You're joking, surely.'

'No. Leave it to me,' replied Charles, and he wouldn't be drawn further.

Court 1 of the Central Criminal Court, the Old Bailey, may reasonably claim to be the most famous courtroom in the world. It is, in fact, named after the street on which it stands, and a court building has stood here since mediaeval times. Since then it has seen some of the worst examples of venality, murder, torture and rape, of which human beings are capable. In the twentieth century alone it witnessed the trials of Dr Hawley Crippen, the first man to be apprehended using the newly-invented wireless telegraph; William Joyce, the fascist Nazi propagandist known to the Allies as Lord Haw-Haw; and the Rillington Place Strangler, serial killer John Christie. All hanged. The cases listed here are invariably the "biggest" of the day.

Charles and Bateman, now fully robed, walk down the central aisle to the benches reserved for counsel, their case papers in their arms. There is a loud buzz of anticipation in the court. Peter looks up at the packed public gallery.

'It's already full up there, and there are a hundred people still queuing outside,' he comments.

As they take their seats and set out their papers the clerk approaches them.

'Good morning, gentlemen. Mr Holborne, I have you down as representing Sir Leo Wise and you, Mr Bateman, the son, Anthony Wise.'

'Correct,' confirms Charles.

'Thank you. I'm told that Mr Anthony Wise has been produced, but that his father was on bail. He has not yet surrendered to custody.' She directs this last comment to Charles.

'I'll go and check,' he says but, as he turns, he spots Stephenson waving at him from the door of the court. The wave turns into a thumbs up and a nod. The double doors open wide, and a wheelchair enters, pushed by Jacquetta. Sitting in it, wearing a grey suit, a white shirt and tie is Sir Leo. His bald pate is hidden by a hat and a blanket is wrapped round his legs. The hubbub in the courtroom quietens as the journalists and spectators realise who is in the wheelchair. Several hundred eyes follow its progress.

The frail man arrives before Charles and Bateman. Charles turns to the clerk.

'My client won't be able to surrender in the normal way. He cannot leave the wheelchair, and there are no facilities for getting the wheelchair into the dock.'

The dock officer has heard the conversation. He opens the wooden door of the dock and steps down into the well of the court to join the others.

'He has to go into the dock,' he says. 'His bail ends by his attendance. And he'll have to go down to the cells during adjournments.'

'That won't be possible, I'm afraid, officer.' Charles turns to his bench, leafs through some papers, and offers a document to the clerk. 'I anticipated this. Please give that to the judge and explain the difficulty. I've already given a copy to the Crown.'

The clerk skims the document, and Charles watches as her eyes arrest at the foot of the page, and widen.

'I see,' she says.

'I'm dying,' says Sir Leo from his wheelchair, with a gentle smile. He now has a rash on his forehead which reaches down the left side of his face to his jaw which wasn't present when Charles last saw him. It looks angry and painful.

'Yes, er ... I see,' stammers the clerk. She holds up a hand to prevent the dock officer from saying anything further. 'I'll speak to the judge.'

She scurries off.

'Where can Sir Leo go?' asks Jacquetta.

'Just wheel him to the end of this bench,' replies Charles. 'He can sit next to me.'

Jacquetta complies and, after some difficulty, finds and applies the brake on the wheelchair to prevent it rolling further into the well of the court.

Another dock officer appears above them, handcuffed to Anthony Wise. The young man is in a dreadful condition. His arm is in a sling and his face is such a mass of bruises and cuts, it's difficult to see undamaged skin. One eye is completely closed with a livid red and purple swelling.

'Jesus Christ!' mutters Bateman, not quite inaudibly. He leaves the group by counsel's bench and goes quickly to speak to his client.

'That's how he was when he arrived in the van,' says the dock officer with a lowered voice.

A third officer appears at the top of the steps from the cells, attached to another man. It is clear that this prisoner has just extinguished a cigarette as his head is wreathed in cigarette smoke which he drags up the steps and into the dock with him. He is about Charles's height, although slighter in build. He has cropped black hair and a thin face.

There is a knock on the wooden panelling behind the judge's seat, and the clerk calls: 'All rise!'

Charles and Bateman move quickly to their seats. At the last second, sliding in next to Bateman, there arrives a short dark-haired man with a beard. Roger Butler, Streeter's counsel. Charles has had dealings with Butler on several occasions over the years. He has no reason to believe Butler is crooked, and when against Charles he has always been courteous and reasonable to deal with, but there is something about the Welshman that Charles dislikes.

Calliope Allinson steps into the QC's bench just as the Common Serjeant enters. The clerk positions the judge's red book and his pens before his seat and takes her place below and in front of him.

His Honour Judge Llywelyn-Jones, the Common Serjeant, is in his mid-sixties. Silver hair peeks out from under his wig and he possesses a strong jaw and an aquiline nose beneath intelligent grey eyes. His practice at the Bar was already well-established at the outbreak of the Second World War, and after a sparkling record in the Royal Navy where he rose to the rank of Commodore First-Class, he returned to his legal practice, making Queen's Counsel within seven years. His judicial career has been no less impressive. Unlike many of his judicial brethren, as long as he considers counsel before him to be competent, he lets them get on with the job without significant interruption. He has a sharp intellect, grasping points quickly and without fuss, thereby shortening cases, which endears him to the Lord Chancellor's Department. His rise to Common Serjeant has been swift.

'Miss Allinson,' he says, once the court has settled into silence.

'My Lord?' she replies, standing.

'Have you been shown the medical report on Sir Leo Wise?'

'I have, my Lord.'

'Given the circumstances I am inclined to extend Sir Leo's bail on condition that he does not leave the court building without my permission. I appreciate that his health may require some flexibility, and counsel may apply to vary that condition if necessary. Does the Crown have any objections?'

'No, my Lord.'

'Thank you. I think, however, that Sir Leo should remove his hat.'

Charles stands. 'My Lord, I appear for Sir Leo. He is an Orthodox Jew, and for religious reasons is required to keep his head covered at all times. Under normal circumstances he would wear something more discreet, but his treatment has caused him to lose all his hair and, I understand, it is a common side-effect to feel the cold very keenly, which he does, and which explains the blanket around his legs. For both these reasons I would request that, exceptionally, he may retain his head covering.'

The judge nods. 'In the circumstances I will not insist. Yes, Miss Allinson?'

'My Lord, I appear on behalf of the Crown in this case. Mr Holborne appears for Sir Leo Wise, Mr Bateman for Anthony Wise, and Mr Butler for Kevin Streeter. Mr Butler has indicated to the Crown that his client will plead guilty to the lesser conspiracy, and the Crown is minded to accept that plea. Otherwise, I believe the case is still contested. I apply for Mr Streeter to be arraigned so that your Lordship may proceed directly to sentence him.'

'Why? Is Mr Streeter to give evidence on behalf of the Crown?'

'He is, my Lord. Obviously it's important that he is sentenced before that occurs so it cannot be said that he's trying to buy a lighter sentence with his evidence.'

'Mr Butler?'

'That's right, my Lord. Your Lordship will have read the Crown's evidence, including that of Mr Streeter. My learned friend Miss Allinson is relying on that evidence in her case, and I'm relying on it in respect of the sentence you pass on him.'

'Yes, very well. Mr Holborne, Mr Bateman, if you wish to leave for the present we can tannoy you when we've completed dealing with Mr Streeter. Miss Allinson, Mr Butler, do you think an hour will be sufficient?'

The two barristers addressed look at one another. 'Perhaps an hour and a half, my Lord?' offers Butler.

The Common Serjeant turns to Charles and Bateman. 'Entirely up to you, gentlemen, but I shall not be offended if you wish to do something else in the meantime. Of course you're welcome to remain.'

'I'll stay,' says Charles quietly to Bateman. He nods towards Sir Leo who appears to be asleep in his wheelchair. 'He's not going to care, and I think you need to speak to your client. He looks pretty bashed up.'

'Thank you,' whispers Bateman. 'If your Lordship has no objections, I'll make use of the time to find out why my client looks as though he has been run over by a London bus.'

'Indeed. I'd like him to be seen by Matron, if you can arrange that? Take Mr Anthony Wise down.'

Bateman nods, bows to the judge and slips out of the bench. Charles settles down to take notes of Streeter's plea and sentencing.

CHAPTER TWENTY-ONE

'Gentlemen, are you ready?'

'Yes, my Lord,' reply Charles and Bateman in unison.

Charles has brought Bateman up to speed. Streeter pleaded guilty and was sentenced to five years' imprisonment, increased by his previous convictions for violence but mitigated by his plea and promise of support for the Crown.

'And your client, Mr Bateman?' asks the judge.

'The Matron has seen him. Yesterday he suffered a severe beating at the hands of three other prisoners, all convicted members of the British National Party. He was examined at the prison hospital and found to have no fractures. He is deemed fit for trial.'

'Very well.' The judge leans over the bench to the clerk below him. 'Arraignment, please. Sir Leo, you may remain seated if necessary.'

The clerk stands. 'Would the accused please stand.'

Anthony Wise struggles to his feet. As the indictment is put to the two accused, Charles turns round to speak to Stephenson in the bench behind him. He had hoped to speak to the solicitor before court sat, but he was late returning from the task Charles set him and only arrived as the judge entered court.

'Well?' whispers Charles.

'I tried, but she won't come. She says she needs to be at home to support her daughter, although I'm not convinced Hannah is actually there. I saw no sign of her.'

'So, is Esther alone in the house?'

Stephenson shakes his head. 'That chap Levy was with her.'

Charles nods. As he turns to face the judge again his eyes land on a tall, fair and rather corpulent man sitting behind junior counsel for the Crown: Detective Inspector Woolley. Woolley is the "officer in the case", the policeman responsible for pulling together all the evidence, acting as liaison between prosecution counsel and her witnesses for the duration of the trial. Under usual circumstances witnesses are not allowed in court until they've given their evidence. It's a sensible rule to prevent liars from tailoring their evidence, making it consistent with what they've already heard. However, Charles and Bateman agreed that, there being no obvious challenge to Woolley's evidence, he might as well remain in court throughout. It would aid the progress of the case, ensuring that documents and witnesses were produced without fuss.

Woolley looks like an archetypal friendly neighbourhood copper, with ruddy cheeks and a round face. As Charles turns to face the front, his eyes lock with those of the policeman. Woolley's eyes are narrowed and there's a sneer on his red lips. His expression is one of loathing, and it's undeniably directed at Charles.

What's that all about?

There is rarely any love lost between the officer in the case and defence counsel, but professional civility is usually required to ensure cases run smoothly. To the best of Charles's knowledge he has never met or spoken to Woolley before. So what lay behind that look?

Charles is only too aware how Jews see anti-Semitism everywhere. Too many have outsized chips on their shoulders; too many take offence where none is intended. Of course, millennia of persecution, murder and expulsion will do that. Nonetheless, he's been guilty of it himself, and he tries to keep in the forefront of his mind that, except within his privileged and entitled profession, where disdain for anyone not "One of us" is the default setting, most ordinary working English people are fair-minded. They don't have a problem with immigrants, Jews or otherwise, as long as they work hard, muck in and accept British values.

He glances back over his shoulder, but the detective inspector now has his head down and is writing.

Did I imagine it?

Maybe. But then Charles remembers Joseph Heller's dictum: *Just because you're paranoid doesn't mean they aren't after you.* He files away his intuition for future reference.

The jury in waiting are entering court.

Another aspect of strategy discussed over the weekend related to the make up of the jury. Each defence barrister has seven peremptory challenges; in other words they can exclude from the jury up to fourteen people in total without any reason. It is obviously a lottery attempting to judge the character of a potential witness merely from their appearance and their name. Unlike in the American system, no questions can be addressed to jurors by either side. Counsel have to make snap decisions immediately after each juror's name is called and before they start to take their oath, in other words, in the space of four or five seconds.

Nonetheless, Charles and Bateman have devised some basic guidelines. Ideally they would like a jury composed of Orthodox Jews old enough to have lived through the war — obviously impossible. Nonetheless they've decided to challenge off anyone under the age of thirty (too little experience of the world); anyone carrying a copy of *The Telegraph* (Charles's personal prejudice against Tories of any age); and anyone who they observe looking unsympathetically at the accused. The last may sound peculiar, but Charles has noted that jurors who stare aggressively at his clients are usually the toughest nuts to crack. On the other hand, they will retain anyone in expensive-looking clothes (less likely to be prejudiced against successful businessmen); men of the cloth of whatever denomination (a belief in justice, and the power of an oath given on a holy book); and anyone who looks like an immigrant, or whose name might suggest such a background (sympathy for hard-working first-generation immigrants such as the Wises, even if not themselves Jewish).

At the same time they need to be alert to any challenges made by Calliope Allinson, as that will give some idea of the complexion of the jury aimed at by the Crown.

The first three jurors to be called are middle-aged white men, but none carries any offensive newspapers and they are allowed to take their seats without challenge from any quarter. The next is a very young-looking West Indian or African woman. As Charles and Peter look at one another weighing their decision, they are forestalled by Allinson who challenges her off. Charles frowns, wondering what their opponent is up to. Next to be called is an elderly woman who joins the jury without challenge, and then another with raw, red knuckles and whose clothing looks threadbare. A working woman, hopes Charles.

The next three potential jurors are all challenged off by Allinson but Charles and Bateman, sharing a glance, can see no logic behind the challenges. The next to be called is a vicar wearing a dog collar. He is allowed to swear his oath without objection by either side. Next comes an elderly man who, Charles thinks, looks Jewish. He too is allowed to join the jury without objection. No one challenges any of the remaining jury members, which include a man and woman who, judging from their skin colour, might come from immigrant families. One gives the oath in a strong Cockney accent, which pleases Charles. Overall, he thinks, not too bad.

'Miss Allinson?' says the judge, inviting her to open the case for the prosecution.

Allinson stands. So too does Charles.

'Yes, Mr Holborne?' asks the judge, surprised.

'I know it's unusual, my Lord, but there is an early point of law upon which I seek your Lordship's ruling.'

'Really? Very well.' The judge turns to the jury. 'Ladies and gentlemen, this sort of thing does happen occasionally during the course of a trial. Because issues of law are for me alone, if counsel has a point of law they wish to raise, they do it in this manner and you may be excused. I know you've only just sat down, but if you follow the jury bailiff, you should have time for refreshments before you're called back in.'

The jury bailiff indicates that the twelve men and women should follow her, and they all file out of court again.

'Mr Holborne?'

'Thank you, my Lord. I needed to raise this before my learned friend started her opening. Your Lordship will have seen the evidence of Dr Singer, the Home Office Consultant Pathologist. It starts at page forty-four of the bundle.'

Charles waits for the judge to find the page and start reading before continuing.

'He gives us an estimate of the date of death of the two men whose bodies were found in the rubble at Seagull Tower. So far as Mr Bartlett is concerned, the Crown's case is that because he was a tenant of a property where redevelopment was proposed, he was killed on the orders of these accused and his body placed in the partially-constructed Seagull Tower. The relevance of Dr Singer's evidence there is obvious. However, so far as Mr Crozier is concerned, the Crown makes no suggestion he has anything to do with this case. They simply say his body was found there and he'd been there for some time. Beyond that, they say nothing about him. Merely to point at the presence of an unexplained body has no probative value, but it creates enormous prejudice for the accused. It appears designed simply to create suspicion. There's no evidence Mr Crozier was a tenant of the London Borough of Newham; there's no evidence WPSL had anything to do with him; there's no suggestion they were responsible, directly or indirectly, for his presence at Seagull Tower. Accordingly I apply for Dr Singer's evidence to be redacted so that it is limited to Mr Bartlett, in whose case a connection is asserted by the Crown.'

Charles sits down.

'Mr Bateman, what is your position?' asks the Common Serjeant.

Bateman rises. 'I support my learned friend's submission. I say this intending no disrespect to Mr Crozier, but in the context of this case the finding of his body at Seagull Tower is simply a "loose end". The Crown's evidence doesn't demonstrate any connection between him and either Newham or the defendants. There's no suggestion he was a tenant, less still that he was a tenant holding up redevelopment.'

'I see, thank you. Miss Allinson?'

'The Crown's case is that Seagull Tower was used for the disposal of the corpses of unlawfully evicted and murdered tenants. The fact that we cannot demonstrate that Mr Crozier was evicted from one of the company's development sites is something the Defence may rely on in due course. On the other hand we can point to the fact that not one but two bodies were found in unfilled recesses on a construction site controlled by the defendants. That demonstrates a pattern of behaviour which, taken with the other unlawful evictions, goes towards proving the conspiracy.'

'Do you agree that, as Mr Holborne says, you have no admissible evidence to prove that Mr Crozier ever occupied a property where the company was developing?'

'Yes, my lord, but we still rely on the inference to be drawn from these facts. We can prove that violence was used which led to one body being found at Seagull Tower, and thus it is reasonable to infer that violence was used leading to Mr Crozier's body being found there as well. The alternative is to suggest that two separate agencies were involved and both chose, by chance, to use the company's building site at Seagull Tower for disposal purposes. That is inherently unlikely, particularly given the restricted access to the site.'

'Do you agree that the prejudicial effect of telling the jury about a second body is substantial?'

'Yes, but so too is the probative value of the inference that can be drawn.'

'Thank you. Anything else you would like to say?'

'No, thank you, my Lord.'

'In that case I rule that Dr Singer's evidence be redacted so that it refers only to the body of Mr Bartlett. I acknowledge that the presence of two bodies at the same site under the control of the defendants, one of which is provably that of a tenant who was obstructing a development, does have some inferential force. But it is too vague to assist the jury and it is clearly and substantially outweighed by the prejudice caused to the defendants. I can think of several other routes by which Mr Crozier could have found himself in the half-constructed tower. He was, according to Dr Singer, a habitual drug user. He might simply have gone there to abuse drugs and died as a result of an overdose. Let's have the jury back in.'

Bateman leans towards Charles. 'Nicely done,' he whispers.

The jury are led back in and, once they have taken their seats, Allinson stands again.

'Members of the jury, my name is Calliope Allinson, Treasury Counsel for the Crown, and I prosecute this case together with my learned friend, Mark Denton, who sits behind me. Two men stand accused, although you can only see one, Mr Anthony Wise, in the dock. His father, Sir Leo Wise, sits in the wheelchair at the end of Counsel's benches. He is represented by my learned friend Mr Holborne —' Charles half-stands and nods towards the jury — 'and Mr Anthony Wise is represented by Mr Bateman.' Bateman follows suit.

'These two men, father and son, are charged with two counts each. Both are unlawful agreements. The first is a conspiracy to murder certain tenants of the London Borough of Newham. Once you have heard all the evidence, and the learned judge has summed up to you and given you directions on the law, the Crown invite you to consider that charge first. If, then, you consider the Crown has not made out its case, we invite you to consider the second, the lesser charge, namely conspiracy to harass and evict such tenants. The difference between the two charges is this: a conspiracy to murder requires that the conspirators, the people who entered the agreement, agree that the tenants were to be, or could be, killed. The lesser conspiracy entails them agreeing that force was to be used to evict tenants, but not that they should be killed.

'Now I'm going to give you a brief summary of the evidence. Nothing I say is evidence. If, having heard all the witnesses, you conclude that the actual evidence is inconsistent with anything I've said, you must ignore me and follow the evidence. My purpose is to give you a framework so you'll understand the evidence when it's called. Similarly, although I'll comment on the law necessary for the Crown to prove its case, all issues of law are for the judge, and the judge alone, and you must follow his directions.

'This case involves a conspiracy, a conspiracy to use violence to remove tenants who had a right to remain in their properties. A conspiracy is simply an agreement to do something that is against the law. There is no magic to the word; it's an agreement. Of course, in the case of most criminal agreements, there is no police officer standing by taking notes to prove it. Normally the existence of the agreement can only be proven by indirect evidence, usually by what occurred thereafter. In this case, however, there was a witness. You will hear from a Mr Kevin Streeter, a bailiff. The job of a bailiff is to evict tenants against whom possession orders have been obtained. To do that is perfectly lawful. However, Mr Streeter has pleaded guilty to entering an agreement to use force to throw out tenants who had rights to remain in their properties. He has already been sentenced for his part. And he will tell you that he was directed to act in that way by Anthony Wise.

'As a result, two people were violently and forcibly removed from their homes. You will hear evidence from both of them. We shall call them "Witness A" and "Witness B" to protect their identities. In the circumstances of this case there is, we say, a risk to their lives if their identities were to be revealed to the defendants. Both suffered injuries. A third person, a Mr Bartlett, was thrown from the first-floor window of his house and, we say, killed. Why, you may ask? I shall explain.

'The defendants control a company known as Wise Property and Securities Limited. Until recently the father, Sir Leo, was the managing director. You may have read about Sir Leo in the newspapers. He is an Austrian Jew who arrived in this country from Europe after the war who, it is said, built the company and his fortune from nothing. Earlier this year he resigned his post as managing director and his son, Anthony Wise, took over. Anthony may or may not have actually taken the formal title of managing director but it is agreed all round that he was in charge thereafter.

'No one living in London can be unaware of the housing crisis. Much of the housing stock of the East End in particular was destroyed during the war, and what remains is in a terrible condition. There are thousands on council waiting lists and thousands more living in slums or even on the streets. In 1967 the London Borough of Newham issued a tender for contractors to bid to demolish large areas of slum properties and build brand-new modern tower blocks. WPSL won the contract over stiff competition. We are concerned with two of the developments, Rochester Avenue and Braithwaite Street. You will see some of the contractual documentation, but you need not be concerned with the details at this stage. In summary, very large sums of money were at stake. On completion of the new tower blocks at these sites, WPSL stood to receive at least two million pounds. However, they had to comply with an agreed timetable, and if they failed to do so they faced very heavy financial penalties.

'You'll be shown documents which demonstrate that the company was in financial difficulties. It costs a lot to demolish old properties and construct new modern tower blocks, and the company would not be paid until right at the end. So it had to borrow. Various banks were very happy to lend WPSL money, but only backed by security. The security offered was mainly the property and land of the development sites, but also included the defendants' family home in The Bishops Avenue, a mansion in the most expensive street in Britain. Some of you may own your own homes and have mortgages, and you'll understand that the bank or building society has lent you the money to buy your homes, but only with the security of a mortgage over the property itself. So, should you fail to pay your mortgage, the bank can seize the property, sell it and recover its loan. Now, obviously, vacant property which is ready for development is worth a great deal more than a property that still has tenants in it. In particular, if those tenants have what is known as "protected tenancies" under the Rent Acts, they cannot be evicted without a court order, which is only granted in a very narrow set of circumstances.

'Here was the problem facing WPSL. At the time when these contracts were negotiated, they were confident they could evict all the existing tenants. However, by the time construction was to start, Parliament had passed the Rent Acts, which gave the tenants rights to remain in the property. Every month the tenants remained, they held up the start of demolition and construction, forcing the company to pay interest on its enormous loans. You'll be shown documents which prove that the banks were getting nervous. They realised they had lent too much. With tenants in the remaining properties and the developments unable to proceed, the value of the security they held fell below the total amount of loans. One bank in particular, Lloyds, threatened to call in its loans, which would have meant the end of the company and possibly the family home.

'So, says the Crown, the scene was set for the unlawful agreement. Everything was at stake. Not merely the future existence of the company and the Wise home in north London but also, we say, the reputation of Sir Leo Wise, who portrayed himself as this philanthropist, intent on providing decent, affordable homes for the working class of East London. That was, after all, the basis upon which he received his knighthood.

'The witnesses will tell you that Streeter arrived at their properties in Rochester Avenue, said he was from WPSL, forcibly evicted them and boarded up the properties. Streeter admits his part in that. The third tenant, Edward Bartlett, was the last remaining tenant holding out against repossession at the second development site, Braithwaite Street. He achieved some notoriety, you may know, because he refused to leave and lived inside his boarded-up property. He gave a number of interviews to the press from his upstairs window. Mr Streeter will tell you that his colleague, a Mr Lane, acting in furtherance of the conspiracy, evicted Mr Bartlett by throwing him through a window on the first floor of the property. His body was found, badly decomposed, in the rubble when Seagull Tower collapsed. Seagull Tower is another of the defendants' developments. Mr Lane has disappeared. We say that he should be standing in the dock with these defendants.

'So, the common thread is WPSL and the developments. The Crown will call a Mr McConnachie, a chartered surveyor employed by the London Borough of Newham and the site liaison officer for the developers at Seagull Tower. He deals with how Mr Bartlett's body was found and it's likely route to that position.

'Finally, the Crown will call Detective Inspector Woolley and Detective Constable Truman. After these facts came to light they arrested both of the accused. During an interview with the police Mr Anthony Wise admitted telling Mr Streeter to use force. If you accept Streeter's evidence, you have first-hand evidence of the conspiracy.

'Interestingly, during the course of that interview, Mr Anthony Wise suggested that the company's plan was for possession proceedings to be brought in court, in his words, "to test the law". There was apparently some scheme to replace the tenants' furniture with expensive furniture which, the company hoped, would remove the tenants' protection given by the Rent Acts. However you will hear that no possession proceedings were ever brought in the county court. This was a lie, we say, to cover up the illegal evictions. The company did not use legal means to evict these tenants. It used violence.

'So far as Sir Leo is concerned, the Crown say that as the major shareholder and, for years, managing director of the company, you can be sure that he knew that force was to be used. In support of that, we shall show you a letter written by him to Lloyds Bank dated 19 April 1969, after the bank pointed out that the presence of the tenants meant that they were over-exposed on the loans. Sir Leo told the bank: "*We are using every means possible to hasten the tenants' removal*" and he guaranteed they would be out within the week. The Crown say that you can rely on that letter to prove that Sir Leo was also part of the conspiracy, even if it was his son who gave the order, because no possession proceedings were ever brought; no order of the court existed authorising evictions and even if court proceedings had been brought, it is inconceivable that possession orders would be granted within a week. The only way it would be possible to evict the tenants within such a short time is by force. Within a week of the signing of that letter, all the tenants had in fact been removed with violence.

'As in all prosecutions, the Crown brings the case and the Crown has to prove it. If, at the end of the trial you are not sure of the guilt of either or both of the accused, it is your duty to acquit. Now, with your Lordship's permission, I shall call the first witness. Mr Ewan McConnachie.'

CHAPTER TWENTY-TWO

Everyone watches as the usher walks to the double doors of the courtroom and Mr McConnachie's name is called. Some seconds later a man enters and is directed down the central aisle towards the witness box. Mr McConnachie is a bespectacled gentleman in an old-fashioned three-piece suit. He looks close to retirement. He carries a bundle of files and plans and has a large rolled-up blueprint tucked under one arm. He bustles to the witness box and takes the oath in a quick and efficient manner.

'Please give your name, occupation and professional address to the court,' requests Allinson.

'My name is Ewan McConnachie and I'm a chartered surveyor employed by the London Borough of Newham at their Stratford Office. I'm the head of a small department of eight surveyors and draughtsmen,' answers McConnachie, struggling to find space on the witness stand for all his documents.

'At the beginning of this year were you working at a site at Seagull Lane, E16?'

'I was. That was the site of a large high-rise development and I was employed by Newham as the liaison between them and the developers, Wise Property and Securities Limited.'

'And what were your duties in respect of the site?'

'I had overall responsibility for the progress of the works from Newham's perspective. My colleagues and I worked with the developers on a daily basis.'

'Were you involved in negotiating the contract between Newham and the developers?' asks Allinson.

'No, I was brought in after that. But I became extremely familiar with it, especially the Schedules, which set out the specifications for the work, the timescales and the penalties for late delivery.'

'What were the penalties for late delivery?'

'It was not a specific figure, and there was a complex calculation, but in general terms it would be in the region of ten thousand pounds per month.'

'Why so high?'

'Well, for every month the council couldn't let flats in the tower, it was losing thousands in rental income. These penalties are set deliberately high to make sure developers hand over on time.'

'Thank you. Was Seagull Tower handed over on time?'

'It was. So far it's the only one. Braithwaite Street is now two months overdue and Rochester Avenue falls due tomorrow, and will probably be six months late at least, as demolition has only just finished. That's assuming they're allowed to proceed at all, which they may not, until the enquiry into Seagull's collapse.'

'That brings me to the collapse. In general terms, what happened?'

'The flats on all twenty-two floors of the south-west corner of the block collapsed, killing four people.'

'Were those four people identified?'

'Yes, they were all tenants.'

'I want to ask you now about another body found in the rubble, that of a Mr Edward Bartlett. Please focus your answers on that gentleman alone.'

'Yes.'

'Was Mr Bartlett a tenant of the council at Seagull Tower?'

'No. He didn't live there. I understand he'd been a tenant at Braithwaite Street.'

'Were you on site when his body was discovered?'

'Yes, I was. I can show you on these plans exactly where he was found.'

'My Lord,' says Allinson, 'the plans are at pages two to six of your bundle, but they have been reduced in size and we have here some full-sized copies.'

She hands a sheaf of large documents to the usher for distribution around court.

'Please continue, Mr McConnachie,' says the judge.

'If you look at the first page, you'll see a plan drawing of the modular construction of the flats. They comprise pre-cast concrete slices. The ceiling of one floor acts as the floor of the one above, and so on. The walls are slices stood on end, bolted to the horizontal slabs. The specifications called for the rectangular gaps that formed the junctions to be filled with concrete. On the next page you can see a sort of latticework of reinforced steel in those corners. All that should have been solid concrete. Unfortunately it appears that many were left as voids, filled with rubbish and so on. When the building collapsed, Mr Bartlett's body was found trapped between the corner formed by a floor slab and a vertical wall slab. We used the crane to lift a personnel cage to view the position. It was too dangerous to climb over the rubble at that stage.'

'Were you able to see his body?'

'Oh, yes. At first I couldn't understand it, because I could see no injuries on him at all. The junction between the two slabs had been maintained and fell without breaking open. He was rather well-protected, actually, by a triangle of concrete.'

'But he was dead?'

'I'm afraid so. The smell told you that immediately. It was obvious he'd been there for some time.'

'In your professional opinion, is there any way in which Mr Bartlett might have got into that position as a result of the collapse? Falling into it, perhaps?'

'Absolutely not. That part of the construction would have been covered up as the building rose. He can only have got into that void while the building was in the course of construction.'

'Thank you. One last question. How many people would have known of the void where the body was found?'

'How many? Scores I suppose. The architects, the developers, the surveyors on site, most of the builders and other trades. Basically, anyone who had plans or who worked on site at the relevant stages of construction. However, I should point out that the voids were supposed to be filled, so most people on site would have assumed that that occurred as the building rose.'

'Thank you, Mr McConnachie. Please wait there.'

Allinson resumes her seat.

'Mr Holborne?' says the judge.

Charles rises. 'Thank you.'

He turns to the bench behind him. Billy Munday is now sitting next to Stephenson. He hands a slip of paper to Charles.

'Mr McConnachie,' says Charles, 'please tell us the dimensions of the void in which Mr Bartlett's body was found.'

'I can scale it from the plans if you like.'

'No, that won't be necessary. An estimate will suffice.'

Despite Charles's comment, the surveyor takes a ruler from his pocket and starts measuring from the blueprint. After a moment he looks up. 'About eighteen feet long, two feet across and a foot and half in depth,' he says.

'So, a bit like a long trench?'

'Yes.'

'If I was walking about on site while this void was still exposed, could I fall into it?'

'Certainly, if you weren't looking where you were going.'

'So, an electrician laying cables, or a plumber fixing pipes would have to watch their feet.'

'Yes.'

'Or a telephone engineer, like Mr Bartlett.'

'Sorry?'

'Mr Bartlett. The deceased. He was a qualified telephone engineer.'

'I didn't know that.'

'Do you know if he was employed by the General Post Office to work at Seagull Lane?'

'No, I wouldn't know.'

Allinson rises. 'Is it the defence case that Mr Bartlett was, in fact, employed there?' she asks.

Charles hands her the slip of paper. 'The defence cannot possibly say. We had no knowledge of Mr Bartlett until this case was brought. But the Crown say they can prove, beyond reasonable doubt, that our clients had him killed and buried at Seagull Tower, and we merely point out that there is another perfectly good, and rather more likely, reason Mr Bartlett was on site. I've given my learned friend a copy of the certificate of completion of Mr Bartlett's Post Office Student Apprentice Scheme issued jointly by the GPO and Catford Technical College in 1951. We don't have access to his employment record but no doubt the Crown can find it. Our enquiries reveal that he worked as a telephone engineer thereafter, sometimes for the GPO and sometimes for other companies. I have copies of the certificate for your Lordship and the members of the jury. Defence Exhibit 1, please, your Lordship?'

'Yes, thank you.'

'Now, Mr McConnachie,' continues Charles, 'at any one time, how many people would have been on site while the development was progressing?'

'Impossible to say. Scores certainly, perhaps as many as a hundred, hundred and fifty.'

'So, very busy?'

'Yes, very. Indeed it was so crowded sometimes that I complained to the developers. They were trying to catch up with the timetable, and sometimes I felt there was too much going on to be able to maintain safety.'

'Thank you. Now I need to explain to you that both Sir Leo and Mr Anthony Wise say they know absolutely nothing about Mr Bartlett, and have no idea how he might have been found where he was. But I would like to explore some possibilities with you, do you follow?'

'Okay.'

'The first set of possibilities is that he was simply working at the site, for example, as a telecommunications engineer installing telephone cables. Was there any security in place to ensure only authorised personnel could go on site?' asks Charles.

'Yes there was, but this was the problem. It was so busy, with tradesmen coming and going constantly, and hundreds of them on site every week, it became virtually impossible to check the identity of everyone working there. That's why I complained to the developers.'

'Did anything come of that complaint?'

'Yes, they did their best, but the nature of the job made it extremely difficult.'

'If I were to ask you for entry and departure logs, that is, a record of the dates, times, names and trades of every person who came and left the site, would you be able to provide such information?'

'No, I'm afraid I couldn't. I don't believe accurate records exist.'

'So it is perfectly possible that Mr Bartlett was there, simply doing his job, but we would have no records to prove or disprove it?'

McConnachie pauses. 'Yes, it is possible, but that wouldn't explain how he came to be lying in a void.'

'Well, Mr McConnachie, you let me worry about that. We'll have some questions for the pathologist. Now let's look at the other possibility, that someone did kill him as the prosecution allege, and placed him in that void. What sort of materials were being brought on and off site?'

'Materials? Everything necessary to construct a tower block. Concrete, steel reinforcement, steels, large sheets of insulation, timber, cable, bathroom equipment such as water tanks, baths, tiles and so on.'

'And these items have to be lifted by crane, don't they, as the tower grows.'

'Of course.'

'The crane doesn't lift, for example, individual toilet bowls, or single rolls of insulation, does it? Materials are lifted in bulk, on pallets, in drums, in crates and so on, depending on the nature of the item, isn't that right?'

'Yes.'

'And the people who work with the crane drivers, in charge of loading these bulk items, are called banksmen, are they not?'

'Yes.'

'If I wanted to get something onto the site, for example a body, I could put it in any of these large containers, couldn't I? The banksmen don't have time to open every pallet, every drum, every crate, before connecting it to the crane and having it lifted into position, do they?'

'No. That wouldn't be practical. They rely on the documentation and the codes written on the containers.'

'Thank you. So, the fact that these accused were directors of the development company does not mean they'd have had exclusive access to the site, does it? Hundreds of people could have found a way of getting a body onto the construction site, because no one was checking all the boxes, drums and pallets being lifted in.'

'That's right, I'm afraid. As I've explained, it was an incredibly busy site and everyone was working under a lot of pressure. Materials were coming in every minute. We would have no way of checking everything to make sure it didn't contain a body.'

'Yes, thank you, Mr McConnachie. Please wait there as there may be some more questions.'

'Yes, thank you, Mr Holborne,' says the judge. 'Mr Bateman?'

'No questions, thank you, my Lord.'

'Miss Allinson?'

'Yes please. You were asked, Mr McConnachie, about how a body might have been taken to that site at a time when there were scores or perhaps hundreds of contractors working there.'

'Yes?'

'If I'd decided to secrete a body in a carton of, let's say, bathroom tiles, and managed to get it past the banksmen and lifted to the relevant floor, who would be responsible for unloading it from the crane?'

'A contractor termed a "slinger-signaller".'

'Thank you. And would the slinger-signaller unpack the carton?' asks Allinson.

Allinson's question tells Charles that she has never worked on a building site, nor done a case involving one. Charles knows the answer, and it's not the one Allinson is hoping for.

'No, not really. Their job is to make sure the load is lowered to the right position and disconnected from the crane.'

Allinson is trying to make the point that whoever might have put a body inside such a container, they could not guarantee being the person to open it. They would risk exposure if anyone but them started poking about inside. It's a good point, but this question won't get the answer she seeks. She decides not to risk another unhelpful answer and gives up the enquiry.

She pauses for a moment and looks at the judge. 'Does your Lordship have any questions of this witness?'

'No, thank you. You are free to leave, Mr McConnachie.'

The surveyor collects his plans and papers, bustles back up the aisle and leaves court.

'Your next witness, Miss Allinson?'

Bateman turns to Charles and raises his eyebrows. Charles leans towards him and whispers.

'I know, I know, it doesn't get us far. It *might* have been possible for someone else to put the body up there but —'

'But why would they?' asks Bateman, completing Charles's question.

'Exactly. I prefer the theory that he was working.'

Bateman wrinkles his nose and shakes his head gently in disagreement. '"The Last Holdout"? The man who was so afraid to leave the property even for half an hour, he had food thrown up to his first-floor window?'

Charles grins and shrugs.

The two men separate and sit upright as the prosecutor calls her next witness.

'Dr Rodney Singer, please,' she says.

Dr Singer must have been waiting just outside the door because the usher has no need to call his name. He strides swiftly towards the witness box. He is a tall, lean man in a double-breasted pinstriped suit and yellow bowtie, and he carries a small folder under his arm. He takes the oath in a quiet voice, looks up and addresses the judge without being prompted.

'My name is Dr Rodney Singer. I am a Consultant Forensic Pathologist, and I have been on the approved Home Office list since 1961. My professional address is Charing Cross Hospital, Agar Street, West Strand.'

Charles stands. 'My Lord, Mr Bateman and I have discussed Dr Singer's evidence and we are agreed that our learned friend may lead or summarise it, as there's no dispute as to what's contained in his post-mortem report.'

'Thank you. I shall leave it to you, Miss Allinson, as to whether you wish to summarise or simply lead Dr Singer through his evidence in chief.'

Allinson nods. 'Dr Singer,' she starts, 'on 7 June 1969 you carried out a post-mortem examination of a body found in the rubble of Seagull Tower, correct?'

'I carried out post-mortem examinations on several bodies from the Seagull Tower collapse.'

'I want to ask specifically about one, that of Edward Bartlett, born 2 September 1917. Would you please summarise your findings in respect of him?'

Singer opens the file and finds the relevant document. 'This was a Caucasian male of average build, close to the stated age of fifty-two years. He weighed 12 stone 7 pounds and was 5 foot 9 inches in height. He was identified by Tag No. 69/SS4615 and by a lightning-shaped tattoo on the left forearm, as Mr Edward Bartlett of Braithwaite Street, London, E1. The state of decomposition suggested a period of several weeks since death. I can give you details if you want?'

'No, that won't be necessary, thank you. Your estimate of the date of death is accepted by the defence.'

'Well, then, the body was fully dressed in brown trousers, a vest and check shirt, a light-weight short jacket, workmen's boots and underwear. The back of the shoulder area of the jacket, and the back of the leather belt holding up the deceased's trousers, had what appeared to be recent abrasions to them. The clothing was removed, and the body showed the following injuries: (1) bruising and abrasions across the back of the shoulders, particularly to the left of the midline; (2) bruising and abrasions to the lower back; and (3) a soggy swelling at the back of the skull over which there was a roughly circular abrasion and some bleeding.

'Examination of the inside of the deceased's vest and the back of his shirt revealed small skin scrapes which coincided with the position of the shoulder and lower back bruising and abrasions.

'Reflection of the scalp and dura revealed a three-inch fracture of the parietal bone. The fracture was depressed at its distal end by approximately an eighth of an inch. Beneath the fracture there was a subdural haematoma of approximately four inches across and eighty millilitres in volume. It was difficult to measure accurately due to the degree of putrefaction. There was also evidence of a contrecoup injury to the frontal lobe. I can run through the histopathological and toxicological results, but they were negative and there was nothing else of relevance.'

'And your conclusions, Doctor?' asks Allinson.

'Death was caused by a traumatic brain injury. This man received a substantial blow to the back of his head. The pattern of injuries to his shoulders and lower back, together with the deposition of skin on the inside of his clothing matching the abrasions to his clothing, suggest that he suffered a fall, most probably from a height, backwards onto a hard surface, landing largely on his head and the top of his shoulders. That caused the fracture and posterior subdural haemorrhage and, as the brain rebounded within the skull, the contrecoup injury to the frontal lobe.'

'Would your findings be consistent with the injuries that might be sustained by a man thrown backwards out of a first-floor window?'

'They would.'

'Thank you, Dr Singer.'

'Mr Holborne?' invites the judge.

'Thank you, my Lord. Dr Singer, was the deceased wearing workman's boots?'

'He was.'

'Thank you.'

Charles glances at the jury and two or three take the opportunity to meet his gaze. One of them actually nods.

Good.

'Now, the soggy swelling at the back of this man's head. If death had resulted immediately, there would be no signs of healing, is that right?'

'Yes. All the repair mechanisms, such as clotting, cease at death.'

'Was there any sign of clotting?'

'It's impossible to be certain because putrefaction was quite advanced, but I cannot exclude it.'

'So it's possible he survived the blow to the back of his head.'

'It's possible. Although I doubt survival would have been prolonged. The depressed fracture of the parietal bone and the bleeding inside the dura would have caused substantial pressure on the brain, as would the contrecoup, or rebound injury, to the front of the brain.'

'Yes, but neurosurgical teams deal quite often with people who suffer from subdural bleeds, patients who walk into Casualty under their own steam, correct? Such patients present with terrible headaches, but their injuries don't inevitably lead to instant unconsciousness and death, do they?' suggests Charles.

'Not always, no. Sometimes the bleeding is sporadic, but the severity of the head injury in this case would have made that less likely.'

'But not impossible?'

Singer looks a little uncomfortable, but after a moment he replies. 'No, not impossible.'

'Indeed I dealt with a medical negligence case in which a fracture similar to this, together with subdural bleeding, were both missed by the Casualty doctor, who discharged my client's husband, only for him to re-present two days later, and die a couple of days after that. So it is possible for there to be quite a delay between injury and unconsciousness in such cases, do you not agree?' persists Charles.

'Mr Holborne,' intervenes the judge. 'I think you are straying into giving evidence. You already have your answer from Dr

Singer that the scenario you postulate is possible but unlikely. You can't expect him to comment further than that.'

'Thank you, my Lord.'

Charles resumes his seat and Bateman stands. He picks up immediately where Charles left off.

'As I understand your evidence, Dr Singer,' he says, 'it wouldn't be unheard of for someone who suffered an injury such as that sustained by Mr Bartlett to go into work, albeit suffering from a severe headache.'

'Firstly, I am a consultant pathologist and so I don't deal with live patients, my Lord, but one does hear of such cases. A patient having suffered this injury would not be able to continue work for very long. It would depend on the speed of the bleeding and how the pressure on the brain accumulated.'

'Thank you,' says Bateman. 'And am I right in understanding your evidence that, if unconsciousness did not occur immediately, it would probably occur thereafter if, of course, the injury was left untreated?'

'Yes.'

'So, putting it in layman's terms, if Mr Bartlett survived the original injury for some hours or perhaps a day or so, went to work, and then fainted or fell unconscious due to the pressure inside his skull, that would not be a surprising series of events?'

'No, it would not be surprising.'

'Thank you,' says Bateman, sitting down.

'Re-examination?' asks the judge of Allinson.

'No, thank you, my Lord. Mr Kevin Streeter, please.'

The usher stays where she is and looks at the dock officer. He nods, bends and shouts down the stone stairs. 'Bring up Streeter!'

A metal door clangs and footsteps are heard coming up from the cells. Streeter, still manacled to a dock officer, appears. The two men sidle past Anthony Wise in the dock, step down into the well of the court, and walk across to the witness box where the usher awaits with a Bible and a card. With a little juggling and shuffling around the witness box, Streeter takes the Bible in one hand and the card in the other and gives the oath.

'Your name is Kevin Streeter, is that right?' asks Allinson.

'Yeah.'

'And your occupation?'

'Licensed bailiff.'

'Mr Streeter, earlier today you pleaded guilty to the second count on the indictment and received a sentence of five years' imprisonment. Is that right?'

'Yeah.'

'By your plea, you accepted that you entered into an unlawful conspiracy with Mr Anthony Wise to forcibly evict tenants of the London Borough of Newham, tenants who were protected from eviction in the absence of a court order. Is that correct?'

'Yeah.'

'Do you work on your own account or for a company?'

'I run a business called Shoreditch Enforcement Services.'

'And you say you're licensed; by whom?'

'I'm on ... well, I was on the list of licensed bailiffs of most county courts in the East London area. I guess I ain't any longer. So, Bow, Shoreditch and so on.'

'Please explain to the jury what a licensed bailiff does,' asks Allinson.

'Sure. If you've bought something on tick, you know, the "never-never", and you get behind in your payments, the company has the right to recover the goods, or the car, or whatever it is. So they use bailiffs to take 'em back. That's one part of the job. Another part is, once a landlord gets a possession order, the tenant has to leave. Only, sometimes, they refuse. So they use us to get 'em out.'

'Do you work alone?'

'I had a chap who worked with me, Kevin Lane, and a part-time secretary and bookkeeper, Mrs Briggs.'

'How long did Mr Lane work with you?'

'About five years.'

'Had you ever cause to think him violent or unstable?'

'The job means you've got to use, you know, persuasion, to get goods handed over, or people to leave their gaffs, 'cos obviously, they don't want to do it. That's why bailiffs are usually big men, and Kev's no different. Every now and then he has to use force but no, I never thought him violent or unstable before all this 'appened. He's actually a very quiet bloke. You might say a gentle giant.'

'Have you ever heard of a company called Wise Property and Securities Limited?'

'Yeah. They've a load of property in the East End and we've done work for 'em.'

'Who did you deal with at the company?'

'For some years it was the MD, Sir Leo Wise, but then he was taken ill, apparently. I can't remember when, probably sometime after New Year. After that I was told to deal with his son, Tony.'

'Did you ever speak to either of them on the telephone?'

'Oh yeah, loads of times.'

'So would you recognise their voices?'

'Of course.'

'Thank you,' says Allinson. 'Now, in addition to doing bailiff work for the Wises' company, did you ever have anything to do with tenants of the London Borough of Newham?'

'Yes. I'd say that was half our work. There's a load of Newham council properties in the area.'

'So, would you ever be involved in executing possession against former Newham tenants?'

'Often.'

'Were you aware of the proposals to redevelop parts of the borough?'

'Everyone was.'

'Did you have anything to do with obtaining possession of Newham properties where redevelopment was planned?'

'Yes. Newham served notices to quit on hundreds of tenants. As always, some refused to move, so we were really busy for a while.'

'Were you asked to do anything regarding those tenants?'

'Yes. The Wises told us to offer them new furniture to replace their old. In return they was to be given new tenancy contracts.'

'Had you ever been asked to do that sort of thing before?'

'No. And it was odd. I mean, most of these places were slums. The furniture was all broken down pre-war stuff. And we was being asked to take dining sets worth hundreds, posh sofas and big American fridges and so on. It was better stuff than I 'ad at 'ome!'

Streeter's outrage is very evident, and prompts a sprinkling of laughter in the court.

'And are you sure that this expensive furniture was being taken to tenants in areas where redevelopment was planned?'

'Oh, yes. We was given specific lists, and the only places we ever went to deliver this furniture was in one of them houses or flats.'

'I see. Thank you. How long did that continue?'

'Not that long. A couple of months, maybe? Then I was told by Tony Wise that the process of obtaining possession was taking too long and we were to use force.'

'How do you know it was Mr Wise who told you?'

'I was told to give him a call, so I did. I knew 'is voice.'

'And what exactly did he say?'

'He said it was all taking too long, and we should use force.'

'Did he say how much force?'

'No. He just said we had to get them out, right away, and do "whatever you need to".'

'"*Do whatever you need to*"?'

'Yeah.'

Allinson pauses long enough to allow the answer to sink in with the jury. Charles watches as a couple make notes of the answer.

Allinson continues. 'But that would be illegal, wouldn't it, if the court hadn't made a possession order first?'

Streeter hangs his head. 'Yeah. I knew it was, 'n' I feel bad about it now. But the Wise company was so important to us, you know, our biggest private client, and I didn't want to lose 'em. He promised me it'd be okay. Said most of them were squatters and druggies anyway and they'd never complain. And 'e offered us double bubble.' Streeter shrugs. 'I couldn't say no, really. I know I should 'ave.'

Allinson pauses again and this time looks at the jury. Charles examines them at the same time. They are all staring at the witness, but he cannot gauge what they are thinking.

'Were you ever asked to go to Rochester Avenue and evict tenants?'

'Yeah, twice. A woman at one end and a man at the other.'

'What happened?'

'Well, they was evicted.'

'How?'

Streeter looks down and pauses. 'The first one, a woman and her two kids were just sort of bundled into the street.'

'Did you need to use any violence?'

'Not really. There was a bit of pushing and shoving and so on. The woman got her hair pulled.'

'I think she went to hospital, didn't she?'

'I don't know about that. She seemed okay, when I left. A bit upset, that's all.'

'And the man? At the other end of Rochester Avenue?'

'He started a ruckus. Tricky bloke, that. Very shouty. Had to use a bit more force with him.'

'What force?'

'I hit him with the jemmy. He goes down on the pavement, and I boarded up.'

'And what about the tenant?'

'What about him?'

The tone of the reply makes Charles look up. Streeter is making a genuine enquiry, as if he can't see what might be wrong with leaving a middle-aged man unconscious on the pavement. There is a lengthening pause while Allinson considers how to respond.

That's a mistake. The longer she leaves it, the more his callousness sinks in with everyone in the courtroom.

Now everyone, including the judge, is staring at Streeter, all except Allinson. She eventually looks up, having decided to move to a different point.

'I now want to ask you about a different eviction. Do you remember where you were on 25 April 1969?'

'Is that the Braithwaite Street job?' asks Streeter.

'Yes. Where had you been working that afternoon?'

'Kevin Lane and I were running through a list of repossessions for Bow County Court. I got a message to call Mr Wise, the son, so I rang 'im. He wanted us to go to 61 Braithwaite Street, Shoreditch, soon as poss, and secure the premises.'

'Was that normal?'

'No. The tenant was a chap called Eddie Bartlett. "The Last Holdout" they called 'im. Well, he'd supposedly been seen somewhere else, so Wise wanted us to go round while 'e was out.'

'What did you do?'

'We went round the next day, me and Big Kev, in the van. Got there about five, maybe a bit before.'

'Tell us what happened,' says Allinson.

'There was a light on upstairs, so we waited for a bit to see if we could see movement. After a bit we decided to knock on the door. No reply. So we broke the lock and began searching the house. That's usual procedure. You have to make sure the property's empty 'cos sometimes tenants hide in cupboards and under beds. I looked around the ground floor and sent Kev upstairs. I was in the kitchen when I heard a shout.'

'Did you recognise the voice?'

'I thought it was Big Kev but I can't be certain.'

'What did you do?'

'I assumed he'd found the tenant, so I ran upstairs. I got to the bedroom at the front of the property and Kev was there, struggling with a bloke.'

'Can you describe the other man?'

'I didn't get a good look, 'cos it was so quick. I'd say in his fifties or sixties, maybe about five foot six. A lot smaller than Kev. Before I could say or do anything, Kev lifted the man clear off the floorboards by his lapels and threw him backwards. The man crashed bottom-first through the bedroom window. There was glass and timber everywhere.'

'What happened then?'

'The geezer fell out.'

'Why didn't you stop Mr Lane from doing that?'

'I had no time,' says Streeter. 'It all happened in a flash! I just shouted something like "What you do that for?" and ran downstairs. But by the time I got to the street, the pavement was empty. I assumed the bloke had run off.'

'What did you do?'

'Well, I ran some way up Braithwaite Street to see if I could find him. I was a bit worried about him, to be honest. But there was no street lighting and I realised I needed a torch. I ran back towards the van but Kev was already in the driver's seat. He drove past me, and called out the open window "I'll get him!" I shouted to him to stop, but he never did. I waited a minute or two and then went back to number 61.'

'Then what?'

'I finished searching the property and there was no one else there. So I boarded up the windows and doors as per instructions. That took me about forty minutes, by which time Kev hadn't returned. I waited on the pavement for a while but eventually picked up my tool bag and walked towards the main road to get a bus back to the office. I assumed Kev was still driving round the streets looking for the tenant.'

'Was that the end of the event?'

'Sort of. That evening I rang Kev's home telephone number but he weren't there. Next morning I woke up and the van was parked outside my place, keys still in the ignition, but no sign of Kev. I've tried to contact him loads of times at his address, I've phoned and gone round, but he's never there. I think maybe he's done a bunk. After a couple of days I began to be suspicious that something must have happened after he drove off.'

'Did you report this to the police?'

'When I saw the newspaper reports of the tenant's body being found in the wreckage of Seagull Tower, I began to think that maybe Kev had found the bloke and, perhaps, done him harm. So I went then.'

'Thank you, Mr Streeter.'

'I want to say I never knew what Big Kev was gonna do. We 'ad orders to use force, not chuck people outta windows. I'd never've agreed to that.'

'Thank you. Please wait there.'

'Any questions, Mr Holborne?' asks the Common Serjeant.

Charles rises. 'One or two, please, my Lord.'

He pauses, collecting his thoughts. He and Bateman have discussed how best to attack Streeter. In theory there's a conflict between Charles and his former pupil, in that only one person could have given the order to use force, and each barrister might have to point the finger at the other's client. That's the very reason separate counsel had to be instructed. On the other hand, the conflict is more apparent than real, because they both need to damage Streeter's credibility.

Charles finds himself faced with a dilemma. Streeter has attempted to minimise the violence he used. He is obliged to, to support his story that he would never have gone to the lengths of murdering recalcitrant tenants. That's helpful to both Wises, as that evidence makes it almost impossible for the Crown to prove conspiracy to murder. On the other hand, Streeter's insouciance towards Mrs Connelly's injuries and his complete callousness regarding the unconscious Mueller were so obvious that Charles could easily demonstrate the man to be a liar. He used a lot more force than he's admitting. While that would obviously be helpful in demonstrating him to be a liar, the more violent the bailiff is shown to be, the greater is the possibility that he might *actually* have agreed to use unlimited force, including murder.

So, a conundrum.

He decides to leave Peter Bateman to resolve it, and goes straight to the heart of the case against Sir Leo.

'You claim, Mr Streeter, to be very familiar with the voices of both Sir Leo and Anthony Wise, is that correct?'

'Yeah.'

'You can tell the two men apart, can you, on the telephone?'

'Yeah, I can.'

'And you're sure that the voice you heard was that of Mr Anthony Wise and not that of Sir Leo Wise?'

'Yeah, I'm sure. The father is German or, at least, he's got a strong German accent. The son hasn't.'

'So whoever gave you the order, you claim, to use force against these tenants, it was not Sir Leo?'

'Yeah, that's right.'

'And you're absolutely sure there was no suggestion whatsoever of killing these tenants?'

Streeter looks outraged. 'I ain't a killer! Nor's Big Kev ... under normal circumstances. We're licensed bailiffs!'

'So, whoever was on the phone, if they'd said "Use fatal force", you'd have said "Absolutely not!" wouldn't you?'

'Bloody right I would!'

'Thank you.'

Charles sits. He's conscious that he's left a lot of work for Peter Bateman to do, but he has confidence in him.

'Mr Bateman,' offers the judge.

He stands.

'You say, Mr Streeter, that you knew the voices of both Sir Leo and Anthony Wise, because you'd spoken to them so many times on the phone.'

'Yeah.'

'So, sometimes they would call you and sometimes you would call them? Is that the picture?'

Charles enjoys listening to Peter Bateman's voice in court. It is gentle and finely accented, but without being annoyingly "posh". Bateman learned quickly to moderate his accent to avoid alienating juries, rather in the same way as Charles had to moderate his, in the opposite direction, to avoid alienating judges.

'That's right.'

'Were you aware that Wise Property and Securities Limited had contracts with nine separate bailiff companies across the East End of London and Essex?'

'Er ... no.'

'Were you aware that the company has a housing management division with twenty-two employees, four of whom are specifically tasked with dealing with rent recovery and repossessions?'

'How would I know the number of employees they have? I only deal with a couple of people.'

'A couple of people in the housing management division?'

'I've no idea what they call their departments — they change all the time — but yes. There's a bloke called Winston Stanley and a woman called Mrs Joyce. I don't remember her first name. We're on the phone all the time. It's the nature of the work. A lot of it's last-minute. You get the possession orders from the court and you need to move quickly.'

'So you would recognise their voices on the telephone as well?' asks Bateman.

'Yeah, of course.'

'What's Mr Stanley's phone number?' asks Bateman quickly.

'What?'

'His telephone number.'

Streeter frowns, puzzled, but answers swiftly. '01 520 1145.'

'And Mrs Joyce's?'

'01 520 1147.'

'And that of Mr Anthony Wise?'

Now Streeter pauses, realising the trap into which he has fallen. 'I can't recall, right now.'

'But you phoned him all the time, you say,' points out Bateman.

'It's changed. I remember now. They changed their phone numbers when the son took over.'

'Okay then, give us the number of Sir Leo Wise. Until recently you dealt with Sir Leo for years, you say.'

'Er … well, it would be a "520" number but…' His voice tails off. Bateman says nothing, letting Streeter stew, and watching his point sink in with the jury.

'You can't remember,' states Bateman eventually.

'Not right now, no.'

'I suggest the reason you can remember the numbers of Mrs Joyce and Mr Stanley is because you used to call them all the time, while the reason you can't remember the numbers of Sir Leo or Mr Wise is because you *never* used to call them. Never.'

'No, that's wrong.'

'Very well. You tell us you regularly spoke to Sir Leo Wise, the managing director of a large stock exchange-listed company, for years. So, what did you talk about?'

'I dunno, stuff to do with their properties, repossessions I was to do, outstanding rent I was to collect, that sort of thing.'

'Perhaps you could give us details of a particular conversation, to illustrate the nature of your discussions?' asks Bateman benignly.

Streeter closes his eyes and adopts an expression of fierce concentration. Bateman takes the moment to look at the jury, one or two of whom are smiling.

'Nah,' Streeter concludes. 'I can't remember an exact conversation. Just work stuff.'

'Not one single conversation?'

'Sorry.'

'I suggest again to you, Mr Streeter, that you had no dealings with either Sir Leo or Anthony Wise at all.'

'That's not true. I did.'

'I suggest it is nonsense to assert that the managing directors of this company would have dealt directly with one of numerous bailiffs, dealing with literally hundreds of properties every week. They had a department specifically for that, and that was your point of contact, was it not?'

'No. I did talk to them.'

'Then give us a single example,' challenges Bateman.

'Okay. There was the call to go to Braithwaite Street.'

'That's the only one you remember, then?'

'At the minute. There was loads of others, but that was the most recent.'

'Very well, let's turn to that. You say you got a message to call Mr Anthony Wise.'

'Yes.'

'Who gave you that message?'

There is a momentary hesitation and Charles see Streeter's eyes flick sharply towards Woolley and back again.

This is going to be a lie, thinks Charles.

'Mrs Briggs, at the office. I called her to say we'd finished the list, and she said she'd had a call asking me to ring Mr Wise.'

'Where were you when you had this conversation?'

'I can't remember,' replies Streeter quickly, evidently deciding that stonewalling is a safer defence against counsel's probing. 'We was still out on the van.'

'So, you'd have had to find a call box.'

'Yeah, that'd be right.'

'So, you find a call box, you call the office and you speak to Mrs Briggs.'

'Yeah.'

'Mrs Briggs tells you that she's received an urgent call from Mr Anthony Wise.'

'Yeah.'

'Did Mrs Briggs tell you she recognised his voice?'

Allinson jumps up. 'Hearsay, my Lord,' she objects.

'Not elicited to demonstrate the truth, my Lord,' responds Bateman immediately. 'In fact, just the opposite. The defence case is that if this call occurred at all, it was neither of the defendants. I'm asking the question to ascertain Mr Streeter's state of belief, not whether it was actually Mr Wise on the telephone.'

'You may continue, Mr Bateman,' rules the judge.

'Thank you. Mr Streeter, did Mrs Briggs say she recognised Mr Wise's voice?'

'No, I don't suppose she would recognise his voice. She just got a message for me to call.'

'Thank you. Did she give you the number to call?'

'I can't remember,' replies Streeter.

'When I just asked you for Mr Wise's telephone number you couldn't remember it. Did you remember it on that occasion?'

'I don't remember.'

This response causes some amusement in the packed courtroom.

'You don't remember whether you remembered?' asks Bateman, smiling.

'You're making me confused!' protests Streeter.

'I'm sorry, Mr Streeter. I'm asking what appears to me to be a simple question: when you spoke to Mrs Briggs, did she give you a telephone number with which to call Mr Wise, or were you able to remember the number that you can't, now, remember?'

'I don't rem—' starts Streeter. 'I don't recall. I 'spect she gave me the number. She'd've had it in front of her, wouldn't she?'

'Very well. So, to summarise, you can't remember but you think she probably gave you the number.'

'Yeah.'

'Which may or may not have been the number you were familiar with, when previously calling Mr Wise.'

Streeter's thin face reddens. 'Look,' he shouts, 'I don't know, all right? The bloke gave me the number and I rang it!'

Charles tugs Bateman's sleeve. 'Bloke?' he whispers. Bateman nods.

Streeter opens his mouth but clamps it shut again.

'Bloke? What bloke?' asks Bateman.

Charles notes beads of sweat emerging from Streeter's hairline.

He's scared to wipe his forehead in case it draws the jury's attention!

Charles looks over at the jury. Every one of them is watching Streeter intently.

They must have seen!

Charles watches a trickle slide down the temple to the corner of Streeter's eye. It evidently stings, as the man makes an urgent movement with his right hand to wipe it away.

'I didn't mean bloke,' he replies eventually. 'I meant Mrs Briggs. She gave me the number, and I rang it.'

'Just a slip of the tongue, was it, Mr Streeter? Confusing your secretary and bookkeeper Mrs Briggs on the telephone, with the "bloke"? Or have we stumbled across the truth?' Streeter doesn't answer. 'Well? Did you receive the instruction to ring Mr Wise from the "bloke"? And if so, what "bloke" would that have been?'

'It was Mrs Briggs. You confused me.'

'Really?' says Bateman, his voice full of disbelieving scorn. 'So, whether it was Mrs Briggs or the "bloke", they told you to throw Mr Bartlett out of a window.'

'No! That was Big Kev, and we was never asked to do nothing like that!'

Bateman has his mouth open to ask his next question but is interrupted by the Common Serjeant.

'Is that a good moment, Mr Bateman?'

Bateman clenches his teeth and forces irritation out of his expression. Charles sighs heavily. They had the witness on the ropes! He looks at the clock. It is only a minute past four.

'May I be permitted to continue for a moment or two?' asks Bateman blandly.

'Will you finish in that time?' asks the judge, equally blandly and with a smile.

'No, my Lord, that is unlikely.'

'In that case I think we'll rise. Mr Streeter, you are still on oath and you are not to speak to anyone about your evidence between now and tomorrow at ten-thirty, understand? Members of the jury, we shall rise now. I shall give you a warning which will apply for the rest of the case. You are not to speak to anyone outside of your number about the evidence at all. This case has attracted a lot of publicity and I'm sure your friends and family will be curious to know what's been going on in court. The difficulty is, if they ask questions and you start answering them, they are bound to say something in response and that might affect your minds. The decision you reach must be of the twelve of you, alone. So it's best not to speak about the case at all until it's over. Sir Leo shall have bail on condition that when not actually in court, he is either at hospital or his home address. Thank you.'

'All rise!'

CHAPTER TWENTY-THREE

Charles and Peter Bateman walk back to Chambers.

'Well done, Peter. You were very effective.'

'Thank you. Still bloody infuriated I was stopped in full flow.'

'Yes, he's given Streeter a chance to regroup. I'd lay a pound to a penny that, despite the judge's warning, Streeter is closeted with DI Woolley somewhere right now, receiving further instructions. Did you notice the way he beseeched Woolley for help?'

'No. What happened?'

'You know how witnesses in trouble sometimes look for help from the officer who took their statement?'

'Yes.'

'I may have imagined it, but I thought I detected that, and something more. Woolley's been staring at me unpleasantly even before the case started. It suggested *mala fides*.'

'Police officers glare at me the whole time,' says Bateman, laughing bitterly. 'It's their visceral dislike of defence briefs.'

'Sure, but remember, your client also thinks there's anti-Semitism at work here. Woolley gives the impression of loathing me.'

'We all loathe you, Charles,' jokes Bateman. 'Woolley's just a good judge of character.'

'Ha, ha.'

'Ever dealt with him before?'

'Never.'

'It could be common or garden anti-Semitism though, couldn't it?' suggests Bateman.

'True,' concedes Charles. 'I'm more intrigued by Streeter's reference to the "bloke". Very revealing. I think the truth slipped out there.'

'I agree. I did wonder if the "bloke" might be Woolley,' says Bateman.

'The same thought occurred to me,' agrees Charles.

'In which case, what's his motive? What's a DI from the Sweeney up to, using roughhouse tactics to evict council tenants? Where's the profit in it?'

'None, as far as I can see. He must be acting for someone else.'

'But who?' asks Bateman.

'That's the question.'

There they leave their suspicions. Charles, who has finished with Streeter and has prepared his cross-examination of the next few witnesses, heads home. He enjoys Leia's bath and bedtime routine, and is looking forward to being there for a change. Bateman heads back to Chambers and a probable late night. He wants to freshen up what's left of his cross-examination in light of the evidence already heard.

At the corner of High Holborn and Gray's Inn Road a No. 46 bus is pulling into the stop. It's less than a mile from here to Wren Street and Charles usually walks, but he's in a hurry and so jumps on. He pays his fare and remains on the boarding platform for what will only be two stops. His attention is caught by a discarded *London Evening Standard* on an adjoining seat. It's the late edition and his eyes arrest on the headline: "*Where Is Big Kev?*"

He reaches over to the newspaper, loops one arm around the pole to prevent himself from falling with the movement of the bus, and reads. Under the headline is a photograph of Sir Leo, evidently taken some time ago because he is the picture of health, and a court sketch of the robed back of a barrister as he questions someone in the witness box. The witness is clearly intended to be Kevin Streeter, but it's not a good likeness and if Charles hadn't been facing Streeter for most of the afternoon, he probably wouldn't have recognised him. He smiles, and reads with interest, disappointed that his name is not mentioned. Without referring specifically to the evidence, the article states that the police are now looking for a Mr Kevin Lane in connection with the prosecution of Sir Leo Wise, and that any member of the public with information as to Lane's whereabouts should contact DI Woolley at Savile Row Police Station. At the bottom of the page is a small photograph of Woolley leaving court. Charles wonders why this enquiry wasn't commenced weeks before, when Woolley first had Streeter's evidence.

Another little mystery.

The house is tidy and Greta has departed for the evening, having handed Leia over. Charles and Sally bathe and feed their daughter and take her upstairs to read to her for a while before settling her for bed. Then they descend to the kitchen to make a meal together.

'This is nice,' comments Charles, as they wash up afterwards. 'I could get used to this.'

'I can't tell you how much better I feel,' agrees Sally. 'I realise now, in retrospect, that every moment I was at work, I was tense with anxiety. I know Maria and Jordan would never have allowed anything bad to happen to Leia, but … I dunno.'

'I understand. And you don't feel like that with Greta?'

Sally shakes her head. 'No. She's qualified for a start, and older. But most of all, she has nothing else to distract her. I know that, when she's here, she's focused solely on Leia, and not juggling with phone calls for gig dates and hiring vans.'

'Good.'

'Have you thought any more about the wedding?'

Charles shakes his head. He and Sally did discuss it with David and Sonia, but the conversation went round and round in circles without any conclusions being reached. 'No. Still undecided about Mum and Dad.'

'And dates?'

'I had a word with Barbara. If we do go for late summer or autumn, there are plenty of gaps. I'm still quite keen to have the reception here. We can all walk from the registry office, so no problems with vehicles and so on.'

'Except for your parents, and my Mum,' Sally points out.

'Yes, but one car or even a taxi would cover that. And the garden looks so lovely.'

'I'm happy to have it here, Charlie, as long we're not doing all the cooking.'

'Of course not. We'll get caterers in.'

Having cleared up, they settle down to an hour of television before bed. NASA's Apollo 11 will launch in a few days, and British TV's coverage of the first human landing on the moon has been extensive. Charles is in the process of tuning the set to the BBC when the telephone rings. Sally picks up.

'Terminus 1525?'

'Hello, Sally, it's Peter Bateman.'

'Hello, Peter. Everything all right?'

'Yes, really sorry to phone you so late but I need a word with Charles.'

'He's just here. Hang on.' She hands the receiver to Charles. 'It's Peter.'

'Peter?' says Charles. 'Still in Chambers?'

'Yes. I apologise for disturbing your evening, but something rather unusual has occurred. You'll never guess who knocked on our door twenty minutes ago.'

'Tell me.'

'Big Kev.'

'What?' says Charles, sitting up sharply.

'He saw my name in this evening's *Standard* and came looking. He's spent the last two hours wandering around the Temple in the dark, checking names on the boards outside Chambers, and finally found me.'

'What on earth does he want?'

'Turns out, he's the giant who watched Bartlett's eviction from behind the window at Mr Martinelli's shop. The witness Billy Munday's been looking for. But there's more. I think you need to hear his story for yourself.'

'Now? Is he still there?'

'Oh, yes.'

'I can get there in fifteen minutes. Can he wait?'

Charles hears Bateman's voice change as he addresses someone else in the room. 'Can you wait quarter of an hour?'

Charles is astonished to hear a woman's voice answer. 'Yes, all right.'

'Who was that?' asks Charles.

'That's Mrs Kev. She's here too, together with Matthew. And before you ask, he's their baby. And that's a whole different story which I think you'll find equally interesting.'

Charles and Peter Bateman find it impractical to fire questions at the Lanes from their desks on opposite sides of the room. Mr and Mrs Lane keep swivelling their heads to respond, and there is an uncomfortable sense that they are surrounded by hostile interrogators, so Charles suggests they all move down to the waiting room. The armchairs and sofas are more comfortable, he can light the gas fire and they can sit in a circle, which will feel less formal. So they troop downstairs. Maude Lane, a quick little woman with intelligent eyes and a no-nonsense manner, carries the baby in a wicker basket. He is wrapped in a blanket and wearing a woollen hat, and he has been asleep throughout. Charles goes to the main kitchen next to the clerks' room and makes a pot of tea, bringing it back on a tray with four mugs.

He and Bateman fall quickly into the pattern of the latter's pupillage. Although he contributes some questions, Bateman takes over note-taking duties while Charles focuses on getting instructions. By half past ten they have been talking for almost an hour. Charles finally sits back in his seat.

'Right,' he says. 'Let me read the notes, and you can correct us if we've got anything wrong. You've worked with Kevin Streeter for about five years. Other than a part-time administrator, Mrs Briggs, it's just the two of you. One morning — you can't remember the exact day but April sometime — you're at the Wimpy in the Lyons Corner House, when a man called Hanrahan arrives. You've been told to wait for him. He and Streeter have met before, and you think he works at Bow County Court. Hanrahan tells Streeter he's got to call Tony Wise, so he goes out and uses the call box outside. Right so far?'

'Yup,' confirms Big Kev.

Charles continues, scanning Bateman's notes. 'Little Kev makes the call but you stay in the Wimpy and finish your breakfast. He comes back and says you've been told to use force on the tenants still in the development sites.' Charles turns to Bateman. 'So, that would appear to be the "bloke".'

Bateman nods. 'Seems likely. We need to get Billy onto Hanrahan asap.'

'Agreed.' Charles returns his attention to the Lanes. 'Have you ever heard Streeter talk of someone called Titmarsh? Shirley Titmarsh, also from the county court?'

Big Kev shakes his enormous head.

'Fair enough,' continues Charles. 'So, your first job is Braithwaite Street, that afternoon. You're to go to the property at a specific time —' Charles turns briefly to Bateman — 'I'll bet that's to synchronise with Woolley — but you can't go, because you have to meet Mrs Lane here at the hospital. You say you'll join him as soon as you've finished. You leave the hospital, you reckon about five. You're pretty sure it was then, because the appointment was at four and it took almost an hour. You head to Braithwaite Street. You're a little early so you pop into the corner shop when you see Woolley drive past in his private car. You know him because he nicked you as a youngster and fitted you up. You hang back inside the shop. Then you see Little Kev break into Bartlett's house, and a few moments later Bartlett comes flying through the front bedroom window. DI Woolley's sitting in his car in the shadows. As Bartlett hits the pavement, Woolley comes racing across the road. But instead of arresting Little Kev, he helps carry Bartlett to the back of the van — you don't know if he's alive or dead — and they both drive off. Have I got all that right?'

Maude Lane looks across at her husband, who nods. 'Yeah,' he confirms.

'Okay,' says Charles. 'If what you say is true, you can prove Streeter's told the court a pack of lies. It also proves links between Woolley, Streeter and Hanrahan. The question is, are you prepared to give evidence?'

282

Big Kev and his wife turn to one another on the couch. Some silent communication passes between them. It is Maude Lane who answers.

'Kev will give evidence, but there are conditions.'

'Conditions?' asks Bateman.

'We're gonna need some help.'

'If you're worried about Kev being prosecuted, the way you tell it, he's done nothing wrong,' says Charles.

'But the police are appealing for information about him, Charles,' points out Bateman.

Charles turns to his former pupil. 'You know, there's something odd about that. They've had Streeter's statement for ages. If they believe it, they'd have been looking for Big Kev here before now. According to Streeter, he's a murderer. Why haven't they?'

'Because,' intervenes Maude, 'they don't want to find him. They know the truth, and they know that my Kev'd be pointing the finger at Streeter. That'd hurt their case. It's the last thing they want.'

'But the newspaper —' points out Bateman, but Maude interrupts him.

'Woolley's been made to put out the announcement. It's the only explanation. Someone higher up who ain't in on it heard Streeter's evidence and ordered Woolley to pull his finger out. He'll never actually try to find him, see? But it's still risky for us. What if some other busybody copper arrests him? What if Kev goes in the witness box but the jury don't believe him? They could prosecute him, couldn't they?'

Charles nods. 'Yes, they could.'

'But that ain't the worst of our problems. You see, Mr Holborne, we got to think about Matthew.'

'What of him?'

'Well, see … Kevin and Streeter found him in an abandoned house. Little Kev wanted him dumped at the hospital, but we decided to keep 'im. The people at Tommy's children's department know he ain't ours but they've let us look after 'im, temporary. They've told us they'll be doing background checks. Kev ain't been in trouble for years, but he was in the past. We've already changed addresses, but we're still in London. One option is for us to take Matthew and leg it good and proper. Get away completely and keep our heads down.'

'But,' points out Bateman, 'you haven't. You're here.'

Maude continues. 'Yes. We don't want to be looking over our shoulders forever, and chances are they'd find us. Kev's face is all over the papers. And legging it would look bad. So, it makes sense to face it now, with you on our side.'

'You've thought this out,' says Charles, admiringly.

'I have,' replies Maude. 'So, Kev will go to court for you, but we need a favour in return.'

'Which is?' asks Charles.

'We want to adopt Matthew. I've asked a couple of lawyers' firms, and they reckon it could be 'undreds if not thousands to go to the High Court to get an adoption order. One refused to take it anyway, said it would be too difficult with Kevin's history. We want you to take the case, Mr Holborne.'

'That's a big ask,' replies Charles. 'And I don't do much child law.'

'Yeah, but you do do that free stuff, doncha? What do they call it, pro something? Seen your name all over the papers for it. Like that woman whose husband was killed, the RAF man. You did her case gratis, right?'

'I do *pro bono* work, that's true. But you really want someone who does this sort of law all the time.'

'Okay. Can you suggest anyone, a lawyer who does adoption work, and does it free?' asks Maude. 'If you can, we'll use them.'

Charles looks at Bateman, who shakes his head. Charles sighs. 'No, I can't. Not many of my colleagues are that public spirited,' he answers sourly.

Maude shrugs. 'There it is then.' She stands, picking up the basket containing Matthew. 'If you knock those notes up into a statement, Kev'll sign it and give evidence exactly the same. But only if you promise to take our case for adoption. You're in the directory, right?' Charles nods. 'So I'll ring 'ere tomorrow afternoon for your decision. All right? Come on, Kev. Shake a leg.'

The big man stands, towering over both Charles and Bateman, shakes hands gravely with each of them in turn, and follows his wife out of the door without another word.

CHAPTER TWENTY-FOUR

'Sorry, chaps, but I need a bacon sarnie,' announces Charles.

He, Bateman and Stephenson are once again walking up Fleet Street towards the Old Bailey. Charles volunteered to stay late in Chambers to type up and photocopy Kevin Lane's statement. Before starting with his painfully slow two-fingered typing, he telephoned Billy Munday's digs. He was a little surprised when the telephone was answered, and he immediately apologised profusely for calling so late, explaining that it was an emergency. Nonetheless the landlady refused to wake Billy and Vivienne in the basement unless a family member had been taken ill. She did however promise to give Billy a message first thing in the morning. Charles had no option but to accept the offer graciously. He got back to Wren Street well after midnight and was, as he feared, woken by Munday the following morning at six. By the time he had given Munday instructions to renew his pursuit of the corner shop proprietor and see if he could track down someone called Hanrahan who might work at Bow County Court, he was too wide awake to go back to sleep.

Despite two cups of coffee, he knows he will perform better on a full stomach.

'Come on,' he says to his companions as he pushes open a door running with condensation. "Mick's", the haunt of most criminal barristers and all Fleet Street hacks, is a London institution. It's all-day breakfast, recently the subject of a price hike but still only seven shillings and thruppence, is a magnificent pyramid of carbohydrate and cholesterol. Fried eggs, beans, sausages, bacon and chips (mushrooms optional at a shilling extra) is Charles's usual breakfast order, but on this occasion he has time only for a bacon sandwich "to go".

Peter Bateman, familiar with his ex-pupil master's unhealthy eating habits, knows Mick's well, but the look on Stephenson's face reveals that their refined solicitor does not habitually frequent greasy spoons such as this. The tall man frowns at the Formica tables, Smokey Robinson's voice blaring from the transistor radio, the steam issuing from the water boiler and the half dozen journalists tucking into their post-graveyard-shift meals. There is some conversation but most of them are engaged in the serious business of eating: jackets off, ties tucked into shirts and, in several cases, trilbies pushed back on their heads.

'Can I get you anything?' asks Charles of the others. Both shake their heads.

'Morning Mr H,' says the woman behind the counter. 'Usual?'

'No, Vera, I wish I could but I've got to run. Bacon sarnie with double brown sauce please, to go.'

'Comin' up,' she says, and she calls the order over her shoulder.

'If that's Charlie Horowitz,' returns a male voice from inside the kitchen, 'tell 'im he still owes ten bob from last week!'

'Crikey,' says Charles, embarrassed. 'You're quite right, Spence!' he calls back, and he hands Vera a pound note. 'Sorry.'

'Horowitz?' asks Stephenson of Bateman.

'I'll let him explain,' replies Bateman.

Armed with his change and a bacon sandwich, Charles hands his robes bag and briefcase to Bateman and proceeds to eat his breakfast as they walk along Fleet Street and over Ludgate

Circus. Bateman and Stephenson pretend Charles is not with them, and chat about the case.

On arrival at the court the two other men go directly to the cells to see Anthony Wise, and Charles heads to the courtroom to meet Jacquetta and Sir Leo. He is surprised to find the daughter, Hannah, waiting there as well. She is dressed in a formal two-piece trouser suit in dark blue and a plain white blouse. She looks older than her years.

'Good morning,' says Charles.

The girl looks pale and tired but she smiles warmly at him. 'Hello,' she says. 'Is it okay if I come in with Dad? I tried to get into the public gallery a couple of times but the queues are impossible.'

Charles turns to Jacquetta. 'Were you intending to come into court today? The judge hasn't objected to you acting as Sir Leo's carer, but I doubt he'd agree to two.'

'I'm happy for Hannah to go in with him. I can wait outside.'

'Sir Leo?' asks Charles, checking with his client.

The old man looks a little better today. Some colour has returned to his cheeks, he's sitting more upright in his wheelchair and he looks more alert. The facial rash has started to scab over. He reaches up to take his daughter's hand.

'I would be very happy to have my daughter beside me,' he says in his thick Austrian accent.

'Okay,' says Charles. 'Hannah, if you wheel your father in and park him where I show you, you can sit on the solicitors' bench behind me. How's your mother?'

The teenager scowls. 'I've no idea. I've moved in with friends.'

Sir Leo is still holding his daughter's hand and draws it towards him. He kisses it. 'It will be fine,' he reassures her, although Charles can see from her face that she doesn't believe it.

'Let's go in,' says Charles.

Ten minutes later, Streeter having been brought up from the cells, Peter Bateman is invited by the judge to continue with his cross-examination.

'Thank you, my Lord. Now, Mr Streeter, you have admitted to reaching an agreement with Mr Anthony Wise to use illegal force against these tenants, and you have pleaded guilty to that charge and received five years' imprisonment, is that right?'

'Yeah.'

'You did a deal with the Crown to give evidence against your co-conspirators in return for a lighter sentence.'

'I don't know about that. I said I'd tell the truth.'

'In return for a lighter sentence,' persists Bateman. Streeter does not answer. 'Did someone tell you that if you gave evidence for the Crown you'd likely receive a lighter sentence?'

'Well, they said if I assisted the police, it'd look better for me.'

'Yes, and that would result in a lighter sentence, right? I mean, Mr Streeter, there is no secrecy about this. Your own barrister asked the judge for a lighter sentence because you gave help to the police, and I have a note of the judge's sentencing remarks in which he says he gave a discount for the fact that you *did* help the police.'

'All right then, if that's how you want to put it.'

'I do. Now, who first offered this deal to you?' asks Bateman.

'I can't remember,' replies Streeter, not looking up.

'Had you met Miss Allinson or her solicitor at that stage?'

'I don't think so. I met them the first day of the trial.'

'So, someone else from the prosecution with authority to offer a deal. Who?'

'I dunno. Mr Woolley, maybe.'

Bateman points across the court at the rotund police officer sitting behind Calliope Allinson. 'Detective Inspector Woolley?'

'I dunno. Maybe.'

'If it wasn't Mr Woolley, who else could it have been?'

Streeter shrugs but does not reply.

'So, by a process of elimination, it must have been DI Woolley. Yes? Yes?' repeats Bateman, more forcefully.

'I s'pose so.'

'So, Woolley says to you: "*Kevin, if you give evidence against your co-conspirators, I can get you a deal on your sentence*"?'

'Not in those words, but something like that.'

'And you know, from that second onwards, that if you implicate Tony Wise —'

'Wassat mean?' interrupts Streeter.

'I'm sorry. If you point the finger at Tony Wise, it's to your benefit.'

'Yeah, so?'

'Which gives you a motive for lying doesn't it?'

'I ain't lying.'

'But you had a motive to lie, didn't you? The more you could shift the blame to someone else, the better it would be for you. Holding up your end of the deal.'

'That's as may be. But I'm telling the truth.'

'I suggest it actually went a bit further. DI Woolley *told you* to implicate Mr Anthony Wise in this conspiracy, didn't he?'

'No, he didn't. He said if I helped the police I'd get a lighter sentence.'

'Possibly, but he specifically told you to point the finger at Anthony Wise.'

'No. I spoke to Tony Wise on the phone. No one told me to point fingers at anyone.'

'In 1941 you were convicted of fraud, weren't you, Mr Streeter?' says Bateman, suddenly changing track.

'Yeah, so? What's that got to do with anything?'

'You were found guilty by a jury at Middlesex Assizes of thirty-one counts of using counterfeit ration vouchers to obtain butter, bread, eggs and other food, which you then sold on the black market.'

'Yeah, and I did me time.'

'Thirty-one counts of dishonesty. You pleaded not guilty, did you not?'

'Yeah.'

'But the jury didn't believe you when you gave evidence on oath, did they?'

'I guess not.'

'Incidentally, why weren't you in the Armed Forces? You were of military age.'

'Chronic asthma.'

'I see. On your release from prison in 1943 you were again convicted of six counts of burglary, bonded warehouses in the East End.'

This question makes Charles look up sharply. The young Charlie Horowitz also acquired experience stealing from bonded warehouses during the war although, in his case, he wasn't caught.

'Yeah.'

'So six more offences of dishonesty. Did you plead guilty or were you found guilty after a trial?'

'Trial.'

'So, again, you gave evidence on oath which the jury didn't believe.'

Streeter shrugs but does not answer.

'I'm not going to go through all of them, Mr Streeter, but you were then sent to prison for four years, and in the period between 1948 and 1958 you were convicted of three further offences involving dishonesty.'

'What of it?'

'Well, you see, the jury has to decide if you're an honest person. They have to decide if they can believe what you're saying about this phone call when you have a long history of lying to get yourself out of trouble, and you had a strong motive to say what the police wanted to hear. I've drawn your attention to forty offences of dishonesty when you lied before juries in the hope of being acquitted, and *they* didn't believe you. So, tell *this* jury why they should believe you now.'

Streeter turns to the jury. ''Cos I'm telling the truth,' he asserts defiantly.

The look of scepticism on the faces of half the jury members is so patent, Charles wishes he could photograph it. They wouldn't trust Streeter as far as they could throw him but, slippery as he is, none of this goes to the heart of the case. Why would he start throwing tenants from first-floor windows unless asked to? And if not by one of the Wises, then who?

'Thank you, my Lord. I have no further questions,' says Bateman, resuming his seat.

'Re-examination, Miss Allinson?' asks the judge.

'No thank you, my Lord.'

'Very well. Take Streeter down.'

The man is manoeuvred out of the witness box, across the court and up into the dock, from whence he disappears down into the cells.

'Your next witness, please, Miss Allinson?' asks the judge.

'Thank you, my Lord. Witness A please.'

After a short delay a slim woman in her forties walks towards the witness box. She has deep rings under her eyes and a pinched, drawn look to her features. She gives her oath in a shy, halting voice which is almost inaudible.

'Now, madam,' says Allinson, 'I shall be asking you some questions first. I'd be grateful if you would turn so that you are facing halfway between the judge and the jury so they can all hear you, and please keep your voice up. I believe you have written your address down for the court, is that right?'

The woman offers a slip of paper in her hand to the usher. The usher walks it to the court clerk, who records the contents, and it is then handed to the judge.

'What is your occupation, please?'

'I'm a housewife,' she answers.

'Before you moved to your current address, where did you live?'

'10 Rochester Avenue. With my two children.'

'What are their ages, please?'

'Seven and nine.'

'Were you renting at Rochester Avenue?'

'Yes, from the London Borough of Newham. I was a council tenant.'

'And how did you come to leave there?'

'A man knocked on the door. When I opened it he said he was from Wise Property. He assaulted me and dragged me out onto the pavement.'

She answers quietly and with an apparent lack of emotion.

'I'm so sorry to hear that. It must have been very frightening. Did he offer any explanation?'

'None at all.'

'What happened to your children?'

'They saw the whole thing. They ran out to me on the street. They still have nightmares about it.'

'What happened then?'

'The man boarded up the property. He wouldn't even let me go in to collect the children's coats.'

'Were you ever able to get your belongings from the house?'

'No. It's been demolished now so I assume they've all gone.'

'Thank you. Please wait there. These gentlemen will have some further questions for you.'

Charles rises. 'Are you aware that a Mr Kevin Streeter has admitted assaulting you in this way, and was sentenced by this judge to five years' imprisonment as a result?'

She shakes her head. 'No, I wasn't.'

'Did Mr Streeter cause you any injuries in the course of this eviction?'

'Yes,' replies the woman. 'He pulled out a handful of my hair with skin attached and when I tried to get back into the house he punched me on the side of the head.' Charles hears the shocked intake of breath of two of the women on the jury closest to him. 'I had bruises everywhere and suspected concussion.'

'Were you taken to hospital?'

'I was, but I discharged myself.'

'Why was that?'

'Because my kids had been taken into care, and I was desperate to find them.'

'Yes, thank you,' says Charles, resuming his seat.

'Mr Bateman?' invites the judge.

'No questions, thank you, my Lord.'

'Re-examination, Miss Allinson?' asks the judge.

'No, thank you,' replies Allinson. 'Does your Lordship have any questions of this witness?'

'No, thank you. You may depart, madam, unless one of the barristers asks now for you to remain. No? Very well. You are released. Next witness, Miss Allinson?'

'Witness B, please.'

A short middle-aged man comes into court. He wears a grey suit and carries a grey hat in his hands. Charles notes that his skin tone is also grey.

He looks like a man painted in monochrome, thinks Charles.

Witness B, known to Charles as Mueller, gives the oath in an accent less strong but not dissimilar to that of Sir Leo.

'Have you been asked to write your name on a piece of paper, sir?' asks Allinson.

'Yes, but I'm not frightened. My name is Herman Mueller and I live at 21 The Drive, London, NW11. I am a lecturer at London University, in the subject of theoretical physics.'

'Thank you, Mr Mueller.'

'Doctor, actually.'

'I apologise. Before you lived at The Drive what was your address?'

'Number 43 Rochester Avenue, London E13.'

'Please tell the jury how you came to leave that address.'

'A man came to the door. I opened it. He asked me my name and I gave it. He said something like "*You were told before*", raised his arm and hit me on the head with something hard. That is the last I remember. I woke up in hospital with a fractured skull. At the time I did not know that the event was an eviction. But when I returned to the house ten days later I found it was boarded up and secured, and I couldn't get in. Demolition had already begun.'

'Did the man gave his name?'

'No.'

'Did he say who sent him?'

'Not on that occasion.'

'Did you understand what he meant by the sentence "You were told before"?'

'Yes. I had seen the man twice before. On the first occasion he was delivering new furniture to one of my neighbours. On that occasion he was all smiles. The second time was about three weeks before he assaulted me. He came to the house with another man and told me that I had to move out within the next seven days.'

'Did he say why?'

'He didn't need to. There were only a few of us left by then. The local council and the developers needed possession to get on with the demolition and rebuilding.'

'Thank you. Please remain there.'

Charles rises. 'Dr Mueller, you mentioned that on an earlier occasion this man came to your property with someone else. Can you describe that other person?'

'He was a giant. Two metres tall, easily, and very big. Light brown hair. His face had … *starke Falten*…' Mueller raises both hands to his own face as if trying to illustrate something. 'I don't know how you would say…'

'Wrinkles?'

'Yes, but not old age wrinkles. Like folds. He looked like … *yah* … a bloodhound.'

'Thank you. Was this giant present on the day you were assaulted?'

'I don't know. I didn't see him but it is possible he was there, perhaps in their vehicle.'

'So he wasn't the man who assaulted you?'

'No, that was the smaller man. Not small, but smaller than the giant. Maybe your height but with a thin face, and dark hair.'

'Thank you. One last matter please, Dr Mueller. I'm going to show you a document.'

Charles extracts a page from his trial bundle and hands it to the usher who walks it across the court to the witness box.

'My Lord, I am showing the witness page 48 in the bundle, which is the letter to Lloyds Bank allegedly signed by Sir Leo Wise. Dr Mueller, am I right in understanding your first language is German?'

'Yes. I was born and brought up there. I came to this country in 1936.'

'If you look at that letter you will see the word "doctor", but it is not spelt as in English.'

'I see it.'

'Is the spelling you see there the one that might be expected in German?'

'Yes. That is the German spelling of the word.'

'And, a little further down, there is the word "market". That also contains a spelling error, if it were the English spelling.'

'Yes. That too is the spelling one would see in German.'

'Mr Holborne,' interrupts the judge. 'Your client is a German-speaker by birth, is he not?'

'Yes, my Lord.'

'So are you putting to this witness that that letter, which bears your client's signature, was written by a native German speaker?'

'I am.'

'You have no obligation to answer this question of course, but is it your case on behalf of Sir Leo Wise that he *did* write the letter to Lloyds Bank?'

'That is not my case.'

The Common Serjeant frowns, staring down at his notes. 'But you are at pains to demonstrate that this letter was written, and misspelled, by a German speaker?'

Before Charles can answer he feels his gown tugged from behind. Stephenson indicates with a nod of his head that Sir Leo wishes to speak to Charles.

'May I take brief instructions?'

'Certainly.'

Charles sidles along the bench and bends his head to Sir Leo.

'Do not take this further,' whispers Sir Leo fiercely.

'But —'

'You have my instructions. If you disobey them, I will dismiss you from the case immediately.'

Charles takes a deep breath. 'I think you're making a mistake. You didn't write that letter, I know you didn't. Nor did Tony. We need to create reasonable doubt —'

'I have given you my instructions.'

Charles lowers his voice further. 'I shall have to record on my brief that I have given you specific advice not to take this course, but that you insist. I will need you to sign it.'

'Do it.'

Charles returns to his seat. 'I have no further questions,' he says.

Neither Bateman nor Allinson have anything else to ask and the witness is released. Allinson is about to call her next witness when the court clerk stands and whispers something up to the judge. The Common Serjeant looks irritated but eventually nods with reluctance.

'I'm sorry, Miss Allinson, gentlemen, but I'm being asked to deal with an urgent matter. So, you may take an early lunch and we'll resume at two o'clock. Bail as before.'

The jury is led out and the barristers collect their papers.

'Chambers?' asks Bateman.

Charles looks at the clock. 'Might as well. We've the best part of two hours.' He turns to Stephenson. 'Would you like to come back to Chambers with us?'

'No, thank you,' replies the solicitor. 'I've got time to get back to the office and answer a few calls.'

'Hannah?' asks Charles.

'Seeing as Dad can't leave court, I'll take him to the public canteen, if that's okay. It'll give us some time together.'

Charles and Bateman walk back to the Temple, collecting sandwiches en route, and enter the clerks' room.

The room is quiet, with all the clerks and secretaries at their desks working industriously. Barbara looks up.

'You two are back early,' she comments.

'Long lunch,' explains Bateman.

'Mr Munday is waiting for you in your room. He said it's very urgent, and he needed to use a telephone.'

'Okay,' says Charles. 'Thank you.'

He and Bateman head straight upstairs. Billy Munday is sitting at Charles's desk, in the process of replacing the receiver on the telephone. He stands, flustered.

'Sorry Mr H … Charles,' he says, moving away from the desk.

'It's absolutely fine, Billy. What have you got for us? Pull up another chair.'

Munday pulls a notebook out of his coat pocket. 'I found Hanrahan. That was the easy bit. He's a clerk at Bow County Court. I chatted up one of the girls on the reception desk. Let me tell you, they can't stand him there! He seems to have rubbed everyone up the wrong way, and she was only too happy to dish the dirt. In fact, you two might know him. He used to be a brief.'

Charles looks up. 'Not Mike Hanrahan?'

'Yup. I was just on the phone to the Bar Council.'

'Do you know him, Charles?' asks Bateman.

'Everyone of my vintage knows him. He was convicted of some offence of dishonesty, forgery I think it was, and got himself disbarred. He's my call.'

'Yes, that's him,' confirms Munday. 'Anyway, Claire, my new best friend, tells me his probation was extended 'cos he did something naughty with a number of cases.'

'Naughty?' asks Bateman.

'She didn't know details. But she confirmed they was all possession cases. Then I got lucky. Some other woman, a senior clerk or someone, saw us talking and tore Claire off a strip. She demanded to know who I was, and was about to have me thrown out. So I told her the truth. Said I was an enquiry agent working on behalf of the two directors, trying to find out why the possession cases were never actioned. She went all quiet for a bit and then told me to come back in fifteen minutes and she'd have something for me. So I did, and she gave me this.'

Munday takes from his coat pocket a single folded sheet of paper and hands it to Charles. Charles opens it, Bateman standing and looking over his shoulder.

'It's a copy of the main court ledger from three months ago, listing all the possession actions received by the court,' breathes Charles. 'And look!' He points. 'Connelly, Mueller and Bartlett!' Charles looks up. 'Who was this woman?'

Munday shakes his head. 'Sorry, Charles. She did say, but I didn't make a note and I've been racking me brains since, and can't remember it. It was an odd name...' he tails off, blushing.

'What?' asks Charles.

'Well, you won't believe me, but ... it was ... Tit-something.'

'Titmarsh? Shirley Titmarsh?'

'Yes! That was it. Titmarsh.'

'Who's that, Charles?' asks Bateman.

'The senior clerk. Been at Bow since she was in her teens. Remember I told you? She's straight as a die, but she wouldn't answer me directly about the possession claims. So she's ready to talk to us?' Charles asks of Munday.

'Sorry, Charles, but she won't do it. Not voluntarily.'

'Then we'll subpoena her,' says Bateman firmly.

Munday intervenes. 'She gave me this on condition it never came from her. She's really frightened.'

'Of Hanrahan?' asks Charles. 'But he's a little runt.'

Munday frowns and shakes his head. 'Didn't get that impression. Someone else, I'd say.'

'This document on its own won't be enough though, will it, Charles?' asks Bateman. 'If we can't say where it came from or who gave it to us.'

Charles thinks. 'I suppose we could subpoena Hanrahan. But he's slippery as hell.'

'And if we show him the document and he says he's never seen these cases before, doesn't know anything about them, we're stuck. We can't go behind it, and the judge won't even let us put it in front of the jury.'

'Maybe.' Charles ponders some more. 'I think we have to issue a subpoena, just in case. We can do that this afternoon when Court rises, and you can serve it on Shirley tomorrow morning first thing, Billy. But tell her, from me personally, that she needn't attend unless we call her, and I'll do everything to avoid that if possible.'

CHAPTER TWENTY-FIVE

'Detective Inspector Woolley, please,' says Allinson.

The ruddy-cheeked inspector rises from behind her, fastens the middle button of his jacket and sidles out of the bench. He takes the Bible offered to him, holds it high and recites the oath in a loud voice without requiring the card. He returns the Bible to the usher, turns to the Common Serjeant and says, 'My Lord, I am Clifford Andrew Woolley, a Detective Inspector at Commissioner's Office 8, West End Central Police Station, Savile Row, W1.'

Charles studies the man as he speaks. He has a very fair complexion and sandy-coloured hair — Viking heritage probably, perhaps via Ireland or Scotland — the sort of complexion that struggles to camouflage emotion. Charles had a girlfriend once, an op room assistant at RAF Duxford, the pinkness of whose face — despite her best efforts — was an unerringly reliable indication of her state of mind (and, to her chagrin, state of arousal). This might provide an opportunity.

'Thank you, officer,' Allinson is saying. 'I think Commissioner's Office 8 is more commonly known as "The Flying Squad", is that correct?'

Charles rises to interrupt. 'My learned friend may lead this officer's evidence so far as my client is concerned. The content of his statement is undisputed.'

'Thank you, Mr Holborne,' says the judge. 'And your position, Mr Bateman?'

'The same as my learned friend's.'

The Common Serjeant frowns. 'I don't wish to tell you your job, Mr Bateman, but may I remind you of the second interview of your client, as recorded by this officer? Is there no challenge to that?'

The judge is being careful not to mention before the jury that Anthony Wise allegedly admitted telling Mr Streeter to use force against the tenants.

'I'm grateful for your Lordship's caution but, as I say, there is no dispute concerning the content of those interviews.'

The judge raises his eyebrows in surprise and makes a note in his red book. 'Very well. Miss Allinson, that confirmation should make your job somewhat quicker. Not to mention easier. You may lead the witness.'

Allinson, equally surprised, nods, and proceeds swiftly to take Woolley through a summary of his investigation, including his enquiries at the county court, his arrest of the Wises and their interviews, and the accountancy evidence which demonstrates the parlous nature of the company's finances. Woolley answers all her questions simply and without embellishment, every now and then watching the judge's pen to make sure he isn't going too fast, and smiling occasionally at the jury.

He's good, thinks Charles. *I'll need to be careful.*

Allinson resumes her seat.

'No questions, Mr Holborne?' asks the judge, expecting none.

'A couple, if you please, my Lord,' replies Charles, standing. 'You told us a moment ago, Inspector, that you made enquiries of the Bow County Court for evidence of formal, lawful, possession proceedings brought by Newham against these tenants.'

'That's right.'

'Do your usual duties often bring you into contact with county court staff?'

'No, my Lord,' replies Woolley, addressing the judge. He turns to explain to the jury. 'County courts deal with civil matters, not criminal.'

'Before you made your enquiries, were you aware of how county courts administer possession claims?'

Charles watches the officer's eyes narrow slightly as he tries to work out where this line of questioning is heading. There is a minute hesitation. If he says he is familiar with county court procedures, he might face a series of questions which demonstrate that he isn't. He takes what looks like the safest line.

'Not really, my Lord.'

'So, I assume you spoke to somebody at the court who knew exactly what records should exist, if an action had been started?'

'That's right, my Lord.'

'Who was that person?'

'I'm afraid I don't remember. To be honest, I thought this was a red herring. Even if possession actions were started at some point, that wouldn't have prevented the Wises from deciding to short-circuit them and use force against tenants in the way. I was passing the court one afternoon and thought I'd drop in. I went to the main desk, showed my identification, and asked them to look up if there had been cases issued against Witnesses A and B or Mr Bartlett. I was told "no". I saw no need to pursue it further.'

'You took no statement from the court official?'

'No. The way I saw it, my Lord, it was no part of my job to prove a negative, especially when it was a throwaway line by *him*,' and Woolley indicates Anthony Wise in the dock with a jut of his rounded chin.

'Can you remember if the official to whom you spoke was a man or a woman?'

'No, my Lord. I make literally dozens of enquiries every week, many of which go nowhere. It's not possible to remember everyone I speak to.'

'I see,' says Charles. 'I have a photocopy here of the entry ledger maintained by the Bow County Court which records all incoming post. Not actions issued; post *received*. I have made copies.'

He hands them to the usher who distributes them to the judge and other barristers.

'If you run your finger down that list, Inspector, you will find several entries starting with "the London Borough of Newham". The list is maintained by the name of the plaintiff, see? And if you run your finger along the page, you will see that three of the proposed defendants were Witnesses A and B, and Mr Bartlett.'

The officer doesn't answer immediately. Charles watches his chubby finger slide down the list and then across the page. 'I can see their names, my Lord, but I am sure that no possession orders were made.'

'I agree, Inspector. For some reason, the progress of the claims was delayed. They were never issued by the court. But it would be wrong to say that none were sent to the court, wouldn't it?'

'So it appears, my Lord.'

Charles continues. 'When Miss Allinson opened the case, she told the jury that Anthony Wise was lying when he claimed that possession proceedings were posted to the county court. This document suggests he was telling the truth, doesn't it?'

'If it's accurate, my Lord, that would appear to be right.'

So far so good.

Charles studies Woolley's face. The inspector has adopted a bland, friendly expression, his head tilted slightly to one side as he awaits Charles's next question with patience, but his creamy skin is pinker than it was a moment ago. Bateman looks up at Charles, who is still hesitating. They have three pieces of a jigsaw, Woolley, Hanrahan and Streeter, but Charles has no idea what picture they create or how they fit together. He has to ask Woolley about the events at Braithwaite Street — his professional rules insist that he does, because an allegation of impropriety against Woolley has to be put to him, to allow him to respond — but going in completely blind is more than extremely risky; it's forensic kamikaze. Charles decides instead to throw a cat amongst the pigeons. He watches Woolley's face carefully as he asks his question.

'You told Mr Hanrahan, a clerk at the county court, to bury these possession claims, did you not?'

Woolley doesn't answer immediately. His face assumes a puzzled expression but in the instant before he mastered it, Charles saw a flicker of shock in his eyes.

Bullseye!

'I don't think I know anyone called Hanrahan,' replies the inspector.

'Really? You've never heard of Michael Hanrahan, former barrister, now disbarred, presently working as a clerk at Bow County Court?'

'Sorry, my Lord. I have never heard of the gentleman.'

'The Defence will be calling evidence to the effect that you know him very well. Where'd you suppose we got this list?' says Charles quietly, brandishing the document in his hand.

Charles has framed this question very carefully. He has not positively asserted that the list came from Hanrahan or that the Defence will actually be calling him, as to do so would be to mislead the court. He has merely asked a question and left the implication hanging. His purpose is deliberately to create the suspicion in Woolley's mind that Hanrahan has changed sides.

Woolley opens his mouth to reply but thinks better of it. His face turns a shade pinker and his eyes dart about the courtroom, first towards the back of the court and then up at the public gallery.

Who's he looking for? Even if we could call Hanrahan, he wouldn't be in court now.

Woolley's eyes finally settle and he turns to the judge. 'Like I say, my Lord, I don't know anyone called Hanrahan.'

'Wasn't he the official to whom you spoke at Bow?'

'No.'

'But how do you know, Inspector? You tell us you can't remember who you spoke to at the court or even if it was a man or woman. So it could have been Michael Hanrahan, couldn't it?'

Woolley looks rattled. A faint sheen of sweat has appeared on his pink forehead. 'Well, my Lord … I … I suppose I might have spoken to someone called Hanrahan, but I wouldn't have known his name. And I certainly didn't tell him or anyone else to bury possession claims.'

Time to go in for the kill.

'Detective Inspector Woolley: you did more than bury the possession claims. I suggest you buried Mr Bartlett.'

'What?' replies Woolley, frowning and apparently mystified. He looks to the judge and is met with a similar expression. Everyone in the courtroom is wondering if Charles misspoke or, perhaps, is joking.

He's trying to buy himself time.

'You heard me correctly, Inspector. I am suggesting that you assisted Kevin Streeter to dispose of the body of Edward

Bartlett after you watched Streeter throw him from the window at Braithwaite Street.'

The charge, now clarified, is so astonishing, so outrageous, that it causes a collective intake of breath in the courtroom. Like a sudden gust of wind through a forest, whispered conversations break out in the public gallery.

'Silence in court!' shouts the Common Serjeant, for the first time revealing something beneath the urbane exterior. 'I will not have the evidence disrupted in this way!' He turns to Charles. 'Mr Holborne! Are you actually accusing this officer of being an accessory to murder? You'd better have some evidence upon which to make such an assertion or you'll be in seriously hot water!'

'I make the assertion on instructions, my Lord, and there will be evidence called to support it.'

The judge continues to glare at Charles. Eventually he sits back and makes a note. 'Very well. You'd better continue.'

However the disruption has diverted attention from Woolley for a moment, and his face is again a blank slate.

'That is a completely false assertion, my Lord,' he says calmly. 'I did nothing of the sort.'

'You understand, Inspector, that I am obliged to put this to you,' says Charles. 'I suggest you were aware that Streeter was going to Braithwaite Street because you either organised it or were told of it in advance.'

Woolley turns to the judge to address him directly. 'Not true, my Lord.'

'I suggest you went there and hid your car in the shadows while Streeter entered the property.'

'Not true.'

'I then suggest that when Streeter ejected Mr Bartlett from the first-floor window, you ran across the street and, instead of arresting him, you helped Streeter place Bartlett inside Streeter's van.'

'That's a lie.'

'You then drove off with Streeter in the van, and that was the last anyone saw of Mr Bartlett. Alive or dead.'

'Complete nonsense.'

Without a further word, Charles silently resumes his seat. He senses Bateman next to him about to rise and puts a gentle restraining hand on his former pupil's forearm. He wants the silence to lengthen. He wants the jury, the public and the journalists present to be forced to reflect on the allegation just made.

For the first time since the trial began there has been revealed a tantalising possibility, an astonishing allegation; one that, if true, would turn the case on its head. He watches them asking themselves: could a member of the Flying Squad actually be implicated in a murder? There isn't a Londoner alive unaware of Met corruption; it's endemic. The Sweeney skims the profits of the very criminals they are supposed to catch; the "Dirty Squad" (formally known as the "Obscene Publications Squad") have an agreement with the principal Soho pornographers, Humphreys and Silver, to turn a blind eye in return for a share of the spoils. There is barely a police station in the Metropolis without an officer or two, often more, being paid by the Krays for information on a daily basis. Indeed, in recent memory, corrupt Met Police officers, hand-in-hand with the Kray twins and their political associates, contrived the cover-up of a paedophile ring to protect the abusers, gangsters and senior politicians on both sides of the political divide. However, the possibility that the court will hear evidence that a senior Flying Squad officer was an accomplice to murder is nothing short of sensational.

For a few seconds the only sound that can be heard is the feverish scratching of journalists' pens. Bateman allows five seconds to pass, then ten. Finally he rises.

'I have no cross-examination on behalf of Anthony Wise,' he says.

The judge addresses the prosecutor. 'Miss Allinson?'

She rises slowly, frowning. 'The Crown is in this difficulty, my Lord. We had no notice of this allegation — I'm not suggesting that Mr Holborne had any duty to make us aware, as we all know the rules don't work that way — but the fact is that, other than the bald allegation, an astonishing allegation, that DI Woolley was in some way involved in the death of Mr Bartlett, the Crown has nothing upon which to re-examine. The witness completely denies the allegation, and until some evidence is put before the court, there is nothing more I can do. I think, after reflection, my position is that I have no further questions for the witness at this stage, but I reserve the Crown's right to re-call DI Woolley later in the case if and when some actual evidence is produced by the Defence.'

'Yes, Miss Allinson, I can see no possible argument against that. Very well, Inspector, you may stand down for the present and return to your seat. And, before you object, Mr Holborne or you, Mr Bateman, I am not going to require the inspector to remain outside while the rest of the evidence is called. I'm going to assume you knew of these allegations and were content to have him sit in court while other witnesses gave their evidence, and I'm not disposed to allow you to change tack now. Right, who's next?'

'Detective Constable Truman, please,' replies Allinson.

As the remaining prosecution witness is called from outside court, the Common Serjeant addresses Charles.

'Is your position regarding this witness the same as that for his inspector? In other words, may Miss Allinson lead the witness through his evidence in chief?'

'Yes, my Lord, that is our joint position.'

'Excellent.'

DC Truman is a slim, rather elegant man wearing what looks like a bespoke suit with a modern cut. This is unusual for a copper. Charles can usually detect Flying Squad officers in an instant; they are considerably more scruffy than most of the gangsters they are paid to apprehend.

Allinson guides Truman through his evidence simply, asking leading questions and obtaining "Yes" and "No" answers, and within ten minutes she has sat down again.

Charles bobs up briefly with 'No questions, thank you, my Lord,' and Peter Bateman gets to his feet.

'As I understand it, officer,' he starts, 'you were present during all of the interviews but simply acted as scribe. You didn't ask any questions yourself.'

'That's right,' replies the young policeman.

'Sir Leo answered all questions with "No comment".'

'Yes.'

'And so did Anthony Wise, during his first interview, at which his solicitor was present.'

'Yes, my Lord, that's right.'

'But he subsequently asked to be interviewed again, in the absence of his solicitor, and this time he did answer questions.'

'Yes.'

'So, during the second interview you'd have had a much better opportunity to form an opinion of him.'

'Well, my Lord, I was only there to take notes of what was said.'

'Yes, you were something of an onlooker. Taking notes, it is correct, but watching the interplay between your boss and Mr Wise.'

'I suppose that's true, to an extent, my Lord.'

'And during the course of that interview, what was your impression of Anthony Wise?'

'I don't know what you mean, sir.'

'DI Woolley read the interview to us. In it he described Mr Wise "rocking". Did you see that?'

'Yes, my Lord, I did witness that.'

'Can you describe it for us please?'

'Well, my Lord, he was sitting in the chair opposite us and was rocking backwards and forwards.'

'A little? A lot?'

'Nothing very much at the beginning but as he became more distressed, it looked as if he might end up banging his head on the desk. That was when DI Woolley asked if he was all right.'

'Had you ever seen anything like that before, when conducting an interview?'

'No, never. In fact I'd never seen anyone act like that before.'

'Thank you. And I believe he was making a noise at the same time, wasn't he?' asks Bateman.

'Yes. A sort of whining noise.'

'Can you describe it for us?'

Truman thinks for a moment before answering. 'One of my colleagues has a younger brother who is … mentally defective. He's nineteen but he has the intellect of a five-year-old. When he's in a car he makes, well, engine noises I suppose you'd call it. He does it with the vacuum cleaner and washing machine as well. It was a bit like that.'

'Did this surprise you? In the case of Mr Wise?'

'Well, it was quite a performance.'

'"Performance"? You thought it was an act then?' asks Bateman.

'Well, I couldn't square it with the fact that this bloke was supposed to have a massive IQ and was director of a public limited company. I mean…'

Truman raises an arm and gestures towards the dock. All eyes in the court follow. Anthony Wise is sitting on the bench in the dock rocking slightly from the waist, his hands clamped over his ears. Now that the court is quiet he can be heard making a little squeaking noise with every exhalation.

'Is that the sort of thing you saw during the interview?' asks Bateman.

'Yes, although it got a lot louder, like he was trying to drown out the questions. And, he wouldn't make eye contact with us, even when DI Woolley insisted. It made him even more distressed, so we stopped asking.'

'And I think one of you, either you or Mr Woolley, expressed the opinion that Mr Wise was preparing the ground for an insanity defence?'

Truman colours slightly and looks embarrassed. 'I don't … I apologise, my Lord. I'm not sure if that was recorded anywhere in the interviews but it is something we wondered about. Perhaps it was mentioned to Mr Stephenson. It did seem very odd.'

'Mr Bateman,' intervenes the Common Serjeant, 'please have a word with your client and get him to settle down.'

'There's nothing I could say, my Lord, that would assist, I'm afraid. Mr Wise suffers from a condition which makes it psychologically painful for him to be the subject of attention like this. Your Lordship may be hearing some medical evidence on that in due course. When the focus of the case moves away from him, I hope he'll be less distressed.'

'That's not going to be easy, is it?' scoffs the judge, evidently irritated. 'He's the bl— the accused!'

The judge managed to prevent himself from inserting the word "bloody" before "accused" but everyone in the court heard it nonetheless. Someone in the public gallery snickers before being shushed.

Bateman thinks better of replying and resumes his seat.

Allinson rises. 'Subject to my last comment, my Lord, that is the Crown's case.'

'Thank you, Miss Allinson. Now,' the Common Serjeant looks at the clock, which informs him that it is five minutes to four, 'I don't think I'll ask you to open your case this afternoon, Mr Holborne, but let's get a prompt start at ten o'clock on Monday. I repeat my warning to you. Bail as before.'

'All rise!'

Charles and Bateman gather their papers.

'I'm going down to the cells to see if Tony's okay,' says Bateman. 'All right if I take Andrew with me?' he asks, pointing behind them to Stephenson.

'No, that's fine. I'll grab a conference room for me and Sir Leo.'

Charles heads out of court, Hannah Wise wheeling her father after him. Their court having risen slightly earlier than the others, they find a conference room without difficulty. Charles slides the "Engaged" sign across the door and sits opposite his client.

'How are you feeling?'

'Not too bad. But I'd like a cup of tea if that's possible. Would you mind, Hannah?'

'Sure, Dad.'

The young woman rises and slips out of the room.

'Here we are again,' starts Charles. 'Not for the first time, I find myself in the uncomfortable position of giving you advice which I think you're going to ignore.'

He points to his brief and the earlier endorsement on it which Sir Leo signed. Where clear advice is given to a client who refuses to accept it, it is essential for the barrister to protect his back by having his warnings reduced to writing and signed by both parties, particularly when the decision may result in the client dying in a prison cell.

'As you have already said, this is my case and you are my mouthpiece,' replies Sir Leo with a smile. The smile is cut short by a wince of pain as he sits back in his wheelchair.

'Yes, of course, that's right,' confirms Charles. 'But it's my duty to do the best I can for you, and lay out your options. If you choose to ignore them, that's up to you.'

'Options? What options?'

Charles leans forward. The old man has more colour in his cheeks and is less breathless than in the days immediately after his chemotherapy, but he is still obviously very unwell. The flesh on his face has shrunk and the planes of his skull are clearly visible. His hands, too, look skeletal; bones with a paper-thin skin covering.

He should be in hospital, thinks Charles, *or at least at home in bed. These are his last weeks. Maybe days.*

'The Crown's case is complete. Allinson may try to recall Woolley but even if she does, his evidence won't affect you. I can tell you in all honesty that you are in as good a position as anyone could be in these circumstances. I'm almost certain that a submission of no case to answer would succeed, even with this judge.'

'How certain?'

'Perhaps as high as eighty-five per cent. The high watermark of the Crown's case against you is the letter written to Lloyds Bank, but it simply doesn't go far enough to prove you were part of a conspiracy to use *force*. I'd like you to instruct me to make that submission. If successful, the case against you will end.'

'But not against Tony.'

Charles shakes his head. 'No, obviously not. Streeter's evidence has been significantly damaged, but he didn't retract his assertion that it was Tony who gave the orders. Tony has no choice but to give evidence that it wasn't him.'

'I know you're not representing him but, in your opinion, what are his chances of acquittal?'

'That's more difficult to call. There are still a lot of moving parts. If Big Kev gives evidence as promised that will further damage Streeter's evidence, perhaps fatally. But it doesn't go directly to contradict his assertion about the phone call. We can raise quite a dust storm regarding the other players, Hanrahan and Woolley, but we're still struggling to prove a motive for why they'd frame Tony.'

'So? What are Tony's chances?'

Charles considers. 'I think definitely better than fifty-fifty, but perhaps not as much as seventy-five twenty-five.'

Sir Leo spreads his hands, palms up. 'In that case, do not make the submission. I will give evidence.'

'And say that it was you, on the phone?' Sir Leo smiles enigmatically but doesn't reply. 'As I've pointed out before, the jury may not believe it.'

'That's a chance I will take. Faced with Tony saying he only admitted it to protect me, and me accepting I gave the order, I think the result will be clear.'

Charles nods. He points to his brief. He has written a second block of text underneath the title "*The Queen versus Sir Leo Wise*".

'This summarises my advice, which is, firstly, to allow me to make a submission of no case to answer and, secondly, not to give evidence.'

Sir Leo leans forward, opens his hand to borrow Charles's pen, and signs. Hannah returns, with a tray carrying three cups of tea.

'Thank you,' says Charles. He watches Sir Leo's hand as it crawls slowly and effortlessly across the page, signing and dating his signature. 'I have one further suggestion,' he says.

'Yes?' replies Sir Leo.

'Under normal circumstances, because your name is first on the indictment, you would give evidence first. I want to suggest that you instruct me to tell the court that you are not going to give evidence at all. In that case Tony will be the first Defence witness. If it goes badly, and you still insist on taking the blame, you can change your plea at that stage without having to give evidence. On the other hand, if it goes well, you'll have kept your powder dry.'

Sir Leo hands Charles's fountain pen back to him. 'If I agree, is there any risk to Tony? Will it look worse for him?'

Charles shrugs. 'I can't think of any.'

'Let me think about it over the weekend.'

'Fair enough.'

Charles moves his case papers from the table to the floor. He sees Hannah looking questioningly at him. He laughs. 'I used to get told off by my pupil master for having drinks on the desk while reading his papers,' he explains. 'I know these are all photocopies, not originals, but the habit stuck.'

As he says this he sees, at the top of the pile of documents by his foot, the copy ledger Billy Munday obtained at the county court. Something catches his eye. He bends to pick it up.

It is indeed a photocopy, but at the foot of the page is something he hadn't spotted before. In black ink is written the words: "*Navy 2162*". Charles turns the page over: blank. He examines the writing more closely. The numbers are very slightly smudged, as if before the ink was dry a sleeve was brushed over them, or perhaps the document was placed beneath another.

'What is it?' asks Hannah.

'It says "Navy 2162".'

'Meaning?' asks Sir Leo.

Charles shakes his head. 'Haven't a clue. It might be nothing. Sometimes when I'm loading the photocopier I accidentally use a piece of paper that already has writing on the back. But the words have definitely been written by hand. I'm wondering if, perhaps, they're a message from Shirley Titmarsh.'

CHAPTER TWENTY-SIX

It is a beautiful Saturday morning in July. The weather is so warm that Charles has been able to open the folding doors onto the garden so he and Sally can eat breakfast in the fresh air. Leia, now almost seven months old, sits in her highchair, babbling to herself and playing with, rather than eating, the mashed banana on her tray.

Sally stands and knocks back the last of her coffee. 'If you don't mind clearing up here, I'll get madam de-glooped,' she says, pointing at Leia. The child's fingers and hair are covered in mashed banana. 'She's going to need a bath.'

'Sure,' says Charles.

'What time are we expected at Sunshine Court?' asks Sally, lifting Leia out of her chair.

'I didn't specify a time, but it'll be lunchtime by the time we get there. They start moving them into the dining room at a quarter to twelve. But I can feed Mum and talk to Dad at the same time. Then a pub lunch in Hampstead, maybe?'

'Have you decided what you're going to say?'

'Pretty much.'

An hour later Charles and Sally step out of the lift onto Remembrance just as lunch is being served. The smell of institutional cooking mixes unpleasantly with the fainter but persistent odour of incontinent dementia patients. Charles immediately spots his parents sitting at a table in the dining room with two others. Their table has yet to be served. He walks across the room, Leia in his arms, greeting carers as he goes.

'Hello Mum, Dad,' he says as he arrives at their table. '*Good Shabbos.*'

Millie is staring, unfocused, out of the window at the tops of the trees that line the large gardens. She does not move or acknowledge Charles. Harry on the other hand looks up immediately.

'Charles, my boy,' he says enthusiastically. 'And two of my favourite girls,' he adds. '*Good Shabbos* to you too.'

Charles bends to kiss his father's cheek. Harry smells of shampoo and, somewhat surprisingly, aftershave. He is wearing a clean shirt and what look like his suit trousers, held up with braces. He eats well enough here, but not as well as he did in his own home when Millie (and, latterly, the home help) did the cooking. He has lost weight. Nonetheless he looks well and better groomed than usual. Charles strokes his father's soft cheek admiringly.

'Nice shave, Dad. Looking very dapper this morning,' he says, teasing.

Harry raises his good arm and points to one of the carers who is dispensing plates at an adjoining table. 'June,' he says. 'She's new, and very patient.'

'Well done, June,' comments Charles.

He bends to kiss his mother's cheek but she does not acknowledge his touch.

'Hello, Sally,' says Harry, gripping her hand gently. 'Lovely as always.'

Sally pulls up two unoccupied seats, sitting in one. Charles takes the other.

'May I?' asks Harry, opening his arms for Leia. Charles hands her to his father, careful to make sure she is sitting comfortably on his lap and that Harry has a good hold of her.

'How's Mum?' he asks quietly.

Harry nods ruefully and pulls an expression which Charles knows means "*What can you do?*" In other words, not great but no worse.

'But we had a good singsong yesterday, didn't we, Millie?' says Harry. He turns back to Charles and Sally. 'That chap with the keyboard? The one who used to do weddings and bar mitzvahs. Your mother was up, singing along. All the words, she remembers, from 1930 in some cases! But when the music stops, she's gone again.' He sighs heavily and changes subject. 'Have you met Alice?'

He indicates the lady to his left. She is elderly, of an age with Charles's parents, and overdressed in a very smart two-piece suit, a pearl necklace and an astonishing dark hairpiece perched on top of her own grey hair. She doesn't look up at the introduction.

'And this is Mr Pelletier,' says Harry, gesturing across the table. 'My son, Charles, and his … his … wife, Sally.'

The man sitting across from Harry fiddles with his hearing aid, but seems nonetheless to have heard Harry, because he immediately smiles and offers a wrinkled hand to Charles, who takes it.

'Jean-Luc,' corrects the Frenchman.

Charles remembers that Pelletier has just celebrated his 100th birthday. 'I've heard a lot about you,' he says. 'You're next door to Mum and Dad, I believe.'

'I am. Your father is an excellent bridge player,' he says in perfect English but with a French accent.

'You're playing bridge again, Dad? That's great!'

Before Millie's dementia became undeniable, she and Harry were stalwarts of the synagogue's Bridge Club, often playing twice a week.

The carers deliver four meals to the table and Charles offers to feed his mother to allow them to help other residents. Harry hands his granddaughter back to Sally and eats unaided, but slowly, stopping frequently to talk to Sally. He always remembers their conversations, listens to her current concerns, in particular the juggling required of her to balance her career with motherhood, and asks intelligent, sympathetic questions.

Charles loves him for it. Millie took offence at most of Charles's life choices, particularly his rejection of her religion and culture and his choice of non-Jewish partners, but her dementia has, finally, defeated her anger. The Alzheimer's has left holes in her brain, and one appears to be where her bitterness used to reside. Harry, silent for years in the face of Millie's antagonism, is now able to express his own feelings. Of course, he remains disappointed that Charles will never be married under the *chuppah* and that Leia will not grow up in a Jewish household. However, in the end, his son's happiness is more important to him, and it is evident to all that Charles is happier now than he has ever been. Harry is able to take joy in that, and he has a special soft spot for Leia, his only granddaughter.

Charles finishes feeding his mother and he and Sally chat with Harry while they wait for the dinner plates to be removed. The Frenchman opposite Harry tries several times to attract the attention of a carer but is unsuccessful. Charles notices his frustration.

'Can I help?' he asks.

'I want to go back to my room.'

'No trifle or ice cream?'

Pelletier shakes his head. 'I need to rest.'

Charles stands. 'I'll take you, if you like,' he says.

'Yes, please.'

He pulls the old man's chair from the table and helps him to stand. Charles casts around for Pelletier's wheelchair but can't see it. 'Did you have a wheelchair? Or a walking frame, maybe?' he asks.

'The frame was here,' says the Frenchman, pointing to the empty space beside his seat, 'but I think someone borrowed it. Here, give me your arm. Go slowly, and I'll be fine.'

Charles walks the old man painfully towards the lobby which serves his and the Horowitzes' suites. Charles pushes open the door with his foot.

'Jesus!' he exclaims.

The room has been ransacked. It looks very like Millie and Harry's room did the previous month. The dressing table drawers have all been pulled out and the contents tipped on the carpet. The wardrobe doors are open and the clothing inside has been shoved on its hangers to one end of the rail. There are papers, books and documents everywhere on the floor.

'Is this —' starts Charles.

'Normal? No.'

Pelletier is breathing heavily and his entire body has started to tremble. Charles is suddenly worried for him. He looks around for somewhere to allow the old Frenchman to sit or lie down that won't interfere with any police investigation.

'Armchair,' wheezes the old man, apparently reading Charles's mind. Charles lowers him slowly into the chair closest to the door. 'Thank you.'

'You know, I begin to think this isn't another confused resident,' says Charles. 'Twice in the space of six weeks, and always this suite of rooms?'

'This is no coincidence,' says Pelletier.

'I'll get one of the carers to call the police,' says Charles, making to leave the room.

'No, wait!' orders Pelletier. 'Please, Charles, do something for me first.'

Charles hesitates. 'I don't think we should touch anything before the police arrive,' he counsels.

'I need you to look under the bed. There are drawers there, on casters. Just look and see if they have been moved, will you? Please!' he insists urgently. 'It's very important.'

Charles draws a deep breath, reluctant, but takes a couple of steps back into the room and crouches down. Careful not to touch anything, he peers under the bed. 'There are two large drawers here with brass handles on the front. They seem to be in place.'

'Good. And underneath them?' asks Pelletier anxiously.

Charles looks more closely. 'Yes, I can see something else. It's … actually I'm not sure what it is. It looks like a picture, wrapped up.'

'Take it out. They can't have found it, but I need to be sure.'

Using his arm and the back of one hand to hold the drawers in place, Charles slides the item from under the bed. It is larger and lighter than he supposed. Kneeling on the carpet, he now has in his hands a board approximately six foot by three foot, covered in what looks like an old felt curtain.

'Do you want me to unwrap it?' he asks.

'Yes, please.'

Charles does so. Inside the cloth is a cork board with a frame, almost completely covered by an enormous map of the world. Stuck into the map are dozens of blue and red drawing pins highlighting towns and cities, the majority in South America, a handful in the Middle East, and others dotted about the globe. Around the periphery of the board are pinned index cards, each headed by a name and full of spidery handwriting in French.

'My hobby,' says Pelletier from behind him.

Charles stares at the map. 'My brother mentioned it to me. You have a very interesting hobby, Monsieur Pelletier. You're a Nazi hunter!' breathes Charles, struggling to believe what he is seeing.

'Not hunter, but tracker, yes. It's not really a hobby, more an obsession. It is the work of my life — or what is left of it. Sometimes I think it's the only reason I stay alive.'

'Do you think it's possible that whoever did this to your room was looking for this?'

'Yes, I do think it's possible.'

'But, with respect, surely the authorities don't require the services of centenarian Frenchmen to track these people down?'

'The British authorities stopped looking years ago. But the Israelis are a different matter. I had two very nice young men visit me from Tel Aviv only last week. Of course my information may only be helpful occasionally, but I have contacts all over the world who feed me titbits, gossip, sightings and so on, which the authorities may or may not otherwise hear.'

Charles turns and points to the pins. 'What's the difference between red and blue?' he asks.

'Red means confirmed identifications and the relevant organisations informed. Blue means sightings or other evidence, but not yet confirmed.'

'Is one of these blue pins for Adolf Eichmann?' asks Charles, pointing at a pin in Argentina.

'No. That monster has been caught and tried, thank God. No, once they're apprehended I remove them.'

'None hiding here, then?' says Charles with a smile, pointing to the UK where there are no pins in the map.

'Nazis? No. But many sympathisers. I have a separate file on them. It's that brown one on the floor, by the mirror, if you want to look,' says Pelletier, pointing to a brown concertina file tied with string. Charles knows that he shouldn't touch it, but his curiosity is too great. He picks it up. The string is still tied which suggests that the burglars did not discover it or, if they did, they might have been interrupted before it was opened. He unties the string.

The file has been maintained carefully and is divided into alphabetical sections "A to F", "G to L" and so on. Charles lifts a document out at random and finds himself looking at a photograph of a senior member of the royal family.

'Really?' he asks, holding up the photograph to show Pelletier.

'Very strong evidence. He was a major funder of Oswald Mosley's British Union of Fascists, and a close friend of William Joyce. You know William Joyce?'

'Lord Haw-Haw.'

'*Oui*, Lord Haw-Haw. Of course once the Germans were defeated the Duke furiously denied any admiration for Hitler. But it is well-documented. The proof is in there.'

Charles replaces the photograph and takes out another document from the same section. 'Who's this?' he asks.

He is holding a large black and white photo of a man wearing hunting clothes. He stands on a heather moor in the Scottish Highlands, a rifle over his shoulder. The man looks vaguely familiar. Charles turns it over. On the back is written: "*Gilly Hamilton, April 1934, Balmoral.*"

'Gilly Hamilton?' he asks.

'Have you heard of the Earl of Menteith?'

'The banker? Yes, of course.'

'Same man. Gilbert Hamilton, the seventh Earl of Menteith,' explains Pelletier. 'He still controls the bank, but he spends most of his time — and makes most of his money — from property development.'

'And he was involved with the Nazi movement here?' asks Charles, puzzled.

'He was a member of the party, and close friends with the Duke. That was the man who used parliamentary privilege to allege a corrupt link between Sir Leo Wise and Keith Joseph, the former Minister for Housing. When they challenged him to repeat the statement outside the House of Lords, and be sued for libel, he went quiet.'

'Sir Leo and Keith Joseph?' says Charles, a suspicion forming. 'This is the supposed "Jewish Mafia"?'

'Yes, of course,' replies Pelletier, looking puzzled. 'Your case, yes?'

'You know about my case?'

Pelletier smiles. 'Your father is very proud of you. He talks about you a lot.'

'Yes, the contract for the tower blocks…' Charles's voice falters. He is staring at the photograph in his hand, his mind racing. 'Is Hamilton, by any chance, a Freemason?' he asks.

'That, I don't know. It wouldn't surprise me, as the Duke is. Why?'

Charles hurriedly replaces the photograph in the file and re-ties the string. 'Thank you, Jean-Luc,' he says. 'You've given me an idea. Do you want me to call the police now?'

'Yes, please.'

He rushes from the room to the office where the shift leader sits at her desk. He tells her what he has seen and she rises immediately and hurries towards Pelletier's room. Charles returns to the table where his parents are being served ice cream. He bends to speak in Sally's ear.

'I've got to go.'

Sally looks up. 'But what about your parents? And the discussion?'

'Jean-Luc Pelletier's room has been ransacked. The police are being called. I think it might have something to do with the Wise case. I need to contact Billy Munday urgently. It shouldn't take me long, and I might even get back before the police arrive. But I've just had an epiphany, and it's really important!'

Sally lowers her voice. 'And getting married isn't?' she hisses, annoyed.

Charles grabs a chair and sits hurriedly. 'Dad,' he says. 'Sally and I want to get married.'

'Charles!' protests Sally, swiping his shoulder.

Harry turns toward them, a spoonful of ice cream halfway between the table and his mouth. '*Mazeltov*,' he says. 'About time.'

'So, will you come? It won't be in a *shul*.'

'Of course we'll come.'

'Mum too?'

'If she's well enough, of course. If not, she'll be fine here.'

Charles turns to Sally. 'See? Easy.'

Sally's lips are compressed in a thin line and her colour is rising. She looks angry, about to explode. Then, against all Charles's expectations, she shakes her head woefully and sighs.

'You're never gonna change, are you, Charlie? Work is always gonna come first.'

'No,' he assures her with sincerity. 'Not always. But sometimes, yes. I'm sorry, Sal. It's just who I am.'

She leans forward and kisses him gently on the lips. 'Go on then. Bugger off. But don't forget we're still here, right? You better come back and get us, Charlie, or there really will be trouble.'

CHAPTER TWENTY-SEVEN

Charles and Bateman step out of the conference room on the second floor of the Old Bailey. They have been there, plotting, since shortly after the court doors opened at half past nine.

Stephenson and Hannah are approaching, Hannah pushing Sir Leo's wheelchair.

'Good morning,' says Charles.

'Mum's here,' announces Hannah urgently.

'Really? Where?' asks Charles.

Stephenson answers. 'She was queueing for the public gallery, but managed to sweet-talk one of the security staff, and they let her in before the queues. She looked drunk to me. And she's dressed up to the nines, as if she were off to the opera.'

'Have you spoken to her today?' Charles asks of Sir Leo.

'No. Not today. We have words, sometimes, when we pass in the house. She is … struggling.'

'*She's* struggling?' replies Hannah, her colour rising. 'You're going to spend your last days in a prison cell, and *she's* struggling?'

'Now, Hannah,' says Sir Leo, 'we've spoken about this. You don't understand.'

'I understand perfectly! How can you do it, Dad? You didn't do anything wrong. She wrote that letter, didn't she?'

'You don't know that,' replies Sir Leo.

'I do!' she says, turning towards Charles. 'Don't I? I heard her shouting at him. She admitted it!'

Sir Leo looks up at Charles, questioningly.

'I'm sorry, Sir Leo,' says Charles, 'but you're my client, and I didn't believe you wrote that letter. I suspected it was your wife, so I asked her. She confirmed my suspicions. I hoped she'd give evidence, but she refused. I thought, actually, she did more than write the letter, but she denied it and I believed her.'

Sir Leo regards Charles steadily. 'You shouldn't have done that.'

'Maybe not. But it makes no difference because, as I say, she won't help and you won't let me pursue it. So the question I'm asking myself now is, why has she chosen to come to court today?'

Sir Leo shrugs. 'She's my wife. Of course she'd be here, if she's well enough.'

'It's that last qualification which troubles me,' says Charles. 'Anyway, have you thought about my advice?'

'I have. I will agree to say nothing for the moment.'

Charles nods. 'Good. Thank you. That keeps our options open. Come on, we'd better get into court.'

'Good morning, ladies and gentlemen,' says the Common Serjeant to the jury as they settle into their seats. 'Thank you for agreeing to start early. Now, are you ready to proceed, Mr Holborne?'

'Good morning, my Lord. Yes I am.' He pauses. 'Sir Leo calls no evidence.'

There is a stir around the court. People whisper and journalists scribble. This was not predicted.

'Very well. Thank you. Are you making a submission of no case to answer?'

'Not at this moment,' replies Charles. 'I reserve my position on that.'

The judge makes a note and then looks up. 'Right. Over to you, then, Mr Bateman.'

Bateman rises. 'I call Anthony Wise.'

Everyone's attention turns to the young man in the dock. He has dispensed with the sling, and the injuries to his face look less fresh than on the first day of trial. A slit has opened between the puffy eyelids that were swollen shut and Charles guesses that he has regained binocular vision. On the other hand the bruising around both eye sockets has matured and there is a large scab of dried blood on his lower lip.

The dock officer attached to him rises first. The young man does not follow suit. The officer looks down at him, waiting, but Anthony remains hunched on the bench, his dark hair flopping over his face. The officer gives an impatient jerk on the handcuffs, which only succeeds in making the bloodied young man look even more like a beaten dog. Charles looks up at the jury in time to see one or two of them wince in sympathy.

Anthony eventually stands, head still down. He is led out of the dock, across the well of the court and up into the witness box. At a nod from the judge, the officer unlocks the handcuffs and steps back down, remaining a few feet away.

Anthony Wise looks as if he is trying to shrink into his own body. He mutters something inaudible to the usher and is handed an Old Testament. He takes the oath card and reaches into his jacket pocket for a yarmulke and puts it on. He proceeds to read the oath, but in such a quiet voice that only those closest to him can hear. He hands back the Bible and card but, to Charles's surprise, retains his head covering. Charles has not noticed any particular religious bent in Anthony Wise and wonders if retaining the yarmulke is performative, a statement that he is religious and his word on oath should be trusted

But an overt display of Jewishness can easily backfire, thinks Charles. *I wonder if this is a tactic agreed with Bateman?*

'Your name and address, please, Mr Wise?' asks Bateman.

The young man replies, his voice again so quiet that none but the officer behind him would have heard him.

'Mr Wise,' intervenes the judge, 'I didn't hear your answer and I suspect the jury didn't either.' Charles looks across at the jury, several of whom are shaking their heads. 'If you wish them to hear your evidence you're going to have to keep your voice up. Turn so you are angled halfway between me and the jury and lift your head, and repeat that, please.'

'Sorry,' mutters Anthony.

He gives his name and address again, slightly louder but still not looking up. His eyes are closed, his shoulders hunched and his hands clasped tightly before him, the knuckles white. There is an unnatural stillness about his posture, as if his entire being were being compressed into the smallest possible space by some intense pressure surrounding him.

Peter Bateman takes him through his evidence in chief quickly, dealing with his takeover of his father's functions and board position when Sir Leo became ill, the company's attempts to obtain possession lawfully by replacing the furniture, and the possession claim forms drafted by the company's housing department on behalf of the council. He gives Anthony the court ledger to examine, and the young man confirms that the entries relate to the possession claims the council were issuing but which, for reasons unknown, were never progressed. This part of the evidence flows well, and Charles notes with satisfaction that the jury are following it intently, several making notes. This last observation is important. In his experience, there is no conclusion to which a juror will cling more firmly than one they have reached themselves. Throughout, Anthony manages to keep his voice audible, albeit only barely so, and he remains completely still in the dock, his head down and, for the most part, his eyes shut.

Bateman moves smoothly to the more difficult aspects of the case.

'Have you ever spoken to Mr Streeter on the telephone or otherwise?' he asks.

Anthony shakes his head. 'No. I have never dealt with a bailiff, whether as an officer of the company or otherwise. The housing management division deals with all that. Members of the board don't deal with day-to-day repossessions.'

'Even in cases such as this, with reluctant tenants?'

Anthony shakes his head. He doesn't open his eyes but he replies, 'No.'

'Even when a new tactic, the replacement furniture, is being deployed?'

'Even then. Members of the board might discuss strategy with the legal department but we don't deal with bailiffs.'

'Thank you. Now, according to the police, you were interviewed twice at the police station. On the first occasion you had your solicitor, Mr Stephenson, with you, and on his advice you answered all questions with "No comment".'

'Yes.'

'The police officers tell us there was a second occasion when you asked to be interviewed again, despite the fact that Mr Stephenson wasn't present. Is that true?'

'Yes.'

'And they say, during that second interview, you admitted being the person who gave instructions to Streeter to use force against the remaining tenants. Did you make such an admission?'

'Yes.'

'So you did say it. Was it true?'

'No.'

'Then why did you say it?'

'Because I realised that my father was going to admit to giving the order and I had to make sure I got in first.'

'Do you know if your father gave that instruction to Mr Streeter?'

'I don't believe he did. He was unconscious in hospital at the time —'

Allinson leaps up to interrupt. 'Hearsay, my Lord. Unless Mr Wise saw his father at the very time of the phone call, he has no first-hand knowledge of it. And your Lordship will note that Sir Leo Wise has not gone into the witness box to give evidence on the issue one way or the other.' She looks pointedly at the jury.

The judge looks up at Bateman. 'Is it your client's case that he was in hospital with his father when this phone conversation occurred?'

'No, my Lord, he wasn't at the hospital.'

'I thought not. Members of the jury, you will ignore that last answer. Witnesses can only give evidence of what they themselves have perceived, in other words what they have seen, heard or touched perhaps. They cannot give evidence of what other people have told them. Move on, Mr Bateman.'

'Mr Wise, whoever actually gave the instruction to Streeter, when you made that false admission, what was your purpose?'

'My father was fighting for his life. He is still. Look at him.'

Most of the jury members look down to the skeletal Sir Leo in his wheelchair. Charles watches their expressions. There can be no doubt that Sir Leo Wise is gravely ill.

Anthony Wise continues. 'His prognosis is very poor. I couldn't bear to see him going to prison for the last few weeks of his life for something he hadn't done. I had to protect him.'

'But the jury may ask, if you admitted making the call only to protect your father, why are you now changing your mind? Why are you now saying it *wasn't* you?'

For the first time Anthony opens his eyes wide and stares straight at Bateman. 'Look at me!' He points dramatically to his face and then to his shoulder. 'I've only been in prison a few weeks! How could anyone endure years of *this*!' He turns to address his father below him. 'I'm sorry, Dad. I can't do it. I wanted to, but I can't.'

Bateman makes to sit down but Charles tugs at his sleeve and nods towards the jury. Bateman understands. Most of the jury members are looking between father and son, weighing the answers just given. Bateman remains where he is, allowing the silence to lengthen. Only then, after several seconds, does he say, 'Thank you, Mr Wise. Please remain there.'

'I've no questions, thank you, my Lord,' says Charles briefly, only half-standing.

'Miss Allinson?' invites the Common Serjeant.

She rises. When she speaks her voice is gentle, almost friendly.

'Mr Wise, have you seen the accounting documents served by the Crown?'

'I have,' answers Anthony, his eyes again closed.

'They demonstrate, do they not, that Wise Property and Securities Limited exceeded its borrowing limit?'

'One bank of several was saying we had, yes.'

'And had that bank, Lloyds, called in its debt, there was a risk the company would collapse, was there not?'

'I believe we'd have found alternative funding,' replies Anthony.

'But the continued survival of the company would have depended on finding such alternative funding, correct? Which can never be guaranteed, can it?'

'No, not guaranteed. But probable.'

'Which means the answer to my question: "Was there a risk the company would collapse?" is "Yes".'

'I'm not disagreeing with you, Miss Allinson. There was a risk, although I don't think it was a very great one.'

'Thank you. And as every month passed without construction starting, the greater became the company's need for additional funds, right? Because every month without handover increased the penalty payable to Newham.'

'Yes.'

'So the risk of default and of failing to find an alternative lender grew every day.'

'Yes.'

'So every day these reluctant tenants remained in possession, the risk to the company grew worse.'

'I have already agreed with you.'

'So the company clearly had a motive to use every possible means available to obtain vacant possession.'

'We needed possession as soon as possible. That doesn't mean we would do anything unlawful.'

'Can you think of anyone else with a motive to use force to remove these tenants?'

Anthony opens his mouth to answer but before he can get more than a couple of words out Charles and Bateman have both stood and started objecting. For a moment there are three voices fighting to be heard in the court.

337

'Gentlemen! Gentlemen!' shouts the Common Serjeant, adding a fourth. 'One at a time, please.'

Bateman gives ground and allows Charles to proceed, but Anthony persists in trying to be heard.

'Mr Wise,' says the judge, but the witness simply raises his voice further. 'Mr Wise!' shouts the judge.

Anthony stumbles to a halt. His eyes are now wide open and he stares around the court, his gaze moving every second, like a grasshopper landing on a blade of grass and then moving instantly to the next.

Charles transfers his attention to the judge. 'My learned friend's question calls for speculation, my Lord. All the accused can say is that they did not make this phone call or in any way use illegal means to evict tenants. They cannot say, or be asked to speculate, who else might have had a motive.'

'I agree, my Lord,' adds Bateman, still on his feet.

He elbows Charles and nods towards Anthony in the witness box. 'He's losing it,' he whispers.

The young man's hands are no longer gripped tight together but are by his side, clenching and unclenching rapidly and he is making little moaning sounds.

The judge is addressing the prosecutor. 'I think that's right, Miss Allinson. This witness cannot speculate on who else might have had a motive. But that's something about which the jury may well be wondering, and you can certainly raise it with them during your final speech.'

'Yes, my Lord. Mr Wise, you confessed to giving this order during your second interview with the police.'

Anthony does not answer. He is looking increasingly agitated, his face contorted as if in pain.

'Mr Wise?' prompts Allinson.

He has started rocking on the balls of his feet.

'Mr Wise,' orders the judge. 'You have to answer.'

The young man's mouth moves, contorts, and his rocking becomes more pronounced.

'Mr Wise!' shouts the judge.

A louder moan escapes Anthony's throat but he manages to utter a single strangulated syllable. 'Yes.'

'You tell us that you confessed, knowing that you would go to prison for something you didn't do?'

Anthony now looks as if in intense pain. His movement in the witness box becomes more violent, no longer merely rocking backwards and forwards but taking half-steps in each direction, his chest repeatedly striking the brass bar.

'Mr Bateman?' demands the judge.

'I'm very sorry, my Lord, but as I explained, this man has a congenital condition —'

'I don't care what he has! You will control your witness or he'll be taken down to the cells! I won't tolerate a performance like this!'

'I assure you, my Lord, this is no performance —'

But the judge has run out of patience. 'Mr Wise, you will answer, or you will be returned to the cells! Mr Wise!'

Anthony moans again but makes no reply. His hands fly to his ears and press hard.

'Officer!' orders the Common Serjeant. 'Restrain that man and take him down!'

The prison officer moves towards the witness box and steps up, reaching for Anthony's arms. Anthony screams and backs away. The officer manages to get hands on him but Anthony is now completely out of control.

'No!' shouts a woman's voice.

Everyone in court looks round for the speaker. It is Hannah. She runs towards the two men, pulling her suit jacket off as she moves. Anthony and the prison officer are now wrestling in the witness box. In a desperate move to get the officer off him, Anthony shoves the man hard and, off-balance, he topples backwards. It is only a short step down to the well of the court, but it is enough for the officer to fall and land on his backside. Anthony stumbles over him, trying to get away, but is grabbed by his trouser bottom and is pulled to the floor. Anthony's cries become louder and his legs thrash. There are tears running from his eyes and snot from his nose. Half the observers in the courtroom are on their feet, including members of the jury, looking down in shock and revulsion.

'Tony!' shouts Hannah, and Charles sees that she too is crying. 'Here!' she says, and she does something so bizarre that it causes a collective intake of breath in the courtroom. She kneels beside her brother and throws her dark blue jacket over his head like a bag.

The judge too is now on his feet, staring, wide-eyed, at the spectacle.

'Hush, baby, hush!' says Hannah, over and over.

She is almost lying next to him, side-on, holding the jacket in place. The officer rolls away and stands, breathing hard, undecided.

The hundred or more people in the room watch, spellbound, as Hannah continues to console and comfort her brother.

Gradually, Tony's whimpering becomes quieter and his legs stop writhing. His head remains encased in his sister's jacket.

'I shall rise,' says the Common Serjeant. 'Officer, you may leave Mr Wise in court unless he makes any attempt to leave.'

CHAPTER TWENTY-EIGHT

The legal team, together with Sir Leo and Hannah, are once again in the second floor conference room. Tony, now much calmer, has been escorted by the Old Bailey Matron and the prison officer to the former's room to clean himself up.

The mood in the conference room is subdued. Hannah, still upset, sits beside her father's wheelchair, clutching a damp handkerchief in one hand and Sir Leo's hand in the other.

'Will he be all right?' asks Hannah of Charles and Bateman. 'With that woman?'

Charles answers. 'Yes, I'm sure he will. I know Mrs Hamlin. I don't know if she has experience of people with Tony's condition, but she's kind and sensible. Also her room is very peaceful.'

'Good,' replies Hannah, 'that's what he needs. It's the over-stimulation. It was bad enough being the centre of attention and under the stress of the case. But everyone shouting at the same time — it was guaranteed to send him over the edge.'

'You were amazing,' says Bateman to her. 'Has that been necessary before, when your brother has an ... attack?'

She nods. 'Yes, but not for years. But I remembered when he was a little boy. Shutting out everything helped. He used to run to his bedroom and bury his head under his pillows. It happened once while we were on a picnic, and Dad used a blanket.'

'It's also the pressure,' adds Sir Leo. 'At its worst he cannot bear to be touched, but once the worst has passed, being held tightly seems to help. I haven't seen him like that since he was a teenager. So, what happens now?'

Forty minutes later they are called back into court. Everyone has assembled, but the witness box and dock are empty. The judge enters, settles, and waits. A couple of minutes later the court Matron, Mrs Hamlin, escorts Anthony Wise from the main doors to his seat in the dock.

'The court is grateful for your assistance, Mrs Hamlin,' says the Common Serjeant. 'Now, I don't require you to take the oath, but please help me on this: is Mr Wise fit to proceed?'

'My Lord, he is much calmer than he was, but I recommend that he be allowed the rest of the day to recover. His heart rate and blood pressure were through the roof, and I think it would be better if he could resume his evidence tomorrow.'

Allinson rises. 'My Lord I object. That performance by Mr Wise was, in the Crown's opinion, a calculated act to avoid him answering questions, and he should not be rewarded for it.'

Bateman rises. 'My Lord, Mr Wise has been examined by a highly qualified psychiatrist whose conclusion is that he suffers from a severe developmental disorder. Indeed the psychiatrist, Dr Rosenfeld, has been in court throughout to watch Mr Wise give evidence —'

Allinson intervenes. 'Medical evidence to explain a witness's performance in the witness box is inadmissible, my Lord! It's a matter for the jury.'

'Mr Bateman?' asks the judge.

'My learned friend might well be right in the normal case. But she has told the court, in front of the jury, that Mr Wise's breakdown was an act. She has raised the issue herself. It must be appropriate for the Defence to call evidence to rebut that suggestion. Unless, of course, she retracts it.'

'Miss Allinson?' asks the judge. 'Do you resile from your position that we witnessed an act, a performance?'

'I certainly do not,' replies Allinson, full of ill-considered forensic outrage.

'I see. Anything to add, Mr Holborne?'

'I agree with Mr Bateman, my Lord. If my learned friend for the Crown had left the matter alone, simply left it for the jury to decide, she might have a point. But she has opened the door herself.'

The judge looks down at his notebook. For a moment Charles thinks he is recording the submissions but as he watches the judge's pen he realises that he is merely doodling as he collects his thoughts.

'Miss Allinson, I place great weight on what Mrs Hamlin tells me. She has been advising judges at this court and helping witnesses and others with medical difficulties for a generation. And if she says she is concerned about Mr Wise being able to continue today, I'm not going to go against that. So we are faced with a delay, which I'm anxious to avoid. If Dr Rosenfeld is here, and able to give evidence immediately, I'm minded to let him. I know I would be assisted by hearing an expert opinion on what we've just seen, and I think the jury would as well.'

He looks across at the jury to see most of them nodding enthusiastically.

'Yes,' he concludes. 'I'm afraid, Miss Allinson, I'm against you. Mr Bateman, would you like to call your witness, please?'

'Dr Yossi Rosenfeld, please,' says Bateman. He turns to Charles and give an almost imperceptible wink.

Rosenfeld's name is called, and everyone watches as he approaches the witness box. Charles is surprised at how good-looking the psychiatrist is, something he had not noticed before. He is tall and slender, with short curly black hair and large brown eyes. He walks confidently, carrying a file of papers under his arm and is once again wearing a yarmulke. Of course, if Rosenfeld is an observant Jew, he would wear a head covering at all times and, most particularly, when swearing an oath in a court of law. But outward signs of Jewishness can be dangerous. Charles faces such prejudice so frequently he is no longer surprised that, despite the Holocaust, the hatred of Jews in Britain has not been sated, merely buried deeper. It is no longer seemly to display this particular prejudice, bearing in mind what the Jews of Europe suffered, but that does not mean that centuries-long attitudes have altered.

Charles is reminded of his mother's oft-expressed dictum: "*Scratch any Englishman and you'll find an anti-Semite*". He never fully agreed with his frightened mother's opinion — neither of his best friends, Sean Sloane nor Peter Bateman, is Jewish and nor is his life partner — but there is enough truth in it to make it a useful rule of thumb.

Rosenfeld gives the oath and hands the Old Testament and laminated card back to the usher.

'Dr Rosenfeld, would you please give your name and professional qualifications to the court?' asks Bateman.

'Certainly. My name is Yossi Rosenfeld, and I am a consultant psychiatrist presently working at the Tavistock Clinic in north-west London. My medical degree was obtained from Tel Aviv University. I qualified as a psychiatrist at Massachusetts General Hospital, which is commonly regarded as the best such institution in the world. I spent five years at that hospital, ending as the co-director of the adolescent psychiatric unit. Last year I was invited to take up a post at the Tavistock Clinic as a Senior Psychiatrist. My specialist subject is neurological developmental disorders.'

'Thank you, Doctor. Have you had an opportunity to examine Mr Anthony Wise?'

'Yes, I have. I have also studied his medical records and spoken to members of his family.'

'Were you in court earlier today?'

'I was. I witnessed the breakdown suffered by Mr Wise.'

'Does Mr Wise suffer from a recognised psychiatric or neurological condition?'

'Yes. Work in this field is still developing, but over the last decade or so it has become generally accepted in the profession that some patients suffer from developmental defects — in other words, present at birth — which affect the way they communicate and interact with others.'

'And what are the features of this developmental defect?'

'There are several, and every patient is different. Some are very severely affected and spend most of their lives in and out of secure psychiatric institutions because they are a danger to themselves and to others. At the other end of the range, some patients function reasonably well in society. They may even have very high IQs, as is the case with Mr Wise. I didn't formally test him, but the records include repeated references to an IQ of over 160.'

'What sort of problems do these patients face?' asks Bateman.

'They find it particularly difficult to understand non-verbal communication. You and I will recognise what some people call body language, but they do not. They will also miss emotions in other people's expressions, for example anger or irritation. Such patients are very literal. So they don't understand the sub-text of what people are saying, or common colloquialisms. They very often don't understand humour. They are extremely logical and understand rules very well. They can be obsessively orderly. They follow rules and can be very upset when forced to do something which they believe breaks them. So, for example, they can become fixed in what they eat, in what order, and the timing of the meals, and if you were to offer them a different meal at the "wrong" time, they would find that very stressful.'

'Anything else?'

'Yes. A very particular feature is their inability to cope with outside stimuli. Many such patients struggle to deal with loud noises, bright lights, too much movement, too many people speaking at the same time, that sort of thing.'

'What happens if they are subjected to such stimuli?'

'Well, you had a perfect example of it a couple of hours ago. It causes them intense psychological pain. Mr Wise's behaviour, of rocking, hitting himself or other objects, screaming, trying to block out the sensory inputs, is absolutely classic.'

'What do experts call this disorder?'

'I have brought an entire file of research papers with me,' replies Rosenfeld, indicating the file on the witness box desk before him, 'and I can tell you that in almost every one, slightly different terminology is used. As I said, this is an emerging field. The presentation itself has been recognised for decades — it is described in medical texts going back more than a century — but only now has any serious research been dedicated to it. The result is that, presently, there is no unanimity about taxonomy. Certainly a sub-group of people suffering from this developmental disorder have something called "autism".'

'Autism?'

'Yes, the term was coined by a Swiss psychiatrist, Eugen Bleuler, at the beginning of this century. Before then people tended to refer to the disorder as "childhood schizophrenia" but I think most psychiatrists now believe that to be too restrictive a description.'

'Thank you. In your professional opinion, is it possible that Mr Wise was faking these symptoms? That is the position of the Crown. He was faking to avoid answering difficult questions.' As he says this, Bateman looks across at Allinson.

Charles takes the opportunity to regard the Common Serjeant. His head is down and he is writing furiously in his red notebook, trying to keep up with the questions and answers. There is no way of telling if he accepts this evidence, but he is certainly paying it attention.

Rosenfeld answers. 'I think it unlikely in the extreme. All Mr Wise's medical records, which go back to his childhood, and the accounts of his family members, support a lifelong condition in which such a response to stressful stimuli would be entirely predictable. A patient such as Mr Wise would find being the centre of attention here, being required to answer questions, and in particular being faced with several people speaking at the same time on such a stressful subject, where his liberty and that of his father are at stake, well, he would find it unbearable.'

'Dr Rosenfeld,' intervenes the judge, 'are you saying that someone with Mr Wise's condition would be unable to give evidence in court?'

'No, my Lord. He is, as I have said, very high-functioning. So he would certainly understand the questions and be able to answer them, as he demonstrated at the outset. But he would find it intensely stressful and there would be a risk of him becoming overwhelmed.'

'You're saying he lost control merely because two barristers were speaking at the same time?' asks the judge, sounding sceptical.

'There were also raised voices, my Lord, including, if you'll forgive me, yours, which would have exacerbated the stress levels. It can take a tiny thing. Dealing with other people causes these patients to function at an elevated stress level anyway. They prefer to spend their time away from others in quiet environments. Merely being in court would place Mr Wise at risk of a breakdown such as that we saw. It could take very little to tip him over the edge.'

'I see. And insofar as Mr Wise is capable of answering questions, does his condition have any impact on whether he understands the truth? So, when we deal with children, for example, or people with a reduced intellect, I have to give the jury a warning about the witness's ability to differentiate between truth and fiction.'

'In fact, my Lord, the opposite is the case. People with autism live by rules. It is what keeps their universe ordered. If anything, they are more likely to tell the truth, firstly because they cannot fabricate stories in their own minds in the same way as other people can. Secondly, because they rely so much on what they perceive to be the rules. Here, the rules require Mr Wise to tell the truth because he has given an oath to that effect, and because that is the law.'

The Common Serjeant pauses, thinking for a moment, before nodding and returning to making his note. 'Thank you, Doctor. I'm sorry to have interrupted, Mr Bateman. Please continue.'

'No, thank you, my Lord, that is all I propose to ask in chief.'

'Mr Holborne?' asks judge.

'No questions, thank you.'

'Miss Allinson, then.'

Allinson rises. 'Let me start with something you just said, Doctor. You claim that people suffering from this … autism, find it very difficult to lie. But Mr Wise admits to lying. It is a fundamental part of his case. He claims he lied to take the blame for something he didn't do, allegedly to protect his father.'

Charles notes the element of scorn in her voice, as if she were inviting the jury to disbelieve the suggestion, just as she does.

'Yes, under usual circumstances making up a lie like that and working out what else would have to follow if the lie were true, would be difficult for someone with Mr Wise's condition. But there is another factor to consider here.'

'What is that?'

'Mr Wise is the son of two Holocaust survivors.'

Allinson frowns. 'What's that got to do with it?'

'There is a lot of emerging research concerning the psychiatric injuries carried by such victims. It's long been recognised. It's been called shell shock in combatants.'

'But Mr Wise is a young man, born here, after the war. He spent no time in a concentration camp.'

'The profession is beginning to realise that the trauma suffered by people like Mr Wise's parents is, in some way, projected onto their children. The children of such victims suffer from intrusive dreams, exaggerated startle reflex and so on, just like their parents, almost as if the trauma had occurred to them. It is extremely common. And — and this, my Lord, is of particular relevance here — it makes these children unusually protective of their parents. One might almost say pathologically protective.'

'Are you really saying,' asks Allinson, the scorn in her voice now plain for all to hear, 'that people with no experience of such events could suffer the same symptoms as their parents? Memories passed down the generations? Pure quackery!'

Dr Rosenfeld opens his folder and pulls out a sheaf of documents. 'If it is quackery as you put it, it is shared by some of the foremost psychiatrists in the world, including several in this country. One of whom was knighted for his contribution to psychiatry.'

The judge intervenes. 'Let me make sure I've understood your evidence correctly, Doctor. You're saying that it's commonly accepted in your profession that people who suffer from the psychological after-effects of, for example, being involved in a war, can pass those psychological problems to their children?'

There is no scorn in the judge's voice — Charles has the impression he is genuinely struggling to understand the evidence — but there is certainly scepticism.

'May I give you an example, my Lord?'

'Yes, if you think it will help.'

'Let's say you're terrified of fire. Some event occurred when you were a child, for example. Ever after that, you take great precautions in your home to prevent there being a fire, and to enable you to extinguish it, should there be one. And you repeatedly warn your children of the dangers of playing with fire and, say, at a birthday party maybe, when a match falls on the floor, you become very anxious to stamp it out. After using the gas ring on your hob, you repeatedly check that the gas has been turned off. Every night you take great pains to ensure your coal fire is completely extinguished before you go to bed. Perhaps you know people like this. Many of us do. Do you imagine your children would be unaware of your fear? They will grow up as cautious around fire as you. Or, to take a simpler example, your wife is terrified of spiders, and screams every time she sees one. She has to call you to deal with it. It is very well known that such fears tend to generate the same fears in children, children who see the fear in their parent's expression, and hear it in their voices. It sends an unconscious message: spiders are something of which to be frightened.'

Charles looks at the jury to see how they are receiving this evidence and sees embarrassed smiles being suppressed by a couple of the jury, both women.

They're no strangers to arachnophobia, thinks Charles to himself with satisfaction.

'Now,' continues Rosenfeld, 'imagine you have undergone the most horrific treatment in a concentration camp. Imagine yourself, a successful and wealthy professional man, stripped of all you have, imprisoned, forced into labour, beaten, starved, reduced to being sub-human. You have watched people all around you being shot, gassed and starved to death. You are the last survivor of your family. Your experience cannot even be imagined by those who have not been through it with you. It seems to me uncontroversial that the psychological damage done will leave scars. As a result, your behaviour will be for ever altered. It is that behaviour which would tend to cause damage to your children.'

'But, Dr Rosenfeld —' starts Allinson, but she is cut off by the judge.

'No, just give me a moment please, Miss Allinson. I want to make an accurate note of what I've just been told.'

Everyone in court watches the judge's pen travel across his notebook. It takes him a couple of minutes to catch up with the evidence. Then he looks up and smiles at the jury. The Common Serjeant at least is obviously taking this evidence seriously, and Charles looks at the jury to gauge their reaction. Many of them are also taking notes, a good sign.

'Miss Allinson?'

Charles watches his opponent evaluate what she has just heard, balancing her need to destroy Rosenfeld's evidence against the fact that the doctor is clearly a very accomplished witness who knows his field.

Oh, Calli, what are you to do? You invited this evidence, and Rosenfeld's too good for you. And every further question risks making things worse!

The court waits patiently for the Crown's barrister to reach a decision. Finally, she does so, and without another word, resumes her seat.

The judge asks Bateman if he has any re-examination, which he does not, and releases Rosenfeld. The doctor collects his papers and starts up the aisle, but Charles catches his eye. He beckons.

'Would you mind staying for the rest of the day, Doctor? In case something comes up?'

Rosenfeld shakes his head. 'No that's fine,' he whispers. 'I'd like to watch anyway.'

Charles points to the solicitors' bench, behind his. 'You can sit next to Mr Stephenson,' he says.

There is a noise, a scuffling sound, above in the public gallery. Charles and the others in the well of the court look up. A distinguished-looking man with a massive salt-and-pepper moustache is just standing up and pushing his way noisily towards the entrance. He wears a grey homburg hat and an overcoat with a fur collar, and is muttering something to a companion who is struggling to follow him past the other spectators. The man is making little effort to keep his voice down. Charles only has a fleeting glimpse of him as he exits the door, but he is certain he hears the words "Complete tosh!".

It takes a moment before recognition drops into Charles's head. Charles held a photograph of him in his hand at the weekend, albeit one taken many years earlier. The person with the impressive moustache, the man who believed Rosenfeld's evidence to be "complete tosh", was none other than Gilbert Hamilton, the seventh Earl of Menteith.

CHAPTER TWENTY-NINE

Court has risen for lunch and the three lawyers eat sandwiches and drink brown liquid masquerading as coffee in the busy public canteen. Hannah and Jacquetta have taken Sir Leo for a walk in his wheelchair somewhere in the court precincts and Anthony Wise has been taken down to the cells.

And he's probably eating a better meal than this, thinks Charles, examining his very dry cheese sandwich ruefully.

Whatever the time of day, there is always a fried breakfast to be had in the Old Bailey cells, and it's as good as any to be obtained in London. In fact, now Charles thinks of it, it's probably the breakfasts available to prisoners and their lawyers in the cells below him that are responsible for his lifelong love affair with crispy bacon sandwiches.

'Here he is,' nods Stephenson towards the door.

Charles and Bateman look round. A giant of a man in a raincoat the size of a tent is filling the double doorway, looking around him.

'Big Kev,' confirms Bateman. 'And, my God, he *is* big!'

'Good,' says Charles, rising to greet his new client. He looks back towards Stephenson. 'Got everything?'

'Don't fret, Charles,' reassures the solicitor, already digging in his briefcase and placing documents on the table. 'It's all ready. We just need signatures.'

Charles spent Sunday evening in Chambers with Mr and Mrs Lane, completing adoption forms headed "Chancery Division" together with bundles of supporting evidence.

'He's not on his own, is he?' asks Stephenson, concerned.

'No. Look,' says Charles.

Only as Big Kev starts weaving his way through the tables towards them do they see that in fact Maude Lane, previously completely obscured by her gargantuan husband, is following behind. Big Kev comes to a halt and waits for his wife to stand beside him. As always, it is the little Cockney woman who speaks for the couple.

'All right, gents?' she asks brightly. 'Got our forms?'

Charles points to the table. 'Everything's here. Why don't you pull up a couple of chairs, Mr Stephenson can start going through them with you, and I'll get you both some drinks. We've twenty-five minutes before we're due back in court.'

'Mr Bateman, do you have any further witnesses?'

'I do, my Lord. Kevin Lane, please!'

The announcement of Bateman's next witness causes the greatest stir to date. Ever since Kevin Streeter's evidence, the tabloids have been full of speculation about the identity and whereabouts of "Big Kev". The fact that the defence is about to call the man alleged to have thrown Bartlett from the window, presumably to his death, is little short of sensational.

Kevin Lane enters court. He has removed his raincoat and wears a new suit, bought, at the instance of Maude, in honour of this occasion.

'Well, he's going to be in court a fair bit over the next few days, ain't 'e?' she'd said. ''E ought to look the part.'

Big Kev now "looks the part". The suit is well-cut and fits him well, but even so Charles can see enormous shoulder and thigh muscles bulging through the material as he strides down to the witness box.

The legal team has spent a long time discussing the best tactic to deploy with Big Kev. Counsel who calls a witness is not entitled to cross-examine him. He is bound by whatever answers he receives. On the other hand, the advantage of having separate representation for clients whose positions almost entirely align is that the other defence barrister can ask almost anything and can keep pressing if necessary, even asking leading questions. Charles will therefore have a much freer hand when it's his turn.

'Before Mr Lane takes the oath, my Lord,' says Bateman, 'I seek permission for him to be excused giving his address in open court. As will soon become apparent, there is a significant conflict in the evidence between Mr Lane and Mr Streeter. One of them almost certainly murdered Mr Bartlett and Mr Lane says it was not him. Accordingly he does not believe that he, his wife or his small baby would be safe from Mr Streeter or his confederates were his home address to be revealed. I have it written here, my Lord, and can pass it up for your Lordship's note.'

'Very well,' says the judge, holding out his hand for the note. 'Swear the witness, please.'

Big Kev reads the oath off the card, stumbling slightly over some words.

'Your name please, sir?' asks Bateman.

'Kevin Lane,' answers Lane, his voice a low rumble.

'And your profession?'

'I'm a bailiff. Before all this 'appened I was working with Kevin Streeter for his company, Shoreditch Enforcement Services.'

'Mr Bateman, I think I need to give Mr Lane the usual warning, don't I?'

'Yes, my Lord, now would be an appropriate moment.'

The judge turns to Big Kev. 'Mr Lane, you are not obliged to answer any question that might incriminate you, do you understand?'

'Err…'

'That is to say, one of the barristers in this court may ask you questions suggesting that you've committed a criminal offence.'

'I ain't committed no offence. Not this time, anyway.'

The honesty of that reply causes some laughter in the court which the Common Serjeant, smiling, ignores.

'Nonetheless. You don't have to answer any question if, in doing so, you might open yourself to prosecution. You're not on trial here, and no Englishman may be forced to convict himself out of his own mouth. It's a rule we have. I'll remind you if necessary.'

'Yeah, got it, your honour.'

'You may proceed, Mr Bateman.'

'Thank you. How long did you work with Mr Streeter?'

'About five years.'

'And what would you do for him?'

'Whatever 'e told me. 'E was the boss.'

'Did you work with him on every job?'

'Not always. For simpler jobs, like rent collection, he would do one list, and I would do another.'

'Who made decisions as to who did what?'

'Mr Streeter. Like I said, 'e was me boss.'

'What was your usual day-to-day work, then?'

'Repossessions, getting tenants outta their properties, taking back furniture what hadn't been paid for. Fings like that.'

'I want to draw your attention to a rather different job you were asked to do in April, a repossession in Braithwaite Street. Do you remember such a job?'

'I do.'

'How did you come to be instructed in that matter?'

'We met Mr Hanrahan at the Wimpy.'

'Who is Mr Hanrahan?'

'I couldn't tell you, 'cept he apparently works for the county court at Bow. He gave us orders every now and then.'

'Okay. What did Mr Hanrahan say or do?'

'He gives Kev a sheet of paper and tells 'im he has to make a call. Kev goes outside to the call box and I stay in the Wimpy. Kev comes back and says we've been told to use force on the tenants still in the development sites.'

'Did he say who gave that instruction?'

Big Kev shakes his head. 'Nah. Not my business.'

'What happened then?'

'Well, Hanrahan's left us with a list of properties and very definite times. We can't go to the properties before or after, just at them times.'

'Thank you. Did you take part in any of these evictions?'

'Nah, but the next day I saw one happening, at Braithwaite Street.'

'Tell us what happened.'

'Well, I had an appointment with the missus at the hospital to do with the baby. I told Kev I couldn't help with this one.'

'Do you know what time you were supposed to be at Braithwaite Street?'

'Yeah, five-thirty. Not before and not after. I said I'd do me best, but he should go ahead in case I didn't make it.'

'What time was your hospital appointment?'

'Err...'

Bateman turns in his bench to face Stephenson, who is already holding out a document for him.

'My Lord,' continues Bateman, 'I have a dated and timed document here from the hospital records, bearing the signatures of Mr and Mrs Lane and recording the detail of the conversation and the decisions taken regarding their baby. I wish to use it to refresh Mr Lane's memory of the exact time.'

Allinson jumps up. 'I object, my Lord.'

'On what grounds?' asks the judge. 'If this document was made at the same time as the conversation recorded in it, and it's been signed by Mr Lane, how is it any different from the police pocketbooks? I gave them permission to refresh their memory of times and conversations from their pocketbooks. Why should I treat this witness any differently? No, Mr Bateman, you may use the document to refresh this witness's memory of the time.'

'Thank you, my Lord. Please look at this document Mr Lane. Can you firstly tell us what it is?'

Everyone in court waits for the document to be handed to the big man.

'They're the notes made by the lady doctor at St Thomas's,' he replies. 'Little Matthew, that's the baby, had to be taken in 'cos 'e was poorly, and this was the discussion about letting us take him 'ome again.'

'Do you see the time recorded in the left margin?'

'Yeah.'

'What time does it say?'

'Four o'clock.'

'Is the time at the beginning of the notes or the end?'

'The beginning. That was the time of the appointment. We had a good old chinwag, as you can see,' Big Kev holds the document aloft and indicates with his stubby finger a complete page of notes. He then turns it over and indicates that the back of the document is also covered in tiny handwriting as well. 'Don't ask me to read it, 'cos I can't. I can't never read nuffin' a doctor writes.'

'Can you tell us what time you left the hospital?'

'It's got to be at least fifty minutes after that. Almost five, I reckon.'

'Where did you go?'

'I left Maudie and the baby and got a bus to Braithwaite Street.'

'What happened when you got there?'

'I was a few minutes early so I popped into the corner shop for some cigs. Then I saw 'im drive past.'

'Who?'

'Him,' says Lane forcefully, and he points directly at DI Woolley, sitting behind prosecution counsel.

'You are indicating Detective Inspector Woolley, is that right?'

'Yeah, DI Woolley.'

'Did you know DI Woolley before this case?'

'Yeah. He nicked me when I was a kid. I recognised 'im all right.'

'Was he in his police car?'

'Nah, 'is private motor. A Vauxhall Viva, with a GB sticker and a nodding dog on the back parcel shelf.'

'Are you sure it was him?'

'Absolutely bloody certain.'

The Common Serjeant raises his eyebrows over his glasses as he looks at Lane, but says nothing.

'What happened then?' asks Bateman.

'Well, 'e goes past me to the shoe factory, which was half a dozen shops up from where I was. It's all derelict now, since the bloke who owned it died. Anyway, he reverses into the rear entrance and turns off the lights. So I'm watching him from the corner shop, waiting, and he appears to be waiting 'n' all, but I don't know what for.'

'What happens then?'

'Coupla minutes later, Kev goes past in the same direction in the works van. I'm getting in a sweat 'cos I think Woolley's there waiting to nick him, but I can't do nuffin'. So we're all there waiting, right? Me in the corner shop with the Italian geezer, you know, the bloke what runs it, Woolley hiding in the shadders up the road, and Little Kev parked up outside one of the houses, lights off.'

'The house outside which Little Kev was parked: were any lights on inside?'

'Yeah. I only noticed after a minute or two as it was getting dark. All the properties on the street were boarded up and empty by then, 'cept this one. There was a light upstairs.'

Charles, writing fast to keep up with the evidence, risks looking up. The rapt attention of everyone in court is fixed on Kevin Lane.

'What happened then?' asks Bateman.

'I'm looking at me watch. I know Kev's doing the same, right? Waiting for half-five. I'm tearing me hair out. I need to warn him, but I daren't. Then, bang on time, Kev gets out the cab with the jemmy. We use it for taking boarding off properties and for gettin' in. He kicks the door, the door goes in, and in 'e goes.'

'And then?'

'Well, there's me expecting Woolley to go racing across the road, but he don't. He just sits in his car. A minute later this geezer comes flying out the first-floor window. Lands on his back and head on the pavement. Horrible crunch, it were. I knew straight off, he was never gonna stand up from that. And it was only then that Woolley comes charging out his car and across the road. I'm expecting him to arrest Kev.'

'Does he?'

'Well, you might have trouble believing this, 'cos I certainly did, but he starts helping Kev lift the bloke round the back of the works van! They shove 'im in, and both drive off!'

Even looking back on the event, Big Kev's astonishment is palpable.

If this is an act, this bloke's worth an Oscar!

'Both of them? Including DI Woolley?' asks Bateman for emphasis.

'Yeah. Bonkers, right? It was only then I realised that Woolley was involved in it. Probably him and Hanrahan too, 'cos it was Hanrahan who gave the message.'

'Did you ever see Mr Bartlett again?'

'Who?'

'The chap who came out of the window.'

'Nah, never. I reckoned then 'e was a gonner.'

'And Mr Streeter?'

'Nah. I knew he was up to his neck in something, and I weren't sure what. I talked it through with Maudie, and she told me to keep clear of 'im, so I did.'

'Maudie?' asks Bateman.

'Trouble. Sorry, your honour,' apologises Lane, looking up at the public gallery. 'Trouble and strife, wife.'

Everyone looks up. Maude Lane is sitting in the front row of the gallery. She is wearing a little blue hat and her best coat.

'So I made up excuses not to go in,' continues Big Kev. 'Then one night Little Kev rings and says "lay low", which I were doin' anyway.'

'Now, I need to put this to you clearly so you can answer it,' says Bateman. 'Kevin Streeter says *you* threw Mr Bartlett out of that window, and he was unable to stop you.'

'That ain't true. He's done a deal with that bent copper —' he nods towards Woolley — 'to keep his arse out of a sling, that's all. What reason have I got to murder the bloke? I'm just a bailiff, working for Little Kev.'

'Thank you, Mr Lane. Please wait there.'

'Mr Holborne?'

'Thank you, my Lord. So, Mr Lane, you've had dealings with DI Woolley in the past, I gather.'

'I have.'

'Can you explain how you first met him?'

Charles and Bateman know that this line of questioning is going to bring out the fact that Big Kev has a criminal record. There's no help for it — the Crown are certain to emphasise it to damage his credibility — but it will do less damage if the information is brought out by Charles, who will be more sympathetic, than by Allinson.

'Yeah. I was seventeen. Never been in trouble with the police. Woolley was a PC in uniform then, and he nicked me on the way back home from a football match. Said I'd been fingered as burglaring a factory. I never did it, but I had a good idea who had, and I refused to name 'im. So Woolley fitted me up.'

'How did he fit you up?'

'Took me round to my gaff saying he wanted to search for stolen tools. Like an idiot I said yes, 'cos I knew there weren't nothing there. And Woolley was such a friendly looking bloke. Chubby red face, you know? Sort of old-fashioned copper. Me Dad, who was straight as a die, always said you could trust 'em. But he planted stuff, an electric drill and a hammer thing they use for knocking out dents in cars. I said I knew nothing about them, but he verballed me.'

'Verballed?' asks Charles, looking at the jury to see if they understand the expression.

'Yeah, made up a confession saying I did it. Said I cried like a baby, too, which was a bloody liberty, 'cos I never cry. Even when me Mum died.'

Charles sees some of the jury members smiling.

They like him, which is half the battle.

Evidence given in criminal courts is often pure fabrication. Sometimes it's a blend of truth and fiction; occasionally, truth and wishful thinking. But it is rarely the truth, the whole truth and nothing but the truth, and on the rare occasion that a witness is transparently, artlessly honest, it stands out, like a diamond shining in the mud. And so it does on this occasion. Big Kev gives his evidence almost like a child, patently honestly, hiding nothing.

'What happened?'

'Two years in Borstal's what 'appened.'

'Were you ever in trouble again after that?'

'I'm sorry to say I was. There's no place like Borstal for learning how to be a criminal.'

'So, Mr Lane, what did you learn?'

'I learned how to burgle, which was funny, seeing's I was there for a burglary I never did. I also learned how to hotwire a car. So after that I was nicked three or four times, all in a row. Stealing cars and burglary.'

'What sentences did you receive?'

'Oh, you know, a bit of bird —' he turns to the jury — 'that's prison, right?' Charles sees the judge hiding a smile behind his hand. 'Then a bit more.'

'When was the last time you served a prison sentence?' asks Charles.

'1952. Three-years, Middlesex Assizes. I did eighteen months. But this time I decided to make use of it, and I learned to read.'

'You couldn't read before?' asks Charles.

'Not really. So I did English and metalwork, and when I got out I found meself a job. First honest job I ever had.' Big Kev turns to the jury and smiles broadly at them, his heavy features beaming with pride. Several of the jury smile back at him.

They're eating this up!

Charles knew Lane would be essential to Tony Wise's defence; he had no idea the man would make such a good witness.

'That was your first honest job?'

'It was. And I've been straight ever since.'

'Miss Allinson will say that you've been convicted of offences of dishonesty in the past, perhaps not as many as Mr Streeter, but each one just as dishonest. Why should the jury believe you rather than him?' asks Charles.

Big Kev shrugs. 'I ain't proud of what I did, but I did me time and since then I've stayed straight. I never want to go back to prison.' He nods at the jury. 'It's up to them, innit? Like I said, we've got the baby now, and 'e's all that interests me. And Maudie, of course.' He looks up to the public gallery. Charles follows his gaze. In the same row of seats, closer to the door, sits Gilbert Hamilton, the Earl of Menteith. Further back and mostly out of sight is Esther Wise in her fur coat.

'Yes. Thank you, Mr Lane,' he says.

Allinson rises. In her hand is Big Kev's CRO docket. She runs through all his convictions in the same way as Bateman did with Streeter, this time in tedious detail. It achieves little. Big Kev has already admitted his past wrongdoing and the sting has already been drawn. She accuses him of lying about the events at Braithwaite Street. He simply repeats his earlier account. She points at the dock and says that Big Kev should be sitting there with Anthony Wise, as he was part of the conspiracy and actually killed Mr Bartlett. The judge intervenes to warn Big Kev, but he says he wants to answer.

'It ain't true,' he says simply.

Allinson tries and tries, but she cannot trip him up. His story remains as it was. Eventually she sits down. There is no re-examination. No further question from Bateman could improve on the impression Kevin Lane has already created.

'Your next witness, Mr Bateman?' asks the Common Serjeant.

Peter Bateman looks down at Charles. Charles shakes his head.

'My Lord, I wonder if we might have a short adjournment to take instructions? I'm not entirely sure if our last witness has arrived at court.'

The Common Serjeant looks at the clock on the wall. 'Yes, very well. Ladies and gentlemen, we'll adjourn for fifteen minutes, which should be enough for you to stretch your legs and perhaps get a hot drink. Bail for Sir Leo as before.'

'All rise!'

Charles gathers his papers quickly and indicates that Bateman and Stephenson should follow him out of court.

'We've no time to get to the conference room,' he says, gathering the others in a quiet corner. He turns to Stephenson. 'Well? Any news?'

Stephenson shakes his head. 'I spoke to Mr Munday this morning before coming to court. He said if he couldn't find Martinelli by two, he'd come straight here.'

'It's quarter past three,' points out Bateman.

'So he's got fifteen minutes,' says Charles, sitting heavily on the stone bench behind him.

The others join him. The minutes tick by.

Finally the court usher puts her head out. 'Ready, gentlemen? The judge is waiting to come back in.'

'Shit!' swears Bateman softly.

The three lawyers rise and file back into court. Charles, at the back, is about to enter when he hears his name called.

'Charles! Charlie!'

He whirls round. Billy Munday is running up the final flight of steps towards him.

'Jesus, you're cutting it fine!' says Charles. 'We're on our way in.'

'Sorry. I had a lead, his son and daughter-in-law in Hertfordshire, but the trains back in were all over the place.'

'And?' prompts Charles.

'Dead end. They've moved too. Staffordshire apparently. The neighbours think that Martinelli senior has retired and moved with them.'

Charles sighs, his shoulders slumping. 'Bugger.'

He is confident that the jury like and believe Big Kev. Where there's a conflict in the evidence of the Kevins, he's pretty sure they'll prefer Kevin Lane's. But having an independent witness who placed the big man in the corner shop while the action was going on over the road would have made it a certainty.

'All right,' he says, deflated. 'Thanks for trying.'

He turns again, about to enter the court, but Munday grabs his arm. 'Not so fast, squire. I ain't empty-handed.'

Charles looks more carefully at Munday's expression. He sees pride and barely-concealed excitement. Munday hands him a document. As Charles reads, his face lights up. He launches himself at Munday and gives the young man a bear hug.

'You bloody genius! You bloody genius!' he exclaims.

'Well,' says Munday, struggling to breathe in Charles's vice-like embrace. 'It was your idea. I just followed orders.'

'Thank you!' exclaims Charles, releasing the other man.

Charles runs into court, straight past the end of his bench and to the court clerk.

'Please can you ask the judge for another three minutes?' he asks hurriedly, his eyes shining. 'We may have a new witness.'

The clerk looks doubtful. 'I'll ask, but the jury's in and the judge is at the door, waiting.'

'Please. Three minutes is all I need, but I have to take instructions before making a decision.'

The clerk rises and starts climbing the steps to the panelled door behind the judge's bench. Charles races back to his seat. He flicks through to an empty page in his notebook, writes a name, rips the page out and hands it to Bateman.

'I want you to call him,' he says to the young barrister, jabbing the paper with his thick index finger.

'What?'

'Please, Peter, I know what I'm doing!'

'But we can't,' protests Bateman. 'We've no witness statement, no deposition. We've issued no subpoena.'

Charles leans in, careful to face the front of the court. 'He's here,' he whispers. 'You don't need a subpoena if a witness is actually in court. No! Don't look round!'

Bateman draws a deep breath and leans towards his former pupil master. 'Charles,' he says in a low voice, 'you've pulled some stunts in the past, but this takes the biscuit!'

'It's not a stunt. Look, we've got Hanrahan, Woolley and Streeter, all clearly involved. But they've no motive! And Big Kev didn't hear who was giving Streeter the order. So even if the jury disbelieve everything else Streeter says, they've still got no evidence to put against his assertion that it was Tony on the phone. There's still a gaping hole in our case on that central issue. But I think I've worked out what's going on!'

'But if he refuses to give evidence, that's the end of it!' hisses Bateman.

'Not necessarily,' insists Charles.

Bateman shakes his head. 'You're mad, Charles.' Charles looks at him, beseeching. 'All right. I'll call him. Although what I'm supposed to ask him, God only knows.'

'I'll tell you what to ask him. Give me a moment.'

Charles sits and starts writing furiously.

'All rise!' calls the usher.

The Common Serjeant enters and takes his place. He looks pointedly at Charles. 'Do you think we might proceed now, Mr Holborne?' he asks drily.

'Yes, my Lord. I apologise. Thank you for the extra minutes.'

The judge turns to Peter Bateman. 'So, do you wish to call any further witnesses, Mr Bateman?'

'Yes please, my Lord. The Defence calls Gilbert Hamilton, the Earl of Menteith.'

Bateman's words cause a renewed stir in the court, with people looking around and whispering to one another. Only one or two of the journalists, those more on the ball, look as if they know what might be about to happen.

The Common Serjeant also looks puzzled. 'Is the Earl present?'

Charles jumps up. 'He is, my Lord.' He turns and points. 'He has taken quite an interest in this case, and has been observing from the gallery.'

The judge looks up. 'Lord Menteith?' he asks, apparently unable to identify the Earl.

The man in the Homburg hat stands. 'I am he,' he says, his voice a deep growl.

'Your Lordship may remember,' says Charles, 'that it was Lord Menteith who accused Sir Leo and his company of being involved in a Jewish conspiracy to obtain the contract from the London Borough of Newham. We believe he may have essential evidence to give.'

'Has a subpoena been served on him?' asks the Common Serjeant.

'No,' replies Bateman. 'But as he is in court, no subpoena is required.'

Charles suppresses a smile. Bateman made the assertion with utter confidence and certainty, despite the fact that sixty seconds earlier he was apparently unaware of the rule.

'I will not give evidence for these people,' says Menteith angrily.

'What, all these *Jewish* people?' asks Charles, pointing in turn to Sir Leo, Anthony Wise, Dr Rosenfeld and then, finally, himself.

'Mr Holborne!' shouts the Common Serjeant. Charles looks up at him, all innocence. The judge shakes his head sadly. 'Don't test my patience. Lord Menteith,' he says, looking up, 'would you like to explain that last comment?'

Menteith glares down at the judge but does not answer.

'I see,' says the judge. He stares at the Earl for a moment and lowers his head. He resumes doodling on his notebook. There is silence in the court and the tension builds. 'Yes,' he concludes finally, looking up again. 'I think we should hear what Lord Menteith has to say.'

'I refuse!' shouts the Earl from his position in the gallery.

'That would not be wise,' replies the judge calmly. 'I'm sure you don't intend to show contempt for this court. Need I remind you of my powers in that regard?'

There is another prolonged silence. Every pair of eyes in Court 1 of the Old Bailey is fixed on the Earl, awaiting his response. The judge continues his doodling, allowing the aristocrat time to reconsider. When the judge does finally look up towards the gallery again his eyebrows are raised and his expression benign, but Charles sees a definite challenge in it.

'Well?'

Menteith looks furious, his chin jutted and his lips compressed in such a thin angry line they disappear entirely behind the silver moustaches.

'Have it your own way!' he shouts, and he whirls around in his seat and stomps up the steps and out of the gallery.

The Common Serjeant nods at one of the officers at the back of the court. The man scurries out, no doubt to ensure the Earl finds his way. Everyone waits.

A few minutes later the door opens again and the Earl appears at the back of the court. The delay seems to have enabled him to control his temper. He strides towards the witness box, head erect, shoulders back, as if on parade. He steps up into the witness box, removes his hat to reveal an impressive thick head of silvery hair to match his moustaches, and puts his hand out to take the New Testament and the oath card offered by the usher. He reads the words in a snarl.

'Your name and address please, sir,' asks Bateman.

'I am Gilbert Alistair Hamilton, seventh Earl of Menteith, Menteith Castle, Lochside Road, Dunhaven, Scotland.'

'Thank you.' Bateman pauses, looking down at Charles's note. 'On 18 July 1967 Hansard records you as having accused the former Minister for Housing, Keith Joseph, of corruption with Sir Leo Wise and others — whom you termed the "Jewish Mafia" — in securing the London Borough of Newham development contract. Your allegation, not repeated outside Parliament, was the subject of many newspaper reports at the time. Does Hansard record your comment accurately?'

'I have no idea. I haven't examined it.'

'Then let's put Hansard to one side. Is it in fact your opinion, or was it in July 1967, that Sir Leo Wise's company secured the contract corruptly?'

Allinson rises. 'I object to this line of questioning. It has nothing to do with this case, and the witness cannot be required to answer a question that might leave him open to civil action.'

Bateman opens his mouth to reply but the judge raises a hand. 'Your second point has no force at all, Miss Allinson. The protection against self-incrimination relates to criminal charges, not civil actions for, let us say, slander. However I'm yet to see how this line of questioning is connected to the case.'

'That will become clear, my Lord, if you will allow me a little leeway,' replies Bateman, again full of confidence. Charles has to admire his ex-pupil who is questioning the witness entirely blind.

'I will allow you a little further leeway, Mr Bateman, but not much,' warns the judge. He turns to the witness. 'What's the answer to Mr Bateman's question?'

'I think there is evidence which should be investigated. I have always said so. Joseph is a Jew, as is Sir Leo Wise. As was the then chairman of the planning department of the London Borough of Newham.'

'So it is the Jewishness of the actors that raises your suspicions?' asks Bateman.

'It is.'

'Thank you.' Bateman looks down at Charles's note. Charles is indicating the second of his bullet points. 'Yes.' He looks up at the witness. 'Were you part of a consortium which bid for that contract?'

'I was.'

'Did you feel that your consortium should have won it?' asks Bateman.

'Of course I did, or else we wouldn't have bid for it,' answers Menteith with an air of exasperation at the stupidity of the question.

'If Sir Leo's company is forced into liquidation and can no longer complete the development, will your consortium bid to pick up the contract?'

'I can't possibly tell you. That would depend on many factors. The simple fact is that Wise's rabble have messed this contract up from start to finish, which only proves that we should've been awarded it in the first place.'

Charles leans across and points to his third and final bullet point. Bateman reads it, turns to Charles and shakes his head. Charles nods insistently. Bateman turns again to the witness.

'So you have a motive to ensure that Wise Properties and Securities Limited goes into liquidation?'

'No!' intervenes the judge. 'You've now used up all your leeway, Mr Bateman. That question is very close indeed to suggesting criminal activity. Lord Menteith I'm obliged to warn you that you don't have to answer any question that tends to incriminate you of any criminal offence. Do you understand?'

'Yes. Thank you, my Lord.'

Charles flaps his hand to indicate that Bateman should resume his seat.

'Mr Holborne? Any questions of this witness?'

'Yes, my Lord. Lord Menteith, do you know Detective Inspector Woolley?' he asks.

'Who? What, that policeman sitting behind prosecution counsel? No, I don't.'

'Never met him?'

'Never.'

'Never spoken to him?'

'Never.'

'Thank you. Do you know anyone by the name of Michael Hanrahan?'

Menteith pulls a face and stares at the ceiling, as if trying to recall the name. 'No, I don't believe I do.'

'Perhaps I can jog your memory,' says Charles. 'Michael Hanrahan is a former barrister, now disbarred for dishonesty, working as a clerk at Bow County Court.' Charles turns to look directly at the jury. 'Dealing with possession actions.'

He scans the faces of the jurors carefully. He can't be sure, but he thinks at least a couple of them have just had a lightbulb moment.

'No,' replies Menteith, 'I don't know anyone of that name.'

'What is Navy 2162?' asks Charles swiftly.

The Earl's face suddenly colours. 'I … I … repeat that, would you?'

'I'm sure you heard me, Lord Menteith. I asked you what is Navy 2162.'

'I don't … I don't…' he blusters, 'I don't think I know.'

Charles pauses and holds a piece of paper conspicuously before him. 'Are you sure, Lord Menteith? Do you wish his Lordship to remind you of the penalties for perjury? I'll give you a moment to reflect on your answer.'

'Damn it, man, how can I be expected to … it rings a bell, all right? I've heard of it, perhaps…'

'Let me put you out of your misery, Lord Menteith. It's the name of a masonic lodge, is it not?'

'Ah, yes, now you mention it, I think it is.'

'A lodge of which you have been a member since 1934.'

'That's possibly correct. I'm a member of several lodges.'

Menteith seems to find something of interest in his fine white shirt cuffs, as he adjusts them minutely, one after the other.

'I'm surprised you don't remember this particular one, because it is a Portsmouth naval lodge, and Portsmouth is where you were based during your naval service —'

Menteith interrupts. 'Like I said, I'm a member of several lodges.'

'— and you've been its chair on two occasions. Is that not right?'

'Possible, I suppose,' replies Menteith, trying to sound unconcerned.

'I have in my hand here a record from Freemasons' Hall, Great Queen Street, London. Now, just so the jury understands, that address houses several lodges where Freemasons conduct their business, but it's also the administrative centre of English Freemasonry, is that not right?'

'Yes,' answers Menteith cautiously.

'And this record states that you are a past Worshipful Master of the Lodge, Navy 2162, and a member of Grand Arch. Do you deny it?'

'No.'

'Now, for those who don't know anything about Freemasonry, there's a hierarchy, is there not, and in each lodge there's a Worshipful Master, a Senior Warden and a Junior Warden. Is that correct?'

'Yes.' Menteith looks as if he's about to say something further, but stops himself.

'And there's a progression up the ladder, in the sense that when the Worshipful Master's year in office ends, he stands down and, in the normal course, the Senior Warden moves up and becomes Master. And the Junior Warden in turn moves up and becomes Senior Warden. Right?'

'Yes.'

'And this team works very closely together, doesn't it?'

'You need to be more specific,' replies Menteith, glaring angrily at Charles.

'The Worshipful Master and Senior Warden are the two principal officers of the Lodge, responsible for its governance and functioning. They work together to initiate new members, perform rituals and ceremonies together, and so on.'

'Yes.'

'In 1965 you were the Worshipful Master of Naval Lodge 2162. And according to the records at Freemasons' Hall, in that year the Senior Warden was one —' Charles makes a show of reading from the document on his hand — 'Clifford Andrew Woolley,' he says slowly, putting a pause between each word.

'So?'

Charles turns to prosecuting counsel. 'Would Miss Allinson please remind us of DI Woolley's full name?' he asks.

'Clifford Andrew Woolley,' she replies heavily, without standing or looking up.

'The name's not that uncommon,' asserts Menteith dismissively. 'Coincidence.'

Charles smiles and looks at the jury. 'Lord Menteith, would you like to guess the name of the Junior Warden at Naval Lodge 2162 that year?'

'Mr Holborne,' says the judge without looking up from his notes. 'Let's not play guessing games. Make your point.'

'Certainly, my Lord. The name of the Junior Warden was … Michael Hanrahan.' Charles pauses for a moment to allow the evidence to sink in with everyone in court. He continues. 'Lord

Menteith, I suggest that when you told the jury you'd never heard of Woolley or Hanrahan, you were lying. They were your close colleagues at that Lodge.'

'Coincidence, I said!' blusters the Earl.

'Mr Holborne,' intervenes the judge again, 'are you in a position to prove these assertions?'

'There's no statement yet from the private investigator who obtained the record, nor from anyone at Freemasons' Hall, but both can be obtained very easily. The investigator's in court. But I have a copy of the original records. If my learned friend wishes to put us all to the cost and delay of obtaining the statements, that may be done.'

'Miss Allinson, are these facts admitted?'

Allinson rises and Charles holds his breath.

In Calli's place, there's no way he'd admit these damning facts without making his own enquiries, if only to delay and pray that something turned up. If Calli plays hardball, this entire line of questioning disappears, at least temporarily, leaving at best a bad taste in the mouths of the jury members.

'I've yet to see the document, my Lord, but assuming it records what my learned friend claims, I anticipate the facts will be admitted.'

Charles exhales.

She's had it! She's given up the fight!

'Thank you,' says the judge. 'You may proceed, Mr Holborne.'

'Lord Menteith, I understand that membership of this particular Lodge is restricted to members of the Royal Navy. Is that right?'

'Present and ex-servicemen, yes.'

'We've yet to make enquiries of the Navy, but would they reveal that you, Woolley and Hanrahan all served in the Navy at the same time, in Portsmouth?'

Menteith does not answer.

'Well, Lord Menteith?' persists Charles.

He still does not answer.

'I'm afraid I must insist on a reply,' says Charles calmly.

Menteith glares at Charles from under his hooded eyes. 'You can insist what you like, you filthy —'

His stops abruptly, apparently thinking better of finishing his sentence.

'Jew?' offers Charles softly. 'Is that what you were about to say?'

'What if it was?' hisses Menteith.

There is a gasp of shock in the courtroom.

'Thank you, Lord Menteith,' says Charles. 'I think that's the only answer I need. Only, perhaps this: you were a member of Sir Oswald Mosley's British Union of Fascists were you not, until 1940, when it was disbanded?'

'I have no obligation to answer anything about my political affiliations!' replies Menteith angrily.

'I am giving you the opportunity to deny it, if you want,' says Charles.

The Earl's lips remain resolutely shut.

Charles waits for several seconds, nods as if to himself, looks hard at the jury and resumes his seat.

'Any cross-examination, Miss Allinson?'

Allinson is deep in conversation with Mark Denton, the Crown's junior barrister, behind her.

The judge waits patiently. Eventually she turns and stands. 'No, thank you, my Lord.'

Charles almost feels sorry for her. Her case looked strong on paper, very strong indeed against Anthony Wise, but it has slowly drifted away, as sometimes it does, and the combination of the evidence of Big Kevin Lane and that of Menteith, have destroyed it. It is obvious to everyone in court that the Earl of Menteith had a motive to ruin the Wises' business, and despite the denials, was pulling Woolley and Hanrahan's strings. He was their Worshipful Master, and their progression through the Lodge depended on him.

Charles is so distracted by his thoughts that he fails to hear the judge speaking to him.

'Mr Holborne,' repeats the Common Serjeant.

'I'm so sorry, my Lord. Yes?'

'I said your client appears to want to speak to you,' says the judge, pointing down at Sir Leo who has his hand raised like a schoolboy in class.

'I do apologise,' repeats Charles. 'May I take instructions?'

'You may.'

Charles goes to the end of his bench and crouches beside Sir Leo's wheelchair.

'So?' asks Sir Leo quietly.

Charles whispers swiftly in reply. 'It could hardly have gone better. We had the junior members of the conspiracy but not the man at the top or the motive. I think we have it all now.'

'And our chances?'

'I think you're certain to be acquitted. Slightly less certain with Tony but —'

'How much?'

'Sorry?'

'Percentage, give me the percentage!' demands Sir Leo, his reedy voice impatient.

Charles shrugs. 'I don't know ... maybe eighty per cent? Eighty-five?'

'No more?'

'Er ... no. You can never be sure.'

'Very well. Thank you.'

Charles nods and resumes his seat.

The Common Serjeant addresses Bateman. 'Is that the case for the second defendant?' he asks, but before the young barrister can reply, the judge's attention is diverted afresh. Sir Leo's hand is raised again.

'It seems your client has more to say, Mr Holborne,' says the Common Serjeant.

Sir Leo is trying to stand. He has shrugged off the blanket around his legs, and is levering himself painfully from the wheelchair. He takes a deep breath, pauses, and then says in as loud a voice as he can manage: 'I wish to represent myself from now on.'

Whispering again breaks out everywhere in the courtroom.

'Silence in court!' shouts the clerk.

'I'm not sure I understand, Sir Leo,' says the judge. 'Are you saying you no longer want Mr Holborne to represent you?'

'Ya, that is right. And Mr Stephenson. I will represent myself.'

'Sir Leo, that's a very unwise course,' warns the judge, 'especially at this stage. Mr Holborne has conducted the case on your behalf very ably and —'

'Are you saying, my Lord, that I cannot dismiss my lawyers?' demands Sir Leo.

'No, that is not what —'

'Then that is what I want. I am of sound mind, and I wish to represent myself from now on.'

380

The Common Serjeant turns to Charles. 'Has this been discussed, Mr Holborne? Does your client understand what he's doing?'

'I've advised my client, my Lord, but he is indeed of sound mind and he can choose to ignore me. Which, apparently, is what he wants.'

The judge stares first at Charles and then at Sir Leo, whose strength has given out and who has collapsed back into his wheelchair.

'Well,' he says, 'if you're sure, Sir Leo, I will record that fact, and thank Mr Holborne for his assistance to the court.'

'Thank you, my Lord. I shall now plead guilty. It was me on the telephone giving instructions to that man … Streeter.'

The conversations in court, bubbling away despite the clerk's admonition, grow louder.

'Silence in court!' calls the clerk again and simultaneously the Common Serjeant barks an order but it makes no difference as both are drowned by the noise.

Then, cutting across all the chaos, there is a piercing high-pitched scream. Everyone looks around for its source. Charles is one of the first to spot it.

Up in the public gallery, Esther Wise has risen from her seat and has descended the steps to the front rail. Her mouth is wide open and her scream continues. All the other sounds in the courtroom are suddenly stilled. Esther has thrown off her fur coat and is no longer wearing her elegant dress but what appear to be … pyjamas!

The scream is abruptly cut off.

She reaches up to her head and tears furiously at her golden hair, pulling handfuls of it out, revealing a bald head. For a second Charles is unable to process what he is seeing, but then he realises: it must be a wig! She has shaven her beautiful hair and replaced it with a wig!

Esther bends at the waist, as if bowing to an audience or perhaps wishing to show her pale white scalp to everyone below her, and the wig flutters down to the benches.

But her forward motion continues.

Suddenly Charles knows with absolute horror what is about to occur but he can do nothing to prevent it. Arms outstretched as if about to take off in flight, Esther's weight shifts, her feet leave the ground, her abdomen slides over the rail and, like a huge bird, she sails gracefully out of the public gallery.

For an instant, a fraction of a second, the world stops, reduced to a single freeze-frame that takes in the barristers, solicitors, journalists, the public, the judge and his staff, some with mouths open in mid-cry, others looking elsewhere, a few pointing at the falling woman. There seems to be no sound except the gentle flapping of the pyjamas against Esther's slim body.

Then the world starts again with an awful wet crunch as her head hits the floor between the ranks of benches and splashes of red are flung in all directions.

She lies still.

The silence continues only long enough for the onlookers to draw breath. Then other screams start from all corners of the courtroom.

CHAPTER THIRTY

The four barristers involved in the case sit around a small table in the robing room. The other courts in the building are still working, and they have the space to themselves.

On the orders of Mrs Hamlin the robing room attendant has provided them with mugs of sweet tea. Allinson, who was nearest to Esther's landing point, has changed out of her bloodied court robes into her day clothes. She is still sobbing. Charles is by her side with an arm around her shoulders. Mark Denton, junior counsel for the Crown, has just returned from telephoning both sets of chambers to inform them of the events. Bateman, who hasn't smoked since he was at university, has asked Charles for a cigarette and sits, staring at the tabletop. Charles notes that his hand is trembling slightly.

Charles himself feels quite calm, almost detached, and he wonders why. Perhaps because he witnessed death and horrible dismemberment during the war which the others didn't. He knows what Sally would say: he learned during childhood to protect the core of himself from the pain of his mother's repeated rejections, by shutting down his emotions. Hence his ice-cold, clear-thinking in emergencies and, presumably, his heroics in the RAF.

She would further say that he *never* processes his emotions. Charles's "stuff" is boxed up and filed away in the dark recesses of his personality, like an enormous aircraft hangar piled high with sealed crates, never to be opened.

Charles wonders if there are now two new boxes: "Responsibility for Esther Wise's Death" and "Damage to Hannah". His heart aches at the thought of the teenager who had no choice but witness her mother's bloody and exhibitionist suicide; the girl who would never be in any doubt that her mother didn't love her enough to stay and stand by her.

The door opens and the judge's clerk enters. She approaches the table.

'One of my colleagues has cleared your desks,' she says, 'and the papers are stacked in their original boxes outside court on the landing. The courtroom has now been taped off by the police while they take photographs and so on. The Common Serjeant has adjourned, and won't continue this afternoon whatever happens.'

Charles is the only one of the four to look up at the clerk. 'Thank you. Are the police requesting our statements?'

She shakes her head. 'No. There were over a hundred witnesses, and your names are on the list, but they've started with the public gallery.'

'And our clients?' he asks.

'Still in the building. That's my principal reason for coming up. The Common Serjeant says he'd like to see you in chambers, if you feel up to it.'

Charles bends to the prosecutor. 'Did you hear that, Calli?' he says softly.

She turns to him, her face blotched and her mascara running. 'What?'

'The judge wants to see us, if we can manage it.'

'Of course.' She stands.

'Peter?' asks Charles. 'Mark?'

'Yup,' says Peter, stubbing out his cigarette. The prosecution junior simply nods.

The clerk gives them a moment more to compose themselves and then leads the way.

She's not able to take them through the courtroom, but Charles discovers that there are other hidden entrances to the Judges' Corridor. They are taken through a panelled door and into a different world. Here there are original paintings on the wall, thick carpet muffles their footsteps and the noise and echoes of the public parts of the building are replaced by an industrious silence reminiscent of a library.

The clerk halts outside an oak door. She knocks.

'Come,' says a voice from the interior.

The clerk half-steps into the room. 'Counsel to see you, Judge.'

'Thank you. Show them in please.'

The four barristers file in and the door closes quietly behind them.

'Please draw up seats,' says the Common Serjeant, pointing to some chairs placed around the periphery of the room. The barristers do as they are invited.

The judge has removed his wig and is standing by a drinks cabinet, pouring amber liquid into a series of small glasses.

'Here,' he says, bringing the tray over to them. 'Scotch. Miss Allinson?'

Allinson takes a glass. 'Thank you, Judge.'

The Common Serjeant offers a glass to each of the male barristers in turn, all of whom accept. He puts the empty tray down on his desk and goes round the back. Instead of sitting, he knocks back the whole of his drink, returns to the bottle and pours himself another glass.

'Help yourself,' he says generally, indicating the bottle. He sits at his desk. 'Quite a case, all in all,' he comments. 'I don't suppose you had any inkling, did you, Holborne?'

'Of what was about to happen? No. Lady Wise attempted suicide a few weeks ago, but she's been under the care of doctors since then, and I was told she was sedated. I can't help feeling I should've suspected something ... like that.'

'And the sudden change of plea?'

'I'm not sure I can talk about that, Judge, if you'll forgive me. At least, not now, while the case is still technically ongoing.'

'I understand. Now, as to that, we're in an unusual, perhaps even novel, situation.' The Common Serjeant turns to the prosecution barrister. 'Miss Allinson, what's the Crown's position regarding Sir Leo's change of plea?'

Charles notes that Allinson has drunk all her whisky and her pale face has a little more colour to it. 'We wouldn't have accepted a plea from either defendant to the lesser conspiracy, forcible evictions. Not at the outset.'

'And now?' asks the judge.

'I'll need to take instructions but in the light of the evidence from Lord Menteith and Kevin Lane, I would expect Sir Leo's plea to be acceptable.'

'And the son, Anthony Wise?'

'I'm in more difficulty regarding that, Judge. It's always been the Crown's case that the son gave the order. That was Streeter's evidence and as to that, at least, there's nothing to set against it.'

Bateman intervenes. 'Except Anthony Wise's own evidence. My Lord, the Crown may not like it, they may even disbelieve it, but we have two defendants; one admits making the telephone call and the other denies it. It can only have been one of them. I don't see how the Crown can accept Sir Leo's plea but continue to prosecute the son.'

The Common Serjeant turns to Allinson. 'I think Mr Bateman has a point, don't you? I also wonder at the public interest at continuing with the trial in the light of Sir Leo's present position. Even though he hasn't been convicted of the more serious offence, even the shortest term of imprisonment I impose is, to all intents and purposes, a life sentence. And there's another matter I must raise.' The judge pauses, looking down. He hesitates before speaking. 'I'd have to recuse myself if the case were to continue on a contested basis.'

All four barristers look up, surprised. 'May I ask why?' asks Charles.

'The rabbit you pulled out of the hat right at the end, Mr Holborne. Navy 2162. I was a Freemason, prior to becoming a judge, although never a member of that Lodge.'

Except for the tick of a large wooden clock on the wall, there is silence in the judge's chambers.

'I wouldn't have thought that that fact alone would prevent you from continuing with the trial, Judge,' says Bateman, 'particularly if you resigned many years ago.'

'The difficulty, Mr Bateman, is that I knew the character of that particular Lodge. Your researches may not have taken you this far yet, but you'll discover that in addition to the Earl of Menteith, at least one member of the Royal family was involved. In the years before and during the war the Lodge became closely associated with the Fascist movement. And, as in the way of these things, once that sort of reputation becomes established, it tends to attract like-minded people. I put on record my abhorrence for some of the attitudes expressed.'

Maybe this explains the easier ride from the Common Serjeant than I predicted, thinks Charles.

The judge turns to Allinson. 'Therefore, if there remain any contested issues in this case, I think I'm barred from continuing. Certainly, if the Crown's position is that Lord Menteith should himself be tried.'

'I haven't had time to consider that or, obviously, to take instructions,' she answers, 'but I think there's a strong prima facie case of perjury, and potentially conspiracy. There's also DI Woolley to consider, and Mr Hanrahan.'

'Precisely,' says the Common Serjeant. 'So, if Sir Leo's plea is acceptable to the Crown, I think I can proceed to sentence him. I can discharge Anthony Wise and that will bring this trial to an end. Any further criminal proceedings that might be brought against Menteith, Woolley and Hanrahan — and, potentially, Streeter for murder — will have to be dealt with by someone else.'

'As I said, Judge, I'll take instructions, but I expect the Crown to agree to that course.'

'Thank you.'

The room falls silent. 'That poor, poor woman,' comments the judge.

'Lady Wise?' enquires Charles.

'Yes, of course, but in fact I was thinking of the daughter. She seems to be the only true innocent in all this, and she has lost her mother in the most appalling way — which she witnessed — and her father, all in one instant. I guess she'll need a lot of support.'

'I agree, Judge.'

'And your client, Peter?' says the judge, turning to Bateman.

'Difficult to tell, Judge. I need to go down to see him. He doesn't react the way most people do. You don't get the usual responses.'

After another pause the Common Serjeant rises. 'Well, thank you all for the professional way in which you've dealt with this extraordinary case. You should probably get back to Chambers; restore some normality to the week. I'll relist for tomorrow at ten-thirty.'

Taking the hint, the barristers all rise and head towards the door.

'Holborne,' says the judge as if in afterthought, 'do you have any idea what was going through Lady Wise's mind to prompt her suicide?'

'Perhaps. Dr Rosenfeld would say that what she experienced in Auschwitz left her psyche extremely damaged. She's suffered periodic depression and other mental illness, but for much of the time she could cope while all the structures of her life were in place. So, the business, her husband, her charitable life, they all supported her and enabled her to function. But once she saw them being removed…'

'I see. And the pyjamas, the shaved head?'

'Oh, I think I know the answer to that.'

'Which is?'

'A group of powerful anti-Semites was bent on destroying her family, and they succeeded. In her mind she was back in Auschwitz. Nazis killed her, as surely as if she'd been taken off the train directly to the gas chamber.'

The judge ponders Charles's answer, and nods slowly. 'Yes, I think you may have something, there.'

The other barristers file out, but Charles hangs back.

'I know this isn't a good time to ask, Judge,' he says tentatively, 'but I might not get another chance to speak to you informally.'

'Yes?'

'I'm thinking of applying for silk in the next April round. Would you consider giving me a reference, based on what you've seen over the last few days?'

'Of course, dear fellow. As I said in open court, you did a sterling job, and I'm happy to say so.'

EPILOGUE

It is three weeks later when Charles sees the notice of Sir Leo Wise's funeral in Harry's copy of the *Jewish Chronicle*. He discusses it with Sally and decides to attend. Given Sir Leo's loss of faith, Charles is surprised at the choice of burial ground. Willesden Jewish Cemetery is the final destination of most of the moneyed and high-profile Jewish residents of north London, sometimes known as the "Rolls-Royce" of London's Jewish cemeteries. Charles assumes that the decision as to Sir Leo's resting place must have been made by other members of the community.

He isn't sure what to expect, given Sir Leo's conviction, but he finds to his surprise that the Jewish community has turned out in force to say farewell to one of their most prominent members. He suspects they too place little credence on Sir Leo's belated and tactical acceptance of guilt.

Charles remains on the fringes of the group for the whole of the service and interment. He is walking back to his car when he sees Hannah Wise saying farewell to other mourners. She raises a hand to attract his attention and indicates that she wants to speak to him. Charles loiters patiently until they are alone in the car park.

Hannah approaches.

'I wish you long life,' says Charles, offering her the customary condolence.

'It was good of you to come,' says the young woman.

'I hope you don't think I'm intruding —'

'— of course not —'

'— but I had a great deal of respect for your father,' replies Charles. 'Plus I wanted to see you, and find out how you're getting on. And Tony of course.'

'It's not usually possible to tell with Tony. I rarely know what he's thinking. He seems unchanged, and he's back at work. He's managed to find refinancing, so the company's still running, and two of the developments are proceeding — not those using the same design as Seagull Tower, of course.'

'That's good news. And you? How are you doing?'

She smiles sadly at him, and Charles notices for the first time that her eyes are not the striking greeny-blue of her mother, but dark brown.

'Well, something rather odd has happened,' she says. She locks eyes with Charles, watching his response as she speaks. 'It turns out that Esther was not our mother after all. Dad told us.'

'Jacquetta,' says Charles.

'You guessed?'

'Not really, but now you say it, it makes sense.'

'Yes, that's how I felt. I think it was always somewhere in the back of my head. Like, I suspected, but never allowed myself to dwell on it consciously.'

'I remember now, your father once told me that he proposed to Jacquetta first, before Esther.'

'Really? He didn't tell us that.'

'What did he say?'

'Not a lot. Just that it was easy to be blinded by Esther's beauty, but she was seriously fucked up by what happened to her in the war. Dad said that, when the cattle trucks arrived at the camp, her parents and siblings were all selected for the gas chambers immediately. But Esther was then a blond, willowy sixteen year-old who looked completely Aryan. So she was spared. She was forced to become one of the camp prostitutes, for the exclusive use of the officers. It damaged her, and not just mentally.'

'Physically too?' offers Charles.

She nods. 'She couldn't have children and, actually, didn't want them. Dad said that side of their relationship was pretty much non-existent from the start. With him, anyway. I know she had a lot of other male friends, but I doubt even those relationships were "normal". I don't think she could connect that side of things with affection. Dad was lonely and, throughout all of it, there was Jacquetta, loyal and steady and in love with him. So the three of them came up with a solution that worked for them.'

'Wow,' says Charles quietly. 'That's a whole lot of stuff to deal with. How has it affected things with Jacquetta?'

Hannah looks down. 'Early days.'

Charles nods. 'So, it turns out you do still have a mother.'

'Yes. And one who says she has always loved me, although from a distance.'

'That's something, then.'

'I suppose so. But I can't shrug off the feeling that I let Mum … sorry … Esther, down somehow. That I should have done more. I was quite a bitch to her.'

'Are you going to get some help with that?'

'What sort of help?'

'The sort of help that Dr Rosenfeld might be able to offer, for example?'

She considers Charles's suggestion. 'You know what?' she says, looking up brightly into his face, 'that's a very good idea. I think I will.'

'Good. Because, Hannah, it wasn't your responsibility to repair your mum. Nor was it your responsibility to mother her. She was the grown-up. You were just a child.'

She smiles and he sees tears in her eyes.

'You know,' she says shyly, 'when you came to the house to speak to Esther, and I was eavesdropping on the landing…'

'Yes?'

'When you came out, and you took my hand and looked at me … I wanted you to hug me.'

'I nearly did,' he says. 'But it didn't feel like my business, and I didn't want you misinterpreting.'

'I know it sounds weird, but I feel that you, me, Dad and Tony have been through something together. Would it be very weird if I asked you to give me a hug now?' she asks.

He smiles. 'Not at all.'

Charles and Sally stand outside the little church in Essex. Sally carries Leia in her arms. The little girl's eyes are wide open but she is calm and peaceful, apparently fascinated by the flickering sunlight through the leaves of the enormous yew tree in the churchyard. She looks delightful in a lacy white dress and bonnet. Sally is, as always, gorgeous in cream-coloured skirt and jacket and a little hat with a veil. Charles wears a formal work suit but was persuaded to forego his stripey barrister's trousers. It's a beautiful sunny day with blue skies and fluffy clouds.

Other people, also dressed in their church best, smile, pass them, and enter the building.

'Ready?' asks Sally.

Charles hesitates. 'Still not sure I can do this.'

'Don't be daft. Course you can. Come on.'

Sally moves down the path and Charles follows. They enter the shadowy interior and Charles is, as always, struck by the smell of polished pews and old books.

Kevin and Maude Lane are just inside the door, Maude holding Matthew in her arms, greeting people as they enter. They too are dressed for an occasion.

'Hello, Charles,' says Big Kev. He shakes Charles's hand and bends to kiss Sally's cheek.

'All set?' asks the diminutive woman of Charles.

'Are you sure about this?' he asks. 'I've never been a godfather to anyone before and, as you know, I'm not a Christian.'

'Course we're sure,' replies Big Kev. 'We wouldn't have no one else, would we, Maudie?'

'Absolutely not. Anyway, you can't back out now. All the cards and order of service are printed with "Matthew Charles Lane". So, you're stuck!'

'It's a lovely name,' says Sally. 'You should be honoured, Charlie.'

'I am, of course I am, but representing you at an adoption hearing is hardly enough to qualify me as godfather!'

Maude leans forward and puts her hand on Charles's arm. 'Charlie, without you this little boy wouldn't be ours. We'll never be able to thank you enough.'

'We're quits, Maude. Your husband paid me back by giving truthful evidence at the trial.'

'Happy to help,' says Big Kev. 'I never heard what happened after the lady … you know…'

Charles sighs. 'Tony Wise was acquitted and his father got three years, although he went straight from the Bailey to hospital, where he spent his last few days. The Prison Service doesn't have facilities for prisoners with leukaemia.'

'That's sad,' says Maude.

'Yes, it is,' agrees Charles, 'but Jacquetta and his children were with him at the end, and he died knowing he'd done his best by them. I think that's some consolation.'

Sally flashes an unnecessary warning glance at him.

'And the property business?' asks Big Kev. 'I was wondering, well, Maude was, if we could pick up the work Shoreditch Enforcement Services was doing, now that Woolley and Little Kev are inside.'

'It's possible. To that extent, Sir Leo's sacrifice paid off. Tony's still running the business and he did find refinancing. So the business is still functioning — at least until the Seagull Tower Inquiry reports. They're even opening the new care home, which is what I think Sir Leo most wanted to protect.'

'Come on, Kev,' says Maude. 'We can talk business later. The vicar's waiting.'

She pulls her husband away, and they walk down the nave, greeting people in the pews on either side as they go.

'Just a sec,' says Charles, putting a gentle hand on Sally's forearm.

'What?'

'I've been thinking. I want us to get married as soon as possible.'

Sally looks up at him, a half-smile playing about her lips. 'What's changed?'

'Nothing. I think I was worrying so much about details that I ... sort of ... froze. Where to have it, who to invite, all that. It seemed intractable.'

'And now?'

Charles puts his arms round her and Leia. Sally smells of shampoo and fresh air. 'None of that seems to matter. I just want us to be together, for ever, and starting as soon as possible.'

'Nothing to do with the Wise case?' she asks. 'You've been a lot quieter since then.'

'Have I?'

'You have. I think the word's "reflective". Unusual for you, and a good thing I'd say.'

Charles smiles fondly at her. 'You know me pretty well, don't you?'

She grins. 'I'm the world's leading expert on Charlie Horowitz, Barrister-at-Law,' she says.

'That you are. And the trial … yes, it affected me, more than most cases. I was reminded that life is short, and things can change in the blink of an eye.'

'Yes.'

'So let's get married soon.'

'When?'

'If possible, before the end of the month, while we've still got decent weather.'

'We'll be bloody lucky to find caterers in time.'

'I think we'll be okay. It's not a big event. Lunch for thirty or forty in the garden. But if not, so be it. We'll manage.'

She reaches up and strokes Charles's face tenderly. 'Fine by me.'

HISTORICAL NOTE

Seagull Lane, London, E16 is just a few streets away from the site of Ronan Point, a twenty-two-storey supposedly state-of-the-art tower block which collapsed only weeks after it was opened. Just like the fictional Seagull Tower, an entire corner of the tower block dropped like a stack of cards, killing four people. The block was almost full, and it is little short of a miracle that the death toll was not much higher.

The Ronan Point disaster occurred slightly earlier than in this book, in May 1968. A resident on the eighteenth floor lit their stove, causing a gas explosion that led to a progressive collapse, one floor after the other. The incident validated growing concerns regarding the flawed design of the building. Anthony Greenwood, Housing Minister, wrote to Prime Minister Harold Wilson on the very day of the collapse expressing concerns about central government culpability: they had "pushed" the design onto local authorities. The "Large Panel System" used pre-cast concrete panels the size of a floor or of a wall. Erection did not require scaffolding; panels were craned up and stood on end to act as walls with others laid horizontally on top to be floors and ceilings.

The Griffiths Inquiry which followed the collapse laid no blame except that, in its view, the Construction Regulations were insufficient, and structural engineers had failed to consider the possibility of progressive collapse. However, later research suggested that the inquiry was a whitewash. The joints between the floor and wall panels were essential but many of the bolts to hold them together were missing. Cavities that should have been filled with concrete were stuffed with rubbish and newspaper (thereby providing the hiding places for the bodies in this book). The developers used unskilled workers paid on a piecework basis; the faster they worked, the more they were paid. Load-bearing walls could be knocked out, as at Ronan Point, if the walls and ceilings were not joined effectively. Technical guidance from 1968 on these buildings actually stated: '*One can hardly over-emphasise the absolute necessity of effectively joining the various components of the structure together in order to obviate any possible tendency for it to behave like a "house of cards"*'.

At the time of writing, there are still over 1,500 of these blocks still standing, 200 of which have twenty storeys or more. They can be recognised easily as they have no gas fittings and a sign informing residents that Calor gas cannot be brought into the building. Many have been pulled down and a fortune spent by councils strengthening those which remain. Nonetheless, following Ronan Point the Ledbury Estate in Southwark was evacuated, a tower block in Leicester is being demolished, and in Portsmouth and Hammersmith and Fulham towers are still being reinforced.

The appalling state of housing in the East End of London is also an accurate portrayal, albeit moved slightly later in time. The devastation caused by the Luftwaffe, together with the deaths of thousands of builders and tradesmen during the war, meant that rebuilding of the East End took years longer than it should have, leaving the weakest and most vulnerable Londoners either homeless or in appalling slum conditions. The scarcity of accommodation led to unscrupulous landlords hiking the rent to the point where families could no longer afford even the meanest accommodation. That eventually led to the passing of the Rent Acts which created rent officers, whose job it was to assess rents by stripping scarcity out of the calculation. The housing situation in the decade between the end of the 1950s and the end of the 1960s bears striking similarities to what is occurring now in London and elsewhere.

Whilst this is not a psychiatric treatise, I have tried to portray the psychological difficulties faced by concentration camp survivors and their children as accurately as possible. Anyone who would like to look at some of the research could start with 'Holocaust Exposure Induced Intergenerational Effects on FKBP5 Methylation' in *Biological Psychiatry* (Vol. 80, Issue 5) as reported in the *Guardian* on 21 August 2015, and 'Concentration Camp Survival: A Pilot Study of Effects on the Second Generation', in the *Canadian Journal of Psychiatry* (Vol. 16, Issue 5).

Finally, the fictional character of Jean-Luc Pelletier is based on a real-life hero, Leon Wilson, whose room was next door to that of my parents at their care home. Leon was, despite his surname, a French Jew, and won the *Légion d'honneur*. There was a photograph on his bedroom wall of the medal presentation by the French president. He served initially in the French Artillery and escaped from the advancing German armies with the British at Dunkirk. In England, having learned to speak English, he enrolled in Field Security in the Intelligence Corps, and fought the rest of the war for the British. After the war he returned to the family home in Paris and learned that his mother, grandmother and three brothers had all been murdered at Buchenwald. He then settled in England with his English wife. You can listen to two fascinating interviews he gave concerning his military life on the Imperial War Museum website. I had the honour of meeting Mr Wilson several times before he died, at the age of 101.

A NOTE TO THE READER

Thank you for taking the time to read the ninth Charles Holborne legal thriller. I hope you enjoyed it. Regular readers of the series will know that there was an overall arc to the first eight books, and I wasn't even sure that I wanted to write a ninth or later book. But I received a lot of very encouraging (not to mention insistent) emails from fans inviting (and in a couple of cases, ordering) me to persist and so *Death, Adjourned* came into being.

Ronnie and Reggie Kray did bring a certain glamour and menace to the first eight books, a feature which following their incarceration, sadly, is no longer available, but London in 1970 was still a seething cauldron of corruption and dishonesty, and there are plenty of potential plots to be found, some of them based on my career at the Bar. If all goes well, and readers enjoy the new direction the series is taking, I could be persuaded to carry Charles into a tenth book...

Nowadays, reviews by knowledgeable readers are essential to authors' success, so if you enjoyed the novel I shall be in your debt if you would spare the few seconds required to post a review on **Amazon** and **Goodreads**. I love hearing from readers, and you can connect with me through my **Facebook page**, via **Twitter** or through my **website**, where you can sign up for my newsletter. If you find any mistakes in these pages I shall be delighted to hear from you. I always reply, and if you're right, I will make sure future editions are changed.

I hope we'll meet again in the pages of the next Charles Holborne Adventure.

Simon

www.simonmichael.uk

Sapere Books is an exciting new publisher of brilliant fiction and popular history.

To find out more about our latest releases and our monthly bargain books visit our website:
saperebooks.com

Printed in Great Britain
by Amazon